Carruther's Peak

David Stant

Pen Press

First published in Great Britain by Pen Press

All paper used in the printing of this book has been made from wood grown in managed, sustainable forests.

ISBN13: 978-1-78003-279-5

Printed and bound in the UK
Pen Press is an imprint of
Indepenpress Publishing Limited
25 Eastern Place
Brighton
BN2 1GJ

A catalogue record of this book is available from the British Library

Cover design by Jacqueline Abromeit

For Clare

Chapter Index

Chapter 1

Boomboomboomboom

'I'm off now, son,' Hugh Tucker said.

'Bye Dad.' Ralph turned over in bed.

'I'm not going to the office. I'm going to Portsmouth. I've been called up for the Navy. I may be away for a long time.'

'Will you be away on my birthday?'

'That's nine months from now. Who knows? There's a war on.'

'Will we be able to come on the ship and see you?'

'Well I don't think so. It's not really for children. Now we must say goodbye so that I can be on my way.'

'Don't kiss me, Dad. You're all stubbly.'

'All right. We'll shake hands. It's more manly. Now you and Veronica must do what Mummy tells you. I'll write a nice long letter as soon as I can and Mummy can read it to you.'

'Thanks, Dad.' He fell asleep.

Hugh went into Veronica's bedroom. She looked like a little doll. He had not the heart to wake her. He sat and looked at her for a while and whispered, 'Bye, my little one.'

He went downstairs.

'D'you know Margaret, I don't think those kids are bothered about anything.'

'They *are* only three and four, darling.'

'Yes, of course. What a time for a war eh?'

He kissed her goodbye. She watched him walk down the drive in his long mackintosh, greasy trilby hat and his father's battered suitcase.

Sure enough a letter arrived a week later. It read:

Dearest Margaret,

The first part of this letter is for you. The last part is a special letter for you to read out to the kids. How have you been coping? Have Ralph and Veronica been good? Are you missing me? I miss you. I've been in the Royal Navy a matter of days and I'm already wondering how long this stupid war is going to last. I dearly wanted to be at home to watch the kids grow up but that is not to be. Who are we to grumble when there are hundreds of thousands of families in the same situation? Dear Margaret I plead with you – however much you love and cherish those children, please please do not turn them into namby-pambies. I'm settling down a bit now, but it was hell for the first few days. I was with a cursing, coughing, spitting, foul-mouthed crew if ever there was one. There were men from Glasgow, Belfast, Sunderland, Bristol – all over the place – and I could hardly understand what most of them were saying much of the time. A Scot asked my name. He remarked that it was a coincidence that we were both called Hugh. So from now on we are Big Hughie (me) and little Hughie. We struck up a friendship. He worked as a reporter for an Edinburgh newspaper. I showed him my photograph of the kids. He told me he'd got four boys, and that he wished he had two girls like me. I told him one was a boy. He apologised and said he hoped he hadn't offended me. He said that the curly hair had fooled him – 'and his pretty face' I added. 'Aye, that too,' he agreed, 'but no doubt he'll grow up to be as ugly as his father.'

Margaret read out the special letter for the children.

Dear Ralph and Veronica (the little scamps),

I won't be going on a ship just yet. I have to learn seamanship first. That means learning to be a sailor, tying knots and all that. I hope you are being good children and helping Mummy. When I come back home we'll go on a walk over Gillity fields like we used to. I've drawn it – look! St Matthews's church hidden in the trees with only the steeple showing, the canal bridge and the haystacks and barns and farmhouses. There's the fence post I used to sit you on, Veronica, so that you could see the church through the trees. Please be good. I shall surely get some leave in a few weeks and we will all be together again.

Love Daddy x x x x

He managed to get leave a few weeks later at the right time to get Ralph into school.

'I don't like the idea of him with all those rough boys at Chuckery Infants. I would have liked him to go to a private school like Mayfield,' Margaret protested.

'We cannot afford private education and that's that. I keep telling you that. Anyway, I'm pleased that he's going to be mixing with street kids. It'll do him good. I've already pleaded with you not to let him become a namby-pamby, with all your fussing round him and choking him with affection, with all your darlings, angels, cherubs, doves and poppets, whatever a poppet is.'

'Well, I' m not going to change,' she said defiantly. "We have two beautiful children and they will have my love constantly.'

Hugh got Ralph into Miss Hickinbotham's class.

'Now what you need, Ralph, are a few pals. It's playtime so let's have a look round. What about these two? They must be about your age. One's your size. One's a big lad.'

'What's your name?' Hugh asked the big lad.

'Dennis,' he said.

'And how old are you?'

'Four.'

'What's your name?' he asked the other lad. 'Tommy. I'm four.'

'There you are, Ralph. Two little friends for you.'

‘This boy’s called Ralph,’ Hugh told them. They ran off, but Ralph clung to his father.

‘Hey, Ralph!’ they shouted. ‘We’ll show you our game.’ Ralph scampered away.

‘I’ll pick you up at four,’ Hugh shouted, but his words fell on deaf ears. Tommy and Dennis were waiting by the boys’ lavatories. The game was to see who could pee the highest up the wall.

‘You’ve got a bigger cock than me,’ Dennis told Ralph, ‘but you’re not as big as me. Tommy’s got the biggest cock but he’s the smallest of us all.’

‘Well,’ Ralph said, ‘I think that when you grow bigger your cock grows smaller.’ They all nodded wisely.

Ralph reiterated the conundrum when they got home. His mother was not impressed. Hugh was amused and scotched the theory that the smaller you were the bigger your cock, by saying, ‘But if Dennis grew up to be a giant he’d have no cock at all.’

‘Don’t encourage him,’ Margaret snapped. ‘I hope you’re satisfied. You can see what’s happening, can’t you? One day among the guttersnipes and he’s measuring his willy and peeing up walls.’

‘That’s what little boys do,’ Hugh assured her.

Another important thing happened that leave. The Tucker family took delivery of their indoor air raid shelter. It was in kit form – almost revolutionary in 1941. Hugh managed to assemble it after hours of cursing, losing nuts and bolts, and leaving bits out so that some parts had to be undone and reassembled. Ralph was his little assistant to whom he issued orders continually, ‘Hold this spanner, son. Hold this hammer. Pass it to me. No, the spanner not the hammer’.

Eventually it was finished, the last job having been to criss-cross some thin steel laths to provide a platform for a mattress. The table top was made of sheet steel. The theory was that when the air raid sirens went off, next door’s

Who's that beautiful lady?' Veronica asked.
'She's an old friend. Her name is Lorna Pitt. You shall her Aunty Lorna. Her husband has been killed in the I want you children to go inside and say to her how you are.' They went inside the house.
unty Lorna,' Ralph said, 'we are sorry that your d has been killed in the war, but we know that he'll leaven.'
how lovely!' She took them in her arms. Tears lown her cheeks. 'What lovely children you are. tty you are Veronica, and my word Ralph, what a boy you are and what a handsome man you will s my little girl, Sarah. Sarah, come and say hello to l Veronica.' Sarah stayed on her chair and would g. 'She's a little bit shy,' Aunty Lorna whispered. his cue to say something really adult.
ct she'll grow out of it. Children usually do.' 's tearful demeanour changed to a faint smile. Ralph to her. 'My little doctor!'

ny and Dennis were sitting high on the wall erimeter of the school playground.
to be in a gang,' Tommy said.
s only three of us,' Ralph argued.
ith three and if anyone wants to join they pay ommy proposed.
ght that was an excellent idea.
we do in this gang?' Dennis asked. 'Break

ot to be good. We have to do good for in Hood's gang did. We should all think nother meeting tomorrow,' Tommy said.
ime we just have adventures,' Ralph

wall!' shouted Mr Sledge, the school ot supposed to be there. Get off home!'

children, Peter and Susan, who were about the same age as Ralph and Veronica, would sleep at one end of the bed and Ralph and Veronica at the other. Margaret and next door's mother, known as Aunty Jo, would sit in the darkened living room smoking continuously and occasionally remarking, 'That sounds near' or 'I wonder who copped that one'.

Margaret always hated the air raid shelter. Her highly polished Victorian dining table had been relegated to the garage. Ralph and Veronica, on the other hand, loved the steel top. Their father had told them that they could do what they liked on it. Stains did not matter. They could even play with Plasticine. Air raid sirens did not bother them. It meant that Peter and Susan came round and they spent the next hour or so talking and giggling. Similarly at school, when the air raid siren sounded it caused jubilation. Everybody was shepherded to the various underground shelters around the playground. When the all clear went, there was always a chorus of moans. It was the signal to return to lessons.

The favourite game for boys at Chuckery Infants School was "aeroplanes". Two teams were picked – English and German. The scrawny or goofy boys were always Germans. Each boy ran around with arms outstretched yelling 'Nyeeeeeeeeoow Nyeeeeeoow' and shooting down his opponents 'rat-tat-tat-tat-tat-tat rat-tat-tat-tat-tat'. The game was controlled by older boys of six and seven who winged around shouting orders. 'You're dead. You're on fire. Lie down you. You're full of holes'.

'I don't like these big boys telling us what to do,' Dennis said one day.

'We could be bombers,' Ralph suggested. 'We could run around with Dennis in front and me and Tommy behind. Dennis is as big as a big boy. They set off with Dennis flanked by Tommy and Ralph dropping their bombs 'Booooooooom boomboomboom booooom'.

'What are you three doing?' a seven year old wanted to know.

'We're Americans,' Tommy said.

'You're spoiling our game,' the seven-year-old protested.

'Good!' Dennis shouted. 'Here we come again. BoooomboooomBooomboomboom boomboomboooom booomboomboooomb.'

The bell sounded for them to go back into school. They were defiantly running at everything and everybody in their way.

'Boomboomboooooomboooomboooomboomboomboo ooo.'

'Wait till I tell my dad about this,' Ralph thought, 'But I can't. He's gone away and he said it might be a long time. I'll put it in a letter. That's what I'll do.'

Margaret sometimes took Ralph and Veronica to see their grandparents, Arthur and Emily Rowley, on Margaret's side, and Harry and Amy Tucker, on Hugh's side. They did not enjoy visits to the Rowleys. They lived in a bleak semi near a railway bridge in that part of Walsall called The Pleck. Arthur Rowley was the archetypal granddad in his rocking chair. He had a gammy leg caused by jumping off a moving tram and getting his foot stuck in the rails. He was a butcher by trade but like so many small businessmen, he had gone bust in the Depression years. He had worked as a postman for a few years – hardly a suitable job for a disabled man – and he had to give it up. His abiding passion was placing complicated small bets on racehorses. Ralph and Veronica had difficulty understanding him, so broad was his Black Country accent. Grandma Rowley was a very straight-laced woman. She was almost always dressed completely in black. She annoyed Ralph and Veronica by continually referring to them in the third person. 'How old are they now?' 'How's the boy getting on at school?' 'They've both got very dirty knees!'

'Can we go home now, Mummy?'
whisper every few minutes.

Their visits to the Tuckers were far
Nan Tucker always hugged them to her
said, 'Well if it isn't my boy's boy and
would open a cupboard in the kitchen
cakes and biscuits.

'All made by me,' she would alw

'Don't let them eat too much
always Margaret's plea.

'Ah, God bless them,' Nan T
not a spare ounce of fat on them.'

Granddad Tucker spent most
couch in the kitchen. He had a
forever making demands on N
cup of tea? Bring the biscuit
Where have you hidden m
beck and call but wheneve
said, 'He worked hard all
fought in the Boer War.
Harry, Colour Sergeant
a great man. At sevent
rest. Anyway I love hir

One day they were s
hedges, when Veron
in a long dress an
hand. Can you see

'Yes, I see t
beautiful than M

They edged
of about sever
lady sat with
and sobbing.
Veronica!
joined thei

‘I’ve got an idea for a little adventure,’ Ralph told them. ‘Come with me tomorrow. I’m going to my Nan’s in Caldmore Road. She’s going to give me a caseball. It’s a bit old, but it’s hard enough. I’ve seen it.’

‘Where did your Nan get it?’ Tommy asked.

‘Before the war she sometimes took in footballers as lodgers. The ball I’m getting was from a famous footballer.’

They were impressed.

‘So this football may have been kicked by hundreds of famous footballers from the Arsenal and everywhere,’ Dennis reasoned. ‘Is this an adventure though?’

‘It would be,’ Ralph said’ if we had to fight off a gang trying to get our ball, but we can call it a half-adventure.’ Tommy, the organiser took over. ‘We’ll meet at the Arboretum gates at 10 o’clock tomorrow.’

‘I’ve thought of a name for our gang,’ Ralph said. ‘We can be the Arbo Gang. We can be a football gang. It’s our ball so it will be our game. I’m looking forward to tomorrow. We’ll get jam tarts, biscuits and everything.’

‘Get down off that wall and go home before I call the Police,’ Mr Sledge shouted.

They met up at ten o’clock and took the long walk to Caldmore Road. Nan Tucker stood out in the yard, hands on hips and demanded to know, ‘And who are these ragamuffins?’

‘They’re my friends, Tommy and Dennis. Dennis is the biggest.’

‘Well you’d better come inside’. They all sat around the kitchen table.

‘You’re sitting there as if you’re waiting for something,’ she said.

‘I said that they could have jam tarts and biscuits’. Ralph explained.

‘I can imagine it.’

She put out plates. Each boy had two of everything – two tarts, two cakes and two biscuits. Nan Tucker went out into the sitting room to answer the telephone, 'Hello'.

'It's Margaret. I've been going out of my mind. Is Ralph with you?'

'He's with me and two of his little friends. He's as safe as houses.'

'Two young guttersnipes, no doubt.'

'Two nice lads.'

'Send him home immediately.'

'All in good time. I'll bring him home myself if you're frantic. Don't you dare come and get him. He'll lose face with his mates. He'll get called a mummy's boy.'

'He *is* my boy!'

'He's with his grandmother and his friends.' She slammed the phone down, went back into the kitchen and poured out three glasses of ginger beer.

'Nan,' Ralph asked' I was wondering if I could have my football now.'

'It was for your birthday. If you have it now you won't get a birthday present.'

'I don't care.'

'All right then, I'll get it.'

She came back with the football. It showed signs of wear and tear, but by the standards of the lads from Chuckery it was in excellent condition.

'There it is,' Nan announced proudly. Tommy picked it up. 'It's a good ball.'

'Can you read what's on it?' she asked.

'W. R. Dean, Everton, 1930,' Tommy read.

'Does that mean anything to you?' Nan asked. They all shook their heads.

'This stupid war is taking away our memories,' Nan Tucker complained. 'W. R. Dean is Dixie Dean. The great Dixie Dean. Ask your Dads. They'll tell you.'

'Nobody knows where my Dad is,' Dennis said sombrely. 'I live with my Mom and my Aunty.'

'I lost my Dad early in the war,' Tommy said, 'He was in the Merchant Navy. I live with my older brother Ron and my Mom.'

'You poor boys! It's the times we live in. Ralph's father is away on the Russian convoys, so there's not a single one of you with a father at home.'

'Nan,' Ralph asked, 'Me, Tommy and Dennis want to swear undying friendship. We want to swear it on the Bible.'

'I've got a big bible, a family Bible. I'll go and get it.' She returned with a heavy black Bible. They gasped when they saw the size of it. She put it down on the table, asking herself why she was getting involved in all this. She asked each boy to put his hand on the Bible and told each in turn what to say.

'I swear that I will protect my friends Tommy and Dennis for life,' Ralph said.

'I swear that I will protect my friends Ralph and Dennis for life,' Tommy said.

'I swear that I will protect my friends Ralph and Tommy for life,' Dennis said.

Good lads,' she said. 'Now be off with you and don't kick that football into the road and get yourselves run over.'

They walked proudly home, taking it in turn to carry the football. They walked past three old men sitting out in the street. Tommy asked, 'Hey mister, have you ever heard of Dixie Dean?'

'Of course we've heard of Dixie Dean. He was a great footballer.'

'Want to see his football?' Tommy showed them the words 'W. R. Dean, Everton, 1930'.

'Well I'll be blowed.'

'That could be valuable one day,' another old man said.

‘We reckon it’s worth seven and sixpence,’ Dennis claimed.

‘More than that,’ the old man reasoned. ‘Ten bob or maybe more.’

‘Ten bob!’ They chorused.

Ralph got home within the hour. His mother was distraught.

‘My little man! You’re back. Come to Mummy. Let me give you a big hug.’ Reluctantly he complied. She changed her tone. ‘What have you been doing all this time?’ He told her in great detail. ‘I’m most perturbed. Swearing on Bibles and starting gangs! Such goings on! You do what I tell you in future, not what that Nan Tucker tells you. What do you want to be in a gang for?’

‘So that we don’t get picked on. We’ve only got three in the gang so far, but we’re going to get bigger. It costs new members sixpence.’

‘This is turning out to be a nightmare,’ she cried. ‘I wanted you to go to Mayfield.’

‘They’re all cissies there.’

‘They’re well-behaved children.’

‘Their mummies pick them up in cars every afternoon.’

‘What’s wrong with that?’

‘Dad wouldn’t like it. He said it would do me good to mix with street kids. I heard him say it just before he left.’

‘You should not be eavesdropping on adult conversations. Go upstairs and wash those grubby hands and knees clean.’

‘I thought you liked us to be little scamps with grubby knees.’

‘Little scamps come from good homes. There’s a big difference between little scamps and street urchins.’

‘Yes, Mom,’ he said resignedly, knowing that he was soon to get what he and Veronica called the ‘Darling treatment’.

'Darling! Mummy knows best. These so-called friends for life will turn on you. They have the morals of the gutter. When you're famous they'll burgle your house and smash up your Rolls Royce with sledgehammers. They'll all grow up to be backstreet criminals. Thank God that, by that time, you'll be at Oxford and your father and I will be so proud of you.'

'Aren't you even interested in the football?' Ralph asked. 'It's signed by Dixie Dean. He was a famous footballer who lodged with Nan Tucker.'

'I know nothing about soccer players except that they're layabouts who should be doing a proper job.'

In the spring of 1945 when the war appeared to be approaching its end, Margaret Tucker announced that they were going on a little holiday in Wales. She had a friend, known to Ralph and Veronica as Aunty Peggy, whose parents had a farm at a place called Stackpole near Pembroke.

'We shall have to change trains in London,' she told Ralph and Veronica, 'so I need you both to stay very close to me as we work our way through the Underground.'

They were very excited about it. This was their first ever holiday. They had never seen the sea and here they were well on their way, fighting their way through the London Underground. They clung to their mother's coat tails as she snapped out her orders – 'This way! Down the escalator! Mind the last step! Come! Turn left! Turn right!' Ralph and Veronica were very impressed. Finally, they were on their train.

They were collected at Stackpole by an 'Uncle Bill', Peggy's father. They piled into his old car and he drove them to his farm. They liked the farm immediately. It had a long veranda. Some days they all sat out enjoying the sun. Ralph and Veronica were given little tasks. Ralph was instructed in chopping wood by Uncle Bill. 'Take the axe then, boy. Not too heavy is it?'

'No', Ralph lied.

'Bring it down with all your might by here.' Ralph swung the axe ferociously and, sure enough, split the log in two.

'Good Boy! Now take the small chopper and chop as many pieces as you can. Hold the log at the end and bring down the chopper. Whack! Whack! Whack! I'll leave you to it.'

'Now Veronica, take this basket here and go all around the yard and under all the hedges and bushes and collect the eggs.'

'That'll keep them occupied for a while,' Uncle Bill told Margaret. 'Veronica's collecting eggs and Ralph's chopping firewood.'

'Chopping firewood!' She shrieked. 'Ralph can't chop firewood. He'll chop his hand off and he won't be able to get into the Boat Race team at Oxford.'

'Stop making a fuss, Margaret,' Bill ordered. 'He's doing all right.'

'But it's dangerous.'

'Dangerous is it? We've been fighting a war for going on six years. That's what I call dangerous. Not chopping wood!'

Ralph appeared half an hour later with a hessian sack. It was so heavy that he had to drag it along the ground.

'Look Uncle Bill,' he shouted, 'I filled the sack. I chopped up every single log.'

'Take it into the kitchen and give it to your Aunty Gwen.' Ralph came up onto the veranda. Margaret clutched him to her.

'Mummy was so worried. Just supposing you chopped your right hand off? You'd have to learn to write left-handed. You'd fall miles behind at school.'

'If I did lose my hand,' Ralph said, 'I'd have a hook put on and I'd be like Captain Hook.'

'That's what is called tempting providence,' Margaret warned.

'He's only having a joke,' Uncle Bill said. 'You'll overprotect him and he'll be afraid of his own shadow. The only thing to look out for here is military traffic. There's a camp just down the road.'

Veronica appeared with a full basket of eggs. 'You'll never guess how many I've got. Twenty seven!'

'And just look at the state of you. Your knees are black. That's through crawling under hedges.'

'She looks a real tomboy that one,' Uncle Bill remarked.

'I'm trying to raise her to be a nice polite young lady,' Margaret protested.

'You've got a battle on your hands,' Bill laughed.

The next day, Margaret took the children to the coast. They walked it, except for Veronica, who insisted on being pushed by Ralph in Uncle Bill's handcart. They had only travelled half a mile when a huge Army lorry appeared suddenly on a bend and seemed to be heading straight for them. They all jumped out of the way. Veronica finished in a ditch. The handcart was yards away.

'Are you all right, Veronica?' Margaret cried out.

'Yes mummy.'

'Come to Mummy then! You poor dear, you're all cuts and bruises. We'll have to turn back home.'

'No Mummy, don't! We haven't got far to walk. There's the sea.'

'Come on then,' Margaret conceded.

They reached the beach. There was a shady area near some rocks where they sat down to eat their picnic lunch. Part of the beach was walled off to form a small swimming hole.

Ralph and Veronica splashed about and each managed to put together seven or eight strokes of breaststroke while Margaret stood on the shore encouraging them until she called them in for their picnic. 'What a lovely day this has been,' she enthused, 'all alone on a lovely stretch of beach with my two little scamps.' She hugged them and smothered them in kisses. 'My little water cherubs! Do you love me?'

'We love Daddy too,' Veronica said.

'Of course you do, but you love Mommy now don't you?'

'But Daddy would be here if he could,' Ralph countered.

Margaret dressed them and they all walked along the beach, Veronica in the handcart.

'And have you enjoyed your first seaside holiday, children?'

'It's been an adventure,' Ralph said.

'Stop a moment,' Margaret ordered, and took her box brownie camera from her bag.

'Stand nearer to Veronica, Ralph. You stay in the handcart Veronica. That's perfect. Click, click, click. There! I can't wait to see it when the film's developed.'

'You'll send Daddy a photo, won't you?' Veronica asked.

That evening Ralph watched through the window as Uncle Bill arrived home, a pole slung across his shoulders and on each side of the pole hung four rabbits. He ran out to greet him.

'Have you shot those, Uncle Bill?'

'I have indeed, young man.'

'Are you going out tomorrow?'

'Probably.'

'Can I come?'

'As far as I'm concerned, yes, but you'll have to ask your mother.'

'She'll say it's too dangerous.'

'I know what she'll say, but leave it to me'

Uncle Bill went into the kitchen. Peggy and Margaret were sitting at the table shelling peas.

'I'm taking young Ralph shooting rabbits tomorrow,' he announced.

As expected Margaret said that it was far too dangerous.

'Guns are only dangerous when they're not handled correctly. I'll make sure he's all right. He asked me if he could come with me. It wasn't the other way around.'

'He can't go,' Margaret insisted.

'He'll be all right with Dad,' Peggy asserted. 'He'll be as safe as houses.'

'He can't go and that's that.'

'I'm going to call him in. Ralph!' Uncle Bill shouted.

Ralph came running into the kitchen.

'I wanted to take you rabbit shooting tomorrow, but your mother won't let me.'

'Veronica and I promised Daddy that we'd do what Mommy told us while he was away in the Navy.'

'I think that your obedience should be rewarded. Margaret, can I take him with me just to watch? He doesn't have to do anything. He can learn something though. So what do you say?'

There was silence.

'He's my only little boy. I worry too much about him, I suppose. Yes, he can go.'

'Thanks Mommy. I'll be good.'

'I hope you will. Now be off with you.'

Uncle Bill followed Ralph out.

'About four in the afternoon we'll go, son. You did well in there. Nobody lost face. You should be a diplomat when you grow up.' Ralph was not certain what a diplomat was, but it sounded quite exciting and he was looking forward to being one in some remote country like Ecuador. He heard voices from the kitchen.

'You're mollycoddling him, Margaret,' Peggy was saying. 'Veronica too, I suspect. Let them do what other kids do. Ralph's a very sensible young lad. He showed his absolute loyalty to you when he said he'd promised his father to obey you. You should be proud of him. No doubt you are. I'm not the one to advise you because I have no children, but I believe most people would say that a child should not be smothered in love or over protected.'

Chapter 2

The Arbo Gang

In 1946 professional football resumed after a seven-year break for war. The nation was stirred and soon football grounds all over the country were packed every Saturday afternoon. Men back from the services, their brothers, sons and fathers, young and old, all flocked to the stadiums. Villa Park, Molyneux, The Hawthorns and Saint Andrews were the biggest Midlands grounds housing Aston Villa, Wolves, West Bromwich Albion and Birmingham City respectively.

Many made their trip to their home ground directly from work. Gates of sixty thousand were not uncommon. The war was over. People craved normality and absolutely nothing was more normal than Association Football.

Ralph became a football fanatic and so did his mates His father, Hugh, invalided out of the Navy near to the end of the war with eye problems, joined the football hysteria and started going to the Wolves home games with a neighbour. Every other Saturday evening, he would arrive home with a crumpled programme in his fist, and over dinner, treat the family to a kick-by-kick account of the whole match, to the utter boredom of Margaret and Veronica.

The Wolves (Wolverhampton Wanderers) were a great team in the immediate post-war years. The Black Country crowd took a lot of pleasing. Only a thumping victory was acceptable and they got it nearly every time. The sight of the old gold shirts on the rampage with the flying wingers Mullen and Hancock was a wonderment. It was an image that Ralph would carry in his mind for many a long year.

Ralph, Tommy and Dennis took to playing in the evenings at The Arboretum (Arbo). The Arbo Gang had grown to a male membership of twelve, netting the founders six shillings, which was in the safe keeping of Dennis, the biggest. Several girls had joined at a special rate of threepence. They hung around near the touchline cheering on their favourite boys. Veronica claimed Tommy as her sweetheart and even had a fight with another girl over him. Ralph was doggedly followed by a skinny, bespectacled girl in plaits named Barbara. She kept on asking him if he really loved her. He would usually grunt 'yeah,' and she would follow up with 'Yes but do you really, really love me?' He would grunt again and she would ask 'Yes, but do you really, really, truly love me?' These tiresome exchanges would continue until he was forced to admit that he really, truly, deeply, sincerely, for ever and ever, hopelessly loved her to the bottom of his heart. By this time they would have reached her garden gate. Ralph was always relieved to get rid of her. Even at the garden gate, she lingered and said, 'I won't kiss you now Ralph. We'll save that for our first date.'

'Good idea,' was always his reply.

The patch of ground where the Arbo Gang played football had been marked out into several pitches, but so many thousands of boots had pounded over the ground that hardly a white line existed. That did not worry them. They would have played a game of football in a swamp. Before the game they would always announce their identity.

'I'll be Tommy Lawton,' Tommy would state.

'I'll be Stan Matthews,' Dennis would claim.

Ralph was always Wilf Mannion. They played until it was dark. The park keeper would arrive swinging his bunch of keys. He would holler, 'Time's up!'

'Who was the best footballer you ever saw?' they once asked the park keeper.

'Well, I saw Pongo Waring at the Villa a few times, but I don't think any of those pre-war players were a patch on this chap Matthews.'

‘We’ve got Dixie Dean’s autograph on our football,’ Dennis told him.

‘Let’s have a look!’ He squinted at the football in the half-light. ‘Whatever was there has worn away.’

‘We don’t care,’ Ralph said. ‘We know it was there and that’s that.’ They sauntered home.

‘It’s no point in us saying who was or is the greatest footballer,’ Tommy said. ‘How would we know?’

How indeed? None of them had ever been to a First Division game. Ralph said that his father had promised to take him to the Wolves sometime where he would see the legendary old gold shirts flying up the field. At present this spectacle, though vivid, was still a figment of his imagination. In the meantime, all three of them got their information from the papers or word of mouth. If the papers said that Stan Matthews was ‘the wizard of dribble’ then he was. Many boys kept scrapbooks with a page for each of the twenty-two First Division teams. These pages would be covered with press cuttings. Ralph’s father used to get wild with him when he cut out photographs from the newspaper before he had even picked it up to read.

One balmy Wednesday evening in September, Ralph was walking home from school when he heard a car horn blow. It was his father with Mr O’Brien from next door in his yellow and black Austin 7.

‘Jump in!’ Hugh Tucker ordered. ‘We’re off to see the Wolves.’

‘Does Mom know?’

‘Yes she does and she doesn’t like the idea of your being with all those rough men, but we’re taking you anyway.’

‘What about my tea?’

‘We’re having fish and chips in Wolverhampton.’

‘Sounds great, Dad.’

Wolves were playing Middlesbrough who had the great Wilf Mannion and the England captain, George Hardwick, in their side. Mannion! The man Ralph had ‘been’ so many times. They saw the Middlesbrough team getting off the coach. They were all sombrely dressed in grey or dark blue suits. Ralph could not pick out Mannion. Maybe he was not playing. Ralph was bitterly disappointed. He had expected to see a team of giants, all ready for kick off, muscles rippling beneath their maroon shirts. Instead they looked no different from his father.

Looking back on it, he could not even remember the score.

He remembered that it was impossible to get near the fish and chip shop so they went hungry. He sat atop a crash barrier, uncomfortable and precarious, with his father's hand behind him to steady him if necessary. The noise from the crowd was overwhelming, as were the odours of cigarette smoke, oily overalls and beery breath. All around them greasy-haired roughs cursed and derided any player who even saw the ball let alone made a mistake. It was a far cry from his innocent comic book world of mighty gladiatorial supermen sportingly battling it out amidst cries of 'Well done sir!' All the way from Wolverhampton Ralph, usually a talkative young man, sat hunched up in complete silence in the back of Austin 7. He had seen his heroes. They banged the ball all around the field without, it appeared, any plan. The crowd booed and whistled for the whole ninety minutes. He vowed there and then that he would never have heroes, not sporting heroes anyway. His heroes, in future, would be explorers or men who walked on a tightrope across Niagara Falls or great authors or artists but definitely not footballers.

Next evening he was back in the Arboretum with Tommy and Dennis ready to go through there established procedure: 'I'll be Tommy Lawton.' 'I'll be Stan Matthews.'

'I'll be Ralph Tucker.'

'But that's your name?' Dennis said.

'That's right. I'm going to be me.'

‘What happened to Wilf Mannion?’

‘Don’t know. Don’t care.’

They played their game, but they were half-hearted and sluggish. They were ready to go home well before the park keeper arrived.

Tommy and Dennis rounded up on Ralph for being miserable and spoiling the game. Ralph told them of his experience in great detail, adding, ‘they were just booting the ball up and down the field and chasing it. They were fouling each other and missing open goals. We could play better than that.’

‘What about Mannion?’

‘I couldn’t pick him out. Maybe he wasn’t playing. It didn’t matter because I’m not going to have a hero again, not a footballer anyway. He’d have to be a tightrope walker or a man who could ride a motorbike at four hundred miles an hour on one wheel.’

‘I’m not having any heroes either after what you’ve told me,’ Tommy decided. ‘I’m definitely not going to be Tommy Lawton. What’s he ever done for me?’

‘So that’s Lawton out and Matthews too,’ Dennis confirmed. ‘We don’t have to be anybody but ourselves, and we’ll tell ourselves that we are the mighty Arbo Gang, better than Arsenal or anyone. We don’t look up to footballers, we look down on them because we’re better than them and we’re only ten and we don’t get paid. What my mom and my aunty and all their friends say about footballers is true. They say that footballers are layabouts. They get paid for ninety minutes a week while working men have to put in long hours and shifts to feed their families. It’s scandalous that footballers can pick up £11 a week for hanging round dance halls and that.’

With this new determination and resolution the Arbo Gang got together a good team, which became the basis for the Chuckery Junior School first team which went a whole season unbeaten. It was a golden age for Ralph.

So much for the romance of football, which, like beauty, is in the eye of the beholder, and dependant on one's age; whether it is the image of Bobby Moore holding up the World Cup, the wizardry of Matthews in the famous 1953 Cup Final or the day back in the thirties when Walsall had the temerity to beat Arsenal and knock them out of the Cup. For Ralph, it was the memory of the Arbo Gang team playing their hearts out on a muddy field with a football that once was kicked by Dixie Dean.

'Maybe we can have just one hero,' Ralph suggested.

In 1948 Ralph took his 'eleven-plus' examination or 'The Scholarship' as it was better known. To his parents delight he got into Queen Mary's Grammar School. Tommy and Dennis did well enough to get into a 'secondary modern school' as comprehensives were then known.

'This won't affect the Arbo Gang,' Dennis asserted. 'Just because Tommy and I are at Edward Shelley School and you'll be a posh Grammar School kid in a silly green, red and yellow cap, we can still stay friends. Anyway, you're still the official holder of the football. Nobody else is going to come up with another one, so it's your ball /your game as usual.'

'We also want to go on seeing your Nan and eating tarts and biscuits,' Tommy said.

'The most important thing,' Ralph asserted 'is that we all swore an oath on the Bible to be friends for life.'

'Yes,' Dennis added, 'and if you break an oath that you've made on the Bible, you can be struck down dead. I know because my mom told me about a man who said he loved her, but he didn't really and the next week he was run over by a tram That was God's way of punishing him for being deceitful.'

'A bit hard on him, though,' Tommy reasoned.

‘No. Deceiving a woman is the worst thing a man can do. My aunty told me that it’s even worse than a man rubbing marmalade in a woman’s hair which happened to her once.’

They parted at the end of Moncrieff Street. Ralph took the long walk to Gorway along the Broadway. His mother was waiting at the door.

‘Where have you been?’ she asked him. ‘Of all days, you had to dawdle home today. Well? Have you some good news for me?’

‘Oh, yes,’ he said casually, ‘I got into Queen Mary’s.’

Margaret shrieked with joy. ‘Oh, come to Mummy, you absolute darling clever boy! My wonderful studious little Ralph. Oh! My adorable son. My cherub, my curly-haired little scamp. Let me kiss you, my angel.’

‘I’m glad you’re pleased, Mom.’

‘Pleased? I’m overjoyed.’

‘What if I hadn’t passed?’

‘It doesn’t bear thinking of. You’d finish up sweeping the factory floor and making tea in some horrible smelly leather works or working down the tip burning rubbish. You’d be drinking stout with a whole lot of low-down men in some vile tavern. You’d get worse and worse asthma through smoking Woodbines.’

‘Wouldn’t you and Dad and Veronica come to my aid if I was in such a terrible state?’

‘Obviously we would try, but by that time it could be too late. You would be filthy and smelly through sleeping rough. You’d virtually be a tramp.’

‘There was a wonderful poet named W.H. Davies who was a tramp.’

‘Well there you are then. He probably failed his eleven-plus and had settled for a life on the road when he could have been the Poet Laureate. The gap between poor and good education is immense when it comes to opportunities.

Thank God you've made the right start. I can imagine you now, punting down the river with an elegant young lady looking admiringly at you. You would be wearing a straw boater above your lovely curly hair. How gorgeous you'd look!'

'I think I'd look like a ponce.'

'Just like your father. In the middle of an important conversation you choose to introduce crudity.'

'I was only joking, Mom.'

'Well-educated young men do not make crude remarks.'

'I bet even the King knows a few crude jokes.'

Ralph saw his father pull his car up on the drive.

'I'm home everybody,' he shouted as he put his key in the door. 'I saw Wesley Taylor outside his house. He's very pleased. His daughter Janice has passed to Queen Mary's.'

'She's not the only one,' Margaret Tucker said proudly.

'You mean Ralph?'

'Yes indeed. Young Ralph has taken the first step to a marvellous career in the Law, the Church or perhaps politics – the second step will be Oxford.'

'Well, don't let us get too excited,' Hugh said. 'Congratulations anyway, Ralph. This is an occasion when I would've liked to have taken you down the pub for a celebratory drink, but I can't. You're only eleven.'

'I'm celebrating in a way, Dad. Tommy and Dennis and I are going to hang around the Arboretum – no particular place. We're just going to tell yarns.'

'Is that little kiosk still there, where they sell ice cream?'

'Yes it is, Dad.'

'Here's two bob, son. You should be able to treat your mates on that.'

'Not half!'

Veronica arrived. 'I'm so excited. I saw Janice Taylor She said she'd got through to Queen Mary's. I asked her about Ralph and she said that he had too.' She flung her arms around him. 'My clever brother. I think Janice

Taylor's keen on you. Why don't you ask her round for tea?'

'Not tonight though,' Ralph told her. 'I'm going out with Dennis and Tommy. Dad's given me two bob for ice creams.'

'You'd better make the best of it,' Margaret told him, 'Once you start at Queen Mary's you won't be associating with the likes of Tommy and Dennis. You'll befriend boys of your own class.'

'Let the boy choose his friends. The class system is on its way out. That's why we've got a Labour government. The old days of the worker doffing his cap and saying "Yes Guv'nor, No Guv'nor" are over. Tommy and Dennis will have the same chances as Ralph. I doubt if either would get a university place but would they want one anyway?' Hugh asked.

The Arbo three ambled along a pathway to the ice cream kiosk. They bought three cones and sat on a park bench to eat them.

'Was your Mom pleased?' Tommy asked Ralph.

'Yes, she was. She was so excited. She rattled on about punting down the river. I don't even know what punting is.'

'I do,' Dennis said. 'It means putting money on dogs and horses. My dad used to do it. Now he's gone and we don't know where he is and it all started with punting. Sometimes I can hear my mom crying. I feel like crying too, but you can't cry if you're in a gang can you?'

'I can't cry either,' Ralph said. 'Nan Tucker told me "Tuckers don't cry" but that doesn't include Veronica or my mother. Shall we have a look at the peacock?' They walked to the peacock's cage.

'I feel sorry for him,' Ralph said, 'cooped up in his cage for years and years and years. Mom used to bring Veronica and me here when we were very little. Veronica could make the peacock display his tail. She used to say, "Open up in the name of the law" and she said it in a kind of squeaky parrot's voice.'

'Let's try it,' Dennis suggested.

'You do it, Den. You're good at voices,' Tommy told him.

'Okay. Open up in the name of the law.'

Surely and slowly the peacock spread his magnificent plumage.

'He's looking at us,' Ralph said. 'He's saying he wants to fly away forever and die in a nice warm place.'

'If I had my way,' Dennis said, 'I'd let all these little caged birds escape too. They should be back in South America or Africa or wherever they started. What boring lives they've got! They jump from one little branch to another. For a bird it's the equivalent of being in prison and who are we to put them there?'

'Fancy another ice cream lads?' Ralph asked.

'I wish you'd pass your eleven-plus every week,' Tommy said.

'There'll be times in life when we may have to help each other,' Ralph said. 'It's one for all and all for one or is it all for one and one for all? Anyway, we've sworn it on the Bible.'

The day came when Ralph was to start at Queen Mary's School. He was excited. A lot of his mother's jubilance had rubbed off on him. Maybe this *was* the day that would define his life – his brilliant career as a diplomat.

He set off early, taking the familiar walk to the Arboretum and catching the inner circle bus to Moss Close. Moss Close had once been a preparatory school but was now the first and second years of Queen Mary's. It was over half a mile from the 'main school'. It had once been a house in its own grounds. The grounds had become playgrounds. The house became the school. It was a rambling old building which Ralph liked immediately; a jumble of architectural styles, originally late Victorian with an Edwardian extension and a pseudo-Jacobean addition where once had been a formal garden. It housed six classrooms, a conservatory and a staff room.

There was an initiation ceremony for new boys called 'the bumps.' Second formers divided themselves into groups of four. They grabbed new boys by the arms and legs, threw them into the air and let them hit the ground – bump! Ralph, in his brand new cap and blazer and carrying a new satchel was an easy target and soon four second formers were onto him. He flung his satchel behind him so that it did not hamper him. He picked out the smallest of his attackers and punched him hard on the nose. Blood poured from his nostrils.

'You're not supposed to do that,' they protested.

'Wait till you meet my two best mates,' Ralph warned, 'then you really will see blood.'

'Where are they then? These best mates of yours?'

'Up your arse!'

The bell rang to call them all into line. Word had spread about Ralph's fictitious best mates. Everybody wondered who they were.'One thing's for sure,' Ralph told himself, 'I'm not going to get the bumps.'

The newcomers were put through an examination similar to the eleven-plus test. This separated them into forms 1 (Remove), Form 1 and 1 (shell). In simpler terms - 1R, 1 and 1S, 1R being the top grade, which theoretically meant that 1R were the top academics of their age in town. Ralph got into 1R. He could not wait to get home. His mother was at the front window.

'Don't get out of breath, darling, you'll bring your asthma on.'

'I won't. I only get asthma when I'm feeling bored or miserable. Shall I tell you what happened?'

'Of course.'

‘We had to take another long test to divide us into forms 1R, 1 and 1S – three classes of thirty. I’m in 1R, which is the top one.

‘That’s wonderful. I’m so, so proud of my little student, so smart in his new school uniform. You did it all for mummy, didn’t you? You could feel me urging you on, couldn’t you?’

‘I did it for Dad too, and for myself and Veronica and Nan Tucker and everybody.’

He heard his father’s key in the door.

‘Hugh!’ she shrieked. ‘Ralph has got into 1R which is the highest grade.’

‘Well done, son,’ Hugh said. ‘I’m parched. I’m going to make us a cuppa.’

‘Well done? Well done? Is that all you can say? He’ll be one of the top thirty boys in Walsall for his age.’

‘What are the bottom thirty like, I wonder?’

‘Typical! You don’t give a damn, do you?’

‘It was only a joke, my dear.’

‘A joke?’ He’s taken the first step to a brilliant career as British Ambassador to – er – Bolivia and to you it’s all a joke?’

‘Si Señora.’

‘I’m talking to a brick wall, aren’t I?’

‘No you’re not. Sit down and calm down. Ralph, come here son. I’m not going to give you two bob this time. I’m going to take you into town on Saturday and buy you an educational present like a geometry set.’

Margaret was hysterical, ‘What a wonderful present! I knew you’d eventually realise the significance of today. How lucky Ralph is to have an educated father. If he were a Chuckery boy, he’d probably be given a bag of crisps or a bottle of fizzy drink.’

‘Let’s get off the class thing, shall we? Let me try and explain something to you. Margaret, I love you dearly. I love Ralph and Veronica dearly. I thought about you all every freezing day up to Murmansk. My main concern was that you were all still alive. I used to make up images of my life after the war. I saw us all on a beach, playing cricket or gathering shells. I saw us walking over Gillity Fields. I saw us around the fire and I would be reading an epic poem to you all, like 'How Horatius saved the bridge'. I never thought much about how Ralph and Veronica were doing at school. If they do well, that's a bonus. If they don't, I won't be crying about it. I'd rather Ralph was average and a nice lad than brilliant and conceited. I wish our kids a good life whatever they do. If they're happy, then so shall I be. And now I'm hungry.'

Ralph settled down quickly at Queen Mary's school. He learnt to play rugby, but he had no intention of giving up soccer or the Arbo Gang. He had a liking for languages and did well at French.

At the end of each month a form list was issued giving the order of merit of the form and analysed in great detail by the form master. The list was very important. At the end of term, the two lowest achievers were relegated to Form 1.The two boys with the highest marks were promoted from Form 1 to 1R, rather like the football league system. Despite his flair for French, Ralph finished twenty-ninth of thirty boys. This was mainly due to his complete failure to master the simple procedures in physics and chemistry. The science master, Mr Fazackerly, the most miserable-looking man in the school and known as 'Spaniel', had a very low opinion of Ralph.

'Tucker,' he said one day, as he watched Ralph get completely flummoxed as to what exactly he had to do in an experiment involving something called a pipette, 'You're like a cow with a musket. Do not touch anything. Sit quietly – somewhere where I cannot see you.'

Things went from bad to worse the following week when he started a fire in the lab. He was called before Mr W. E.

Tregorran (known as 'Wet'), the headmaster of Moss Close, to explain himself.

'I'm rather inept and clumsy at some things, sir,' he pleaded. 'That, and my not knowing what I'm doing, makes things rather hard for me. Apart from Aristotle jumping into a pool, scientific knowledge does not seem to stay in my head, sir.'

'It seems that way,' Mr Tregorran sighed. 'You're certainly no Isaac Newton. In fact I think, at this stage, we can safely assume that science or anything remotely connected with science will not be your forte in life. Therefore, I am taking you out of physics and chemistry lessons, mindful of the historic borough of Walsall becoming engulfed in flames. You will spend the time previously taken up by physics and chemistry in linguistic revision. You are dismissed.'

'So I'm not getting the cane, sir?'

'That can be arranged. Now get out!'

Chapter 3

The Nine-Inch Trophy

October 1951 saw Clement Atlee's Labour Party replaced by Churchill's Conservatives.

'It's not necessarily going to work out,' Hugh told Ralph.

'How come, Dad?'

'Churchill was the right man for Britain at war, but is he the right man for Britain at peace?'

'You tell me, Dad.'

'How should I know?'

'You're the top man when it comes to discussions in the pub, or so you say, so tell me what you think. We've got a special Form 1VR discussion period tomorrow and I want to have my say. I've noted down a few things that you've told me.'

'But it's your own ideas you'll need to put across, not mine. Tell me, what do you think will happen over the next few years?'

'I can't speak from experience, Dad, because I've led a very sheltered life. One thing I do know is that the equality that everybody hoped for just hasn't materialised. Tommy and Denis have got none of the things that I have – Monopoly, dinky toys, Meccano, encyclopaedias, a big garden, a car, seaside holidays to come. So where's the equality?

'I think that people are disappointed and Churchill is the man to turn to. And maybe some people are a bit remorseful and they wished they'd voted for the Conservatives in 1946. If Churchill led us through the war, we should have given him the chance to lead us through the peace.'

'You've got a point there, son. I'm one of those people who naively expected a brave new world. Well, we've got the Health Service. I suppose that's a start. Real equality would mean breaking down the class system, but do we want to be like the Soviet Union? No. The class system is firmly ensconced and Churchill, however great a statesman he is, epitomises it. We haven't heard the last of the Labour Party though. They'll be back aiming for Utopia again, cuddling up to the Trades Unions. Strikes and strife is where we're heading, son. Remember who told you first – Hugh Tucker, The Oracle!'

'Can you see into the future then, Dad?'

'Wish I could. I know somebody who can.'

'Who?'

'Your mother's friend, Aunty Lorna. I think you met her once during the war.'

'Yes. I remember it as if it was yesterday. We called her 'The Beautiful Lady'. What does she see in the future?'

'Things that may happen. She doesn't always get everything right. She's almost a clairvoyant.'

'Anyway, Dad, thanks for your ideas.'

'Not at all. I'm glad you're interested in politics. Good luck for tomorrow. Remember to put your point over forcefully and don't let hecklers put you off.'

The next morning the desks in form 1VR were repositioned to form a three-tier semicircle. The form master, Mr Cox, a man known and liked by all for his fairness and firmness, called them to order.

'These two-hour discussion groups are being held simultaneously in forms 1R,2R,3R & 1VR.' he said. 'It is not a debate. It is more of a forum. We invite you to air your views and invite anybody with similar or opposite views on the same subject to have their say. A small trophy will be awarded to the person who impresses the adjudicator most. I am the adjudicator. I'll start by bandying a few notions about:

'The country has just had a change of government. Is this important to you? Would you rather be dismissive of all politicians and say quite cynically that they are all the same? How important are elections? Who are Labour? Who are the Tories? Who are the T.U.C? What do they stand for? Is class an issue?

'Before anybody speaks let me warn you that there will be no heckling, no remarks from the floor, no booing and no deviation from the topic which is 'Britain under successive governments'. Who'll start the ball rolling?'

Ralph raised his hand eagerly.

'Yes? You, boy. Announce yourself.'

'R. M. Tucker, sir. Gentlemen, may I pose this question? Is Churchill the right man for Prime Minister? He was an indomitable force throughout the wartime coalition government. He was a great leader and brought us through a war. He was the man for the occasion. He was the right man for Britain at war. Is he the right man for Britain at peace?'

'Good point, Tucker. Come on, come on you dozy lot. Is anyone going to challenge that?'

There was silence.

'All right, Tucker. Since you're the only one with a tongue in his head, elaborate!'

'Yes sir. A lot of middle-class people were shocked when Clement Atlee won the 1945 General Election. They thought it rather an affront to the heroic Churchill. I have often asked this question of my elders, that is to say: Why did Atlee get in so easily? The answer was always the same. Nobody but nobody, especially ex-servicemen, wanted to live in Britain as it had been in the 1930s, with poor health and housing, unemployment and poverty. They wanted a radical change and could not imagine Churchill, a Patrician, achieving that change. They perceived that an upper-class politician would not understand how bad conditions really were.'

'Excellent, Tucker. Now let's have some different ideas, you sleepy lot.'

A boy put his hand up.

'At last.'

'Blenkinsop, sir. Socialism is another name for communism. There is a secret plot to enforce a Soviet-type system here. The protagonists are communist workers and Trades Union leaders. My father told me.'

'I see,' Mr Cox said, 'What kind of work is your father in, Blenkinsop?'

'He's got a building business, sir. Communists have wormed their way in and have caused two strikes already.'

A boy's hand shot up.

'Lancaster, sir. That's all rubbish, Blenkinsop. If they wanted to impose a Soviet-style government they could have done so by having Communist candidates in all the constituencies. They didn't and there isn't a single Communist MP. Your father's probably underpaying his men. You're the meanest boy in the form and now we know where you get it from.'

'Don't you insult my father, Ginger Nut!'

'That'll do!' Mr Cox ordered. 'We don't want this to develop into a slanging match. Let's get back to the main business.'

'Cavendish, sir. Well, sir, even though some people get a bit hot-headed about Communists and Socialists, we cannot take the subject lightly. A 'them and us' situation exists. 'Them' being the working class and 'us' being the more comfortable middle class. This is hardly likely to change under Churchill. We could return to the thirties. We could have a situation where the poor get poorer and the rich get richer. Churchill is a die-hard, let's face it. I think that he should be highly honoured by his country for the valiant stand he has always taken against tyranny, and then should be asked to retire gracefully after a year and be replaced by an experienced Conservative front bencher, of which there are many.'

'Oakley, sir. Churchill is an Empire man. He fought in the Sudan and was a journalist in the South African War. He stands for a Great Britain that is regrettably losing its possessions. He is not the man to oversee this handing over of power. I hope the Tories do well, but I think there should be a younger leader – somebody nearer to the people.'

'Well done, Oakley.'

The discussion went on for two hours until Mr Cox rang a bell. 'Thank you, boys. You did very well. It is encouraging for me to hear how eager, nay passionate, you are about your subject. Nevertheless, you were nearly all reading from notes that you had prepared the night before, with parental help I suspect. That will not be allowed again. The purpose of these discussion groups is to increase your awareness and to make you more articulate.

'The next discussion group will be in four weeks' time in the assembly hall. Two teams of ten will discuss the issue of women's rights. I shall select our team. The opposition will be from the girls' school, so expect a few fiery little ladies to put you in your places. No hanky-panky. No passing notes and giggling. No trying to get a glimpse of a young lady's navy blue knickers.'

'Today's trophy goes to Tucker, who was the only boy who spoke without reference to notes.'

Ralph ran through the park, past the greenhouses into the wooded area of the 'arbo', past the poor peacock, on towards the main road, onto the Inner Circle bus, off at Birmingham Road and another sprint home. Margaret saw him through the window and went to the front door.

'My clever little man's early and he looks so happy. I wonder what he has in store for me.'

‘Guess what? I won the trophy for the best speaker at the discussion group. Here it is, look! It’s a nine-inch statue of Benjamin Disraeli holding a big sheaf of papers and there’s a plaque which is going to be engraved ‘R.Tucker 1951’. It’s called ‘The Disraeli junior public speaker’s award’.

She threw her arms around him, almost crushing him. ‘Oh, my wonderful clever boy. Let Mummy hold you for ever and ever. This is a watershed, a turning point, an indicator, an omen, a platform for a brilliant career in the House of Lords.’

‘But I’m not a lord.’

‘That would present no problem. You’d be a friend of the Prime Minister and you’d get knighted for services to something or other.’

‘Services to asthma?’

‘Of course. I knew your asthma would come in useful one day.’

‘But we shouldn’t look too far into the future. I’ve only won a nine-inch trophy.’

‘Yes, but these trophies will get taller and taller, the more you progress in your public speaking career.’

Veronica came in and asked what the celebrations were for.

‘Ralph has won a trophy for his brilliant public speaking. I wouldn’t be surprised if we got phone calls asking him to speak at village halls up and down the country.’

‘I’m in the next discussion group in a month’s time,’ Veronica said casually. ‘It’s boys versus girls. Janice Taylor’s in the team too. I expect she’d like to see your nine-inch trophy, Ralph.’

‘Now, now Veronica. You don’t have to turn everything into a smutty joke.’

‘I didn’t mean to do that. I’m very proud of my brother.’

‘Good girl. And you’ve done very well by getting into the team.’

‘It was voluntary. I picked myself.’

'Yes, but you had the confidence to be a volunteer. Just supposing you both won a trophy? Can you imagine the potential? Brother and sister in the House of Lords? Sir Ralph Tucker and Lady Veronica Tucker. It's a pity it's such a common name – Tucker. My family name would be more appropriate.'

'What, Rowley?' Veronica asked.

'Why, yes indeed. "A frog he would a wooing go. Hey ho' said Rowley."'

'What about little Tommy Tucker who sang for his supper?'

Margaret took hold of both of them and held them to her bosom. 'My little scamps. You make me so happy.' The smile left her face. 'Your father's coming down the drive.'

The day arrived for the second discussion group. The teams were ordered to announce themselves.

'Boys!' shouted Mr Cox, 'Cut this noise out and introduce yourselves, surnames only.'

'Tucker' 'Blenkinsop' 'Lancaster' 'Oakley' 'Gregg' 'Mackintosh' 'Deacon' 'Venables' ' Spratt.'

'Good. Girls please. First name only.'

'Janice' 'Mona' 'Alice' 'Janet' 'Irene' 'Barbara' 'Veronica' 'Brenda' 'Shirley' 'Yvonne.'

'The subject is women's' rights,' Mr Cox announced. 'Consider these factors – equal rights, equal opportunities, attitudes towards women, women's contribution to the war effort, women in government. There are a few topics. Who'll start the ball rolling?'

'Veronica Tucker.'

'Begin Veronica.'

'Certainly women should push themselves more and show confidence. When we've got something to say, let's say it. We should be aiming for half of all MPs to be women, half the police force and half the fire brigade. These are simple jobs. All a policeman has to do is whack wrongdoers with his truncheon. All a fireman has to do is make sure he's pointing the hose in the right direction. Women could get these jobs. It's a matter of personality. I'm the shortest of the girls' team by three inches. I need a strong personality and a strong will, otherwise I'd get picked on. So ladies, don't be shy or embarrassed like Janice Taylor over there who's blushing bright red because she's opposite my brother and she fancies him.'

There followed an outbreak of clapping, cheering and booing.

'Now, now.' Mr Cox said. 'You were going quite well, Veronica, until you decided to get personal. What do you have to say about this, Janice?'

'I am blushing. I can't help it. It's because I am attracted to Ralph Tucker because he's well built and gentlemanly and he has lovely curly hair and dreamy eyes.'

The claps and whistles reached a crescendo.

'Veronica Tucker's only thirteen. She thinks that she's got confidence, but it's really just cheek. She's still a tomboy climbing trees and building dens in the garden and she can be as cheeky as she likes because her mother forgives her for everything. This is not a little girl's debate it's a women's discussion. I'm developing as a woman. I shall be wearing a bra soon. I'll prove that I'm not shy.' Janice vowed.

She stood on a chair, pulled up her gymslip and revealed her navy blue knickers to a chorus of cheers from the boys and screams from the girls.

'Order!' Mr Cox shouted. 'Sit down Janice. If this session is going to develop into a circus, I shall call a halt to it. Do you understand?'

There was a muffled acknowledgement.

'Blenkinsop, sir. My dad says that women working in offices are nothing but a nuisance. They've got no interest in anything but varnishing their nails. They never stay long because they all get pregnant.'

‘Lancaster, sir. We were having fun until you decided to shoot your mouth off Blenkinsop.’

‘Who asked you for opinion Gingerballs?’

‘Sit down, Blenkinsop,’ Mr Cox ordered. ‘Have you got anything worthwhile to say Lancaster?’

‘Yes sir. It’s not that men and women are unequal, it’s just that they’re different.’

‘How did you work that out?’ Blenkinsop asked

‘That’s enough from you,’ Mr Cox said wearily. ‘Sit down and shut up. Continue Lancaster.’

‘Yes sir. Women and men have different functions both anatomically and socially. So it is hard to talk in terms of equality.’

‘Let me cut in here,’ Mr Cox asked. ‘Finish what you have to say Lancaster, but in future you must not, I repeat *not* read from a script or a notebook.’

‘Yes sir, sorry sir. Women have the difficult task of child bearing, whereas men are expected to fight in wars. Man feels it within himself to make supreme sacrifices and in return, he expects his womenfolk to provide his comforts. Of course, we live in a country where social mores are changing, but I wanted to point out that the sharing of duties between men and women is as old as time.’

‘Thank you, Lancaster. There were some good points there.

‘How about you, Tucker, you’re the present holder of the trophy. Have you got anything to say before the trophy is handed over to this month’s winner?’

‘The only thing that I have to say, sir, is that I have enjoyed the debates and I shall bring in the trophy tomorrow from the engraver. My father wants to know who is paying the engraver. I told him that the school would pay against a receipt. I hope I’m right. Janice Taylor should not have said what she did about my sister, but I like Janice so I’m willing to kiss and make up.’

With that he walked over to Janice Taylor, put his arms round her and kissed her. The kiss developed into a snog. Veronica rushed over to kiss Ralph and told Janice that everything was forgiven and soon everybody was kissing everybody. Somebody sat herself at the piano that was used for hymns every morning and started to play a sort of boogie-woogie music. Soon everybody was dancing around the assembly hall with absolute abandon. The Headmistress arrived on the scene with Mrs Glossop, the PT instructor. Eventually, order was restored and they were sitting down in teams again.

'By popular demand,' Mr Cox announced, 'the winner is Janice Taylor. Please do not resume your dancing and kissing. You've had your fun. Now get back to your form rooms and do some work.'

'Quite a handful these lot, aren't they Albert?' Mrs Glossop said to Mr Cox.

'What a fiasco!' Mr Cox sighed. 'To think that in twenty years' time, this lot will be running the country.'

Chapter 4

Ode to Janice Taylor

Hugh knocked on Ralph's bedroom door.

'Are you in there, son?'

'Yes dad. Come in.'

'You look awful, boy. Your face is as grey as ash.'

'I'm a nuisance.'

'Of course you're not. You've got very bad asthma.'

'I should be doing something.' He was finding it difficult to get the words out.

'Don't tax yourself.'

He put his hand on Ralph's forehead. It was hot and damp.

'Why are you sitting in a chair, Ralph? Wouldn't it be better to lie down?'

'It's easier sitting.'

'We'll be having dinner soon. Will you be able to eat anything?'

Ralph shook his head. His father left him.

They ate their dinner in silence. They all hoped that sometime, in the not too distant future, there would be a way of controlling asthma. A cure would be asking too much. There would perhaps be a spray or some magic pill that could be carried on the person. The medication that he was presently on did nothing to improve him. It simply made him woozy and light-headed. His attacks rarely lasted more than two days. It was an insidious thing. He could be fine one moment and seconds later, he would be wheezing and struggling for breath. Then, simple tasks like dressing or tying shoelaces became impossible. He never used asthma as an excuse for missing games or PT. In fact, he loved rugby and always gave it everything just to prove to people that he was not an invalid.

'I'll go and see him after dinner,' Margaret said, 'then Veronica, then we'll leave the poor boy with his books and hope and pray that he'll not have too difficult a night. I only hope that he'll be well enough to take his GCEs. What causes these attacks, I wonder? Doctor Brice says it's bronchial. Doctor Logan says it's a nervous condition.'

'Can I come in darling?'

'Yes mom.'

'How are you?'

'It's easing off. I'll be okay.'

'My instinct is to take you into my loving arms and soothe you and call you my angel and my dove. That is because I love my children so much. That will change now. You're sixteen. I'm not going to fuss around you anymore. I don't think I'm doing you any good. I think that, deep down, I never wanted you to grow up. You were both my little scamps. I've pampered you too much. One day we shall lose you and Veronica. You'll go your separate ways. You've both got strong personalities. You'll do well. As your father said a very long time ago, if you and Veronica go through life without causing anybody to worry about you, and in turn making someone happy that will be good enough. But though I'm saying all of these things, I have to lapse into the 'old' mother for just one last time for when I look into your eyes how can I help but love you so overwhelmingly? You are so beautiful.'

'I understand what you're saying, mother and it's a great relief.'

'I shall, of course, still be proud of you. I always will. You'll feel better now. I know you will. I'm going to send Veronica up.'

'My poor brother,' Veronica said, 'You never complain do you?'

‘No. Any news of any sort?’

‘I saw Janice Taylor today. She asked about you. She’s got quite big tits now. She showed me.’

‘Well I wouldn’t be interested,’ he said.’

‘Liar!’

‘I’ve got to concentrate on my GCE revision.’

‘All work and no play makes Ralph a dull boy.’

‘I don’t care. I shall be a boring old codger at a university, lecturing on the Icelandic sagas or something.’

‘No you won’t. Don’t be a martyr. Do you want me to ask Janice Taylor to come and see you, or not?’

‘She wouldn’t come. Ever since that chaotic discussion group, she’s hardly spoken to me.’

‘She was waiting for you to make a move.’

‘We were only fourteen. I thought it was all a lark in the assembly hall. Everybody was kissing everybody. Mind you, we’re sixteen now, so it’s different. I’m talking too much.’

‘You’re feeling better though, aren’t you?’

‘Yes, but I mustn’t get too excited.’

‘Of course not. I’ll go across to the Taylor’s’ house and bring Janice back.’

He threw his *Richard II* aside. He had lost his concentration. Janice Taylor would be here soon. He felt considerably better. His breathing was almost back to normal. He heard voices near the front door.

‘Janice!’ he heard his mother say. ‘How lovely to see you. We haven’t seen you for ages.’

‘I’ve been concentrating on ‘O’ level revision.’

‘Veronica will take you up to see Ralph. Don’t get him excited.’

He heard them on the stairs. ‘Come in Janice.’ he asked eagerly.

‘Poor Ralph,’ she said, ‘are you very ill?’

‘I was but not anymore.’

‘He mustn’t get excited,’ Veronica ordered.

‘I was going to show you something, but if it’s going to make you ill, I won’t.’

‘Maybe I could get a little bit excited without it harming my long term health.’

‘Come on Ralph! Be positive, like you were at the discussion group all that time ago.’

‘Show me then.’

She unbuttoned her school blazer, then her blouse.

‘D’you like them?’

‘Y-yes,’ he managed to say.

‘Janice!’ Hugh shouted from downstairs. ‘Your father just phoned. You’ve got to change out of your school uniform in time for your visitors.’

Hurriedly, she adjusted her dress.

‘Shall we see you again soon?’ Margaret asked.

‘I hope so, Mrs Tucker. There’ll be other times.’

‘You’re developing into a nice young lady. Give our regards to your family. By the way, your blouse is not done up properly. You’ve got all the buttons in the wrong button holes. Come here, let me put it right for you. There! I presume that you dressed in a hurry.’

‘Yes, well – er – we all make mistakes.’

‘Of course we do, my dear. There’s no need to blush.’

‘I bet you feel better now, dear brother,’ Veronica said.

‘Yes, I do as a matter of fact, but Janice seemed to intimate that when she said ‘other times’ she meant when I was ill.’

‘She did actually. Janice sees you as a dying poet like Bishop Percy Shelley or Lord Biro. She thinks you’re twice as good looking when you’re ill. Your eyes are dreamier and you’ve got an invalid poet’s sickly complexion. She wants you to write a poem for her called ‘Ode to Janice Taylor’. She likes life to be romantic.’

‘I see,’ he said gloomily.’ Who, pray, are Bishop Percy Shelley and Lord Biro?’

'Romantic poets.'

'They are *Percy Bysshe Shelley* and *Lord Byron*.'

'Well, near enough. I thought it was Lord Biro because they named a pen after him.'

'I cannot believe that you go to Queen Mary's.'

'Poetry's not my subject.'

'What is your best subject then?'

'Biology – the study of living orgasms.'

'Organisms for God's sake! I might just as well be having a conversation with Mrs Malaprop.'

'Dear brother, dear sickly brother. Admit it. You're suddenly perfectly well. All this stuff about not getting excited is crap. It's the opposite way round. When you relax and have fun you get better. When you're all moody and depressed and into your shell, is the time you get your asthma attacks. Don't tell me you haven't had fun this evening. I'm really pleased that you and Janice are going to be friends or maybe more than just friends. Who knows? Next time she sees you, she's going to let you feel her left tit.'

'What's wrong with the right one?'

'Nothing. It's just that she's a respectable girl and she has strict rules like one tit at a time.'

'So I've got to fall ill, and write a poem to play out my part in Janice's romantic fantasy.'

'I told her that you write poetry.'

'I'd try to, but it usually comes out as doggerel or verse. 'Ode to Janice Taylor' is not my kind of thing. Through being an interfering little monkey, you've given me extra stress which could lead to asthma.'

'Come off it! We've been through all that before. Here's a notepad. Get that brain working. I shall be back in half an hour. When I come back I shall want you to read me the complete masterpiece, which will make me weep with emotion.'

'Your half hour is up. Have you done it?'

'As a matter of fact, I have. Shall I read it?'

'I'm all ears.'

'Ode to Janice Taylor:

I wish I were the almond tree that grows outside your windowpane.

Then would I see your beauty over and over again.

Then would I see your face in sleep, Its innocence compelling.

There I would see your bosom fair, with its proud buds a swelling.

But I am not that almond tree, nor shall I ever be,

but you are always in my mind, my heart and memory.'

'My wonderful brother! It's beautiful.'

'You'll be the one to give it to her. You'll be the 'go between'. That's the way things were done in the days of Lord Biro.'

He put the poem in an envelope and sealed it. In his best broad nib calligraphy he wrote upon it, 'Ode to Janice Taylor' by Ralph Tucker.

'Give it to her on the way back from school.'

The school day dragged. He looked at his watch. It was only three o'clock. Mr Old, the history master, droned on about the American War of Independence. Twice he rapped out 'Tucker! Pay attention, boy'.

After an age the school bell rang and classes were over.

'Did you give it to her?' he asked Veronica when they were home.

'Of course.'

'What did she say?'

'She just smiled and said she'd read it when she got home.'

'So all we have to do is wait,' Ralph said.

'Don't be that optimistic, Ralph. She may do nothing, but she's bound to be pleased with it. My guess is that she'll be calling at about seven – after dinner.'

Margaret Tucker came in. 'I hear that you're writing verse to young ladies.'

'Only one.'

'The only one being Janice Taylor? Did you keep a copy? Shall I read it?'

She put on her spectacles and read it. Her face remained expressionless. She handed the poem back to Ralph.

'There was a time when I would have hugged you and heaped undeserved praise upon you. Those days are gone. This is the work of an infatuated boy is it not? A bit of Tudor stuff is in there too. If I were a sixteen-year-old, I think I'd like it. It's innocent. It's as innocent as you and Janice are. It's too much, I suppose, to hope that you remain that way for long.'

Hugh arrived home, kissed Margaret and sank into his armchair.

'Do I detect an air of expectation?' he asked. 'Are we expecting somebody?'

'Possibly, Dad. Possibly Janice Taylor.'

'The comely wench who was here the other day? John Wesley Taylor's daughter?'

'She asked me to write a poem to her.'

'Let's hear it then.'

Ralph read it out.

Hugh listened intensely before saying, 'Good stuff, Ralph, especially the proud buds swelling. Let's have dinner shall we? I'm starving. I think she'll go for it, even though proud buds might conjure up a picture of green nipples.'

Sure enough Janice arrived at seven o'clock. Veronica let her in.

'I wonder if Ralph would like to walk with me across the Oval,' Janice asked.

'I'm coming,' Ralph announced. 'Let's go.'

'It has been nice to see you again, Mr and Mrs Tucker,' Janice said politely.

Ralph put out his hand for her to take, but she did not take it. He wondered if something was wrong. At her suggestion they sat down on a bench.

'Ralph,' she said, 'I don't expect that anybody in my life will ever send me a poem like that. It's honest and innocent. I shall keep it in my scrapbook and when I'm a boring old lady, boasting of her youthful conquests, I shall read it out. The fact is, though, that when I mentioned 'Ode to Janice Taylor to Veronica, I was only joking.'

'Ah, well! So it's not the start of a grand courtship. I never thought it would be. Veronica's a bit mischievous at times. She wants to be a matchmaker, I think. Well I, for one, am not going to be a lovesick adolescent.'

'Nor I, Ralph. But I think we can be loyal friends.'

'What do your parents hope for you, Janice?'

'They have high expectations. University, a degree, a noble career in medicine or the law, teaching, journalism, local government. That sort of thing – no parties, no alcohol, no dates. Marriage to the right man at the right time. These are my father's wishes. My mother is not consulted. If she were, I think she would merely wish for my happiness.'

'My situation's similar, but it's my father who is stoical. My mother's expectations were impossible to live up to. I was to be in the House of Lords. I was to have a great career in the Diplomatic Corps. I was to be an Ambassador.'

'You're talking in the past tense.'

'I know. She's changed her tune completely. She's in agreement with my father now. Boy, what a relief! As long as we try to lead good lives and are happy and do no harm to others, we will have done enough to make them proud.'

'How I wish I were in your situation. I have to be ambitious for my father's sake. He's stern but a good man. The truth is that I simply don't see myself as a pillar of the community. I want to drink in pubs and go to the pictures and dances and parties.'

'I can't think of anything useful or intelligent to say except to quote my dear grandmother Tucker, who's very wise. Quote "To thine own self be true. Thou canst' not then be false to anyone," Unquote.'

She squeezed his hand.

'Was that a platonic squeeze?'

'Yes, my darling boy. It was a mildly intimate, platonic squeeze.'

It was late summer in 1953. GCE 'O' level results were out. The stamped-addressed postcard that Ralph had prepared all those weeks ago had finally landed on the doormat. He read from the postcard that he had passed English Language English Literature, Maths, Art, French, Latin and Greek. He had failed History and Geography, his two favourite subjects. Maybe, he surmised, he would have done better in History had it been English History rather than European. He was uninspired by the likes of Bismarck and Metternich. Similarly, he would have done better in Geography had there not been so many questions about layers of chalk and coalfields.

Hugh and Margaret were ecstatic but chose not to show it. The Margaret of old would have hugged Ralph and smothered him in kisses and called him her dove, her cherub, her angel, her poppet and so ad infinitum. The revised Margaret took him by the shoulders and said, 'I'm proud of you'. He knew how hard it was for her to stem her exuberance and how hard it was to simply say what she did.

'For you to be proud of me, mother, is all I want.'

Hugh decided to phone John Wesley Taylor.

'Wesley, it's Hugh. Would you and Rita like to come over this evening for a celebratory drink?'

'I don't drink, Hugh.'

'Tea then.'

‘We’d love to. We’ve had good news. Janice got nine subjects.’

‘Ralph got seven. See you at seven, with Janice, of course.’

They arrived exactly at seven o’clock. John Wesley Taylor was a punctual man. Margaret had brought out the best china and had made a mountain of sandwiches. They sat around the table, Veronica, Ralph and Janice still in school uniform.

‘I’d like to drink a toast to our children.’ Hugh raised his teacup. ‘Cheers!’

‘Cheers!’ they said in chorus.

‘Janice will tell us what subjects she passed in,’ John Wesley announced rather formally.

Janice stood and recited clearly, English Language, English Literature, French, German, Geography, Biology, Maths, Advanced Maths and History.

Everybody clapped.

‘You next, Ralph.’ Hugh ordered.

‘English Language, English Literature, French, Latin, Greek, Maths and Art.’

More clapping.

With formalities over, the younger element were sent to another room.

‘Children should be seen and not heard or should it be not seen or heard and banished?’ Veronica muttered.

‘We’re children, aren’t we?’ Ralph said. ‘We’ve just got to put up with it.’

‘When does childhood end and adolescence begin?’ Janice asked.

‘About now I’d say,’ Veronica claimed. ‘I’m skipping adolescence. I’m going straight to adulthood.’

They decided to play Monopoly even though Veronica habitually cheated. Ralph would finish up with a house on the Old Kent Road while Veronica had hotels in Mayfair.

‘Maybe that’s going to be the pattern of our lives,’ Ralph sighed resignedly. ‘You’ll be Lady Veronica and I’ll be in the gutter.’

‘Hope so,’ Veronica grinned. ‘I shall drive my Rolls Royce past you and cover you in mud.’

She threw the dice. ‘Five – one, two, three, four, five. Dammit! I’ve got to go to jail.’

Janice did not understand the game.

‘Haven’t you got one at home?’ Veronica asked.

‘No. I don’t think my father would approve. He’d say it was a game based on monetary greed.’

‘He’s dead right.’ Ralph agreed.

‘You don’t like it because you never win,’ Veronica told him.

‘Well, it’s hardly a game of skill is it?’

‘Janice!’

‘That’s my father. I’ll be off. Bye Ralph, bye Veronica.’

‘I reckon she has a miserable life at home,’ Veronica said after Janice’s departure. ‘Mr Taylor looks very stern. I bet she’s not allowed to do this or do that.’

‘Ralph! Veronica! Come down now!’

‘We’ve had the teetotallers’ party. This is the drinkers’ party.’

‘Let’s call it the moderate drinkers’ party shall we, Hugh?’

‘Yes, of course. This is a special occasion. It is not the commencement of a steady decline into alcoholism, but it’s about time you kids had a little drink. Veronica, you shall have a sweet sherry.’ He poured out her drink. ‘Do not drink yet because I have to propose a toast.’

‘We’ve already drunk a toast,’ Veronica said.

‘That was with teacups. This is a different toast anyway.’

‘Ralph, you shall have a scotch and soda. Your mother and I shall continue drinking this excellent red wine. In fact I think we ought to open a third bottle. This is vintage wine, a present from Aunt Lorna. Raise your glasses! The toast is the family!'

'The family,' they cried in chorus.

'We're very proud of our children. We want you to do well in life. We know that we haven't been a very good example.'

'You've been great parents,' Ralph said.

Hugh poured out another two glasses of the excellent red wine and sent Veronica into the kitchen to bring in some more. 'Might as well make a night of it,' was his excuse. 'Now, the thing is we (well, mainly your mother) were namby-pambying you. For my part, I wasn't showing enough interest in you and spending too much time down the pub. Well, that's all changed,' he went on, pouring himself another glass of red wine. 'Now where was I?'

'You were talking about change, Dad' Ralph told him.

'True. I was just testing you in case you weren't paying attention. From now on, you kids are not doves or cherubs or poppets. Darling's allowed. As always your mother has had her own way. There may be difficult times ahead.'

'You sound like Churchill, Dad' Ralph said.

'We will fight on the beaches!' Veronica put on her gruffest Churchillian voice.

'Why don't you both shut up. I've lost my train of thought,' he poured out two more glasses of red wine. 'Where was I?'

'There may be difficult times ahead,' Ralph suggested.

'Did I say that?'

'Yes darling,' Margaret intervened, 'that's what you said. It was a very clever thing to say and I'm proud of you for saying it. Only a man like you could have said it.'

'Said what?'

'Said what you said. I'm looking you straight in the eye and you look ten years younger,' she said dreamily.

'You look twenty years younger, my dear,' Hugh said.

'You look thirty years younger,' she countered.

‘We’d better go to bed before we’re too young to be alive. You kids clear up all the mess before you come to bed and leave that red wine alone. It’s too strong for you, even for your mother and me.’

Hugh and Margaret stumbled up to bed.

‘They’re both drunk,’ Veronica said. ‘Is this the new family regime?’

‘Hope not,’ Ralph replied. ‘Just listen to that noise from their room – grunting, squealing, banging and shouting!’

‘Is that it?’ they heard Margaret shriek.

‘Well, better than nothing!’ he roared back. ‘I’ve had too much to drink!’

‘What a let-down!’ she cried.

‘What would Janice have thought, I wonder?’ Veronica asked.

‘She’d probably have enjoyed it. What a hopeless family we are.’

Chapter 5

York Rock

'There may be difficult times ahead,' had been Hugh's Churchillian prediction some weeks before, and now, sure enough, difficulties arose.

Ralph had entered the sixth form (Humanities). Classes were much smaller, a surprising number of pupils having left at the end of fifth form at sixteen years of age. Doubts began to seep into Ralph's mind about the value of a classical education followed by university and National Service or the more favoured option of National Service before university. Either way, he would not be in the workplace until the age of twenty-four.

Masters continually encouraged him to look forward to a brilliant future without being specific as to what form this brilliant future would take. He had vague ideas about the law, politics, journalism, teaching, and the Colonial Service. The latter had some appeal, but at the end of it all would he be a boring old codger recounting his forty years in British Honduras or The Gilbert and Ellis Islands? His head was pounding with apprehension and uncertainty. He had a series of asthma attacks. He spent long hours in his room swotting. Latin and Greek had suddenly become incredibly taxing. He was no longer an instinctive learner as he had been as a fifth former. The sixth form operated a loose discipline with plenty of free study time. Sixth formers were not bound to participate in the cadet force, the scouts or games. He fell out of love with rugby after having had an asthma attack just after a scrum. He felt ashamed, even though he had no need to, but it was all part of a general malaise. He stayed in the cadets even though he had always hated it. He thought it useful to keep his hand in at soldiering, even though he could not imagine the regular army being the slightest bit like the cadets. He had absolutely no friends in the sixth form. There was a cliquey atmosphere. Twelve of the sixth form were prefects and seemed to revel in bullying smaller boys. Those in the cadets (or the Corps, as it was generally known) were warrant officers or under officers and strutted around as if they were on the parade ground of the Grenadier Guards. He kept in touch with his old Chuckery mates. Tommy Ward was working with his brother as a plumber. Dennis Holmer worked in a foundry. They still all went down to the arbo and kicked their Dixie Dean football about. It was the only exercise Ralph was getting. After the kick-about Tommy and Dennis took him to a pub – The Spring Cottage. He never had a penny on him to pay his way and felt rotten about it. His only other company was Veronica and Janice. He valued his brother–sister relationship with Janice, even though Veronica insisted that they were in love. They played scrabble in Ralph's room in the evenings after homework. Veronica always came out with words that did not exist.

'D O O K' she said one evening. 'The K is on a treble so that's nineteen altogether.'

'What's a dook?' Ralph asked.

'It's in the dictionary.' She was looking in the Nuttalls Dictionary.

'Yes, but what does it mean?'

'A seabird, native to Indonesia with orange and black plumage.'

'Let's have a look.'

'Don't you trust me?'

'No.'

'So, you don't trust me. That means that you don't love me.'

'Of course it doesn't. I just wanted to check it out, that's all. It didn't sound right.'

'I'm not continuing to play in this distrustful atmosphere.'

'Don't then.'

'You're jealous because I always win. Even your smarty-pants lady-friend can't beat me.'

'Nobody can beat you if you're making up words that don't exist.'

'I hate you!'

'Go and eat a dook.'

Sometimes in the evening Ralph and Janice would take a stroll around the Oval which backed onto The Firs (Tuckers' house). The Oval was Ralph and Veronica's name for it. In fact, it was a rectangular cricket ground. Invariably, there were three of them taking a stroll, as Veronica would tag along. The conversations were getting boring for Veronica. There were continual soul-searching's, as to whether or not they would be continuing at school and going on to university. If they 'dropped out', how disappointed would their parents be? Would they live to regret it? Were they cut out for academia in the first place?

'Shall we, shan't we, shall we, shan't we, shall we join the dance?' she mimicked one night. 'Make a decision you ditherers.'

'There are so many aspects to it,' Janice said. 'I'm not certain that I want to be a student in dowdy clothes. I want to wear nice dresses and stockings and suspenders and go to parties. What's university going to do to my femininity?'

'You could become Professor of Underwear at Titfield College Oxford.' Veronica suggested. 'Let me put an end to all your indecisions. Firstly Ralph. Ralph, you're hating school and all those toffee-nosed, pompous twits like Blenkinsop. You're having bout after bout of asthma. You're looking podgy. Leave school. Get a job. Get some money. Dad won't mind and Mom thinks the sun shines out of your arse. If you got a job as a builders' labourer, she'd tell everybody you were a construction manager or something. Secondly Janice. Janice, you're not a bluestocking or whatever they call them. Look at you! You're bursting out all over. You're a good-looking woman in school uniform. You're an adult. Get a good job like a legal secretary or something. Act like a woman. Surely your father isn't that strict, is he? Appeal to him as a man of God. And that's me, Veronica Tucker, signing off until this time tomorrow. Thank you for listening.'

'I've been listening, good sister. Trust you to put it in simple terms like that. It makes sense. I'm going to get any old job tomorrow. Tell Dad. Hand in my cadet's uniform. Get a sub off Dad so that I can buy Tommy and Dennis a drink. What am I now? I'm a penniless invalid and definitely an outsider in the sixth form. I'm never going to be a prefect and I'm never going to be higher than a Lance Corporal in the cadets and who cares anyway?'

'As soon as I'm in funds, Janice, I'm going to take you to the pub. If you're worried about your father finding out, then suck some peppermints before you leave for home, so your breath won't smell.'

'You don't know how much I look forward to that, Ralph. A big foaming pint of beer! I haven't got a clue what it tastes like but I bet it's nice.'

'It's not very nice the first time you taste it, but it gets better and better.'

Ralph told his father next day that he wanted to leave school. Hugh stared hard at him in silence for a while and then said quietly, 'All right son. Let's have a little walk to the Wheatsheaf pub shall we, and discuss it!'

He gave his father the whole story. Hugh listened, nodding occasionally. Then they drank their beer slowly.

'So what do you think then, Dad,' Ralph asked tentatively.

'In under a thousand words?'

'As long as it takes.'

'Well, firstly I'm disappointed, but I understand your reasons. Bang goes your mother's dream of Oxford and punting down the river and all that ethereal stuff. I know she's changed and I'm sure I shall find a way of explaining how it can no longer be, but it has been her vision since you were a small child. Strictly speaking, it's *you* who should be talking to your mother about it.'

'I'm willing to do that.'

'I know you would be. Anyway, let's put family reactions aside for a while and deal with matters in hand. You were going for an 'A' level in Latin, Greek and Ancient History – the so-called classics. Everybody knows that there is not a single job in the country, outside teaching, that requires knowledge of Caesar's Gallic wars or how to conjugate Latin verbs. The classics are a sort of test of intellect aren't they? A passport to articulate, persuasive brilliance. Maybe that's all bullshit too. The classics have no practical use. Dead history in dead languages – that's my opinion. I can understand that you've fallen out of love with your subjects. What does displease me is that you have taken advantage of the rather loose discipline exercised by the sixth form and declined to play games. That's out of character for somebody who loves soccer and rugby. It's given you plenty of time to mope around feeling sorry for yourself and your asthma's getting worse. Another pint? It'll be your last.'

They took a break from talking. Since he could remember, he had been in awe of his father's wisdom, but Ralph had the feeling that he was going to get more than wisdom. He was going to get the bollocking he deserved.

'Are you ready for this, Ralph?'

'Yes Dad.' He felt like a naughty child.

'Get out of your stupor! Start playing rugby again. Join my old club, the Humourists. They share Queen Mary's fields. Take your books, your cadet uniform and everything that belongs to school back. Simply tell one of your form masters that you have left school. I do not want any heart to heart talks with the Headmaster about your throwing away the chance of a marvellous career. You're going and that's that. I'm going to give you a sub of £20. When you've done two months' work I want it back in full. Get a job, any job – clerical, manual, menial, whatever. Give your Mom half your money each week. You'll start to learn the value of money. We'll get you through a driving test in my car. That'll help you if get a job where you need to know how to drive a van or something. Get fit, and not just rugby, do what you used to do. Swim. Run. Walk. Get off your arse.'

'I won't let you down, I promise. Changing the subject, do you know Trevor Blenkinsop's father?'

'George Blenkinsop? I know something about him. He's a jerry-builder. He made himself a pile of money just after the war. Do you want to know about Herbert Blenkinsop?

'Who was he?'

'Father of George, grandfather of Trevor, he was well known in Walsall as a card sharp.'

'That's very useful information, Dad.'

Hugh slumped into an armchair.

'Are you all right, Hugh?' Margaret asked. 'You look drained.'

'Come and sit on my lap. I've got something to tell you.'

'Sit on your lap?' she asked incredulously. 'I haven't sat on your lap since before the war. I'm still in my apron.'

'Apron or not, come here.'

'Is this all part of our new start?'

'I suppose it is.'

'So what was the long conflab with Ralph about?'

He went through everything that had been, said ending with the words, '…so there goes your hope of dreaming spires and punting down the river and all that.'

'I'm glad in a way. You know how clumsy he is. Suppose he toppled the boat over and he and his beautiful society girl got caught in the rapids and were carried out to sea never to be seen again.'

'What's your reaction to leaving school and all that?'

'I'm not surprised. The exaggerated aspirations are over. For the first time in our married life I agree with what you say. I'm going to ask him to promise me to get himself some professional qualifications, either commencing now or after his National Service. Letters after his name – good idea?'

'Good idea. Something practical.'

'I never really took to the idea of learning about ancient Greeks. We need to live in the present. Socrates would be no good in this day and age. He'd be two thousand years behind the times. He wouldn't be able to drive a car or anything.'

It was the Friday before the school term was to break up for Easter holidays. The combined cadet force of Queen Mary's Grammar School was preparing to muster, thence to march to the playing fields for the Brigadier's inspection. Ralph walked through the school gates in school uniform minus cap and tie, his battledress and web equipment in a bag. He spotted Under Officer Blenkinsop strutting round like a popinjay. Ralph walked straight in front of him.

'Where's your uniform, Corporal Tucker?' he asked.

'In this bag and the best place for it too.'

'You're talking about the Queen's uniform, Tucker.'

'I wondered whose it was because it doesn't fit me.'

'Who the hell do you think you're talking to, Tucker?'

'A pompous twit, son of a jerry-builder, grandson of a cardsharp, pompous twit from a criminal background with delusions of being an officer.'

'You're going to be on a charge for that and you still haven't told me why you're not in uniform.'

'I've left the corps and I've left school. You may be a big shot here, Blenkinsop but wait until you get called up. You'll just be a little sprog with a crew cut. You've been playing school politics haven't you? You've got your little clique and you're making sure that nobody enters it and you're prepared to protect your little coterie by fair means or foul. All the decent lads have left. You and your high-minded cronies are the reason I'm leaving. I used to love coming to school. Now I hate it. Are you listening to me, Blenkinsop? Don't march away you coward.'

Ralph raced out of the gates and caught up with Blenkinsop at the rear of the leading platoon. He pushed him aside. Blenkinsop replied by swinging a haymaker punch, which missed Ralph but hit a third former in the second platoon. Soon the whole column was in disarray with cadets breaking ranks and attacking senior ranks. Sergeants and Warrant Officers were soon involved. It seemed that disgruntled third formers, already sick of being bullied by upstart NCOs, had pulled down the trousers of at least seven seniors and thrown their web belts over a wall. It now appeared to be a grudge brawl between rebellious third formers and the 'Little Hitlers' of the fifth and sixth forms.

Ralph had chosen his time to walk casually away from events and watch from a distance. When discipline was finally restored and the men were back in their platoons, they were given a stern lecture by the Maths master, Colonel Kershaw, about the disgraceful conduct of his cadets, of whom he had once been proud. There would be a full investigation and some boys would be dishonourably discharged. A cheer went up from the third formers, who were obviously the ringleaders of the riot.

Ralph sauntered to his form room and left all his books on his desk. He then strolled across to the Quartermasters and left his bag by the door. He walked through the main gates and across the road to the Arboretum. He walked past the 'bottomless lakes' as Nan Tucker always referred to them, sat down on a park bench and silently addressed his old school:

'Farewell Queen Mary's founded 1554. Floreat Regina and all that – a school song I never learnt. I thought that Queen Mary's would be the platform for a great career in something or other, but that is not to be, which is just as well. I shall go my own way. I shall not attend any Old Boys dinner nights. That's for men who want to stay boys.

'I never intended to start a school riot. All I wanted to do was tell Blenkinsop and his little jumped-up friends what I thought of them. How was I to know that a third form mutiny was about to come to the boil? It did not surprise me. Why are potentially psychotic pupils of seventeen to eighteen years of age encouraged to bawl at, pick on, bully and victimise younger boys? Is it our one-eyed, misguided Englishness that decrees that to suffer purgatory at school is beneficial in the long run? Maybe times will change. I doubt it though.'

Now he had the task of finding himself a job. Tommy had mentioned a man named Jeff Pyke in Walsall Wood who had a builders' yard called Quality Building Supplies and had a vacancy sign on the wall. Ralph decided that it would be better to go home first and change into old clothes. He then set out on a three-mile walk to Walsall Wood until he got to the site. There was a huge sign over the main gate, which simply said QBS. He walked through the entrance. At first sight it appeared to be a junkyard. Closer examination revealed a variety of reusable stock – broken paving slabs, old chimney pots, kerbstones, bricks, garden ornaments, plant pots, roof tiles, rocks for rock gardens, fence posts, poles, pit props, floor boards, window frames, doors, deck chairs, wrought iron gates, offcuts of marine ply, large mirrors, rolls of wire netting, rolls of barbed wire, toilet bowls, sinks, lattice work, reclaimed timbers – quite an assortment.

A tall skinny man in his late twenties came over to him and asked, 'Can I help you?'

‘I’ve come about the vacancy. I got to know about it from Tommy Ward.’

‘Ronnie Ward’s little brother? Yes, I know him.’

‘Well, Tommy’s my best mate.’

‘Well that’s good enough for me – friend of a friend so to speak. You’re in. It’s only temporary. We’re short of staff. It’s cash only. No questions asked, know what I mean? Fiver a week in your hand. Working hours – 8.30 to 5.30, half an hour for lunch. What’s your name?’

‘Ralph Tucker.’

‘I’m Jeff Pyke. You look a well-built lad, Ralph I’ll give you a start. I’ll show you what you’ve got to do. A monkey could do it. Everything in this yard’s got a price on it. You take the money. The customer takes his goods. Simple common sense! If anybody tries to bargain with you, tell them to piss off – politely, of course. We’ve got no till so we give you a float. Most of the customers come by car or van. Always insist on loading their slabs or whatever they’ve bought. There’s a pile of old blankets over there. If you’re loading into the boot of a car, put a blanket down first.

If anybody requires home delivery, see the lad in the office. His name’s Stan. I call him Stan the van man because he drives the van. Any questions? Too bad if there are. See you tomorrow at 8.30. Bring sandwiches and a cup. We brew up at 11 am and 2 pm.

There was a spring in the step of Ralph Tucker as he walked back home. Three miles a day seemed easy. Six miles was a bit daunting, but he knew he would do it. Well, he damned well had to.

He burst into the house eager to give his parents the news. He found them in the living room. Margaret was sitting on Hugh’s lap.

‘I’ve got some good news for you,’ Ralph announced. ‘I’ve got a little job.’

‘That’s nice dear,’ Margaret said.

'Don't you want to know what the job is?'

'Tell us,' Hugh sounded bored.

Ralph gave them all the details, to which his father replied, 'So, you'll be walking six miles a day and loading slabs and rocks for eight hours in between. If you don't get fit now, you never will be.'

'I'll be ready for my dinner when I get home each day. That's for sure.'

'I bet you're hungry now, aren't you? It's been quite a momentous day,' Hugh said.

'Yes. I'm hungry. I'm looking forward to it.'

'You'll have to go down to the Fish and Chip shop, darling,' Margaret told him. 'I'm afraid that I haven't cooked dinner today. It's something you always took for granted, isn't it? The fact is, that apart from holidays, today is the first ever day that I haven't cooked an evening meal.'

'I'll go and get some fish and chips then?' Ralph said morosely, 'Shall I get four?'

'Of course. You've got that £20 that your father gave you. You'll have to break into it.'

Ralph knocked on Veronica's door.

'Are you in there? Are you bored?'

'Bored stiff.'

'Come for a walk with me to the fish and chip shop.'

'Okay, I'll be out in a minute. I've lost a shoe. No, I've found it. Here I am.' She appeared at the door. They set out across the Oval.

'I got myself a little job today,' he announced. 'But more on that later. What is going on with Mom and Dad?'

'I don't know. It's incredible. It could be a second honeymoon.'

'She hasn't bothered to cook tonight. Hence our little trip to the fish and chip shop.'

'Is this the mother who has spent seventeen years fretting over us?'

‘Seems like it. She couldn’t give a damn. Do we like the revised, broad-minded, casual parents or do we prefer the old models – one overambitious for us and overprotective towards us and the other fitting in just for a quiet life?’

‘I like the modern Hugh and Margaret, but I don’t want fish and chips every night.’

Ralph liked life at the builders’ yard. The six-mile walk became second nature. The work within the yard was arduous to begin with, but he soon got used to it. Sometimes they kicked their heels for long periods, but normally there was a steady flow of business. He wore gloves for loading the slabs and rocks, but his forearms got scratched to hell, especially when handling garden rocks which were stored in metal cages.

It appeared that Jeff owned the business and was the general factotum, foreman, buyer, and salesman. Stan the van man did very little more than his title suggested. Ralph was often called away to unload supplies coming in, which he thought should have been Stan’s job, but he kept this minor grudge to himself. Stan was a likeable man and Ralph got on well with him. On reflection, the summer of 1954 at QBS would be one of the happiest times of Ralph’s life. Jeff instructed him to put himself on self-employed status and pay a weekly stamp. That way Jeff was able to pay him as a contractor. It was easier than installing a PAYE system.

‘You haven’t listened to a single word I’ve said, have you Ralph?’

‘It’s too hot, Jeff.’

It was midday and it was indeed extraordinarily hot. Ralph, Stan and Jeff sat on a pile of bricks swapping yarns or rather, listening to yarns. Ralph and Stan, having had limited experience of life, did not have as much to say as Jeff. They were but boys, whereas he had served in the Korean War, been a market trader and had even been homeless and down and out at one time.

‘What was Korea like?’ Stan asked.

‘If you’ve got three or four hours to spend one night in the boozer, I’ll tell you. I was in the Middlesex regiment. I carried the Bren gun for eighteen months.’

‘Where did you go?’ Stan asked.

‘Mainly in the opposite direction to the way we were supposed to go,’ Jeff laughed. ‘What a fiasco! You’ll have to do it, you two – National Service. Take my tip. Sign on for three years. You get regular soldiers’ pay.’

‘But you’re in for a year longer,’ Ralph countered.

‘What’s a year in your three score years and ten?’ Jeff reasoned.

‘I’m going to join the Guards,’ Stan said, ‘the Grenadiers or the Coldstream.’

‘You’ll never get in,’ Jeff quipped. ‘You’re five foot fuck all.’

‘I’m five foot eleven,’ Stan replied indignantly.

‘Now, now Stanley. It’s only a joke.’

‘A mate of mine was in the Coldstream,’ Stan told them. ‘He was on sentry duty outside the Palace and this sexy American tourist had herself photographed with her hand on his dick.’

‘Well, wasn’t he asking for trouble, being on duty with his dick out?’

‘Of course he didn’t have his dick out. Her hand was on his dick, but his dick was in his trousers.’

‘This sort of devalues the story doesn’t it?’ Jeff argued. ‘I mean, being on parade with your dick out is definitely a court martial offence, whereas just having a hard on is something that can’t be helped.’

‘You’re spoiling it. She had her hand on his dick, right? And she was a bit of all right, right?’

‘Right.’ They said.

‘And she asked him what time he was off duty, but he couldn’t say anything. He just had to stay dead still as if she wasn't there, even though his dick was getting harder and harder.'

'Why was that then?' Jeff asked.

'Because… forget it! You've spoilt the story.'

Ralph spotted a stout middle-aged lady walking towards the cages of rocks.

'Here's a customer,' Ralph said and walked over to the stout lady.

'Can I help you ma'am?'

'I want twelve rocks.'

'Would you like York rock?'

'Is it the best?'

'There's no such thing as best when you're talking about rock. York rock is most people's favourite, but it all depends on individual taste.'

'I don't want a lecture on rock. I'll have York rock.'

Ralph fetched a blanket and put it on the back seat of the stout lady's car.

'What are you doing that for?' she demanded to know.

'I'm going to load the rocks on top – some on the back seat and some in the boot.'

'What?' she shrieked. 'In a Mercedes?'

'Do you require delivery to your house, ma'am?'

'Yes I do. I shall require them to be carried to the bottom of the garden. My husband would have done it, but he's in Hong Kong.'

'In that case I'll liaise with our transport department.' Stan and Jeff had returned to the shade of the office.

'Job for you, Stan – delivery for that shapely young lady.'

'She's not shapely and she's not young,' Stan whined.

'Her husband's in Hong Kong,' Jeff said, when they had loaded the van. 'You could be well in there. If she puts her hand on your dick.'

'Pack it in!' Stan cut in, 'Just – just bloody well pack it in!'

Chapter 6

Not Blenkinsop?

To use Jeff's expression, they 'larked about' whenever there was a quiet period at QBS. 'You might as well have some fun,' was his opinion, 'Because soon you'll both be in some dreary barracks getting abused from 'arsehole to breakfast time.' I've never quite understood that saying.

'I'm not even thinking about it,' Ralph said. 'I'm seventeen. I'm happy now and that's all I care. I could do with a bit more money, but I'm not grumbling.'

'On the subject of money, Ralph, I never told you about our little bonus scheme, did I? Sometimes, we get a good price for something – better than list price. We leave price labels off and wait for the customer to make an offer. We only do it for stuff that comes our way via house clearances. Sometimes, we get an offer that's way over the top. We accept it and split the profit between the three of us.'

'That sounds good Jeff,' Ralph said. 'What sort of things can we make a bit of black market money on?'

'Those full length mirrors for a start. I got them for next to nothing and I haven't got a clue what they're worth.'

'They're old, I bet,' Ralph said. 'They're ornate, I reckon they're worth something. I'm going to find out. You've given us a nice incentive, Jeff. It puts a whole new slant on things.'

'We could become antique dealers,' Stan said eagerly.

'I bet my dad knows someone who'd give us a valuation.' Ralph told them that his father was District Rating Officer for the Birmingham wards of Market Hall and Ladywood.

'Aren't those poor areas?' Jeff asked.

him twenty years. What he doesn't know about antiques isn't worth knowing.'

'I understand you have a few items of interest, Mr Pyke?'

'I have indeed, Claude.' He took him to the mirrors. 'They shouldn't be stored outside,' Claude said. He had a good look at them.

'These are nothing special. Round about the 1880s I'd say. They're very attractive. I'd say from £10-£15 maximum each. If you leave them out in the weather they'll be worth nothing. Get them under cover. Set a minimum of seven quid each on them. Sorry if I've disappointed you.'

'Not at all. I just needed a price on them so I'd know whether what I was asking was too high or too low. Let's have a look at these pictures shall we?'

They went inside the office. Jeff cleared a space in the clutter for Claude to view them. He got through the pile rapidly saying 'print –print –print'. Then he stopped and said, 'Ah, this looks interesting.'

It was a domestic scene, mother, child, two dogs asleep, shafts of sunlight from the window, household paraphernalia everywhere.

'That's my favourite,' Jeff lied.

'And so it should be,' Claude told him. 'D'you see the signature? Matthew Hasting Beaumont, a very highly regarded artist from Yorkshire. This picture's dated 1895, that would be towards the end of his life. His paintings are rare. As many as twenty of them were destroyed in a fire at his home at the turn of the century. This is definitely not a print. It's an original oil. It needs cleaning.'

'How much is it worth?' Jeff asked eagerly.

'Over the next few decades paintings like this will increase in value. In the year 2000 this painting may be worth £15,000 - £20,000. You could keep it as an investment.'

‘That’s based on economic growth. What if we have another Great Depression? My business is based on quick cash turnover. Today’s price is what I need on that picture.’

‘I would have it in my gallery at a selling price of £800, after cleaning. I’d give you £500 cash now.’

‘It’s a deal.’ They shook hands. ‘Are any of the other pictures worth anything?’

‘Worthless. The frames might be worth a bit. You could get rid of them at a few bob each.’ He counted out the money into Jeff’s hand, all in low denomination notes. It took a long time to count it all out.

‘Good deal?’ Hugh asked Jeff.

‘Good deal.’

‘We did well,’ Jeff said. ‘Five hundred in notes in my hand. I’ve got to put some money into QBS. This kind of money only comes up once in a while. I’m going to give you a hundred quid each and put three hundred into the bank. Is that fair?’

‘It’s not the three-way split you promised, Jeff, but it’s fine by me.’

‘Me too,’ Stan said.

‘Right, let’s count it out shall we?’

He counted out two piles of pound notes and ten-shilling notes onto the table. They each picked up their share.

‘I’m booking a taxi for you,’ Jeff said. ‘I don’t want you walking home with that sort of money bulging out of your pockets.’

‘Why don’t you build a little gallery here and display work by local artists? If you sell anything you take a cut.’

‘Stan, we’re not gallery owners. We’re not antique dealers. We are what we are. We wheel and deal a bit and sometimes we get lucky.’

‘Fine, fine,’ Stan said, ‘it was just a thought. I’m a bit of an artist myself.’

‘Yeah?’ Jeff said. It was the most disinterested ‘yeah’ that Stan had ever heard.

Ralph was in his room. Veronica knocked on the door.

‘Friend or foe?’

‘Janice Taylor ready for a bit of hanky-panky.’

‘Come in! Oh, it’s you, scruffy sister. What a let-down.’

‘What are you doing?’ Veronica asked.

‘Trying to write some poetry, well verse actually or doggerel, I suppose.’

‘You’re not going back into your shell, are you?’

‘Far from it. I’m happier than I’ve ever been. I spend my working day loading slabs and rocks and stuff into vans and cars. I work with two decent blokes. We laugh and joke a lot. Why am I telling you all this? You already know it.’

‘Why are you trying to write poetry then?’

‘To keep my brain active.’

‘Well, talking about active brains, I’ve got my GCE results and I doubt there’ll be a family celebration. I got four passes – English, Biology, Maths and History. I scraped through in all four.’

‘You did well, little sister. Four subjects equals four kisses from me. Mom and Dad might be disappointed, but I shall always be proud of you. You’re my tomboy. You make me laugh. You’re a dirty-minded little scallywag, but I love you. I think I might give you a little present for your efforts. A poetry book maybe – the works of Lord Biro.’

Margaret called them down to dinner. The table was laid for all the world as if it were Christmas Day, dazzling white table cloth and serviettes, sparkling cutlery, and an array of drinks on the sideboard.

‘What’s all this about?’ Veronica asked.

‘It’s for you darling,’ Margaret replied. Veronica began to cry. Margaret took her in her arms.

‘You did well, my darling. You tried your best. I’m very proud of my little scamp. You don’t need university. You’ll do well. Your father and I will always be proud of you.’

‘We’re going to partake of a little aperitif before lunch,’ Hugh said and poured out four dry sherries. ‘Now for the toast. The toast is to my lovely little daughter who is small in size but big in personality.’

‘It’s all too good to be true,’ Veronica sobbed. ‘Something’s going to happen to spoil it all.’

They ate their gigantic meal of roast beef and Yorkshire pudding. Ralph ate at twice the speed of everybody else. Ever since he had worked at QBS, the long days had given him a voracious appetite. Having consumed his main course, trifle, cheese and biscuits, Drambuie and coffee, he went into the living room, flopped onto the sofa and fell fast asleep.

‘D’you think he’s becoming a bit uncouth?’ Margaret asked.

Janice Taylor called round a few days later and asked Ralph to walk across the Oval with her. They walked hand in hand to a spectator bench and sat down. Janice had some news for him.

‘We’re leaving Walsall – something to do with my father’s job.’

‘Different church you mean?’

‘No. He’s not tied to the church. He’s a lay preacher. His real job is the manager of an electrical goods shop in Bloxwich. He’s been promoted to a bigger branch.’

‘Where?’

‘Portsmouth.’

‘Portsmouth? That’s the end of the world. I won’t be able to see you.’

‘You can phone or write. Don’t look so sulky, Ralph. Ours was supposed to be a brother– sister relationship, wasn’t it?’

'Yes. Platonic was the word we used. I suppose I took it for granted that you'd always be here.'

'So did I. I wished many a time that I wasn't an only child and that you and Veronica were my brother and sister.' She burst into tears. He put his arms around her.

'This isn't just platonic is it, Ralph? This is romantic. This is when lovers have to part. I feel that this is a portent of our future. I feel that this is not an end in itself. Do you feel that way, Ralph?'

'No. I'm still in shock. I expect it will hit me later on. At the moment I'm just thinking of Portsmouth. We went there on holiday just after the war. My dad was stationed there. I didn't like it much. I pulled a face on all the photos that Mom took. I was seasick on the ferry to The Isle of Wight and refused to go on the ferry to Hayling Island. I was a right little sod.'

'You've never been a right little sod to *me*, Ralph. You've always been loyal, upright and true.'

'I never asked you when you were going.'

'The day after tomorrow.'

'So this is possibly our last time together?'

'It is, I'm afraid. We're calling on various relatives all day tomorrow – excruciatingly boring. So this is definitely adieu.'

'Then let us walk back with our heads held high.'

Ralph sat in the kitchen head in hand.

'What's the matter, darling,' Margaret asked.

'Nothing.'

'Don't irritate me, Ralph. What's the matter? If it's about Janice Taylor and family moving to Portsmouth, I already know. It's the end of your gymslip romance, It's certainly not worth moping over.'

'You just don't understand. It's an event that could shape our future. Fate has given us a chance to test the true depth of our love by our being apart.'

‘Stop talking such a lot of adolescent drivel. I thought you’d put all that behind you when you went to work with Stan and Jeff.’ There was a pause and a sigh from Margaret. ‘Ralph darling, I still love you and Veronica as I always did and believe me, if or when any great sadness befalls you, you have your mother’s breast on which to lay your head, but Janice Taylor’s departure is not such an occasion. You must start to learn what is important and what is not.’

Veronica entered.

‘Try and knock some sense into this brother of yours, this boy whom I love and cherish, who, at present, is irritating me to death with his sickly poet routine.’

‘Is this about Janice Taylor? Buck up, good brother. If you never see Janice again, at least you’ve seen her tits.’

‘Now, now, Veronica. You don’t have to be that crude about it,’ Margaret said.

‘I’ve just about got the message, now,’ Ralph said. ‘All right. Gymslip romance. Thing of the past. Blah blah blah. I’ll get over it. I’ve got to grow up.’

‘I could tell you something that would definitely put you in a ‘who cares?’ mood,’ Veronica told him.

‘All right, tell me.’

‘There was a school dance last week – The Harvest Ball – and guess who took Janice Taylor in his daddy’s Jaguar?’

‘I don’t know and I don’t care. I’m supposed to know what’s important and what’s not and this is definitely a ‘not’.’

‘Wait till I tell you. You’ll know it’s not a ‘not’. Question: who took Janice to the ball? Answer: Trevor Blenkinsop?’

‘What? Blenkinsop? That jumped-up pompous toad of a man? He started the cadet riots. He swung a punch at me and it missed and hit a third former. There’s not an ounce of good in him. Well, I reckon that news just about seals it. I’m finished with deceitful women. I’m going to do what Stan’s cousin does.’

‘What’s that then?’

‘He’s got a rich woman of forty-five hidden in the leafy suburbs who knows exactly what she’s doing, if you know what I mean.’

‘I hope you find one,’ Veronica yawned.

‘Sorry if I’m boring you.’

‘Oh, that’s okay, good brother. It’s just that talking about love and romance is boring. I’m never ever going to get myself into any emotional tangles. I’m skipping adolescence, going straight into adulthood, and marrying the man that I’ve already chosen, although he doesn’t know it yet.’

‘Who’s the lucky bloke?’

‘Obviously, I can’t tell you, but you will know in due course. Don’t start guessing either. It’ll drive you crazy.’

Chapter 7

Bashful and Doc

In October 1954 Ralph presented himself to the secretary of the Humourists Rugby Club in their little clubhouse and bar on the edge of Mayfield playing fields. The bar was packed.

'Is Mr Ray White in?' he asked.

'That's him,' the barman pointed. 'That bald-headed bloke in a blue shirt.'

Ralph walked over to him. 'Mr White?'

'That's me.'

'Ralph Tucker.' He put his hand out to shake hands.

'Ralph Tucker? Hugh Tucker's boy? I don't believe you. You're far too handsome to be Hugh Tucker's son. How is the baldy headed old reprobate anyway? Is he still airing his political views in the Dog and Partridge pub?'

'Yes, he's still trying to change the world.'

'He was a tough player. I expect he's told you.'

'No. He's modest.'

'Well, I'll tell you. He played hooker. He was always in the thick of it. He threw a few punches too. Let me buy you a pint. I presume that you drink. You can't join unless you drink.'

'I drink, but I'm only seventeen.'

'You look eighteen. I'll get all your details for your membership card and you can collect it next time you call. I'll need seven and sixpence from you. Fancy a game next Sunday? We're playing a side called the Chasers from Cannock. Cannock Chase – get it?'

'Don't I have to have a trial?'

'Trial? That's a laugh. We're lucky to scrape together fifteen blokes under forty, never mind trials. This is the Humourists boy. Jokesters first. Rugby players second. Our posthumous patron is the great Jerome K. Jerome, the best writer of humour the English-speaking world has ever known or ever will. To become a life member you have to have read all the great man's books and you must sit for a test. This is not a joke. It's compulsory.'

'Nobody could say that you're not trying to stay fit,' Hugh said to Ralph over dinner. You're doing a ten-hour day if you include getting to work and back. You're having a kick-about with your Chuckery mates and now you're a Humourist rugby player. Sure you're not overdoing it?'

'If I am I'll soon find out. We're playing a game on Sunday against a team from Cannock. Ray White asked how you were. He said that you used to throw punches in the scrum. Did you?'

'Never. Well once or twice, maybe a few times. I'm glad you've joined them but don't get involved in any heavy drinking culture. You shouldn't be drinking anyway.'

'Be reasonable, Dad. This is Walsall. What's this stuff I've got to learn about Jerome K. Jerome? Is it some bull they tell rookies?'

'No it's not bull. Jerome was Walsall born and we're proud of him. You've got to have a thorough knowledge of his works. Jerome's buffoonery is the basis of the club. There's not much humour about and the Humourists rugby club fills the void. They're very serious about their humour!'

'That's a contradiction in terms.'

'No it's not. It's humour.'

'Oh, I see. Well, I don't see. I'll take your word for it, until I become a fully-fledged buffoon.'

'Your mother's quite pleased with you, y'know. So am I. We just need to get Veronica fixed up with a job and we're finally free of unrealistic ambition.'

'And you've got a spring in your step.'

'I shouldn't be telling you this. We've got a proper married life again. We reckon we're a modern couple. Maybe we're not, but we feel modern. Your Mom's got her figure again. She was a damned good-looking woman in her time.'

Veronica got a job at a chemists in Caldmore Green, very close to Nan and Granddad Tucker's house. She saw them most lunchtimes. Nan Tucker loved a gossip.

'I understand that Maggie Rowley has transformed herself into a normal human being,' she said one morning.

'Nan, Ralph and I don't like you referring to our mother as Maggie Rowley. It's almost as if she's not worthy of being a Tucker. My father and all her friends call her Margaret. We love her and always have and will whether she is transformed or not, and that's an exaggeration anyway. My parents have simply made a few decisions, one was to stop over protecting us, another was to improve their marriage, my mother's lost weight and started to take a pride in her appearance. My father tells us that she's always been a 'damn good-looking woman' and she is a classy woman. Everything's fine at home. For the first time in a lifetime we're all happy.'

'Well, I'm pleased to hear it,' Nan snapped. 'You've certainly put me in my place haven't you?'

'We still love you, Nan. All I'm doing is defending my mother.'

'I go along with the saying, if you've got something to say, say it. Well, you've said it.'

'A lot of things were wrongful! Mother's expectations for us were ludicrously high. We've been assured that, as long as we lead good lives and cause no wrongs to others, we shall be the subjects of their pride and happiness.'

'So it's all quiet on the western front,' Nan said, 'which is all very well for now, but are you going to stay in that little chemists shop forever? Is Ralph going to spend his life 'larking about' as he calls it?'

'Dad wants Ralph to get a professional qualification – letters after his name – after he comes back from army service.'

'My boy knows what he's talking about so I'm sure my boy's boy will comply. And I'm sure we'll all live happily ever after until the next family row brews up.'

'You're a real Job's comforter, Nan.'

Granddad Tucker was in his usual place, snoozing on the couch in the kitchen.

'It's little Veronica! You brighten my day. Tell that brother of yours it's about time he called too.'

'He works long hours at QBS. It's a six-mile walk there and back and it's an eight-hour working day in between. When he gets home he's done in.'

'Why does he walk six miles? Why doesn't he buy a bike?'

'He's trying to get himself in good nick for the Army next year.'

'I was forgetting that. He'll do all right, will my boy's boy. I've got a photo that I'm going to give him when he goes. He can carry it for good luck. He can look at it and tell himself that if his Granddad could do it, then Ralph Tucker can. Open that drawer my little one. Pass me that brown envelope.'

He sorted through papers for a while and then said, 'Ah! Here we are.' He passed her a large photograph.

'Colour Sergeant Harry Tucker, Royal Welsh Fusiliers, 1884–1904,'she read. He was in dress uniform, stern, stiff and formal.

'You look ever so fierce and proud, Granddad, with that great moustache.'

'I was fierce. I was a man to be obeyed and from what I hear, you take after me a bit. Off you go and let me finish my snooze.'

The winter months came and life was more serious at QBS. The golden days of summer when Stan and Ralph, shirtless and bronzed, posed in front of the stack of full-length mirrors, were long over. In fact, the mirrors had all been sold for £7 each. To Jeff's delight, he picked up a cool eighty-four quid.

Jeff called them together.

'Now, listen lads. Poncy posing is over and there's work to go be done. We're going to go through a very busy period right up to Christmas Day. Garden ornaments are popular gifts.'

'What garden ornaments?' Stan asked.

'See that van over there. It's full of stuff. Unload it and you'll see for yourselves. Here's a checklist Ralph.'

Ralph took the list and read it out. 'Twenty owls, fourteen lions, thirteen cats, five flamingos, three of seven dwarfs (Sneezy, Bashful and Doc), eight kestrels (some damage to wings), nine Santas emerging from the chimney, eleven giant mushrooms, one bust of Julius Caesar, two of Lloyd George and Marlene Dietrich.'

'Put them over there,' Jeff ordered.

'These are bloody heavy,' Ralph complained.

'And they're out of proportion,' Stan added, 'the owls are twice the size of the lions.'

Finally they were able to line all the ornaments up, check them off and sign for them. The only casualty was Sneezy who had lost his head.

'Maybe he blew his nose so hard that his head blew off.' Stan ventured.

'Where did you get this lot from, Jeff?' Ralph asked.

‘From an old bloke in Brownhills. He’s been illegally occupying a patch of ground since 1920. The council have just got round to kicking him off.’

‘Poor old man!’ Stan said.

‘I offered him a price for the lot plus some chimney pots. He jumped at it. D’you reckon they’ll sell?’

‘It just depends on what’s in fashion. Four foot high concrete owls could be the future, in which case Jeff, you’ll need a new distribution centre,’ Ralph said.

‘Yes,’ Jeff said dreamily, ‘QBS International. Reusable Resources Specialists.’

‘You don’t want to get too big,’ Stan advised. ‘You lose track of what’s going on.’

‘There’s an old lady looking at the busts,’ Ralph said, ‘I’ll see what she wants.’

‘Hold it,’ Stan told him. ‘She’s not old. She’s about forty and she’s about the best-looking woman to come into the yard for months so I’ll attend to her.’ He rushed out. ‘Watch she doesn’t put her hand on your dick!’ Jeff shouted after him.

‘Can I help you, madam?’ Stan asked.

‘That’s not Marlene Dietrich,’ she said. ‘The other one could be. The hair is the same, but I think that one is Joan of Arc.’

‘Maybe they went to the same hairdresser,’ Stan reasoned.

‘And that’s definitely not Julius Caesar. It’s William Wilberforce.’

‘It said Julius Caesar on the packing list.’

‘Well I can assure you that Julius Caesar did not wear spectacles.’

‘Well, I can only apologise for the confusion. Please rest assured that I’ll take it up with our historical research department. Next time you call here, the whole matter of wrong identity will have been corrected.’

‘Thank you, young man. I’m impressed with your attitude if not with your general knowledge.’

‘Why don’t you buy a Santa emerging from the chimney? There’s no possibility of mistaken identity is there? I mean, Father Christmas is Father Christmas. No doubts.’

‘I shall think about it.’

‘May I say that you are a very attractive lady?’

‘You most certainly can. And may I say that you are a most handsome young man.’

‘I look forward to our next encounter and wish you adieu.’

‘Don’t overdo it, young man. I may or may not return to purchase something. She walked to her car, smiling and waving at Stan as she drove past him.’

He walked dreamily back to the office.

‘That was a long chat for a ‘no sale’ wasn’t it,’ Jeff remarked. ‘Did you get a date?’

‘No, I didn’t get a date, but I had something that I’ve not had since my first day at QBS – an intelligent conversation. It seems we’ve got our busts mixed up. Julius Caesar is William Wilberforce and Marlene Dietrich is Joan of Arc. I said I’d check it out. I think I’ve persuaded her to have a Santa emerging from the chimney.’

‘Very well done, young Stan. While you were out there being intelligent, we sold Bashful and Doc for ten bob each. As for the busts, I don’t think anybody knows who they’re really supposed to be. They might have been nicked from public places. The old bloke in Brownhills was probably taking the piss when he gave them names. I think we could sell them as doorstops.’

Jeff had been right in his forecast that they would be busy up until Christmas. They worked right up to Christmas Eve. They stayed as long as there was daylight. Stan reckoned that Jeff would have them working under floodlights if he could.

‘This is the post-war boom economy we’ve all been waiting for,’ Jeff announced. ‘Garden shops are going to be big business. Anyway, Merry Christmas and a Happy New year. We’re open on 27th, 28th, 29th and 30th December. Otherwise your time’s your own. Here’s your Christmas bonus. He gave each of them a bundle of worn ten-shilling notes. Ten quid each, right?’

‘Mean bastard,’ Stan muttered when Jeff was out of earshot.

‘Ten quid’s, ten quid,’ Ralph said. ‘You’ll think of this day when you pick up your first measly army pay. Have a nice Christmas, Stan.’

‘You too Ralph. See you on the 27th.’

Christmas for Ralph, as far back as he could remember, was hosted by Nan Tucker. Everybody said, ‘It doesn’t seem five minutes since last Christmas. How time flies!’ Ralph had been promoted to adulthood, which meant that he drank bottled beer and played cards with the menfolk – his father and his uncles Bryn, Jacob, and Sid and his two grandfathers Tucker and Rowley.

‘Full house!’ Granddad Tucker shouted.

‘How can that be a full house, Dad?’ Bryn asked.

‘Three threes and two twos.’

‘Well I see two threes, two twos and an eight.’

‘It must be these new glasses. An eight can look like a three can’t it?’

Granddad Rowley threw his cards across the table.

‘What’s the use of playing when he can’t tell three from eight?’

‘He’s an old man,’ Ralph defended his beloved grandfather.

‘So am I, an old man, but I can tell three from eight.’

‘Calm down,’ Bryn said and put the cards away.

Normally at this point Bryn threw in a probing question to get a debate going.

‘Do you think old Winnie will last in charge much longer?’

‘No,’ Uncle Sid said. ‘Too damned old like some of us. Eden’ll take over.’

‘Another toff!’ Grandad Rowley complained.

‘You’ve got to have a toff,’ Sid insisted. ‘The Prime Minister’s got to talk with world leaders like Eisenhower. You can’t have Britain represented by some upstart Trades Union bloke in a flat cap. We don’t want Bert This or Sam That.’

‘That’s a bit snobbish isn’t it, Sid?’ Bryn asked.

‘No, it’s common sense,’ said Uncle Jacob. ‘He should also look smart. A nice dark well-cut suit is what’s needed. Just imagine making a suit for Anthony Eden! I bet he’d pay a good price.’

‘Aren’t we getting off the subject slightly,’ Ralph suggested.

‘Yes we are. Every time Jacob’s here we finish up talking about suits. Let’s get back to Prime Ministers. I’ve seen them come and go,’ Granddad Tucker said. ‘Gladstone, Salisbury, Gladstone, Salisbury, Gladstone, Rosebery, Salisbury, Balfour, Asquith, Lloyd George. Toffs? Maybe Gladstone wasn’t a toff. Nor was Lloyd George.’

‘Nor was Ramsay McDonald between the wars,’ Hugh added.

‘Baldwin and Chamberlain were toffs,’ Sid said, ‘but who cares? To hell with them all!’

‘We’ll drink a toast to that,’ Hugh said. ‘Prime Ministers!’

‘Prime Ministers!’ They replied in chorus ‘To hell with them.’

‘The Queen!’ roared Sid.

‘The Queen,’ they chorused. ‘God bless her!’

Nan Tucker and Veronica brought in the cold ham, beef and turkey followed by cheese, crackers, bread and butter and a bottle of Drambuie.

'If you've solved the problems of running Britain, we'll eat,' Nan Tucker ordered. 'You do the carving, my boy,' she told Hugh. She then proceeded to pour out a miserly drop of Drambuie for all the guests. The next event on the programme was 'entertainment time'. This was Christmas 1954. Television had not yet taken over. Families still entertained themselves. Uncle Sid was always first on the bill. He announced that he would recite the epic poem 'How Horatius saved the bridge in the brave days of old.'

Lars Porsena of Clusium
by the nine gods he swore
That the brave house of Tarquin
would suffer wrong no more.
By the nine gods he swore it
and named the trysting day,
and bade his messengers go forth
from East and West and South and North
to summon his array….

Though they heard the same recital every year, everybody under the influence of beer and Drambuie gave a hearty cheer.

Ralph got to his feet. 'I'd like to read you one of my monologues. Granddad Rowley will like this because it's all about a racehorse. It's a bit long so if you're ever so bored, you tell me to stop.'

'Stop.' Veronica said to laughter.

Ralph began.

Of all the great racehorses that passed through Tilers' yard.
The finest was the chestnut, the mighty Beauregard.

He carried the well-known colours of the Noble Lord Carew.
Yellow cap and tunic with seven hoops of blue.

The first race that he ever had as an unknown two year old,
He knew the trainer's orders. He ran as good as gold.
'Fifth place will do us nicely,' said the crafty fox Carew.
We'll give him two more runs like that to show what he can do.

They kept the same old jockey - Tommy Flynn. Why not?
Tommy would get to know the horse and find out what he'd got. 'Tommy,' Mr Tiler said,' You'll be on Beau at York.
The Noble Lord Carew and I have had a little talk.

So, Tommy, don't make him look good. Aim for a midfield spot.'
'But Mr Tiler,' Tommy said, 'this horse has got the lot.
He should have won his first race, but he did what he was told.
Now you're asking more o' the same, which frankly, leaves me cold.

So sure enough, he ran at York and finished some way back.
Tommy did not like it much. He would have liked a crack.
And now the race was over, he whispered in Beau's ear,
'Sorry about this, young 'un. Your time will come don't fear.'

Beau's next race was at Catterick, again with Tommy Flynn.

'This is our time, Beau,' he said. 'This time we have to win.'
Beau drifted in the market, right out to twelve to one.
And that was when Carew burst through and put a thousand on.

The bookies slashed the odds to ten and now the rush was on.
Nines, eights, sevens, sixes, fives, fours, three to one.
So now Beau was the favourite. Tommy whispered in his ear.
'Just run your own race young 'un, and get well in the clear!'

Then head on for the winning post and give it all you've got.
Which is exactly what he did and he outpaced the lot.
He started winning races all up and down the land.
Tommy always spoke to him, and told him what was planned.
Tommy never used the whip for Beau knew what to do.
Mr Tiler loved that horse and so did Lord Carew.
They raced him at six furlongs. They raced him at a mile.
They raced him at ten furlongs. He always won in style.
When Beauregard was three years old the stable all agreed,
They'd run him in the Derby. They knew he had the speed.
On a glorious day at Epsom, the starters were on view,
The best of British bloodstock, French and Irish too.

The Queen asked her adviser, 'Who do you think will win?'
He said, 'I fancy Beauregard, ridden by Tommy Flynn.'

'Do you mean the number two horse in yellow with hoops of blue?
The owner is that scoundrel, the Noble Lord Carew.

Yet Carew has been successful at everything he did.
Yes, I'll back Beauregard to win. Stick on a thousand quid.' Then the Derby field were off like the charge of the Light Brigade.
It was a blur of colour and what a sight they made!

'Steady up there young 'un,' said a nervous Tommy Flynn.
'We're switching to the outside, in case we get boxed in.
We're lying sixth I reckon, with not much ground to gain.
We'll track that Irish raider, who's going like a train.'

Just then the Pride of Galway burst clear from the pack, pursued by mighty Beauregard, who was not that far back.
With half a furlong left to run, they found the going hard,
The Pride of Galway leading the Mighty Beauregard.

'Relax there Beau,' said Tommy Flynn, 'things are going fine.
We're gaining ground with every stride. We'll catch him on the line.'
And so they did and how the crowd cheered him, young Beauregard, owned by the Noble Lord Carew. The pride of Tilers' yard.

The performance drew loud applause. Granddad Rowley said it was like listening to a race commentary on the radio. Hugh was rather surprised that his son knew so much about racing. Ralph stayed on his feet to announce that his mother would now sing a song that would bring back childhood memories, as she sang it to her own accompaniment on the piano.

Margaret stepped forward. She wore a tight turquoise-coloured dress. Even Nan Tucker had to concede that she looked glamorous.

'Thank you my darling Ralph. I'm very proud of you. I shall now sing The Minstrel Boy. The minstrel boy to the wars has gone. In the ranks of death you will find him. His father's sword he has girded on…'

She belted out the song. Her bosom heaved with the effort. She had a powerful voice and so popular was her rendering that everybody called for more. She obliged by singing, 'If I were the only girl in the world.' She was loving the limelight and was smugly aware that 'Maggie Rowley' had upstaged Nan Tucker.

Uncle Jacob did a few conjuring tricks involving corks which he appeared to push through the table, quite convincing if one did not get too close.

In no time it seemed to be one o'clock. Like the ploughman of Gray's *Elegy*, the Tuckers and their relations homeward plodded their weary way.

Chapter 8

Garden Party

One evening Ralph decided to cover half of his journey home by bus. This would be his routine from now on, he promised himself. Staying fit was one thing. Putting oneself through it was another. He wanted the extra time to get out a bit more in the evenings.

'You're home early,' Margaret remarked.

'I used the bus. I was starting to get really weary. Fitness has been replaced by exhaustion.'

'You mustn't overdo it darling.'

Hugh and Veronica arrived and they ate together. Ralph said he'd got business to discuss with Tommy and Dennis, and left. He knew that they would be in one of three pubs. His first choice was the Windmill and sure enough they were there.

'It's Ralphy,' they cried, 'Just in time to buy a drink.'

'You're looking super fit as usual, Ralph,' Tommy told him, 'But on closer inspection, a bit weary.'

'That's what I am but not any longer. I shall be using the bus more.'

'You're not too knackered to buy us a drink are you?' Dennis asked.

'Of course not. I'll get them in.'

'Cheers, lads!'

'Listen, chaps,' Ralph said. It's not that long before our eighteenth birthdays is it? Mine's May 31st.'

'So's mine,' Tommy said.

'I'm the baby', Dennis told them, 'born June 1st.'

'Now listen to this,' Ralph ordered. 'If we do National Service the chances are that we won't be called up until November or later, when we'd be eighteen and a half.

Whereas if we sign on as three year regulars we could join up earlier. We could also make sure that we were together in the same outfit.'

'This needs some serious thought,' Tommy pondered. 'Three years is a long time.'

'Yes,' Ralph agreed, 'but if you think of it as part of your three score years and ten, it's nothing.'

'If we join,' Dennis asked,'Who do we join?'

'We join the Grey Jackets. We have the Staffordshire knot as our cap badge,' Ralph said.

'Yes. Good thinking Ralph!' Tommy agreed. 'They're stationed at Lichfield. That'll be handy.'

'The Depot's at Lichfield,' Dennis added, 'but the Battalion are in Cyprus. There's dozens of our mates there. So what are we going to do? Get ourselves into some trouble just so we can be together and get our arses shot off? All in the name of friendship?'

'You're out of order, Dennis!' Tommy argued. 'That's what the Arbo Gang is all about isn't it – one for all and all for one? Or is it all for one and one for all? We stay together. Just supposing we all go our own ways and we all find ourselves in a regiment of Scousers or with Geordies saying 'Why aye, mon' and all that. They take the piss out of our accents just as we do to theirs. I can't be bothered with trying to understand accents so I say let's be regulars and make our own decisions. What do you say, Ralph?'

'I say we go for the money. A National Serviceman in training gets four shillings a day. They deduct a shilling for a haircut, a few more for National Insurance and they put some more into a Post Office Savings Account. You have to march the length of two barrack blocks, salute an officer and he gives you a quid to spend on Blanco and Brasso and egg and chips in the Naafi.'

'Yes, I've heard that,' Dennis said. 'Blokes have told me just what you've just told me, Ralph.'

'Well, I'm not soldiering for a bloody quid,' Tommy affirmed. 'Let's go for three years.'

'Three years with the colours,' Dennis said. 'Sounds romantic doesn't it?'

'But it's not', Ralph said.

They drank to it. The toast was 'three years of Hell'.

Summer came. Ralph told Jeff Pyke that he wanted to finish in mid-July so that he could rest up before leaving for basic training.

'It's up to you, Ralph. You're on self-employed. You go when you like, but if I take anybody on in the meantime all I can give you is a day's notice and then you're finished. The same applies to Stan. He wants to finish around the same time as you. I must admit that I'll miss you both. We've had a laugh and a joke and that's how work should be.' The office phone rang and Jeff went in to answer it. Stan was sitting on a pile of bricks eating his sandwiches Ralph sat opposite him on some rocks.

'So you'll be off too then, Stan?'

'I haven't been called up yet, but it's matter of time. I'm eighteen years and nine months.'

'Maybe they've forgotten you.'

'Oh, Ralph. Please don't say that. I'm desperate to go.'

I want to get away from here. I don't understand why some blokes moan about it so much, who knows where you might finish up? Places you'd never see as a civvy – Hong Kong, Malaya.'

'Cyprus?'

'Yes. That'll be okay.'

'Active service. You could cop it.'

'Long odds. Say a battalion of seven hundred men lost five of them. That's 140 to 1 against. Would you back a horse at those odds?'

'My granddad has backed horses at over 100-1 and won.'

'Anyway I don't want to lay odds on death. It's too morbid.'

'Why don't you come with Tommy, Dennis and me? We're going down to the recruiting office in James Watt Street on July the 14th. We're going to sign on for 22 years with the option of finishing every three years. Think about it. We'd be together. You'd have mates. That's very important in the services.'

'I'm going to give it plenty of thought. If I decide yes, I'll have my cousin Duggie with me.'

Ralph knew that Stan would decide to string along with the Arbo Gang even though he had always regarded the whole concept to be childish and had told Ralph so. As predicted, Stan was waiting near the Midland Red bus stop with a tall wiry youth whom they guessed was Duggie. They introduced themselves and piled onto the next red bus.

'This is our day of destiny,' Ralph announced, 'the 14th of July.'

'Bastille Day,' Duggie told them.

'I never thought of that,' Ralph said.

Everything had gone through smoothly. The recruiting sergeant had been keen to get them into the Guards, but they stuck with the Grey Jackets. Subject to a date for a medical examination yet to be advised, they were all attested and would report to Whittington Barracks in Lichfield on 24th August 1955.

One evening at dinner, Hugh let it be known that a garden party would be held the following Saturday to celebrate their 20th wedding anniversary.

'Who'll be there?' Ralph asked.

'A lot of relatives that you haven't seen for a long time. In some cases, you've never seen them. Some are friends from before the war.'

'Will there be a bar?'

'Yes, Ralph. There will be an adequate supply of bottled beer on ice. I shall be personally be supervising the dispensing of spirits and Aunt Lorna has kindly donated two cartons of red wine.'

'Do you mean Aunt Lorna the beautiful lady?' Veronica asked.

'That indeed would be an accurate description,' Hugh confirmed.

'We shall need both of you kids to look after 'Front of House' as it were,' Hugh instructed. 'Greet everybody as they arrive. Say who you are and find out who they are. Lead them through the garden and offer to get them a drink.'

The day came. It was hot. Guests began to appear in the early afternoon. For the most part, Ralph and Veronica were ignored. They approached people and attempted to shake hands but to no avail. It was not working out. Among the adults there were hearty handshakes and roars of laughter.

'How are you, you old reprobate?'

'Not as well as you, you old rascal.'

'Haw haw haw haw haw.'

'Roar roar roar roar roar.'

Everybody was an old codger, an old rogue or an old boozer.

'Squeal, squeal, squeal, squeal'

'Chuckle chuckle chuckle, chuckle.'

'I think we're redundant,' Veronica said. 'A lot of ignorant people if you ask me.'

'Where are our favourites like Uncle Bryn and Uncle Sid and Nan Tucker?

Just then a roly-poly woman with three chins put her arms around Veronica.

'Well if it isn't little Veronica. What a pretty dress! Did you make it yourself or is it a thirteenth birthday present?'

'I'm seventeen,' Veronica snapped. 'Who are you?'

'Why, I'm Auntie Gladys, of course.'

'You nearly squeezed me to death. I am instructed to tell you that alcoholic beverages are served at the bottom of the garden and the buffet will be located outside the French windows.'

'That's told her! What a liberty!'

A huge man in tweeds, sweating profusely came up to Ralph and said, 'Ralph?'

'That's me.'

'You made it then.'

'I live here.'

'No, I meant that you'd made it to the party. I heard that you'd been getting very bad asthma attacks.'

'Not so much lately, but I'm allergic to tweed.'

'Oh dear!' He looked distressed.

'I'm only joking.'

'Thank God for that. Just like all the Tuckers, joking all the time. I'm Uncle Percy. Of course, I'm not really an uncle. I used to play golf with your Uncle Bryn.'

'The liquid refreshments are at the bottom of the garden, Uncle Percy. If you get too hot in that tweed jacket, I'll relieve you of it and put it somewhere safe.'

'That's kind of you. You're a very obliging young man.'

Uncle Percy walked away.

'He was a decent old boy,' Ralph said to Veronica.

'Some of them are all right. Most of them are awful. I never imagined that Mom and Dad had so many fat, smelly, boozy friends. I thought they'd all be glamorous like Lorna.'

'If only.'

'They must be nearly all here by now. Let's go through to the garden. I've had enough of being kissed by frumpy women and whiskery men with abdominal breath.'

'Hold on for a little while. Lorna hasn't arrived yet.'

‘There she is!’ Veronica cried. ‘I knew she would make a grand entrance. She’s all in white again. I swear it’s the same dress that she wore all those years ago.’

‘She’s made some pretty daring alterations hasn’t she? The dress is split completely up one side.’

‘And her left nipple’s showing,’ Veronica whispered, ‘but what a sensational looking woman.’

‘What legs! Or rather what leg. I think we can assume that both legs are the same.’

She seemed to float across the lawn. She was carrying two large cartons of wine as easily and casually as if carrying two shopping bags.

‘Do you know what, Ralph? This may sound a bit far-fetched, but you could conceivably get off with Lorna. Just look at this bunch of mediocre, half-drunk cretins. If I were Lorna Pitt, I’d try and trap the best looking man here. That’s you, Ralph. Don’t panic, don’t blush, don’t be shy. Just strike up a conversation.’

‘I’ll need some Dutch courage then. I’m going to grab myself a bottle of beer first.’

‘If you don’t try for this, I’ll never talk to you again Tucker. You’ve got the chance of getting yourself a real woman who’ll instruct you in the art of love. Older women love gorgeous young men.’

‘All highly exaggerated and makes me a gigolo. Anyway, what have I got to lose? I’m off.’

He walked up to the beer area, took a bottle of beer from the ice box, applied his bottle opener to the bottle cap. Beer spurted out all over Lorna’s dress.

‘What a start,’ he muttered. ‘I’m sorry!’ he almost sobbed. ‘I apologise profusely. I’ve ruined your dress. I shall buy you another one. I shall save my money until I’ve got enough to buy you the dress of your choice.’

‘Enough, enough, young man,’ she cut in, ‘it’s not that serious.’

She laid her hand on his arm and said, 'Don't worry about it.' She looked at him and smiled. He thought that she was the most beautiful woman he had ever seen. Her eyes dwelt on him again and he wondered if it was 'that look'.

'That look', according to braggarts and self-acclaimed womanisers, meant that you were 'in'. It was the cue to say something witty, complimentary and possibly memorable.

'You are without doubt the most gorgeous woman at this party,' he told her. 'You have laughing eyes, the figure of a goddess and shining olive skin. You are a vision in white and I like your hat.'

'Thank you. You have discerned very early in our relationship that I am a woman of unparalleled beauty. I'm glad you like my hat. I must say that I've never liked the hat much but, of course, on me it looks good. Thank you all the same. I shall reward your compliment with a kiss. She threw her arms around him. Her hug was like a vice. Her kiss was deep and prolonged. He was oblivious to everybody and everything but her. They finally broke apart. She soon gained her composure, but he was trembling with excitement.

'You seem flushed and agitated. Let's take a little walk, shall we?'

They walked through the gate at the bottom of the garden which led directly onto the Oval, stopping to sit down on a spectator's bench.

'Do you know who I am?'

'Aunt Lorna – Lorna Pitt.'

'Yes, and you're Ralph. I met you eleven years ago. You were seven. You were a beautiful boy then and you still are. You said something very nice to me. You said that you were very sorry that I had lost my husband in the war.'

'Which I would have been told to say, I imagine.'

'No doubt, but you added a bit of your own. You said that you were sure that he was in Heaven. I thought that was so sweet of you. I burst into tears and hugged you like mad.

You played with my little girl, Sarah. You are the same age. I used to think what a lovely couple you and Sarah would make one day, but it was not to be. Sarah's now pregnant to a fellow student who has since done a disappearing act. I'm very cross with her for being so naughty. Well, at least I'll have a little grandchild to fuss over and I'm glad about that. Tell me Ralph. What do you do for a living?'

'I was working for a company called QBS. They sell building supplies and all sorts of junk salvaged from demolition sites – some weird things too like four feet high concrete owls. There were only three of us. It was hard work loading stuff on and off vehicles, but we had a good laugh. It's all over now. I'm giving myself a break before I leave for the army on August 24th.'

'So you've got about three to four weeks off then. I've suddenly got a great idea. Would you like to earn yourself some money working for me?'

'I was going to rest up but as it's you, I'll say yes – very eagerly too.'

'Come with me.' She held out her hand and he took it. 'Look across the Oval. Do you see that immense gothic house in the trees?'

'I see it. I know it. I've walked past it many a time. There's a drive bordered by cedar trees and high hedges.'

'It's my house. It's Stanhope Hall. I've been there alone since Sarah left to go to Cambridge. The regular groundsman-cum-gardener retired some months ago and I've never replaced him. The consequence is that the grounds are a jungle. You would have to work hard every day. I estimate that there's four weeks work there, but you might cram it into three. You'll be well rewarded. I shall show my appreciation in a very personal way. Are you excited? I am. I'm sure that we'll get along well. Oh, you're such a gorgeous boy.'

'How old are you, Lorna?'

‘I’m forty-three. That’s twenty-five years older than you. Do you mind?’

‘I haven’t really taken everything in.’

‘You will. Just try to relax. Think calmly about it. An older woman of unsurpassed beauty and an incredibly handsome young man eager to be taught the art of love. A femme fatale. Let’s walk over to the house shall we? Then you’ll see what I mean about the gardens.’

They walked up the cedar-lined drive to Stanhope Hall. Lorna had not exaggerated the woeful state of the gardens. To get them in order would be a formidable task, but he knew that he could do it. She showed him where all the tools were. He checked what he needed, a scythe, an axe, a bandsaw, spades, forks, trowels, rakes, shears and two hand mowers. He was looking forward to it. The manual work would maintain his fitness levels for his basic training. He told Lorna that he would need to start at 6.30 am to get a long enough day in. She told him that she admired his enthusiasm and handed him two keys, one for the tool shed and one for the kitchen to call in and make himself a cup of tea. She worked at Royal Oak Insurance from 9 am to 2 pm most days. She was the branch accountant and claimed to work more or less when she liked.

‘Let’s see how the first day pans out,’ she suggested. ‘Then we’ll get into a routine.’

‘Until tomorrow,’ Ralph said and made to leave.

‘You’re not going are you? Are you worried that they’ll miss you at the party? Don’t worry. Most of them will be three parts sloshed. Anyway, we still have a little job to do. We have to get that beer stain out of my dress, so come back into the kitchen. What do you suggest?’

‘You could take it to the dry cleaners.’

‘And put another one on. Yes, that’s a good idea. Let’s take it off then shall we? I really don’t know what dress to put on to replace it. To hell with it. I’m not going back to the party so I don’t need to bother.’

She lifted the loose white dress over her head and threw it onto a chair quite casually. She was now completely naked but for high heels; gloriously naked, solid as stone, statuesque, proud and haughty, her long copper hair falling over her shoulders, her triangle of wiry pubic hair a veritable forest, a perfectly proportioned woman in her prime. Ralph was transfixed, paralysed, unable to speak.

'You wanted to see me, didn't you, Ralph? I haven't made a fool of myself have I?'

'N-no. You're incredible.'

'Would you like to get to know me better?'

'Of course.'

'I shall expect you at 6.30 tomorrow.'

He ambled back to the party. It was earlier than he thought, barely eight o'clock. The party was still in full swing. The manic laughter had, if anything, increased and the haw haw haws and roar roar roars seemed louder than ever. The temperature had dropped and guests had started to drift back into the house through the French windows. Somebody was playing the piano. A group were singing 'Roll out the Barrel.'

Veronica was sitting in the tree house, Ralph had not seen her. She leapt down onto him, landing on his shoulders. They fell in a heap in the dirt.

'I'm very curious,' Veronica said. 'I saw you kissing Lorna Pitt on that bench and so did Mom and Dad incidentally. Then you walked hand in hand like lovers across the Oval and vanished near the cedar trees. I know she lives in the big house in the woods. So I reckon you were in her house giving her one.'

'No I wasn't and that's the absolute truth.'

'Something happened, Ralph. I watched you ambling back over the Oval. You were like a man in a dream and you looked sort of happy but smug. I want to know why.'

'Well, I've got a nice little cash job for the next three and a half weeks looking after Lorna's gardens, which are spread over a wide area and as overgrown as the jungle. I'm looking forward to it. It'll be hard work but rewarding.'

'Plus?'

'Who knows?'

'I'm getting really annoyed. Are you about to embark on a torrid affair with a woman in her forties who will educate you in the art of love? Is this gardening a front for you to be Lady Chatterley's Lover?'

'The gardening is not a front. It's a genuine job and it's not going to be easy. As far as an affair is concerned, the only hint I've got is that she will show her appreciation for my work in a very personal way. She also said that she was sure that we would get along well and told me I was such a gorgeous boy and things like that.'

'Well, go on!'

'Do you want to hear more you dirty-minded little madam?'

'Yes please, darling brother. I'm squirming with excitement.'

'When we were in the house, she asked how we should get the beer stain out of her dress. I suggested that she could take it to a dry cleaners. She agreed and nonchalantly whipped off the dress and slung it on one side. She was naked except for high heels. I was in shock. I thought I was dreaming. She's built like an Amazon. She's got enormous knockers. She let down her hair. It's a dark copper colour. It's luxuriant. It falls down well past her shoulders. She's incredibly vain and conceited. When you pay her a compliment, she agrees with you.'

'Oh, brother Ralph. I cannot take any more. My depressed, misguided, asthmatic, penniless, introvert brother. You deserve a change in fortune.'

'I'm not penniless, nor shall I be.'

'Anyway, Mother wants to speak to you. She's in the house somewhere and she's had more than a few large glasses of wine.'

He found her quite easily. She was sprawled in armchair. She wore a tight blue dress. She looked good.

'Help mummy off this chair.'

He pulled her up. She staggered. She kept saying, 'I'll be all right.'

'Let's get you outside in the fresh air, mother. Hold onto me.'

She steadied a bit. They made it to a garden chair. He sat next to her on a beer crate.

'Are you ashamed of me? Here's mummy nearly drunk whilst her two little scamps have been models of good behaviour.'

'There's no harm in getting a bit inebriated, Mother.'

'Not for a man there isn't. They do it all the time, but a drunken woman is a pitiful sight.'

'Of course she isn't! It's a party. Everybody lets themselves go, don't they? That's what parties are for. You're not a pitiful sight. You're the best looking woman here by far.'

'Except for Lorna Pitt.'

'If you say so.'

'I know so. Son, I wanted to have a little chat with you about her. I think I should sober up first. Go into the kitchen and make me a cup of coffee, very strong in a large cup. No milk, no sugar.'

He was back ten minutes later. The party was starting to break up and the roars and squeals of laughter receded as guests drifted away.

'Have you enjoyed your evening, darling?'

'Immensely, mother.'

'We saw you walking hand in hand over the Oval with Lorna Pitt. You looked for all the world like young lovers.'

'There's something I have to tell you about–'

'You don't have to tell me anything,' she cut in. 'I'll tell *you* – she wants you to put in a month's hard labour to get Stanhope Hall's gardens into shape. You will have to work long hours from what I've been told, but you won't have far to go to work. You'll be stopping with Lorna. Even though she may not have said that yet, it *will* be the case. Your father is rather flippant about the whole thing. He talks in terms of 'getting your end away' and all that. Typical male. He says that if you're old enough to serve your country, you're old enough to have a fling with a sensuous rich widow. I suppose that would apply vice versa. Lorna lost her husband in 1944 and spent the next ten years or so bringing up a daughter on her own. Maybe she thinks she's due for a taste of the good life too, and if that includes a handsome boy lover so be it. She will, no doubt, invite you into her fantasy world, but you will soon be undergoing basic infantry training so if anything is going to bring you down to earth, it's the army. You can take it that I'm not a hundred per cent approving of your affair. I'm not against it either. Frankly my dear I don't give a damn, as Rhett Butler said.'

'I'm glad you feel that way, Mother.'

'The mother of old would have berated Lorna for stealing her son and turning him into a gigolo. She would have barred you from the house until you renounced Lorna completely. So be glad that I've decided to try and be a more modern mother. Mind you, I hope you know what you're letting yourself into. Lorna in her prime was an outrageous woman, and from the way I saw her flouncing across the lawn today in a dress leaving nothing to the imagination, I guess she still is. She is a dominant, self-indulgent, vulgar woman. She has a huge intellect. She's generous to a fault. She's loving. She's an enigma. She always seems in good health, yet she can drink men under the table.

'Now there's something else to tell you. Your father and I are taking a holiday. He's got a month's accumulated leave and if he doesn't take it now, he'll lose it. We're off tomorrow morning for Eastbourne. Some old friends of ours, who were at the party, own a hotel and we've got a rock-bottom rate. We're leaving you and Veronica to clear up the mess. Keep an eye on the house. Veronica will stay with Nan Tucker. Where shall you stay, Ralph, I wonder?' she smiled. 'Kiss me, my little scamp and wish us a good time.

'Now, now, Ralph! A proper kiss please. That's better. My, but you're a lusty lad. When you and Lorna Pitt get together it's going to be like a Walls ice cream van hitting a brick wall.'

Chapter 9

Stanhope Hall

Ralph and Veronica were up early. Hugh and Margaret rose soon after. Ralph loaded their suitcases into the car and wished them a great second honeymoon.

'You have a good time too, son,' Hugh winked.

'You both look very glamorous, I must say,' Veronica told them. Margaret wore a summer dress. Hugh wore an oatmeal-coloured baggy suit and a Panama hat.

'You look like Mr and Mrs Robert Mitchum,' Ralph said.

'Did we give you the address and phone number of the hotel?' Margaret asked.

'Yes yes,' Veronica sighed. 'Now be off with you and drive carefully.'

They decided to make a start on clearing up. They cleared away bottles, plates, half-eaten snacks, ashtrays overflowing with cigarette and cigar butts. They repositioned all the chairs and swept the paths. There were over a hundred glasses lying on the lawns that had to be brought in and washed. After an hour of concerted effort, they had everything shipshape. Ralph suggested that they get inside, away from the summer heat. They went into the gloomy but cool living room, espying en route a carton, recognised as one of the two that Lorna had brought. Three full bottles remained. They drank two bottles between them and fell asleep.

Three hours later they came out of their stupor simultaneously. They had anticipated mighty hangovers, but they felt fine.

‘It’s probably good quality wine, knowing Lorna,’ Ralph suggested. ‘Thank God I’m not hung-over. I’m due at Stanhope Hall at 6.30 am tomorrow.’

Ralph was up at the crack of dawn and striding across the Oval to Stanhope Hall. He reached the Hall at exactly six thirty as arranged. He sat on a wall, took his notepad out and listed his tasks. There were seven hedges to be pruned and cleared, eleven flowerbeds to be weeded and dug over. Four lawns to be mown. Many paths to be cleared, slabs to be laid again in the patio area outside the kitchen and overgrown shrubs to be pruned or removed. He decided to tackle the lawns first, starting with the smallest.

The grass was almost waist high. He began swinging the scythe. It was very hard going at first, but he stuck with it and got into a rhythm. He loaded the loose grass into a wheelbarrow and took it to an out of sight area where he commenced to build up a compost heap. The lawn needed three scythings to bring it down to a mowable height. He fetched the largest hand mower from the tool shed. It was completely seized up. He poured some oil into it and got it mobile, but it still would not cut. He found a carborundum stone on the tool-shed shelf. He sharpened the blades and finally the mower began to cut the grass down to a manageable level. The mower loosened up and he was able to ‘put the lines on’ the small lawn. It had taken him two hours. Lorna came out of the house.

‘I’ll have to go now, Ralph. Tomorrow we’ll get into a routine. I’ll cook you a full breakfast every morning to keep you going all day. You seem to have made inroads already. I’ll see you at two thirty or thereabouts.’

He started another lawn using the same method. This lawn was much larger and awkwardly shaped. Again he got into a rhythm as he swung his scythe, but his stamina was beginning to sap both physically and mentally as he tried to come to terms with the enormity of his task. He decided to take a break. He went into the kitchen and made himself a cup of tea. He emptied the contents of the biscuit barrel and wolfed down all the broken biscuits and even the crumbs, so ravenous was he. He returned to his labour. The sun was strong on his back but he continued, telling himself that it would get easier day-by-day. Lorna appeared at two thirty.

'You've been working like a Trojan by the looks of it,' she enthused. 'You're dirty and sweaty too. Call it a day. Have a beer. We'll have a little chat.

'You will have gathered that I occupy only this small corner of the Hall. That's not going to be forever. Over a period I'm going to get it all converted to flats, but in the meantime I'm here on my own and rather lonely. It occurs to me that, as your parents are away, you may as well stay here. I shall feel safer with a man in the house. In fact, I'd go further and say how nice it would be to have a man in my bed. I've got a nice big bed. We could have some jolly good fun.'

She said it all in such a matter of fact way, in her deep 'jolly hockey sticks' accent that it seemed compulsory to say 'Yes'. In fact 'yes please'.

'Good. My next question, Ralph, is, are you a virgin?'

'Yes. I have to admit it.'

'We'll soon fix that. Get out of those dirty working clothes, leave them in the kitchen. Have your shower and I'll see you in the bedroom. I'm really looking forward to it.'

He did what he was told and emerged refreshed from the shower. He opened the bedroom door.

'Oh, yes! What a physique! What a golden boy! Are you excited? I am. I've been thinking about it all night. What an erection! Now then, Ralph. Don't worry about your weight on me. I'm very strong and look! I'm in position for you. I'm so excited. I bet you are too. It would be inconceivable that you didn't know what to do.'

A shaft of light from a gap in the curtains threw a silvery line across her back as she lay motionless on the bed.

'Did I do it right?' he asked nervously.

'Yes, silly boy, you did it right, but it was all so frantic.'

'My backs bleeding,' he said, 'from your nails clawing into me.'

'So sorry, darling. Next time you must not go at it hammer and tongs. I know that you're a tender and gentle person and that is the way you should make love. Lie here a while with me.

'This is a lovely time, Ralph, the time after making love. I call it the golden time. You are my Beautiful Boy now. For how long I know not, but while you are mine, I shall make you happy and you shall make me happy in return.

'Now there are things I must tell you and if I come over as school-ma'am-ish, so be it. I put lovemaking on a pedestal because it is a most wonderful thing. I loathe and detest all the vile slang and ugly oaths that demean it. Apart from four letter words commencing with an F or C, the following are verboten – shag, screw, knock off, shaft, cock, dick, tool, fanny, pussy, minge, arse, knockers, boobs, tits, Bristols. Oral or anal sex is an abomination. Permissible are breasts, buttocks, bottom and my very favourite word – bosom – the enclosure of the breasts and arms. Do you understand, Ralph? I'm sure that you do.

'There is absolutely no future for us, Ralph. I am your mother's age and I cannot have any more children. You will want to live the normal life of a young man, pursuance of the opposite sex being a priority. I can stay with you through the period of your military training and beyond maybe. After that you are on your own.'

She sensed that he looked perplexed. 'I think I've given you enough lecturing, you poor confused boy. Come lay your curly head upon my bosom.'

'I was just thinking. Suppose we were hopelessly in love at the time when we had planned to go our separate ways?'

'I shall never let you become hopelessly in love with me, Ralph. You shall have your own life. You will make your mark. In that respect, I am ambitious for you. Being hopelessly in love? I think not. I could bewitch you, seduce you, overpower you with my beauty, but I shall not do so. Our love will be light-hearted. We shall have fun. Do you feel excited? *I* do. I think little Ralph would like to visit little Lorna again in her house in the forest.'

'Dare I ask?' he wondered. He did not have to ask.

'Even by my high standards that was commendable.'

'I can relax.'

'You should always be relaxed, always be confident about your performance. I will make a lover of you. I shall make a man of you. We have blissful days ahead of us. Try to forget the Army. It will be purgatory. Similarly, don't dwell on your daily tasks. They are not daunting. You will succeed.

'Now as this is your first evening, I have prepared a nice dinner for us. Evening meals normally will be very basic. Tonight we have chicken salad and red wine. Shall we dress for dinner? I think we should. Ralph, walk back to your house and bring with you all that you will need for your sojourn here including some nice clothes.'

He walked back across the Oval to the house. Veronica was there.

'Just checking things out,' she said.

'I was about to do the same thing.'

'Liar! I know what you've come for. You've come for your gear to take it back to Stanhope Hall. My burning question is – have you shagged her yet?'

'We don't use words like 'shag'. They are permanently taboo.'

'So how do you describe it then?'

'Love is a wonderful thing and should not be demeaned by vile slang.'

'Tell me, for heaven's sake. Describe it!'

'Little Ralph visits little Lorna in her house in the forest.

Veronica was convulsed with laughter. ‘Is that the little Ralph that lives in your pocket? Forgive me if I go into hysterics. Lorna’s got you trapped, boy! She’s got you trapped in her fantasy world. For the final time, how many successful trips has little Ralph made?’

‘Two,’ he said. It sounded flat

‘So I’ve wheedled it out of you at last. I shall know what to ask next time. How many calls did little Ralph make today?’

‘There’s no need for you to be asking at all. You’re treating an important subject as a joke. I am only too happy to be living in Lorna’s fantasy world. I’ve got the army coming up and that’s going to be hell by all accounts, so yes, I’m in Lorna’s little fantasy world. I admit it.’

She walked over to him and kissed him, ‘I’m sorry I was facetious. I really do care about you.’

He walked back to Stanhope Hall with the battered old suitcase that he had inherited from his father. He took his case into the bedroom and hung his clothes in the wardrobe. He sneaked a look into Lorna’s side of the wardrobe. Apart from the navy blue outfit she wore to work, there was very little there.

‘I don’t have many clothes,’ she admitted. ‘That’s why next week you will be taking me to a rather chic dress shop in Malvern, we hope. In the meantime, I’ve found rather a daring dress that I had forgotten I had. It’s from Hong Kong. As I remember, it was very expensive.’

‘I imagine so,’ Ralph said.

It was turquoise and gold, extremely tight, but doctored by Lorna to fit her. In truth, she was oozing out of it. She looked voluptuous.

They sat down to dine. She lit two candles. She filled their glasses and proposed a toast to loss of virginity.

‘This is the wine that you took to the garden party,’ Ralph remarked. ‘Veronica and I had two whole bottles between us and we never even had a hangover.’

'Nor will you,' Lorna said. 'There is a story concerning this wine. In 1935, an officer in my father's regiment owed him a huge amount of money in gambling debts. He simply did not have the funds to pay him, but his family were wealthy wine importers so he arranged to pay my father in wine. Now I have half a room full of it. I think I shall be drinking it forever. Cheers!'

'Cheers!' Ralph replied, 'I shall drink to a golden time. The golden late summer sun. The golden times when I lay my head upon your breast. Your golden skin. Everywhere is golden for us. Even the Oval is golden in the evening. But the most golden of all is you, Lorna. How did you get that overall golden tan?'

'That's not a suntan darling. That is I. I am this colour. I am half English, one quarter Paraguayan (Spanish) and one quarter Paraguayan (Guarani). The Guarani are the largest single group of Indians in Paraguay. I am immensely proud of my Guarani blood. In The War of the Triple Alliance, Paraguay lost three quarters of its population and the Guarani fought to the bitter end.

'My grandfather was General Raul Ortiz. He was a soldier, a land owner, and timber exporter. He was very rich. My grandmother was Maria Carrero Ortiz, a Guarani. We visited them after the 14-18 war as I remember. My father, Colonel Edwin Stanhope, one time Colonel of the Grey Jackets regiment was posted to Asuncion in 1911 with a vague title – Military Attaché or something. That is where he met my mother and that is where I was born in 1913. He was home in time to go to the trenches in France. Miraculously, he came through the Great War. Shall we replenish our wine? I think we shall. I absolutely worshipped my father and the feeling was mutual. I was thoroughly spoilt. I was allowed to behave outrageously. He always dismissed it as high spirits.

'I could have had any single officer in the battalion and I played the field. I married Captain Roger Pitt who was *so* handsome but I lost him at Arnhem.' She paused and stayed silent for some seconds. 'We won't pursue that. Not today. It's highly inappropriate. I have lots to tell you, Beautiful Boy. We shall have lots of quiet times. Shall we have more wine?'

At six o'clock Ralph was already at work on the lawns. However purposefully he swung his scythe, he struggled. The scythe was blunt. He sharpened it as best he could using the carborundum stone. It cut well for a while, but soon he was finding it difficult again. He switched to using shears, but they soon became ineffective. He decided that the only way out of it was to have the mowers, scythe, and shears professionally sharpened. In the meantime, he continued but his labours were in vain. He was relieved when Lorna called him into breakfast.

He asked Lorna if he could use the car to go to Chuckery later that morning.

'Have you got a licence?'

'I passed a test using Dad's car about a month ago.'

'Why do you need the car? Can't you walk it?'

'I want to take the mowers and other things to be sharpened by a bloke I know. They'll all go in the back of the car.'

She handed him the key to the old Morris Minor.

'Have I done something wrong?' he asked.

'You never said if you enjoyed your big breakfast.'

'It was great. I'm sorry I said nothing.'

'Forget it,' she sighed. 'Men are men. I still love you.'

'I thought we were not supposed to become hopelessly in love.'

'I never said anything about being hopelessly in love. I only said that I loved you. Do you know, Ralph, that in Russian there are forty words for love, or so I have been told, forty words yet we have only one – and thus how sad, how inept, how confused one can become. My love for you is love for a virile young man who shall make me happy. Now be off with you and be about your tasks.'

He went into the tool shed to take out the mowers. He was conscious of a diminutive figure coming up behind him. There was a scream of 'Dear brother!' Veronica ran to him and jumped upon him, landing with her arms around his neck and legs around his waist.

'Get off,' he ordered. 'You'll crush the breath out of me. What are you doing here anyway?'

'We're closed this afternoon. I finished at ten thirty and here I am.'

'I thought chemists were open all day.'

'It's done on a roster system but enough of this boring talk. I've got something to tell you. Yesterday evening I took a little stroll through the dusty streets to Moncrieff Street and surprise, surprise, there was Tommy Ward sitting on a wall drinking a bottle of Tizer. I asked him if he'd take me for a drink in the Duke of York pub. I reminded him of the days when I always cheered for him, when you were all playing football in the Arboretum. He said that I'd grown to be a real cracker. We got to know each other again. He's a very serious man. He's determined to get his plumbing business off the ground and expand it. At the moment he's in a quandary. He wished he'd never signed on for three years. It's putting too much pressure on his brother Ron.'

'Yes, I know this Veronica. He's my best mate.'

'Well, I'm confident that he'll be your brother-in-law once he's back on Civvy Street. I asked him if he had anybody to write to when he's away. He hasn't. As a matter of fact, he's never had a girlfriend. So we've agreed to exchange photos and write to each other while he's away. He's taking me to the pictures tomorrow night in Caldmore Green. We're seeing *Shane* It's a Western isn't it? Just my type of film, plenty of people getting shot. Anyway, what's your verdict?'

'I'm delighted. But – and it's a big 'but' – don't get bored with writing and stop. Promise me you won't go out with other blokes. Three years is a long time. There'll be periods of leave, but it's still a long, long time. Please, please, don't let Tommy down.'

'I absolutely promise faithfully and eternally on the Holy Bible.'

'Good. I believe you. I can't hang around. I've got work to do.' He jumped in the car and sped off to Chuckery.

'You're here,' Ralph said.

'You sound surprised.'

'I am surprised, Tommy I thought you'd be out on a job. I called here on the off-chance. I'm on my way to see Ted in Walsingham Street.'

'You mean the bloke who sells leather belts and dog leashes and that. That's Reg.'

'No, Reg is the bloke who cuts keys.'

'No he doesn't. He's a cobbler. You're thinking of Ray.'

'No,' Ralph said, 'I've got to see the bloke who sharpens knives and saws and mowers and that.'

'That's Cliff,' Tommy said. 'Why didn't you tell me in the first place? You never said what this elusive chap did. If you'd said he was a knife sharpener, I'd have told you – Cliff.'

'Anyway, that's who I'm off to see, but before I go…'

'Before you go,' Tommy grinned, 'You wish to congratulate me on my engagement to Veronica in November, which will be our first leave. You're behind this aren't you, Ralph?'

'No, Veronica's her own woman. She made the decision.'

'Come off it, you're the matchmaker and I owe all my future wedded bliss to you, Ralph Tucker, founder of the Arbo Gang. We'll piss this army service in. Piss it in! All for one and one for all or is it one for all and all for one?'

'I must be going. I've got a lot to do.'

'Fair enough, Ralph. Cliff's at number 87.'

Cliff was a grizzled man of maybe fifty, but one could never tell ages in these streets. A lot of people had been through a lot and looked old and wrinkled before their time. Ralph unloaded the mowers and tools.

'What have you been doing, son?' Cliff asked, 'Trying to scythe down walls and mow rocks? There's a fair amount of work here. Leave the whole lot with me for an hour.'

Ralph took a leisurely walk to The Walsall Arms via a newsagent's and settled down to read his newspaper over a pint.

When the hour was up he walked back to Cliff's workshop.

'It's all ready for you,' Cliff said. 'Seven and six the lot. That's cheap because the mowers were in a real bad way. Follow me.' They went down the entry to a small patch of lawn behind Cliff's house.

'Try them.'

Ralph tested both mowers. 'Smooth as silk. Thanks Cliff.'

'They'll do the job,' Cliff assured him. 'Where are you working?'

'Stanhope Hall. I'm doing all the grounds.'

'Stanhope Hall. That's the house in the woods isn't it? I've been there when I used to do knife sharpening door to door. I thought twice about calling at Stanhope Hall. It looked a bit like a haunted house. I thought to myself, nothing ventured, nothing lost. The lady of the house let me in by the kitchen entrance and guess what? She hadn't got a stitch of clothing on.'

'No kidding?'

'It's as true as I'm standing here. A lovely looking, big powerful woman she was. Olive-skinned, massive knockers, nipples like hazelnuts. I sharpened three big kitchen knives for her. She watched me. I was as nervous as a kitten. It gave me a hard-on for the rest of the day. I can tell by your face you don't believe me. I thought *you* might have seen her.'

'The lady I'm working for always wears a long black skirt, white shirt and black blazer. She dresses like a policewoman.'

'A policewoman? That's just about as far away from the lady I saw, as it's possible to be. Never mind. Let's get this lot into the car. Be careful when you unload it, the scythe's razor sharp.'

Ralph was back at Stanhope and hard at work by early afternoon. He decided to work straight through until seven pm to make up for the time he had lost already that day. He was soon back into his rhythm. The scythe was cutting the long grass like a knife through butter. Barrow load by barrow load, the grass cuttings were tipped onto the compost heap. Each time he unloaded, he jumped on the grass to compact it.

He told himself that he was enjoying his work. It was certainly peaceful and there was a sense of achievement about it. The work was rewarding in a self-indulgent way too. He felt strong. He knew he was fit. He knew that he looked good. He loved the sun on his body. He spied Lorna walking down the drive.

'You've done well,' she told him.

'Not *that* well. I lost a lot of time getting the tools sharpened so I thought I had better work through to about six to make the time up.'

'What an honest, upright young man you are! This is day two of twenty-four and you're conscious of losing time. However, do as you will, and be showered and changed for dinner which is sausage and mash – good stodgy stuff to replace lost calories.' She went inside the house. He continued at the same pace. His objective was to scythe the second lawn of four so that it could be mown next day. In the event the target was too ambitious. He had to leave about a third of the big lawn un-scythed. He went inside, showered and dressed. Lorna brought in the sausage and mash and poured out the red wine.

'Life is strange is it not, dear Ralph. You could have been a toffee-nosed sixth former learning about the one-eyed Cyclops and Caesar's Gallic Wars, pale and podgy and asthmatic, moody and sorry for yourself. Instead you are the virile young lover of a woman of spectacular beauty and eating sausage and mash with vintage wine which is the absolute in thing at the present time.'

'Do you ever remember a man who sharpens knives calling here?'

'A bit off the subject, darling, but I have a vague memory of a scrawny little man who seemed rather nervous in my presence.'

'Because you had no clothes on,' Ralph replied.

'No. That's not true. I was wearing high heels and a large straw hat. It's all coming back to me. I remember thinking, Why can't these door-to-door men be well-built, good-looking men rather than the weedy specimens that come round these days? Some of them have the temerity to call me 'love' or 'Sweet'art' If a gorgeous youth like you, Ralph, called here, he could sharpen my knives any time.'

The days passed quickly. His sojourn at Stanhope became a placid routine. Somewhere in the future was the army, basic training, Cyprus, leave, Germany, the end of the affair, civilian life, grim reality and a variety of emotions. It was easier to live in the present. Outrageous, vulgar and dominant as she was, Lorna was never going to allow his time at Stanhope to degenerate into an orgy. She organised his pleasure. She rationed his excesses. In every respect save his working day, he abandoned himself and his time to her. She liked to be the seductress but so submissive was he that seduction became unnecessary. Their love was light-hearted though not superficial. Conscious of the fact that someday their affair would be over, pleasure replaced passion. In his heart he knew that no experience in his life would ever equal the joy and ecstasy of his time with Lorna, and he was sometimes on the verge of becoming maudlin. Lorna always sensed his moods and talked to him, comforted him, and, in her words, 'tried to shake the boy from the man'.

On day eight he updated the schedule in his notebook. It read thus:

4 lawns —all mown and edged
11 flowerbeds — 3 weeded and dug over, 8 remaining
7 hedges — 5 pruned and cleared, 2 remaining
Paths —all to be weeded and weed killer applied
Patio area —slabs to be laid again
Shrubs — all to be pruned or dug out

He showed his notebook to Lorna. She pronounced it 'well on time' and suggested that they took the day off, got away from Stanhope and took a trip to Malvern. They were on the road by nine o'clock, Ralph in shirt and flannels, Lorna in a dowdy long brown skirt, one of Ralph's check shirts and, bizarrely, walking boots. She had subbed him£10 to be deducted from the gardening bill.

'You can use that to buy me a nice lunch in Malvern,' she told him.

The trip was a small adventure for Ralph. Driving was a newly acquired skill and once he was clear of the suburban wilderness of the West Midlands and into the country, he began to enjoy it. They made their way through a labyrinth of streets in Worcester before picking up the Malvern sign.

'We shall go to the dress shop first,' Lorna decided. 'It's very exclusive and rather expensive. We lived here for a short time between the wars. It's rather snobbish is Malvern, full of retired military men and civil servants. My father opened an account for me. I'm assuming it still exists. I hope the shop hasn't changed. The assistants were always subservient and grovelling, which are two qualities that I always look for in staff. Turn left at this garage, then first right. There it is. 'Lucy Palmer Est. 1904'. Aren't we lucky? There's a parking space right outside. Come back in about forty minutes to load all my stuff into the car.'

Ralph sat for a while in a little park near the Winter Gardens, then ambled around the rather aloof town. He wandered aimlessly past toyshops, craft shops, antique shops, coffee shops, cake shops and bookshops before retracing his tracks back to Lucy Palmer est. 1904. He had anticipated simply loading her purchases into the car and driving off, but that was not the case. He entered the shop to be greeted by pandemonium. A shop assistant came up to him and asked if he were Mr Pitt.

'Well, er–' he began.

'He's my young virile lover,' Lorna shouted. 'He's a wonderful man in an emergency. He'll soon sort this appalling mess out. Ralph Tucker is his name, a name for the future.'

'Mr Tucker,' the assistant seemed close to tears. 'We're having problems with your – er – lady-friend. Mrs Pitt refused to use the changing room because it was too poky, so we took the unusual decision of cordoning a section of the shop off. She keeps putting dresses on and throwing them off. Sometimes she wanders off 'browsing' in full view of the public. She's wearing nothing but a pair of boots!'

Ralph sought the help of the manageress. He told her what was happening. She told the assistant, who was in hysterics, that she would take over.

'Now then, Mrs Pitt. Can we assume that you have purchased everything in this pile?'

'Absolutely,' Lorna said.

'Then let's get it all parcelled up shall we?'

She folded the clothing expertly and put it all in bags.

'There you are, Mrs Pitt,' she said calmly. 'What a lot you've bought.'

'At last! Some decent service,' Lorna said. 'Let me know the total and I'll give you a cheque. What on earth was the fuss about? All I was doing was trying dresses on.'

'Of course, Mrs Pitt but you had no underwear on.'

'That's just one of my eccentricities. Why should my superb body "cause embarrassment to other customers" to quote your assistant?'

'Some people are more sensitive than others I'm afraid,' Mrs Pitt. 'It's possible that many women would be jealous of such a curvaceous figure.'

'Yes, that's a strong possibility. I suppose you do get a few fuddy-duddies in here. For future reference, I do not wear underwear, nightwear, cosmetics, perfume or jewellery.'

'Point taken, Mrs Pitt. I think now would be a good time for you to dress.'

'Of course.'

To the manageress's relief, Lorna put her skirt and shirt on. She took out her chequebook and signed a cheque. I'll leave you to write in the amount,' she said. I've put my address in the back, but I assure you it won't bounce on you.'

'Stanhope Hall,' the manageress read out. 'That account goes back a long way.'

'I wish you good day,' Lorna said, 'tell that assistant that I forgive her. She was probably overawed by my presence.'

Ralph loaded the parcels into the car boot. 'Where to now?' he asked.

'Leave the car. We'll stroll into Malvern and find a little place for a snack.'

'I've seen a cake shop near here,' Ralph said.

'That'll do. You can buy me a big piece of gateau.'

They found the patisserie and ordered gateau and coffee.

‘I was very impressed with you today in that dress shop my Beautiful Boy. You were very calm and collected and sorted the problem out. You reminded me of my poor Roger. He was like that. Officers have to be like that. I’m hoping that you will pass WOSB or whatever they call it and get a commission. I think your mother would like that too.’

‘So would I. An officer’s life would be far, far preferable to a ranker’s.’

‘I would love to see my young lover with pips on his shoulders, but perhaps I have no right to wish that. There’s a danger that I would start to think of you as the son I never had. I know how much your mother loves you. I can do a lot for you. I can keep you fit and strong, bring out any talent that I’m sure you have and, bluntly, make a man of you but never mother you. Come on, let’s pay the bill and drive out to West Malvern and we’ll go for our walk.’

They took a walk along well-worn pathways to a cairn that marked the highest point. They rested at the cairn for a while and then plodded back. He felt like a child again. He and Veronica had been on that same walk with their mother. It was near to the end of the war. Childhood seemed a long time ago. It would never come again. ‘Damn good thing,’ he told himself.

‘You seem lost in your own little world,’ Lorna remarked.

‘Yes, I was. I was having self-indulgent thoughts as ever and thinking about how times have changed for me.’

‘They’ve changed for me too,’ she said. ‘Hold my hand.’

‘You look comical in those boots.’

‘Comical? You mean a figure of fun? I hope not. I couldn’t go walking in the hills in high heels could I? I do admit that I have rather large hands and feet. Normally, this minute flaw in an otherwise perfect figure goes unnoticed. I was forgetting that you are still, in many ways, a gauche youth.’

'I didn't mean to upset you.'

'I forgive you.' She squeezed his hand. 'Did you enjoy our little day out? I know you did.'

The shadows had lengthened. The temperature had dropped a degree or two. It was a balmy summer evening. They drove their leisurely way home.

In what was rather pretentiously called The Great Hall at Stanhope, there were three very large framed portraits, all the work of the renowned artist Cosmo Whacksparrow, whose remarkably long career spanned eighty years. In fact his untimely death – he fell off a chair whilst changing a light bulb – had been reported quite recently.

The largest portrait was of Sir Herbert Stanhope. The brass plaque read:

Sir Herbert Stanhope 1855-1925

Founder and owner of Stanhope Pen Nib Company Ltd

Lord Lieutenant of Staffordshire 1919 to 1922

At each side of Sir Herbert were the portraits of his two sons. The brass plaques read:

Lieutenant Colonel Edwin Stanhope 1885-1950

Commanding Officer of the 38th Regiment (The Grey Jackets)

Godfrey Stanhope 1889-1951 Indian Civil Service

Surrounding the stern faces of the Stanhope elders, there was a sombre display of the stuffed heads of stags and moose. Ralph sometimes strayed to this area of Stanhope Hall to sit in the eerie gloom and think. He tried to relate the features of Lorna to her father, uncle and grandfather but he could not. He had once asked Lorna, but she was also at a loss to explain. One rumour was that she was the daughter of a rich hidalgo from Paraguay. Lorna argued that, if such was the case, why was she the apple of her father's eye, spoilt, indulged, never blamed. Would that be the behaviour of a cuckolded man, a man whose daughter danced naked on the Brigadier's table at some minor function? A brazen act dismissed by her father as 'high spirits'. She told herself over and over that she must – absolutely must – be Colonel Stanhope's daughter. The ultimate proof of his love was to make her his sole beneficiary. Her two brothers had decided to take up careers outside the Army. Edwin Stanhope was reported to have been bitterly disappointed. There was more than an element of spite in his actions.

It was day fourteen, Ralph updated his notes as follows:

Lawns —complete
11 flowerbeds — 7 weeded and dug over, 4 remaining
All cut and cleared, all pruned.
Selected shrubs to be dug out
7 hedges shrubs
Patio area outside kitchen
3 sycamore trees
Complete re-slabbing required, sand and cement needed
All to be pruned (recent decision)

He decided to tackle the slabbing first. He borrowed the car and drove to QBS. He was amazed to see Stan. 'I thought you were taking time off before the big day when we cease being individuals and become numbers?'

'It's not going to be that bad is it, Ralph?'

'Hope not. Did you sign on for twenty-two years with the three year option?'

'Yes I did. I changed my mind about the Guards though. I reckoned there'd be too much bullshit – kit cleaning day and night and marching around in red tunics and bearskins.'

'But on the positive side, what about all the lady tourists grabbing your dick?'

'Not that again! Anyway I've joined the Grey Jackets.'

'When's your call up date?'

'August 24th.'

'We'll be together.'

‘My worst nightmare.’

‘There’s worse to come. Tommy and Dennis will be with us.’

‘Is that Tommy Ward and Dennis Holmer? I know them from school. My cousin’s joining on the same day too – Duggie Jennings is his name.’

‘That’ll be great, five of us all mates. You need that in the Army.’

‘So what can I do for you, Ralph?’

‘I need some sand and cement.’

‘They’re over there. Just pick up what you need. I’d help, but I’ve got a bad back.’

‘Skiving bastard!’

‘I’m only kidding. I’ll load them on for you. I’ll give you an offcut of marine ply to do your mixing, on. Are you laying a path or something?’

‘Re-laying more like. It’s part of a big gardening job at a big house – Stanhope Hall.’

‘Stanhope Hall, eh? I’ve been there when I was cleaning windows. I’d finished the job and I wanted to get paid. So I went to the kitchen window and told the lady of the house that I’d like to get paid. She shouted back that she was still in the bath, but she’d be down in a few minutes.

‘It was it was a deep voice and very posh. Now imagine this. She suddenly appeared in the kitchen stark naked, not even a towel round her, her body all glistening with soap and water – I’d say she was about thirty. What a body! I could go into raptures about it. I only have to think about it and I feel horny. You don’t even look surprised. You don’t believe me, do you? Nobody ever believes me, but as God’s my witness I swear it’s true.’

‘The lady there now’s about fifty and she dresses like a policewoman.’

‘Nah! A policewoman’s about the furthest away from what I saw as it’s possible to get.’

‘See you on 24th Stan – Walsall railway station.’

He called on Jeff to say farewell. Jeff wished him the best and said, 'And don't forget, Ralphy, in three years' time when the Queen gives you the royal boot, come and see me. I'll be big time by then. I might have an opening for you. I might not.'

He drove back to Stanhope Hall stopping at the house en route. There was a letter for him. He opened it. It was from his mother and read:

My darling Ralph, (We are allowed darling, are we not?)
How are you getting along with Lorna? I don't mean in a physical sense – I'll take it for granted that you are wallowing in youthful ecstasy. I really mean is she mothering you? Is she treating you like the son she never had? If so, I'm very angry.
We are having a marvellous holiday. We've been walking, swimming, dancing, sailing – you name it, we've done it. We feel great. Mind you, I think I've worn your father out somewhat. We shall not be home just yet. We are going to miss bidding you farewell on August 24th. Well, we would not have gone down to the station anyway. You're only going to Lichfield after all. So this letter is just to wish you luck and success. Oh, I do hope you get a commission.
Love Mother and Father X X X X X

It took him five more days to complete the Stanhope Hall grounds project. Two complete days were spent on the patio area. He was very pleased with his efforts. What had once been a patch of wobbly slabs choked with weeds was now solid and cemented in. Pruning the sycamore trees with a handsaw was another difficult task, which took a whole day. All in all he was very pleased with himself and invited Lorna to take a guided tour with him.

'You have performed a Herculean feat, my Beautiful Boy. I shall not ever let my gardens get in such a dreadful state again. I shall take on a man for two days a week to stay on top of the work and next spring, I shall have it planted out and it will be a blaze of colour. Let's go inside shall we.'

She sat down at the little desk in the corner from which she administered the Stanhope Estates which included other substantial properties in the town.

'You are to be well rewarded.'

'I didn't do it just for that.'

'Of course you didn't. You have made it a labour of love'

She wrote out a cheque.

'I am paying you £100.'

'But that's a–'

'Pray do not protest. I have forgone the £10 sub I gave you for the Malvern trip.'

'Then I shall forgo the cost of sand, cement and blade sharpening.'

'Let's not talk pennies. Here's your cheque. We shall walk into town and bank it this afternoon. I also want to have a photo of you – top half only, no shirt. Then maybe you can take me for a coffee or something. I shall wear one of my new two-piece outfits that we bought in Malvern. Which would you prefer, beige, maroon or cerise?'

'I bet they all look good. I'll say maroon.'

They were home by mid-afternoon. It seemed strange to Ralph to have absolutely nothing to do. He sank into an armchair. She sat on his lap – all twelve stone of her, as was her habit.

'What a weight!'

'You love it though, don't you? I think we should celebrate the completion of the grounds. I'll prepare the old standby – chicken salad. We'll open a few bottles of wine and have some jolly good fun, not necessarily in that order. Now, with only a few days to go I think that you should be celibate. It's all very well you being fit, but we don't want you arriving for basic training feeling worn out or hung over for that matter.'

'So we cram everything into tonight and rest up until August 24th?'

'That's basically it – you may feel like doing some visiting.'

'Nan Tucker's the priority. Mom and Dad will still be on their extended holiday.'

'Have you enjoyed your stay with me, darling?'

'Of course! What can I say? It's been ecstasy, even the work. As a matter of fact that has made it better. It's given me an objective.'

'And have you fallen in love with me?'

'Nearly. The Russians would have a word for it, no doubt.'

'Nearly is honest and realistic. Nearly is as far as it should ever go. It should be light-hearted and indeed it has been. I shall miss you though. I shall miss you in my bed and I shall miss you being around.'

By seven o'clock the meal was prepared and they sat down to dine and drink their wine.

'This is the last such occasion for at least three months but don't let us dwell on the future. You'll find out soon enough. Shall we pour the wine? I think we shall.'

Chapter 10

The Grey Jackets

'My boy's boy!' Nan Tucker pulled him to her apron. 'You *are* looking well. You look fit, bronzed, handsome and hard working. I think this recent life of labour has put some rough edges on you but never mind. I think there's a gentleman inside you bursting to get out. Yet you choose to live with the Widow of Gorway, whilst there must be young ladies out there who'd be throwing themselves at you if they only but knew you were available. What happened to the buxom one, the preacher's daughter?'

'She did a rotten thing to me. She went out with another man who is my sworn enemy.'

'Well, you seem to have got over it. You should not have 'sworn enemies' by the way. You should put disagreements behind you. You started a riot in the street, didn't you?'

'No. It wasn't me. Blenkinsop threw a punch at me, but it missed and hit a third former and that started the riot.'

'Blenkinsop? Son of a jerry-builder, grandson of a card sharp. Scum of the earth, that family.'

'Well, it was Blenkinsop who went out with Janice Taylor.'

'Now I'm beginning to see it,' Nan said. 'No wonder he's your sworn enemy. She'll regret it for the rest of her life will that Janice Taylor. She spurned the handsomest lad in Walsall.'

Ralph heard footsteps and saw Veronica pass the window.

'Here she is, my little treasure,' Nan Tucker said.' She's going to be trouble to nobody.'

'Talking about me?' Veronica asked as she entered.

'Yes. I was about to say that you will be no trouble to anybody. You've picked young Tommy Ward and that's the end of it.'

'Exactly, Nan. I'm not going through all this courting stuff and dinner dances and being stood up by some worthless oaf and standing outside the Savoy in the pouring rain. I've skipped adolescence too. I'm not going to be moping around and miserable like Ralph sometimes used to be.'

Nan Tucker poured Ralph a glass of Guinness. He went into the next room to see Granddad Tucker.

Granddad Tucker lay snoozing on the couch. Ralph shook him by the shoulder.

'If it isn't young Ralph.'

'How are you, Granddad?'

'Ready for the knacker's yard, boy.'

'Surely not.'

'God should take us when we're eighty. What use is an old codger like me?'

'We all care about you Granddad – me, Nan, Veronica, my Dad, My uncle Bryn, everybody,'

'I hear that you're off to the army soon, Ralph. You'll make it. You're a strong lad. Your asthma seems to have gone. You're educated too. You could be an officer. It's a funny thing you know. As you get older your memory for times long gone gets better. On the other hand, your short-term memory all but disappears. My twenty army years seem like a dream. It's hard to believe that I was ever there in Tralee. The Curragh, Cairo, Southern India, Burma and that dreadful war that we never should have fought – the Boer War. Yes, twenty years and I can name every man in B Company, even now. How long is it that you've signed on for?'

'Twenty-two years, with a three year option.'

'Three years is an eternity when you're young. You'll find it hard when you come back. I did. I'd loved being

Colour Sergeant Harry Tucker of The Royal Welsh Fusiliers; it was 'yes colours', 'no colours', 'three bags full colours', but when I was back in Civvy Street I was one of the hoi polloi again and nobody gave a damn about me. The army looks after their own. Civvy Street don't give a damn.'

'But I'm tired now, boy. Come again soon.' He was asleep immediately.

'How do you put up with that snoring, Nan?' Ralph asked.

'Love, boy's boy. I hope you find it.'

'Is that a barbed remark, Nan?'

'Yes it is, boy's boy, because what you have now is not love. It's infatuation.'

With seemingly endless time on his hands, Ralph wandered back to Stanhope Hall. Lorna arrived home minutes later.

'When we took out our mini vow of celibacy,' she said, 'What was our decision on alcohol?'

'We never made any decision,' Ralph told her.

'In that case, it is banned with effect from midnight tonight. Up until then we can be decadent and drink wine.'

She sat on his lap and watched as he winced.

'I'm too heavy for you, aren't I?'

'A bit.'

'But you let me do it, don't you? You let me do it because you're nearly in love with me, don't you? I can twist you round my little finger, can't I?'

'Yes, but I purposely let things happen. I vowed when my stay commenced that I would fit in exactly. It has made life uncomplicated. It's been the key to our relationship.'

'Yes, how right you are. You're not a jealous person, are you?'

'I can be. I was jealous of Janice Taylor.'

'I'm not talking about school romances, Ralph. You have never asked about other men in my life. Is it that you don't care?'

‘I purposely shut any thoughts of that out of my mind. What you mean to me is more important than what you may have meant to other men. There again, I think I’d like to know something. We’ve got time on our hands.’

‘What a strange boy you can be. There have been comparatively few men in my life, Ralph. My early years were spent in India, as you know. Probably every single officer in the battalion had been my escort at some function or other, but that was always as far as it went. The British Army sets a high moral standard. Eventually somebody I really grew to love came bursting through the formal system. He was Captain Roger Pitt. He was an upright, athletic and rugged young man. He was extremely popular. When he entered a room he would impress the throng immediately. I was incredibly conceited then as I am now. I thought him the only man in the Grey Jackets who was worthy of me, given his build, his looks and personality. So we were married and happy. We lived in married quarters. Sometimes army life became tedious. We had a small circle of friends. Roger got on with being an officer. I spent my time doing rather useless things like playing bridge. I went astray. I had an affair with one of Roger’s platoon commanders, a young second Lieutenant – Gerard was his name. It was all frantic and furtive. He was, I thought then, incredibly handsome. Sometimes you remind me of him. Maybe that’s why I have this obsession with your becoming a second lieutenant. I want another Gerard.

‘Roger found out by way of Gerard’s batman – a little sneak whom I have dreamt of giving a punch on the nose for many a year. Roger’s only words to me were, ‘I’m a bit cut up about this old gel. I’ve told Gerard to keep his mouth shut otherwise I’ll give him a damn good hiding. If it happens again, I’m afraid it will be divorce.’ He seemed to see it as something to be kept from the Regiment as a priority. He did not seem affected by the event itself. There was no attempt to talk about it. It had happened. The divorce threat was obviously real. In 1937 Sarah came along. We were fiercely proud parents. We were happy again. You know the rest. I was left with a child to raise. I could not and would not bring men into the house. I mourned for Roger. A more spinsterish existence one could not imagine, even though gossips assumed that I was a loose woman and referred to me as the Merry Widow of Walsall and that sort of thing. When Sarah left to go to university I was on my own, still glamorous, unbelievably not scarred by war. I decided to find myself a man. I was clueless. I amused myself by appearing naked before milkmen, postmen, salesmen, odd job men, and all to no avail. Most of them were reduced to jibbering fools by my unparalleled beauty. There were some nice ones. There was a young window cleaner. He had curly hair. He was a lot like you. So thus ends my uneventful love life, darling. Final stop was the garden party.'

'I'm glad you told me all that, Lorna. I think I understand you a bit more.'

'There were a lot of things I was going to tell you before you left but no matter. We shall write to each other. What I now omit to say will be said in due course by letter. Please do not send me letters all about your training. I already know it all. You will be cleaning and Blancoing and Brassoing, running, marching, drilling, and on and on and on. Remember that I was an army daughter, an army wife and an army mother, bred in the army, married in the army, widowed by the army. Neither do I want to read lovelorn letters.'

'It doesn't give me much scope,' Ralph protested.

'Of course it does. Send me some poetry and I promise to send you a critique. Send me a few comical letters. Believe it or not you'll have a few laughs. It won't be all bawling and shouting.'

She passed over a photograph.

‘Here’s your photo of me. I’ve got nothing on but nothing showing either. Artistic, don’t you think?’

‘I shall keep it next to my skin.’

‘Good man! Don’t pass it round. When you’re in barracks there will, no doubt, be more than a few guttersnipes boasting of their sexual prowess in the most vile and crude terms. Promise me that you will never include me in any disgusting banter.’

‘I promise.’

‘There’s some more news for you. My brother has a cottage in Devon, which I’m going to rent for us when you get back on first leave. Three or four days will be long enough. It’s not far from the beach at a ramshackle little village called Wanstock. It’s a rudimentary sort of place but comfortable. It’s got central heating. Don’t forget we’ll be well into November. There’ll be hardly any visitors.’

‘Can we have a nude swim every morning?’ he asked.

‘Absolutely. We can walk and run on the beach too. There’s nothing much more than the beach anyway, except for the pub and the general store. Everywhere else will be closed.’

Ralph telephoned Tommy and asked him what the drill was for Thursday.

‘Be on Walsall station at about ten. We’ll all be there. There’ll be me, Dennis, Stan the van man and Stan’s cousin Duggie. Is anybody coming to see you off?’

‘No. We’re only going to Lichfield aren’t we? It’s not as if we’re off to join the Foreign Legion.’

‘I’ll join the legion, that’s what I’ll do.’ Tommy sang. ‘I tell you, Ralphy, ‘we’ll piss this army lark in.’

Ralph and Lorna sat out in the afternoon sun.

‘You did a great job on this patio, Ralph. Those wobbly slabs were getting me down. It only remains to mow the lawns before you go.’

‘They’ll be done, Lorna, no problem. In the meantime I’d like to sit peacefully!’

Tommy had cheered him up. His apprehension about the army had gone. He told himself that what would be would be. She must have read his thoughts.

‘You look so calm and carefree, my Beautiful Boy. That is the best way to be when the future is unknown. I have strong premonitions. There are tough times ahead of you. I see a son for you. You are on an island. There are ships unloading in a port. I see a name on a ship in white letters on black. I see the letters RON. This place is where your son is conceived.’

Having dutifully mown all the lawns the day before, Ralph awoke as always in Lorna’s iron grip. He savoured the moment. It was August 24th. Eventually he disentangled himself. He rose, showered, shaved and put casual clothes on. He packed a minimum of baggage. There had to be enough room left to pack his civilian clothes when he came home on his first leave.

Lorna dressed in her new beige outfit and walked with him to the end of the drive. She did not kiss him. She held him for a while and released him.

She watched him move silently away across the Oval, his father’s battered old suitcase in his hand, hair plastered down as best he could, soon to be sweepings on the barber’s shop floor, a 1950’s man, one of a naive, bewildered and ultimately lost generation. He looked back once. She smiled and waved.

Later that morning she walked into town and collected the photographs of Ralph. She bought a picture frame and put the best of the three photographs in it. She called at a coffee bar. A large man walked in just after. There was only one free table. She sat down. He asked if she minded him sitting there. She said, ‘Not at all’. He wore a business suit. It looked expensive. There was not a single crease in the jacket. The trousers, on the other hand, had razor sharp creases. He looked to be in his forties. He was well over six foot. 'Now that,' she told herself, 'is my type of man. Ralph is a big lad but this man!' Desperately, she searched for a talking point. She found one.

'Is that an opal?'

'I believe so.'

'It's unusual for a wedding ring.'

'It *was* a wedding ring. I'm divorced. I've always liked it so I wear it.'

They drank their coffee in silence. 'I have to rush now,' he said. Nice meeting you.' She watched as he paid at the counter. Something fell from his pocket. She picked it up. It was a business card. She put it in her handbag. When she was out in the street again she read it:

INDUFAS Ltd Industrial Fastners, Russell James, Managing Director (followed by an address and telephone number).

She was certain that he had dropped the card on purpose. 'I'll keep this in reserve,' she said to herself, 'it's odds on that he's a callous handsome devil. But maybe not and maybe it was meant to be, to get my mind off Ralph.'

Ralph arrived on the platform for the Lichfield train. The others were all waiting and the chorus went up 'Ralphy!' Ralph introduced himself to Stan's cousin Duggie. Dennis was wearing a tweed jacket, corduroy trousers and a deerstalker hat.

'Why the get up?' Ralph asked

'Just a bit of fun. I'm Charles Cholmondeley, 46th Earl of Tipton.'

'Accent and all?'

'Even posher than yours, Ralph. Cut glass!'

They all piled into a compartment.

'This is it lads,' Tommy said, 'the first day of a three-year journey.' The train moved out.

‘Are you honestly going to try this Earl of Tipton stuff, Dennis?’ Ralph asked, ‘Because if so, we’ll have a rehearsal. I’ll be the sergeant. What is your name?’ he roared.

‘Charles Cholmondeley 46th Earl of Tipton.’

‘Give me your real name you ‘orrible little man!’ he roared even louder.

‘Why dammit, man, I already have done so. I might remind you that I am a friend of the Colonel.’

‘I don’t care if you are a friend of the fucking General, Give! Me! Your! Effin! Name!’

At this point the sergeant explodes. The compartment of six burst into laughter.

‘Bet you don’t do it,’ Duggie said.

‘How much?’ Dennis asked.

‘Five bob.’

‘Five bob? That’s too high for me. Shall we say half a crown?’

‘Done. Shake hands on it.’

The atmosphere had lightened as the train rattled its way to Lichfield City station. A sergeant and three corporals were waiting for them.

‘There’s your sergeant, Dennis,’ Tommy said, ‘I wouldn’t recommend upsetting him.’

He was the archetypal regular army sergeant: bull-necked, barrel-chested, immaculately turned out and a voice like thunder.

‘Line up!’ A corporal shouted. ‘Line up here! You! Come here! Stand here! Now line up behind him.’

The sergeant arrived with his millboard.

‘Right! Stand still! You! Teddy boy! What are you doing?’

‘Lighting up, Sarge.’

‘Lighting a cigarette?!’ The sergeant roared. ‘Put it out! Put it out! Put it out immediately. That goes for all of you. The only time you can smoke is when you’re off duty inside barracks or at a break during training and only then if told that you can smoke. Do you understand?' Nobody replied.

'Do you understand?' A few muttered yes.

'Yes what?'

'Yes, Sarge.'

'What is a Sarge? I am a sergeant – S.E.R.G.E.A.N.T– but in this regiment it is normally spelt S.E.R.J.E.A.N.T. All right,' the sergeant said quietly. 'Welcome to the Grey Jackets. I have to check your names off, starting with you Sherlock Holmes. Name?'

'Cholmondeley.'

'I don't have a Cholmondeley here.'

'Algernon Cholmondeley, 46th Earl of Tipton and a friend of the Colonel.' He had expected the sergeant to roar like a lion and call him a few unpleasant things. Instead the sergeant went up to him and whispered through gritted teeth, 'Tell me your correct name or I will hammer you into the ground like a tent peg.'

'Holmer, Sarnt!' Dennis said.

'Good. Now have I heard the last of the comedians?'

'Yes, Sarnt,' they all shouted.

The sergeant checked off the remaining names and said, 'Let's start again. My name is Sergeant Edwards. These are Corporals Williams, Albert and Dean. You will at all times address all NCOs by their rank. Get on the vehicle!'

Thousands of young men went through the so-called 'sausage machine' of National Service in the 1950s. Some handled it well. For others it was purgatory. The public's attitude towards National Service was positive. They thought that a long period of harsh discipline was good for the wayward youth of the country whom they wrote off as Teddy boys, cosh boys and all manner of derogatory terms emanating from the emerging 'James Dean' culture. The theory was that all these wastrels would have some sense knocked into them and return to Civvy Street as well-dressed, upright law-abiding citizens. It did not exactly work out like that. Eighteen-year-old burglars resumed their criminal careers as twenty-year-old burglars. National Service changed young men but not necessarily for the better. Polite lads became rough diamonds. Rough diamonds became polite lads.

Having been given the runaround all day with so much shouting and yelling that it had reached the point of becoming meaningless, the 'new draft' – as they would be known until the next draft came along – were ensconced in barracks. They had all had their hair shaved off unceremoniously by a barber who would have made a good sheep shearer, so fast did he turn curly haired youths into shaven-headed recruits. They had been issued with blankets, sheets, mattresses, pillows, one pair of second best boots, one pair of best boots, two battle dresses (one for best), gaiters, web-belts, pouches, small pack, large pack, water bottle, bayonet scabbard, rifle sling, kit bag, three shirts, one tie, cap badges, Holland patches, berets, socks, braces, gloves, greatcoats and 'housewives' (sewing and darning materials). Other items had to be purchased – Brasso, Bianco, boot polish, toothpaste, shaving kit and all toiletries.

One man complained to Sergeant Edwards that his mattress was badly stained.

'They're all badly stained,' Sergeant Edwards barked.

'But this one's really badly stained, Sergeant.'

'I don't want to know. This is the army not the fucking Ritz Hotel. Hundreds of brave men have wanked on these mattresses and their name lives on. Does anybody else have a silly complaint? Good. I'll wish you goodnight!'

'Goodnight, Sarnt,' they screamed in unison.

'You're getting the idea.'

The National Servicemen were told that their pay to begin with would be twenty-eight shillings a week. A shilling would be deducted for a haircut, anything left after other deductions would be deposited on their behalf into a Post Office Savings Account. Weekly pay, in effect, was £1 a week for which one had to march the length of a barrack room, get given a £1 note by an officer, state clearly, 'pay and paybook correct, sah', salute, about turn and march out again. For some men who had earned good money in heavy industry, the pay was a joke. However, one learnt thrift in the army. You needed to put some money aside. If you had an item of kit stolen, you paid for it yourself. You had to take it on the chin. If you thought the world was unfair before, then your conclusions were confirmed in the armed services.

The new draft was split into two squads named after battle honours. Each squad was housed in one barrack room. The squads were named Central India and Lucknow. Ralph, Dennis, Tommy, Stan and Duggie were lucky enough to stay together in Central India squad. Each man was allocated a bed space with a steel locker and metal frame bed.

It was only early evening but most of the new draft was ready to drop to sleep. This was not possible because they had to watch a demonstration on how to apply Bianco on their webbing and Brasso on their brasses without it getting on the Blancoed area. Then followed another demonstration on how to bull their best boots. It involved burning polish on a teaspoon handle and covering the boots with hundreds of whirly patterns. A pair of bulled boots was a work of art.

Ten o'clock came and with it the order 'lights out' and by this time they had all had enough.

Ralph awoke to the sound of reveille. 'Hell!' he muttered, 'I'm in the army.' All over the barrack room the order was repeated ad infinitum –'Get up! Get out of bed!' as NCOs marched through banging beds. Oh, what Ralph would have given to be in Lorna's strong arms. Instead, here he was walking zombie-like to the ablutions. On each bed a denim jacket and trousers had been thrown, regardless of whether or not they would fit. Denims were about the ugliest item of clothing that a soldier wore, but they were good enough for shaven headed sprogs as they were already being called.

Today they were to be given Tetanus and TAB inoculations. The effect would be to make them feel as if they had a heavy dose of flu with aching limbs and a muzzy head. To counteract this they were kept on the move. They were marched to meals and back. They cleaned the barrack room. They dusted, swept and polished anything metal. They Blancoed and polished, cleaned and dusted. They were even taken for sessions in the gym.

Ralph, Tommy, Dennis, Stan and Duggie made it clear from the onset that they were close mates. Even though Stan and Duggie were not keen on the idea, they dubbed themselves the Arbo Gang. Who knew when they might have occasion to unite in defence, but it was just a subtle hint that nobody was going to piss them about.

Despite their weariness, sickness and bewilderment, the new draft got through the hellish weekend.

'I told you we'd piss it in,' Tommy boasted.

By Monday morning, the twenty recruits of Central India Squad had cleaned their equipment and dressed ready for inspection. Each man stood at ease in his bed space ready for inspection by the platoon commander, Mr Ribbons.

'You haven't forgotten my half crown, have you Duggie?' Dennis asked.

'Be quiet!' roared Sergeant Edwards. 'Listen to me carefully – Lieutenants and second Lieutenants are always referred to as Mister. When Mr Ribbons reaches the door I shall give you the order Shun! On hearing this command, you will stamp in your left foot to bring your feet together in the attention position. Your feet will be at an angle of forty-five degrees. Do you understand?'

'Yes, Sarnt!' they shouted.

‘Good! You’re getting the idea, Mr Ribbons is here. Central India Squad Shun!’ He screamed, and twenty left boots slammed down hard on the floorboards.

Ralph’s bed was first on the right as Mr Ribbons entered.

‘Tucker,’ Mr Ribbons said, reading the name from the temporary label taped to the locker, ‘ have you been in the cadets?’

‘Yes, sah! I was in the C C F at Queen Mary’s school.’

‘Good experience and a good turnout.’ From the corner of his mouth Sergeant Edwards said, ‘Well done Tucker.’

Mr Ribbons spoke to every man, occasionally finding fault.

‘Not a very good shave’ or ‘Boots could do with more work’ or ‘Beret at the wrong angle’. When he reached Dennis he said ‘Ah, Holmer! I’ve heard about you. The man in the deerstalker. Nothing wrong with a little attempted humour, Holmer, provided you take your duties seriously.’

‘Sah!’ Dennis screamed. Mr Ribbon’s inspection seemed to take an age. When he finally finished, he took up a position by the stove to address them.

‘Considering the very short time that you have been here, your turnout is praiseworthy. It is difficult to look smart in denims but there is evidence that you have all done your best. Now you must work very hard over the next twelve weeks to maintain and improve your standards.

‘So welcome to the Grey Jackets, an infantry regiment with a great history. Regimental history will be included in your training. Absorb what you are told and remember it with pride. For the rest of your lives you will be proud to have been a Grey Jacket. The first Battalion are presently on a tour of duty in Cyprus and it is said (but not confirmed) that they will be there until May 1957. The majority of this intake will be sent out to the Battalion in Cyprus after training. You will be on active service. We have an important job to do there.

'We have you in two squads, Central India and Lucknow to foster a spirit of competition. You should already be thinking about victory over Lucknow. Anything Lucknow do, you must do better. Anything you do, they will try to do better. There are no prizes at the end of your training. You will have pride and a sense of achievement.

'You arrived here on Thursday, a bunch of backstreet toughs, Teddy boys, gawky school leavers, namby-pambies and dance hall Romeos. You will leave here an immaculate, well-drilled, confident, able and devoted unit. Some of you will become NCOs or even officers. Always do your best. Use your intelligence. Develop your skills. Obey orders. Develop your stamina. Maintain high standards of personal hygiene. Take a pride in the most menial of tasks. Do all these things and you have nothing to fear. Fail to do any of these things and we will make your life hell. Carry on Sergeant Edwards.'

'All right lads,' Sergeant Edwards said quietly when Mr Ribbons had gone, 'Stand easy. That means that your feet stay where they are. Mr Ribbons gives a good pep talk doesn't he?'

'He should be in the House of Commons, Sarnt,' somebody said.

'How did it make you feel?'

'Ready to fight World War III,' the same man said.

'World War III?' Sergeant Edwards laughed. 'He'll be pleased when I tell him that. Mr Ribbons is a good officer. I've been with him for four new drafts. He's honest and well, normal I suppose. Don't be overawed by the army. It's full of normal people doing difficult jobs. This is your first day's training. We get rid of the waffle early on. From 1300 hours today, we'll have you working. Until that time here is your final lecture. It won't be as inspiring as Mr Ribbons' but you'll get some hard facts.

'You've probably been given ideas of what National Service is like from brothers or pals who've already done it.

The press call National Service the sausage machine, don't they? God knows why. Anyway, whatever you've been told, forget it. We don't care how things are done in the RAF or the Sherwood Foresters or the Royal Artillery or anybody for that matter. We are the Grey Jackets. We wear 'Holland patches' on our collars. We have a glider on our shoulder flashes. We are different. We are special. Think of yourselves as special when you're tired, weary and dirty. Forget the myths and the barmy saying that you get 'bollocked from arsehole to breakfast time'. We don't even understand it! Let me give you the rules so that nobody can be in any doubt.

'You will not be victimised or bullied under any circumstances. You have good officers and NCOs who will always be aware of the situation.

You will not be reprimanded or punished in any way for making mistakes. You will be instructed again so that mistakes can be eliminated.

You will be punished for disobeying an order, being absent without leave, insubordination, conduct to the prejudice of good order and military discipline which includes fighting, drunkenness, striking a comrade and whatever is deemed to be a punishable offence. Is that clear?'

'Yes, Sarnt!' The cry went out louder than ever. The slog began – running, marching and drilling.

The barrack room became a sort of home from home, a haven. Personalities emerged. Dennis's buffoonery provided some comic relief. He did a passable impersonation of Mr Ribbons and his numerous pep talks: 'You did very well on the rifle range today, Jennings. You will remember this day until you die and you will feel proud that you were a Grey Jacket. To be a Grey Jacket is special. The ugliest Grey Jacket in the regiment is better looking than the most handsome Grenadier Guardsman in the army. Remember this until you are an old man who is so old he has forgotten how to speak. He only remembers one word in the whole of the English language, which is…?'

'Grey Jacket!' they would shout.

Tommy seemed to be regarded as a leader. He picked up the art of soldiering very easily. After just one demonstration, he was able to strip and reassemble the Bren gun. Ralph could demonstrate similar skills but only because he had learnt them in the cadets. Basically Ralph was clumsy and inept. To begin with they were suspicious of his nearly posh accent. They reasoned that he would not be a mate of Tommy or Dennis if he were really posh, so they accepted him. Stan the van man retained his ridiculous nickname. His naiveté sometimes left him wide open for practical jokes. Duggie took to soldiering even better than Tommy. He liked to spin yarns. He seemed to have had a lot of jobs and these were the subject of his anecdotes. Sex seemed to be the main topic of conversation the 'guttersnipes' that Lorna had warned him of with their tales of sexual prowess. Soon everybody got bored with these self-promoting womanisers. Duggie Jennings was the first to crack. A charmless moron named Barnard was the most annoying and seemed incapable of ceasing his obscene drivel. Duggie told him, 'I'm getting sick of listening to your crap, Barnyard or whatever your name is. If you're such a great lover, you must have the biggest cock in the county. That's not what I saw in the showers last night, so let's see what you're made of. Come on lads. Give us a hand.' They debagged him.

'Who's got a little willy then? Have a look at this, lads. It must be all of an inch long.'

'It's the bromide in the tea,' Barnard protested.

'You must have drunk a gallon then, to have shrivelled your dick that small.'

This was the turning point. It was agreed to ban sex talk for a week unless somebody came up with something really interesting like shagging a sheep.

‘Or a donkey,’ somebody muttered.

There were long periods of silence in the barracks at night as men wrote home, showered, cleaned their kit or played cards. Ralph wrote home to Hugh and Margaret, Veronica, Nan Tucker and Lorna. It was hard to write anything more than a dull letter given the circumstances. Lorna was the hardest to write to because she had already told him that she did not want to hear about the army. Neither did she want to receive lovelorn letters. Despite this, Ralph had to tell her that he missed her arms around him in the mornings. To his surprise she wrote back quickly.

Stanhope Hall, September 55

Hallo my handsome Grey Jacket

Well, what a hypocrite I am saying that I didn’t want lovelorn letters. I ache for you. I loved you for just being around, but I loved you most in my bed. I feel like sending you a long sad litany but you don’t want that, do you? You’re probably so dosed up with bromide you’re not even thinking about any jolly good fun in bed, are you? You might not be but I am. How I wish you get a commission and I could walk with my dashing young 2nd lieutenant on my arm. In my present mood I am only capable of writing silliness like this. So please write to me – write anything. In the meantime, I shall gather my thoughts together and write a proper letter.

Love Lorna. I’m going to have my bath now.

Sure enough another letter arrived from Lorna a few days later. She informed him that she had taken on an old boy called Fred to look after the grounds.

‘He looks about sixty odd, but he’s tough and wiry. He comes on Monday Wednesday and Friday mornings.’

She went on to tell him that the work will go ahead shortly to convert the whole of Stanhope Hall into flats, all en suite. Stanhope Hall will live again as it must have done when Sir Herbert Stanhope was head of the house. Her other news was that her daughter Sarah would be arriving in the New Year and that the grandchild was due in February 1956. She concluded:

'So that's the news. I am assuming that you are in robust health – marching, drilling, crawling through the undergrowth, and doing all things infantry. I am assuming that you are used to eating pigswill and sleeping on a bed designed for a man of five foot six (the average height in the Crimean War). What a formal, dull letter this is turning out to be. I want to say something about the way I feel, to be truthful I feel numb. You had become part of my life, indeed almost all my life – what more can I say? Your absence is intolerable. I'm a stupid woman, fast heading for middle age and I know that one day, we shall part but until that day I love you.

Lorna

The weeks began to fly past. There was continuous activity from reveille to lights out. There was literally no time to think, no time to brood, build up resentment, feel homesick, feel lonely or feel dejected. Central India knew that they were doing better than Lucknow. It was in the fifth week of the twelve that Sergeant Edwards and Mr Ribbons called them together. Mr Ribbons spoke first:

'At the moment you will be pleased to know that, on our points system, Central India Squad is well ahead of Lucknow. You have excelled on the rifle range, in the gym and on the parade ground. Lucknow are slightly ahead on weapons training, fieldcraft and map reading. Your smartness and general demeanour has been excellent and has earned you points.

'We are not yet half way through training. Things can change. Do not be complacent. Now, before I hand you over to Sergeant Edwards, I am told that you do a passable impersonation of me. Is that so, Holmer?'

'Passable is about all it is, sir.'

'Let's hear it then.'

'Here and now, sir?'

'Here and now.'

'It doesn't seem right, sir.'

'It's an order, Holmer.'

'Yes sir.'

Dennis got to his feet and began:

'Good morning men, stand at ease, stand easy. I much regret to inform you that Central India Squad will not be going to Cyprus. You will be going to Mars to fight in the War of the Worlds. You will collect your spacesuits from the QM at 0800 hours tomorrow and your Death-Ray guns from the armoury at 1000 hours. This war is in its 746th year and is forecast to continue for another 394 years, so it goes without saying that most of you will not be coming back. There will, however, be good opportunities for promotion. When you arrive on Mars you will be shocked to see how scruffy some of the International Force are. Such scruffiness will not be tolerated in the Grey Jackets. You will wear your spacesuits with pride. You will keep your helmets polished. Remember that you are a Grey Jacket and be immaculate at all times. A 394 year posting is tough but you will take it on the chin because you are Grey Jackets. Do not fraternise with Martians. Some of them have as many as five heads and it would cost you a fortune to buy them drinks. Good luck chaps. Who are you?'

'The Grey Jackets!' they roared back.

'Thank you, Holmer. That was amusing. Humour is good for morale. But remember that your duties and your training come first.'

Sergeant Edwards took over.

'You have an easy morning ahead of you. One by one you will be called in to be interviewed by Major Roade and

I don't want to hear any cracks about 'Halt at Major Roade ahead' are you listening Holmer?'

'Yes, Sarnt.'

'Good. Major Roade is, in civilian terms, a personnel officer. He will assess you not on your time in the unit, but rather before you were called up. Basically, we want to know what sort of a bloke you are. The assessments are kept on your file in the Orderly Room and are very important. They are normally referred to when promotions are discussed. Answer questions clearly and truthfully. Do not pretend to have qualifications you do not have. Do not lie. You will be called in, in random order. Listen for your name. Is that clear?'

'Yes, Sarnt!' they shouted back.

'Ward! Stand, quick march left right left right left right halt!'

'Private Ward, sir.'

'Sit down, Ward. It's probably the first time you've ever been asked to sit since your call up, is it not?'

'Yes, sir'

'What was your occupation, Ward?'

'Plumber, sir.'

'We've got water coming through our bedroom ceiling from somewhere. We could have done with you this morning. I think my wife has got things sorted out.'

'Contact me if you need any help, sir. I've got some tools in my locker.'

'I appreciate your offer. What were your pastimes, Ward?'

'None sir. No time. My brother and I are trying to build up a business and we're on call at all times.'

'So who is looking after the business while you are away? I see you're a regular. Three years is a long time to be absent from a business.'

'We've got temporary help, sir.'

'I see. That is all, Ward. You seem an ambitious chap.'

‘I hope that you do well.’

Tommy was marched out.

During the course of the morning Ralph, Dennis, Stan and Duggie were marched in. Ralph was first.

‘What was your occupation, Tucker?’ Major Roade asked.

‘I worked for a building and garden supplies company sir, loading and unloading vehicles and attending to customers, but it was really a fill in job between school and the army.’

‘Were you wise to have left sixth form?’

‘The future will tell, sir.’

‘I see that you were in the C C F at Queen Mary’s school. Did you find it good experience?’

‘I disliked it, sir – not the soldiering part – there were too many fifth and sixth formers acting like little Hitlers.’

‘Overzealousness. Sometimes a reaction to failure elsewhere, such as sport. Have you got a sport?’

‘Rugby, sir. I played for a club called the Humourists.’

‘I’ve heard of them. What about pastimes?’

‘I try to write poetry, sir.’

‘Have you read the war poets?’

‘Like Wilfred Owen, sir? Yes, I have.’

‘You could go for a commission, you know. How do you feel about that?’

‘It appeals to me, sir. It’s my parents’ wish too. My father was a Naval Officer. My grandfather was a Colour Sergeant in the Royal Welsh Fusiliers.’

‘You must not wish to try for a commission for that reason, however commendable it is. You must want to do it yourself. You will be approached again. I wish you success.’ Ralph was marched out. Next it was Dennis’s turn.

‘What was your occupation, Holmer?’

‘Foundry man, sir.’

‘Did you like it?’

No, sir. It was too hard but a job is a job.’

'What would you really like to do?'

'Act, sir, be an actor, act on the stage'

'You're a sturdy fellow. You could play Falstaff.'

'One day I will.'

'I hear you're quite a comedian too. You arrived here in tweeds and a deerstalker hat and pretended to be a toff.'

'It was just to put people in a good mood sir.'

'I'm told that it was very irritating. Mind you, you need a sense of humour in the services. You are an interesting chap with unusual ambitions and I think your personality will bring you success of some sort.'

Stan the Van Man was next.

'Known as Stan the Van Man, eh?'

'Not my idea, sir.'

'What was your occupation?'

'I worked at the same place as Tucker, sir'

'The building supply company? Did you like it?'

'Yes, sir, we used to lark about a bit. It was good fun but hard work at times. We did our work though. Larking about was for the quiet times.'

'Good attitude, Compton. What are your ambitions?'

'I was very good at art at school. I want to develop that commercially. I've got a photographic memory. I want to put that gift into use.'

'There has been some talk about a war artist out in the battalion. I'll make the appropriate comment on your file and who knows? Good luck Compton.'

Duggie was the last man in the whole of Central India Squad to be interviewed.

'What was your occupation Jennings?'

'There were several, sir.'

'The most recent.'

'Driving a van delivering car parts, sir.'

'Was that a good job?'

'Dead end job, sir.'

'What would you really like to do?'

'Work my way round Canada or Australia or somewhere. Write travel books. Learn a foreign language. I wouldn't mind going to sea. I've got a lot of ideas and three years is plenty of time to think about.'

'You seem an independent sort of chap, Jennings. By the standards of the Grey Jackets you are well spoken. The chance to try for a commission is not out of the question at some future date. Does holding the Queen's Commission appeal to you?'

'Just give me the chance, sir.'

'Good. Try to concentrate on one thing at a time, Jennings, and I'm sure you will do well.'

Corporal Dean arrived to march them away. Sergeant Edwards went into a small office where Mr Ribbons and Major Roade were waiting. They sat around a table.

'A most refreshing morning,' Major Roade said. 'I've met a man who volunteered to do a plumbing job for me, a poet, a budding Falstaff, an artist with a photographic memory and a man who wants to thumb his way round Australia. Any comments? Sergeant Edwards? Comments? Nigel (Mr Ribbons)? Any comments?'

'Ward is my bet for best recruit,' Sergeant Edwards asserted.

'Jennings and Tucker are officer material,' Major Roade said. 'Agreed Nigel?'

'I've got reservations,' Mr Ribbons said. 'They are similar personalities, which may be why they are close friends. At times they both lack concentration.'

'I'm impressed with them. The assessment is over. Thanks for your comments.'

'You came out of there all smiles, Ralph,' Duggie said.

'So did you. Did he mention the word commission?'

'That he did.'

'What did you say?'

'Just give me half the chance. What did you say?'

'Something similar.'

'We'll just have to see what happens.'

Ralph could not wait to write to Lorna that evening.

Dearest Lorna,

I know that you do not want me to write about the army but this is worthwhile information. I was interviewed by a Major Roade today. He told me that I would be considered for a commission and that I would be approached later. It all sounds a bit vague, doesn't it? Anyway, it's encouraging. Just thought I'd tell you.

On another subject, do you remember once saying to me that in Russian there are forty words for love? I've tried to write a poem on the theme. Here it is.

I search a trinket box of memories
for an old Slav I met, a maudlin migrant,
far from his sepia world, who said,
'In Russian there are forty words for love.'
Yet we have only one word,
a single silver piece in the rich plum pudding of our own
tongue, for love of wives, of dogs, of continents –
love hate, love lost and unrequited love,
Or folksy love to out of tune guitars.
'My love is worn like grass upon the lawn,
and tomorrow I wed another dear John.
She signed it love but really not true love.
Not true love is a solitary X;
Potential love is a faint and wispy X.
Two Xs are for Christmas cards to Aunts.
Three Xs are for grandma on your mother's side.
Four Xs are for friends you think you lost.
Five Xs are as fake as artificial flowers.
Would one give such flowers to one's own true love?
Five Xs in a domino pattern? Very rare.
In Soviet days, they graded love from one to forty.
Enigma died with the last Czar.

Soft consonants were blown on the wind to perish on the vast loveless steppe.
There had been a time when syllables dripped vodka and promises were icicles on wooden walls.
Desire then, was an itch in the breeches of Konstantin Gavrilovich Treplev.
Adoration was unthawed in the pale sun.
Yearning was an ikon's shadow waiting till summer came and lovers chose the word to melt the innocence of winter virgins.
During this time the poorest, the dispossessed, migrated to the English-speaking world, where love was strange and almost wordless.
Their generation learnt to be inarticulate.

Tell me what you think. Don't say anything is good when it isn't. Good honest and constructive criticism is what I want.

He also wrote to Veronica that evening.

Dear adorable little sister Veronica,

How I miss you and how I love you. Are you keeping up your correspondence with Tommy? I never ask him. He's quite a private person. He's doing very well. He's favourite to win best recruit. We're all chasing him. It's all getting very competitive. I'm glad about that. I'm competitive. Mind you, I don't cheat, unlike a certain person who invented scrabble words like 'dook' – remember? Well I'd give a hundred quid to be playing scrabble with you now and I wouldn't mind if you cheated.
I know that you'll be wanting to spend your time with Tommy when we're home on leave in December, but I wish we could have one little holiday together with Mom

and Dad. It seems that suddenly our childhood is over and teenage years too. I don't think Dad will get the time off. I think he used it all when they went to Eastbourne. Anyway, it's just a thought. I shall be going down to Devon with Lorna as you know, but I think it will be no more than a week, if that. In any event, I shall be spending a big percentage of my time with our little family. Are you going to get engaged to Tommy or not? I hope you will. I want you to be happy, good sister and Tommy too. Oh boy! When I think of it! I've got to get through basic training, get some leave, go to Cyprus, get more leave, go to Germany and it's all over – 'a piece of piss' to use Dad's navy slang. Easy!

Can you believe that I haven't seen a female for five weeks? There are married quarters here, but we never see any wives or kids. Maybe they leave and enter camp by a secret door – a big iron door guarded by a wizened old sergeant major. It's eerie. Is Whittington the village of the damned? Why am I writing all this stuff? Because I'm a boy I suppose.

'All right, now pay attention!' Sergeant Edwards roared. 'This morning you are going over the assault course. This exercise usually takes place later in your training. You are only in your seventh week, but you have made good progress. I must stress that this is only a practice. Some of you may not make it the first time. You will told to try again. When every man in the squad has mastered it, we cease. We try again in two weeks' time. Are there any questions? No? By the right quick march.'

'I'm going first,' Ralph said to Tommy. 'Get it over with. It's too nerve-racking hanging around waiting.'

'I agree,' Tommy said. 'I'll go second.'

'Shut up!' Sergeant Edwards shouted. 'You will go in the order we send you, but since you are keen, Tucker and Ward, you shall go first and second.'

‘There it is, lads!’ Sergeant Edwards pointed to the first obstacle. ‘Strenuous but not impossible.’

They stood in line. Sergeant Edwards gave them some last-minute instructions emphasising that it was a matter of individual effort. They were not to assist one another.

‘Off you go then!’ He tapped Ralph and Tommy on the shoulder after which he called them by name at one-minute intervals.

Ralph got to the first obstacle, a wooden hill 45 degrees up and 45 degrees down. He got up successfully, stumbled coming down but regained his balance and lumbered on to the next obstacle, a solid brick wall. No footholds and seven feet high. The only way over it was to grasp the top (if you were tall enough – shorter men had to jump for it) and pull yourself up by sheer arm and leg power. He struggled over and carried on to the water jump. He knew this one from his cadet days. It involved swinging over a stream on a rope. The secret was to let go of the rope as soon as you hit the opposite bank, hanging on for too long meant that you eventually fell into the drink. He got across with no mishap. Then there was a pit to jump over. He only just made it and had to throw himself forward on his hands and knees to ensure landing on the bank. He sensed that Tommy was close on his heels. They reached a sheer wall face covered in netting to aid ascent, but it did the opposite. He continually got his feet entangled. Tommy was within a few yards of him, but he was struggling too. He made the tricky descent down on the netting. He was conscious of yells and curses behind him as he crawled through a long piece of pipe with very little room to manoeuvre. On emerging from the pipe, there was yet more crawling to be done under netting. The crawl seemed to go on forever. The next obstacle was a square dugout almost as deep as the ‘pit’ he had jumped over earlier, which had two logs across it to walk over. To maintain balance was a matter of working out the right speed to go. Too fast and you fell. Too slow and you fell. He kept a steady pace and nearly made it. He went back, tried again and succeeded. Finally, there was a rope slung across a timber framework. It was necessary to propel yourself 'hand over hand' along the rope, and to let yourself down on a single rope and sprint to the finish line.

Ralph and Tommy could not believe that they had done it. They sat triumphantly near the finish line smugly watching the others stumble and fall. Sergeant Edwards and the three training corporals shouted encouragement. One by one, men made it home amidst a chorus of screams and oaths. Only a few stragglers were left. Sergeant Edwards ordered everybody to fall in, however far across they were. He announced that the non-finishers would be given another chance in two weeks' time.

'Well done lads,' he said. He called Ralph aside. 'Tucker, I've got some medical data on you. Apparently you're asthmatic.'

'I was asthmatic throughout childhood, Sergeant, but I seemed to lose it when I left school. I haven't had an attack for some time. I hope it's not on my medical records.'

'No, son, it's not. It's private information. You did all right on the assault course. I never pick out one individual for praise but on this occasion – yes. My little boy gets asthma. He's only seven. I feel so sorry for the little chap.'

'I hope he grows out of it, Sergeant.'

'Thanks Tucker.'

Sergeant Edwards called the three training corporals together – Williams, Albert and Dean.

'So what do you think of Central India Squad then lads?' Sergeant Edwards asked.

'Verging on excellent,' Williams said. 'I've been involved in four intakes and this one's the best. There are maybe four or five strugglers, but we'll get them up to scratch. There are no thick men, no skivers and no scroungers. We've hardly had to shout at anybody.'

‘Mind you,’ Dean said, ‘the battalion is the true test.’

They all nodded wisely.

Ralph was reading a letter from Lorna. Duggie came over and sat at the foot of his bed.

‘I reckon you’re reading the same line over and over again,’ Duggie said.

‘Yes I am. It’s about the cottage my girlfriend and I are going to rent for a few days when we get leave in November. It’ll be cold, but we don’t mind.’

‘You’ve got your love to keep you warm, as the song goes.’

‘Yes, we have.’

‘Got a photo?’

‘Yes. I’ll show it you, but this is strictly between you and I, Duggie. Strictly and absolutely. Lorna would be beside herself if she knew that her photo had been bandied around a barrack room.’

‘We’re supposed to be best friends, aren’t we?’ Ralph passed him the photo. ‘Sensational!’ Duggie said. ‘It’s an artistic pose isn’t it? Nothing showing. Well, maybe half a nipple. Ralph, may I ask how old she is?’

‘Forty-three.’

‘They’re the best.’

‘Who are?’

‘Older women. They know what they want. They don’t tease you. They want you to make them happy. I’ve been there. Do you want to hear the story?’

‘Go on then.’

‘My last job in Civvy Street was delivering car parts, mainly to the trade but sometimes to private houses. One day I was delivering to the other side of Wolverhampton. A place called Penn. I expect you know it. My last delivery was to a big house. I knocked on the door. A lady in a dressing gown opened the door. I asked her to sign for the parcel. She said, ‘You look all in. Have you had a long day?’ I told her that I had. She asked me to come in and have a cup of tea. We started chatting. It appeared that her husband was out in the Far East and her son was at university. In no time it seemed that we were in her bedroom. She was hungry for it. Things happened so quickly that we never even exchanged names until three hours later, when she told me that her name was Gwendoline. She told me that I'd 'done very well' like a teacher to a pupil. I asked if I was one of a stable of lovers. "Well, there are a few, but I'm willing to give you an uninterrupted run. You're a nice looking boy. I prefer boys." The affair went on for two months. It got more and more furtive and complicated. I was in trouble a few times for not bringing the van back to the depot to be locked in the compound. Things came to an abrupt end the day her husband came back. She hadn't even told me. She saw a car about a half-mile away and told me it was her husband's Mercedes. I dressed frantically and jumped out of the window into some bushes. Seconds later the Mercedes pulled into the drive. I stepped out from the bushes deciding to meet my doom. Her husband got out of the car. "I know what you've been up to, my lad." I managed to stutter "w-what?" "Yes, I know what you've been up to," he said again. "W-what?" "You've been pissing in those bushes, haven't you?"

'I'll tell you what Ralph. I've never been so relieved to hear that in all my life. I told him that the parts were on the kitchen table, jumped into the van and I was away like the clappers.'

'I don't want to sound naive, Duggie, but did you love her?'

'Yes, it was a sort of love. I was bewitched if anything. I miss her. She'd got class and warmth and a figure a little bit podgier than your Lorna, matronly I'd say. She was always telling me stories. Once she heard me whistling in the bathroom. I was whistling 'Speed bonny boat'. She said that the song was apt. I asked why and she said, "The song is about the young pretender and you are my young pretender." She told me the tale of Charles Edward Stuart. She did things like that. She would say, "Did you enjoy that Douglas?" I would say yes. She would say. "Good! And in return you must make me happy".'

'Can you understand why I get irritated by little grubs like Barnyard?'

'Yes I can. Let's take a little stroll down to the Naafi.' Over egg and chips and two bottles of stout, Ralph told Duggie the story of his life since the garden party. Duggie listened attentively and at the end remarked that he and Ralph were kindred spirits having had a shared experience – the love of an older woman.

'It all seems a bit poncy though, Duggie. Let' s settle for 'good mates'. Anyway our stories are different. Your affair is over. Mine is only threatened. Yours was in secret. Mine is in the open. But what the hell! It's all in the past. The future's our journey round Australia.'

A letter arrived from Lorna.

Stanhope Hall Date: who cares?
My Beautiful Boy,

Time is getting on. I bet you're anxiously awaiting my critique of 'In Russian there are forty words for love.' Words of praise are welcome to a soldier, are they not, for the army rarely give out praise. I've had a few glasses of wine, but I think that will help me. I think much poetry is best read and understood when one is inebriated. Such is my condition now – inebriated and dishabille. And so to the critique. I think you are in love with words, but you come up with some wonderful images – the Soviets grading love from one to forty, Enigma dying with the last Czar, syllables dripping vodka but my favourite is an itch in the breeches of Konstantin Gavrilovich Treplev. Who the hell is he? I think he's a Chekhovian character in a play where everybody talked but nothing happened. I don't know whether I like all the stuff about the letter X. As a matter of fact X is the most unsuitable letter in the alphabet to represent a kiss. It should be '0' for the shape of the lips. I like all the last verses about winter virgins. I wish I was your Russian winter virgin and you are taking off my furs, all except the hat. I miss you a lot

Love Lorna 0 0 0 0 0.

Chapter 11

Told You We'd Do It

Dearest sister Veronica –
did you say anything to Mom and Dad about a little holiday? Just the four of us. A united family just for a few days. Let me know.

Tommy's promise that we would 'piss it in' is starting to look a reality. We're nearly into November. We've got the rehearsals coming up for the passing out parade and a few things in between. I bet Tommy tells you all the army stuff, doesn't he? I may be wasting my time telling you. So I won't. It will be nice to see a woman again. I've forgotten what they're like. They're a different shape from us aren't they? I've written you some verse – well doggerel actually. Do you remember that awful holiday we had at Auntie Joyce's boarding house in Rhyl, when it rained every day? I've turned it from miserable to lively. I wrote it to cheer myself up one evening.

<u>1947 – Rhyl's best year</u>
The teacher asked, 'How many of you will have holidays this year?
To her surprise, twelve hands shot up. Thus she demanded, 'where?'
A doleful little girl said, 'Rhyl'
'Rhyl,' said the boy next to her.
'Rhyl Rhyl Rhyl,' they said in turn.
Rhyl was tops for sure.
I asked my mother when I got home, 'Are we going away to the sea?'
I never expected her to say, 'There's a strong possibility.'

'We've had an invitation from Aunt Joyce and Uncle Phil. They've taken over a boarding house right on the front at Rhyl.'
This Rhyl must be a wonderful place I thought to myself in bed.
It's almost as if there's nowhere else in the world to visit instead.
There was a survey nationwide to find Britain's best resort.
Rhyl was top with a hundred per cent. The others all scored nought.
A questionnaire, which covered the world, finally proved Rhyl's case.
The Taj Mahal and the Pyramids were just not in the race.
Rhyl was the best place in the world, so the world all came to her.
Tribesmen from Mongolia came, and Greenlanders in fur.
Aztecs came from Mexico, Incas from Peru,
Argentinian Gauchos came, Pirates and their crew.
All around the hills they camped. They danced a merry jig.
Aborigines cooked witchety grub and Maoris roasted pig.
Oh, what a clamorous scene was this! Hark to the flute and drum.
Hear the raucous sea shanties of the sailors drinking rum.
I woke up in a tiny room with a single shaft of light.
Outside the rain was splashing down, as dawn pushed out the night.
I looked out through the window. The mist was all around.
Ragged seagulls strutted through puddles on the ground.

And somewhere out there was the sea. It looked a dirty brown.
A pale sun tried to break the gloom of this old seaside town,
'Are you all right in there, my son?' It was my father's voice.
I heard other voices too, my mother and Aunt Joyce.
'Did you sleep well?'
Whose voice was this? It must be Uncle Phil.
'Breakfast is in ten minutes time. Welcome boy, to Rhyl'.

Written by Ralph Tucker for his sister Veronica, shortly before he became Poet Laureate in November 1955

Winter loomed. It began to get colder in the barracks in the evenings. The only heating was an old pot-bellied stove in the middle of each room. The recruits themselves were responsible for getting a good fire going. They took it in turn to go out scavenging for wood. Empty ammo boxes were grabbed immediately at source – the rifle range – and brought back for fuel. The back of the Naafi was a good scrounging area. There were often broken pallets and beer crates. The area behind the dining hall yielded some good items, packaging and paper, sometimes fruit boxes. They discovered a good stock of wood near the perimeter fence where trees had been pruned.

Lighting the fire each evening became a ritual. From a tiny pile of wood splinters wrapped in paper to a good roaring fire was a thirty-minute exercise. Then they would all sit as near to the fire as possible and swap a few yarns whilst cleaning their kit. Sex having been banned as a topic because it only reminded them of the womanless place they were in, their favourite tales were family yarns. Christmas at Nan Tuckers was Ralph's speciality.

It was November 1st. Mister Ribbons inspected them on muster parade.

'Stand them at ease, Corporal Dean,' he ordered.

'You have worked well and have only got three weeks to go.'

A cheer erupted from somewhere in the rear rank.

'Quiet!' Corporal Dean shouted. Mr Ribbons resumed his address.

'Over the next five days we will get all the basics out of the way – finalised, finished – this includes PE tests at the gym, the rifle range and fieldcraft. You will, however, have one night exercise, one route march and one map reading exercise in the time between now and passing out. You have all mastered the assault course. Apart from what I have told you, the emphasis will be on drill and your run up to passing out parade. Both squads will be involved in this. It is not, repeat not, a competition. It is something that we have to get right. I mean absolutely right, and we shall rehearse it until it is absolutely right. One of you will be selected as best recruit. This is a great honour as well as an achievement. The passing out parade will take place on 24th November at 1130 hrs. Your parents, wives, girlfriends and other relatives are instructed to be seated in the temporary stand by 1045 hrs. Because the regimental band is in Cyprus, you will march to the band of RAF Stafford. After the final rehearsal on 23rd November, you will be advised of your postings. I can tell you in advance that you will all be joining the first battalion in Nicosia, Cyprus.

'You will proceed on embarkation leave from 24th November (immediately after the passing out parade) to 0800hrs on 15th December. The exact date of departure is not known. You are unlikely to fly out until after Christmas. You will therefore get an extra bonus – more leave for Christmas. It seems that you are having nothing but leave. The army has gone soft,' he shouted, 'What do you think, Corporal Dean?'

‘I think that they should all go home, sir. They must see their mummies and daddies, and open the presents that Father Christmas has given them, not forgetting their Christmas stockings with an apple and an orange in and extra little surprise presents for being good boys.’

‘I’ve heard enough,’ Mr Ribbons said. ‘March them to the range and back here for drill at 1430 hrs.’

Home
Letter from Miss Veronica Elsie Tucker
Date optional
My dear, dear, darling brother.

Yes we shall all be having a holiday together. Dad says he’s taking time off whether or not he’s entitled to it. The City of Birmingham Treasurers Rates Department can go hang. He’s put in ten hard years since the war. So we’re all going to the Derby Dales, which is where they went on honeymoon in 1936. Mom is overjoyed that we want to have a family holiday. She’s so happy that she keeps bursting into tears. Of course, you’ll have your naughty little stay in Devon first. I’ve seen Lorna a few times. She looks a bit down in the dumps. She didn’t think she’d miss her virile young lover so much. She knows that the affair has to end, but she still wants to keep in touch regularly when you’re in Cyprus. She says it’s for your sake. It’s an anchor for you. Sometimes I feel so sorry for you both. She’s almost a clairvoyant isn’t she? She sees a golden-haired girl with a parasol, so she says. Most unusual I’d say. Lorna says that this golden-haired girl will marry Ralph. Is she saying it to ease her sorrow or to force herself to admit that Ralph will go his own way – which you will. I have a daydream that Tommy and I and you and the golden-haired girl are all growing old together.

But enough of this stuff. It scares me. Lorna's strange. What a great brother you are. How many brothers would send their sisters a whimsical poem? I remember the holiday well. It was awful, wasn't it? Where do you get your weird ideas? Are you a reincarnation of Lord Biro? I've got all the gen on the passing out parade. Dad and I will be there. Mom will be at home preparing a nice meal. Do *not* go to Stanhope Hall to collect any clothes. Stay with us. Passing out day is our day. I'm not seeing Tommy either until Friday. Well obviously, I'll see him at the parade, but I won't be with him if you know what I mean. I'm getting in a muddle am I not? You can work it all out. I think there's an evening set aside for you, Tommy, Dennis and Dad to have a booze up at the Dog and Partridge pub. It'll all work out.

Tommy will be going back to work to help Ron out. What an absolute pain in the bum he is, but I love him. This will be the last letter,

all my love Veronica.

For days Central India Squad and Lucknow squad pounded the square to the roars of the NCOs. Sergeant Edwards' voice echoed throughout the depot. Whatever the virtues or otherwise of screaming out orders and roaring out criticism, it all seemed to be working and by final rehearsal day they were moving with precision. Their timing was spot on. Their bayonets were dead in line. Their forearms swung in unison. Their boots and brasses sparkled. The RAF Band struck up the regimental march. They felt proud. This was the final rehearsal. It had gone well. There was a discussion between NCOs and Officers. They had picked out some minor faults. They broke away. Mr Ribbons marched over to Central India squad.

‘Pay attention please. That was up to the standard required. Do that tomorrow and you will have done yourselves proud. March them off and fall them out, Sergeant Edwards. Tell Ward that he has won ‘best recruit’ and go through the drill for handing over of his award. Re-emphasise that they must keep the good standard tomorrow.’

They did. The twelve weeks were over.

‘I told you that we’d piss it in,’ Tommy boasted. ‘I told you, Ralphy. I told you, Den. I told you. Stan and Duggie.

‘And you’re to be congratulated for winning best recruit,’ Ralph told Tommy.

‘I’ll go along with that,’ Dennis said.

‘There’s my dad and Veronica,’ Ralph walked over to them. Hugh shook his hand and said ‘Well done, son’. Veronica saw Tommy, sprinted over to him and jumped into his arms.

They all piled into Hugh’s ancient Lanchester car – Hugh and Ralph in front, Tommy, Veronica and Dennis on the back seat, three kitbags, three sea kitbags, and three suit-cases in the boot or wherever they could fit them. Veronica beamed with happiness as she clung to her man, immaculate in his best battledress. They sped along the road to Lichfield, thence Walsall. They sang all the way. They sang the songs that were popular at the time. This was pre-pop music time. There were no divisions in music, no heavy metal, folk, rock, country, skiffle. This was soon to come. In the meantime everybody, young and old, sang the songs that came over the radio, songs like Christmas Alphabet: C is for the candy hanging on the Christmas tree. H is for the happiness for all the family. R is for the reindeer pulling Santa’s sledge at night. I is for the icing on the cake, the sweetest sugar cake. S is for old Santa, who gives all the kids a treat, and on and on.

They sang, ‘River of no return’ and ‘Davy Crocket’. Ralph and Veronica used to put their own words to songs.

Their version of Davy Crocket was this: Born on a mountaintop in Cannock Chase, You never saw such an ugly face. They put him in a rocket and they shot him into space, with nothing but a bottle of beer. Davy, Davy Sprocket, the man with a cauliflower ear.

'Where shall I drop you boys off?' Hugh asked.

'Top of Moncrieff Street's near enough,' Tommy said. Hugh pulled up and unloaded their gear onto the pavement.

Tommy kissed Veronica a short goodbye.

'She'll be down to see you with the first sparrow,' Hugh said. 'Be sure of that, Tommy. And as for you lads, no doubt we'll all get together for a few ales over the coming weeks.'

'That we will, Mr Tucker,' Dennis assured him.

They drove on.

'It's a strange experience is your first leave isn't it son. The world looks unreal. You realise that there is a life outside the barracks. You don't know it yet, but you're already institutionalised. Now you'll have to get through the day without being told what to do.'

'I think I'll manage it, Dad.'

'I'm sure you will. We're nearly home. There's your mother already at the front door.'

'My little scamp, grown up to be a soldier!' She took him in her arms. 'Oh, my son! I'm reverting to my previous persona. I shall smother you with love. You deserve it after your privations.'

She was dressed in a tweed suit with a long skirt, a beige blouse, dark stockings and court shoes.

'You look great, mother. You look like one of the county set. You should be in *Staffordshire Life*. Your hair looks good. You're my beautiful mother.'

She pulled him to her again.

'There's a special relationship between us, isn't there?' she whispered.

'Of course, mother.'

'Of course, I've always known how to dress, which is more than I can say for Lorna Pitt in her threadbare office clothes or her dowdy brown skirt and men's shirts.'

'Now, now mother. I took her to a posh dress shop all the way down in Malvern and she bought a lot of stuff. As for her wearing men's shirts, it's simply practical. She needs room in that area if you know what I mean.'

'Yes, we know what you mean, son,' Hugh cut in. 'Let's drop the subject, shall we? We don't want a debate on a day like this.'

'I bet you'll be glad to get out of that uniform, won't you, son?'

'I'm off to change now.'

He went into his room, undressed and began hanging his uniform on coat hangers and putting everything neatly in the wardrobe. There was a knock on the door.

'Can I come in?' Veronica asked.

'I'm undressed.'

'Completely?'

'Completely.'

'Good. I'm coming in.'

'What do you want?'

'I want to see your manly body.'

'Well here it is. Not a spare ounce of fat.'

'I'm impressed except for your shrivelled up little willy, or little Ralph as he is known. Lorna's going to be rather disappointed.'

'Why are we having conversations about Lorna Pitt? First mother, now you. Let me assure you that, when the time comes, Little Ralph will do his duty, as will Little Tommy when he meets Little Veronica.'

'That will be tomorrow,' Veronica said.

'Let's have an aperitif, shall we?' Hugh suggested and poured four dry sherries. 'We'll drink no toasts just yet. Let's just relish the time we have together as a family. What do you think of your mother, Ralph? Doesn't she look good? I'm a lucky man. I've got a classy new wife, two good-looking kids that are about to flee the nest, a car that's just about ready to conk out, a job I hate, no hair, no teeth, nightmares that I'm still at sea and freezing to death and a demob suit that I've never worn and I'm the happiest man in England, well Walsall anyway, maybe not all Walsall. I'm the happiest man in Gorway.'

'Stop raving on, Dad,' Veronica pleaded. 'Let's get dinner started. Sit down at the table, you lazy men. Mother and I will serve you.'

Margaret had done them proud. Their dinner menu included celery soup for starters, the good old standby of roast beef and Yorkshire pudding to follow with choice of vegetables – cabbage, cauliflower, peas, green beans and roast potatoes. They shared a huge trifle for sweet. There were four bottles of Lorna's red wine on the table. Cheese, biscuits, port or liqueurs rounded off the feast.

They stayed at the table, satiated, drinking their powerful wine like lemonade. Hugh got to his feet and cried out, 'Here's to your wonderful mum, the master chef or should I say the mistress chef, for preparing this veritable banquet. Here's to young Ralph who's been through three months of soldiering and still remains the genuine lad he has always been, but I should mention that his table manners are now atrocious. Here's to my little Veronica who has always been the apple of my eye.'

'Here's to Dad for putting up with us,' Ralph said. A cheer went up and they drank heartily. They were all in various stages of inebriation and one by one retired to bed.

Ralph awoke at six o'clock awaiting reveille, blown over and over again. He waited for the yells and screams of NCOs as they stomped the length of the barrack room banging the beds and shouting, 'Get out of bed, get up, get up you horrible sleepyheads,' There was silence. He felt bloated and sick and far from home. He rolled out of bed and fell onto the floor. He looked up at the walls and saw the little picture library he had assembled as a boy – 'Kings and Queens of England.' He knew where he was. He felt dizzy. He climbed back into bed and fell asleep once more. It was 9 o'clock before he stirred again, when his mother brought him in a large black coffee.

Gradually he unscrambled his thoughts and realised that he was on embarkation leave with a day to himself and a drink with his mates tonight. Maybe he should see Nan Tucker.

Yes, that was what he would do; he would skip breakfast and stroll into Caldmore.

'Well if it isn't my boy's boy.' Nan Tucker hugged him. 'When did you get home? Don't you look fit? Am I your first call? Or have you been with the Gorway widow?'

'One question at a time, Nan. I got home yesterday afternoon. I had a big meal with Mom and Dad and Veronica last night. I strolled down to Caldmore and here I am.'

'And how are you?'

'A bit rough to be honest.'

'That's Maggie Rowley's cooking for you.'

'Now, now Nan. I've come here to see you and Granddad, not to listen to you running down my mother.'

'You're your mother's boy.'

'Yes, yes, I'm a mummy's boy, smothered in affection. If I've heard it once, I've heard it a hundred times. She's my mother, I love her. Dad loves her, Veronica loves her. She cooked a wonderful meal. I'm feeling rough because I had too much wine that's all.'

'Was it that rotgut wine that the Gorway widow's been giving away for years?'

'It's good stuff, Nan, and in future I would like you to refer to my mother as Margaret and the so called Gorway Widow as Lorna. I'm going in to see Granddad.'

Granddad was lying on the couch as usual. He was actually awake, a rare occurrence.

‘Young Ralph! I thought it was you when I heard voices, raised voices I may add.’

‘I was arguing with Nan.’

‘That’s something I’ve been doing since 1904, boy. What were you arguing about?’

‘She keeps referring to my mother as Maggie Rowley. She’s Margaret Tucker and has been since 1936. Nan seems to be inferring that my mother’s not good enough for her son.’

‘Your grandmother’s got a bee in her bonnet about quite a few things. She’s got a long memory. It comes from her side of the family. Let’s get onto soldiering shall we? So you re off to Cyprus.’

‘December 15th – just in time for Christmas under canvas. Word has it that we’ll be there until May 57, then we’re back to Blighty for a while before we leave for Germany in September 57. In August 58 my time will be up.’

‘I shall try and stay alive until then.’

‘That’s jolly decent of you Granddad.’

‘How the hell I managed to stay alive this long, God only knows. I thought I was a goner a few times in South Africa. Thank God I was unfit and a bit too old for the Great War, the so-called ‘war to end all wars.’ What a misnomer that turned out to be. The Boer War was my war. They didn’t fight fair those Boers. They fired at us from behind walls and everywhere. Every man was his own general. You never knew where they were. Well, now we’ve got campaigns like Cyprus and Malaya. At least we knew who were Boers and who weren’t. Who are these EOKA blokes and where are they and what the bloody hell are they throwing bombs for?’

‘They used to be fighting for union with Greece. That was called ENOSIS. Now they’re fighting for independence and it’s called EOKA.’ Ralph told him.

‘Give them independence and get out of the place.’

'But that could lead to Civil War – Greek Cypriots against Turks.'

'The Turks? They're always getting in on the act. Bah! I'm not even going to try to understand it and I'm too old to care. As long as my curly-haired little grandson comes home safe and sound, that's all I care. Mind you, you're not so little now are you? You're a sturdy lad. So goodbye, boy's boy and make peace with your Nan.'

He came back into the kitchen. Nan Tucker gave him a going away present. 'Still in the wrapper, those playing cards, when you've worn the spots off it'll be time to come home.'

She burst into tears.

'Come on, Nan. Don't upset yourself.'

'I'm a nasty gossipy old woman aren't I? I'll take back what I said about your mother and your lady-friend. They'll be Margaret and Lorna from now on. That does not mean that I approve of Lorna's relationship with you, nor do I approve of your mother's condoning it. I can see how a naive young lad could be easily seduced by a shapely, strapping, good-looking, wealthy woman. I'll wager she can twist you round her little finger. Listen to your grandmother, boy's boy. End the relationship. I'm a moralising old woman, I know, but she's twenty-five years older than you. That's a generation. She's only two months off being a grandmother. Believe me, when your first grandchild arrives, it's the most important thing in the world and you hope for more and more. That new child will spend two thirds of its time on Lorna's lap. Your nose will be put right out of joint, young Ralph and that would be a good time to start disentangling yourself.'

'I'll be in Cyprus, Nan. There's nothing to be disentangled from.'

'Maybe I've got my dates wrong but you know what I mean, consider all the pros and cons including the operation the historicrectory or whatever it's called.'

'I know what you're saying, Nan. I've had a few lectures on the subject. I'm going to do my best to please everybody or 'appease' everybody. I'm spending a few days with Lorna at a cottage by the beach. It'll be peaceful down there at this time of the year. We can talk things over. She wants us to write regularly from Cyprus. That I agree with. It's going to be a long spell there and I need someone who will send me witty letters and someone to whom I can write witty letters. Surely the family will have no objection to that. Do you also know that Mom and Dad and Veronica and I are going on holiday together when I come back from Devon? Nan, rest assured, I shall not marry Lorna. I shall not make her my mistress. I shall always be conscious of my family's wishes, but I shall do what I consider is the right thing. Can I say fairer than that, Nan?'

'No, son, you can't.'

He said his farewells and left.

Ralph set off for the Fullbrook pub at 7.30. The Arbo Gang plus two honorary members were already there.

'Ralphy!'

'Cheers Lads!' There was already a pint waiting for him.

'Let's park ourselves around this large table,' Tommy suggested.

'So what's the purpose of this meeting?' Ralph asked.

'I'll make it short and sweet,' Tommy said. 'Today, I went to a jewellers and bought an engagement ring. I'll show it to you.' He reached into his jacket pocket, pulled out the ring and placed it on the table. 'What do you think of that?'

They all politely told him it was a nice ring.

'It cost a pretty penny,' Tommy said.

'When will you give it to her?' Ralph asked.

'On the day that you all leave for your little break up in Derbyshire. I'm going to do it properly. I'm going to ask your Dad for his daughter's hand in marriage. I shall then go down on bended knee and ask Veronica to marry me.'

'That's the way to do it, Tommy, correctly, like the old days. I'm impressed,' Duggie said.

'Like *Pride and Prejudice* or *Jane Eyre*,' Dennis said.

'Or the Owl and the Pussy Cat,' Stan added.

'Who was the husband and who was the wife in the Owl and the Pussy Cat?' Duggie asked.

'It would be Owl as husband and the Cat as wife,' Dennis maintained. 'Pussy is female.'

'It's not pussy in the sense of a fanny,' Duggie argued. 'It's pussy in the sense of a pussy being a pet name for a cat.'

'Come on, lads,' Tommy implored. 'This is a big day for me and we're talking about marriage one minute and pussy the next.'

'Same thing, Tommy, as you well know,' Duggie said. 'Anyway, subject closed and Tommy's round.'

Tommy came back with the drinks and asked rather smugly, 'So who else has good news on the female front?'

'I had a lady once,' Duggie said sadly. 'She taught me how to love. One day it all ended. Her fading beauty haunts me. Gwendoline was her name.'

'I have a lady now,' Ralph said. 'She taught me how to love.'

'It wasn't the same one as Duggie's was it?' Dennis asked.

'No it wasn't. You've spoilt it all now.'

'It was all getting a bit boring.'

'Really? Well let's hear your contribution,' Ralph demanded.

'I'm not bothering about women at the moment,' Denis said.

'When I'm a star of stage and screen, women will be throwing themselves at me, so why bother chasing them?'

'Dream on, Dennis,' Duggie said.

‘I took a girl out once called Shirley,’ Stan said ‘She was reputed to have the biggest knockers in Friar Park. We went to the pictures. It was a gangster film. She didn’t like it much and started blaming me. There was one bloke who should have been shot but wasn’t and there was another bloke who shouldn’t have been shot but who was. I told her that she ought to write to Twentieth Century Fox. There was one last chance of turning the evening from disaster to success and that was to get a feel. Some hopes of anyone getting a feel. I swear her bra was made of stainless steel. There’s a poem in there somewhere.’

Everybody cheered. ‘Stan the Van Man!’

‘Trust Stan to make us laugh each time,’ Tommy said, ‘And do you know, Stan. You’ve got a great gift. You can laugh at yourself.’

They drank and sang until ten o’clock. Ralph told them that he had to drive down to Devon next morning and left. He was merry. A mild classification of inebriation. He sang to himself as he walked. Cyprus, the army, the future were all well out of mind. It was next stop Devon and his little fantasy world with Lorna.

Chapter 12

Wanstock

Ralph rose early next morning and packed clothes and sundries to cover all eventualities. He said his short farewells and strode off across the Oval with his battered suitcase, heading for Stanhope Hall.

Lorna was waiting by the faithful Morris Minor. She looked the personification of elegance in a tweed suit, the skirt of which finished at knee height. Her hair had been cut to shoulder length, apparently because her new style would not hamper her swimming.

'How do I look?'

'I'm not searching my head for superlatives. I'll just say that you look great – at any level whatever that means. How about me? How do I look?'

'You look like my Beautiful Boy. Now pack your case into the boot. My clothes are all on the back seat along with a good supply of wine. Petrol, oil and water are all checked. Here are the keys. Jump in and away we go. Be careful. Do you know the way?'

'A38,' he said, 'Bromsgrove, Droitwich, Worcester, Gloucester, Bristol, Burnham, Taunton, Exeter, then where?'

'Ashburton, Buckfastleigh, South Brent, then B-roads until we get to Wanstock. I'll give you directions.'

'What's the cottage like?

'You'll love it. Just wait until you see it. I'll let it be a surprise for you. Rest assured it will be nice and cosy. It's got central heating. There's also a log fire which is more romantic but also more hard work.'

'Couldn't we get up really early, get a good fire going, have our swim and dry ourselves in front of the fire?'

‘All sorts of ultra-pleasurable rituals can be arranged, darling. Leave all the hedonistic details to me. Now watch for signs and get us out of this labyrinth and onto some country roads.’

‘Devon, here we come. Ah, the open road!’

‘You sound like Toad of Toad Hall.’

‘Yes. That’s right. It was an exciting novelty for Toad and it’s a novelty for me too.’

Unspoilt rural England passed by. Winter was well upon them. The trees were bereft of leaves and the fields were ploughed. They reckoned to be well past Gloucester by midday. The intention was to stop at a pub, have an hour’s break before covering the last stretch. They stopped at a rather bleak hostelry called the New Inn and entered the lounge, which was certainly in contrast to the nondescript exterior. A wood fire burnt fiercely and there was a buzz of conversation. Ralph asked Lorna what she would like to drink and she said, ‘the same as you. From now on that will be my order. If you’re drinking pints of bitter then so shall I. It makes life simpler.’

‘It’s absolutely fine by me,’ he agreed, and brought back two pints of bitter.

Everybody seemed very polite especially a constant flow of elderly gentlemen who passed their table on the way to the Gents. Without exception they doffed their caps and said, ‘Mornin Ma’am, Mornin Zur.’

‘Perhaps they think that we are the Squire and his good lady. We’re both in tweeds.’

‘I think there’s a simpler explanation,’ Ralph replied.

‘I think you should try to tug your skirt down a little further.’

‘Well the answer to that is that I can’t. It’s knee length. If I’ve made a few old gentlemen happy then so be it. This skirt may be short by 1955 standards, but you just wait till the sixties. Skirts will get shorter and shorter until – well until they can’t get any shorter.’

‘I’m looking forward to those days,’ Ralph said.

They drank their beer and left to cries of ‘Mornin ma’am.’

They set out on the final stretch of their journey.

‘I bet you’ve been looking forward to this, haven’t you, Ralph? I know *I* have. I’m really excited at the prospect of our having some jolly good fun together. This is all innuendo, isn’t it? Does it irritate you? I don’t think so. I think you like it.’

They drove on through the afternoon.

‘This is the turn-off!’ Lorna cried. ‘Slow down Ralph.’

She put him through a series of ‘turn rights’, ‘turn lefts’ and ‘Straight ons’ for thirty minutes. Finally they came to a sign for Wanstock.

‘Now, d’you see that white bungalow near the outcrop of rocks? That’s it. That’s our home for five nights – Beach Cottage. We’re right on the beach. There looks to be a hell of a wind blowing but who cares? I know we’re going to have lovely time. I just know it. Don’t drive straight down yet. I want to check out the general store so drive on and take first left. There we are! It’s open. The pub’s over there look – The Ship Inn. It’s a lively place at night as I recall.’

Ralph turned back and forked along the narrow bumpy track that led to Beach Cottage.

‘There’s a stone in that wall with a splash of red paint on it. Take the stone out, Ralph, and you’ll find a set of keys. There’ll be a large rusty one for the kitchen and a Yale key for the front door.’

Ralph brought the car to a halt, jumped out into the fierce wind and extracted the keys. He handed them to Lorna so that she could let herself in, and set about unloading the car.

He stepped into the cosy warmth of the cottage, dumped the baggage down in the kitchen and took himself on a tour. There was a large kitchen, a bedroom, a dining/living room and a bathroom. He was impressed.

‘I really like it,’ he told Lorna.

‘I knew you would.’ She put her arms around him and kissed him. ‘This holiday is for you, Ralph. It’s a gift from me to my Beautiful Boy. If that makes you a gigolo, who cares? We are away from the moralisers. We’re adult enough to know that we’re in a relationship that is ultimately destined to end. This holiday is going to be a golden memory one day. I could never have let you go to Cyprus without such a memory. You deserve it.’

‘What can I say? What a gift! And considering that this gift includes your love, your body and your mind, I feel that I should, in turn, give you my love, body and mind.’

‘What a blooming rigmarole! Let’s get all these clothes hung up in the wardrobe, and then we’ll be ready. And if you say ‘ready for what?’ I shall punch you on the nose.’ She rolled up her man-size fist.

‘Boy, will I be glad to get these itchy tweeds off.’ In seconds she had whipped off her jacket and skirt. ‘Come on, Ralph! Hurry boy! Speed it up a bit. Let’s have a look at you. Basic training’s done a good job on you. Fit and lean, eh? Remember our first time? It was so wonderful and exciting. Little Ralph did so well. Now, here he is again. He hasn’t changed much. He’s grown a bit. I bet he’s excited. I know I am. I’ve been excited all day. I’ve been really looking forward to it. Come on, Ralph. I’m in position’

Rain lashed against the windows. There was a mist on the sea. A blustery wind seared through the high grass of the dunes.

‘I don’t care about the future,’ she said, ‘For now I love you. I will have other men, but you will always be the one. Even our light-hearted lovemaking becomes a wondrous thing. Come, boy. Lay your head on my bosom. Let my strong arms enfold you.’

‘I’m glad that our lovemaking is light-hearted. I’m glad that we apply humour to our love. This is ecstasy.’

‘Let it stay that way. Forget the world. Forget time. We’ll eat when we’re hungry. We’ll drink when we’re dry. Forget the world out there. It doesn’t exist.’

‘Not even the pub?’ Ralph asked.

‘You absolute cretin!’ She tightened her grip on him so fiercely that he gasped for breath.

In time they grew hungrier and Lorna prepared a basic meal of corned beef, mashed potato and baked beans.

‘Dinner preparation is not my forte as you well know. I’m more of a big breakfast cook,’ Lorna admitted. ‘Never mind. This should go down well enough with a couple of bottles of wine. We won’t go to the pub. We’ve got all the time in the world to go there. It’s been a long day. I think we should have a little party of our own and then crawl into bed.’

‘Ralph, Ralph! Wakey wakey! Come on! It’s our nude swim. It’s seven thirty. Follow me!’

They ran past the rocks, through the dunes and onto the beach. From there it was a fifty-yards run to the water.

‘Run, Ralph, run!’ She was sprinting like an athlete, holding down her huge breasts with her right forearm. ‘How can she be so fit?’ he asked himself. They ran into the bay until the water was deep enough to swim in. She powered through the water swimming what is now called front crawl but was, in those days, referred to as overarm. Ralph could not match her for speed. She slowed to let him catch up and they swam together in a full circle in the bay. The water was almost calm. At other points along the front, the sea was crashing down. Lorna would not let him rest. She took him on a further half mile run as far as an old abandoned boat lying upside down in the dunes.

‘Now for the interesting part,’ Lorna told him. ‘You have to piggyback me to the cottage. I’m only twelve stone eleven. You can do it, Ralph. I know you can. If you don’t I shall know what a little namby-pamby you are.’

‘Me? A namby-pamby? I don’t think so.’

She jumped on him, locked her forearms together and gripped his waist with her thighs. He supported her as best he could but staggered around for a while. Then he steadied himself and began the laborious walk to the cottage. He concentrated on putting one foot in front of the other.

From the corner of his eye he spotted three middle-aged couples approaching them at right angles on the way to one of the tracks that led off the beach. They were almost certain to meet.

‘What do I do now?’ he asked breathlessly.

‘Just carry on, you silly shy boy.’

Inevitably they reached the couples, all well wrapped up against the cold. They all cried out a hearty ‘Good Morning’. One of the group was tempted to remark, ‘The cold seems to have affected your manhood, young fellow.’ He prodded Ralph’s penis with his stick. ‘The old John Thomas has shrivelled up a bit, hasn’t it?’

Lorna felt obliged to interrupt. ‘Once we get into the warmth of little cottage that will soon come up.’

Apart from feeling tired in every muscle, Ralph was getting increasingly embarrassed. Lorna made her customary announcement that he was her virile young lover. After what seemed an age of small talk they finally got under way.

‘There you are, Ralph. If you just act naturally, you will find most people will be charming and polite.’

‘I didn’t think they were charming or polite. That old chap in a balaclava prodded me with a stick where it really hurts. We’re nearly at the cottage now. Can I let you down?’

‘As soon as you reach the back door, Ralph. Rules are rules. It’s like the assault course. You must cross the line which, in this case, is the back door.’

‘To say that I shall be glad to lower you down is an understatement.’

They went into the kitchen, the warmth hit them. Lorna began to prepare a huge 'gardener''s breakfast'.

'You did very well, Ralph. Now you can imagine what a beast of burden has to endure day in day out. I noticed, when we were talking to those old timers, you had the resigned look on your face of a patient old camel who is destined for a life of continual hardship.'

'Am I destined for a life of continual hardship? Is that what you see for me?'

'Not physical hardship, darling, though there is a bit of that. Let us say that you have a difficult life ahead of you. Knowing how to face hard times is an important thing. You probably think, "What does this rich widow know of hardship?" Well, I do know a lot and I will always help you if you need me. I'm helping you now. This has to be more than a carefree little break by the sea. It has to be a special time in your life. Breakfast coming up.'

After breakfast, Ralph decided to carry out a recce of Wanstock. It was a rudimentary place with no streets, only tracks between haphazard clusters of buildings. The general store was little more than a giant wooden shed. It was dimly lit and open limited hours in the off-season. The gift shop, the artists' materials shop, the souvenir shop and the second-hand bookshop were all closed, though they all displayed notices on their front doors with telephone numbers in case of need. All the shops were housed in a rather ugly bungalow directly opposite the general store. The only other building was the Ship Inn. It was completely in character with the rest of the village – ticky-tacky fifties style badly in need of a coat of paint. The Inn sign of a sailing ship had faded completely. Nobody seemed to give a damn in Wanstock. He decided to call in for a swift half pint and was most surprised to find that the pub was three quarters full. It seemed that Upper Wanstock, about half a mile to the north was mainly a retirement community. It had no pub so the Upper Wanstock villagers used The Ship Inn.

Ralph sat himself down, nodded a hello to the elderly gentlemen around him and sipped his beer. The walls were completely bare but for a large, badly written sign board which simply said: TALENT CONTEST 7.30 NIGHTLY.

'That could be fun,' he thought and made his way back to Beach Cottage.

He found Lorna asleep on the bed. He did not want to wake her. He touched her. She turned over onto her back.

'It's my Beautiful Boy,' she said sleepily. 'I must have fallen asleep after that enormous breakfast.'

'I did a little recce of Wanstock,' Ralph told her. 'Not much to see really, but what do we need? We've got enough – saltwater, rocks to explore, sand dunes, a beach, a cottage, a general store, a pub, howling winds, torrential rain, occasional sun and love.'

'Not to mention lots of jolly good fun so stop waxing lyrical, young man and get your clothes off. But, you're right,' she said. 'We have got enough here to be deliriously happy. Tomorrow we'll do a bit of rock exploration. You may wear trunks, Ralph. We don't want little Ralph getting scratched on a jagged piece of rock, do we? Tonight we'll go to the pub. We might as well go in for the talent contest too. There's no prize. It's just a bit of fun. What songs do you know? A lot I bet. D'you know, 'If you were the only girl in the world'?'

'Of course.' he said.

'Then that's what we'll sing.'

Ralph thought ahead, conscious of Lorna's vow to drink with him pint for pint. He was almost certainly going to have to carry her home. How to avoid such a backbreaking experience? He had an idea. He had seen an old wheelbarrow in the garden of Beach Cottage. He carried it through the dunes and along the beach, parking it at the rear of The Ship Inn. It seemed highly unlikely that anybody would steal it. He found a large carton, which he broke down and put it on the floor of the barrow. He walked back to the cottage feeling quite pleased with himself.

'Come on, Ralph. Where have you been? I'm getting us a gourmet meal. Gourmet sausage and gourmet mash. We want to be at the pub by 7.00 o'clock to get some seats. I'll have to find something sort of 'pubby' to wear. I left all my good quality stuff at home. What shall I – I know.' She went away and returned with two long dresses. 'I bought these in a charity shop. I would call them kaftans. They were a mixture of russet, crimson and yellow ochre. They're threadbare now. They're diaphanous. I would wear my tweed jacket on top.'

'Wear one,' Ralph said. 'It'll look great. You'll look great. You *are* great. Are they low necked?'

'Well, yes. I've done a bit of doctoring. They're very low necked. That could win us the talent contest? Maybe not, but it'll add a bit of sparkle to the evening. Let's put one on and I'll show you.' She pulled on a Kaftan, and asked 'What d'you think?'

'I think you should wear your tweed jacket on top.'

'Come on. Let's be off.'

The pub was filling fast when they arrived. They found themselves a seat and Ralph ordered two pints of bitter.

A burly man was walking round the tables, a flat cap held out. People were putting slips of paper and money into it.

'Talent contest, sir. Talent contest, sir. Just put your names in the hat with two bob per name, if you want to be in it. It's ten bob to the winner, but it's traditional to immediately put your ten bob prize back in the charity box for cancer research.'

The MC took up a position by the bar. 'Ladies and Gentlemen, Usual rules. I'll need the help of a lady in the audience to draw the names out so that I can put them in order. How about that glamorous lady in the tweed jacket, the elegant squire's lady? Would you like to draw the names out, ma'am?'

Lorna stepped boldly up to the bar. She was a powerful presence. The lights shone through the threadbare kaftan. Her sturdy body in all its glory stood in clear silhouette. She was the centre of attention and she knew it.

'And what is your name, my dear?'

'It's Lorna.'

'Lorna will draw out the names.' He announced.

She put her hand in the cap, took out a slip and said clearly 'Albert.'

'Albert,' the MC repeated.

'Maggie,' Lorna said.

'Maggie,' the MC repeated.

On it went – Norman, Betty, Alf, Barry, Winnie, Janet, Archie, Max and finally Ralph and Lorna.

The entertainment got under way. In the final days before Rock and Roll, popular music was in its death throes but everyone knew a tune or two. It was customary to sing along with the so-called entertainers. Ralph and Lorna found themselves belting out 'Old Man River', 'My Old Man Said Follow the Van', 'There'll Be Bluebirds Over the White Cliffs of Dover', 'I'll Join the Legion That's What I'll Do', 'By a Babbling Brook, in a Shady Nook' and numerous other songs of that uncomplicated era when a song was a song for all ages. Ralph and Lorna were on their third pint.

'We're up to Archie,' Lorna said. 'You sing, Ralph, and I'll harmonise.'

Archie had finally finished his laborious rendering of 'Widdicombe Fair.' Max was singing 'Clementine' and Ralph and Lorna were raring to go.

'If you were the only girl in the world, and I was the only boy, nothing else would matter in the world today. We would go on loving in the same old way. A garden of Eden just made for two, with nothing to mar our joy...'

By this time the whole pub was singing in unison. At the end of it there was wild applause. There were three possible explanations for this – either they were all glad to reach the last song or they genuinely thought that 'If you were the only girl in the world' was the best song of the evening or, and most likely, they liked Lorna's see-though dress. Their names were announced above the hubbub, and they went through the rather peculiar practice of picking up their prize and giving it straight back.

The villagers began to leave. The singing was over. Ralph and Lorna swilled down their fourth and last pint of beer.

'What a brilliant evening,' Lorna said, 'and I kept up with you pint for pint. Mind you. I'm starting to feel a bit tipsy.'

'I'll get you home all right. Follow me. He led her to the wheelbarrow. 'You're carriage awaits, ma'am. I've put some cardboard down to prevent you getting dirty. Here we go then.' He trundled her down to the beach and they headed off towards Beach Cottage.

'When you commence your new life as a party-going young man in his twenties, I hope you don't imagine that young ladies will be all that impressed with a lift home in a wheelbarrow. However, a woman of the world, as I am, would certainly be won over by the inventiveness and eccentricity of it all.'

She fell asleep. He delivered her to the back door and carried her to the bedroom. He lay her on the bed, undressed her and moved in beside her.

'Ralph, Ralph, come on! It's swimming time followed by rock exploration. Put your trunks on. Leave your boots by the dunes. Run, Ralph run past the rocks, through the dunes and onto the beach. Get some speed up, boy. Now into the water. Swim two circles. Good lad. Swim with me.'

She moved effortlessly through the water. He was in awe of her. Finally they came back to shore and collapsed on the sand. They walked leisurely back to where their boots lay and put them on. He was amazed that Lorna took a size fourteen. The only other time he had seen her in boots was at the dress shop in Malvern and on that day he had been rather preoccupied.

'Those are the rocks,' Lorna said, pointing towards the large grey jagged outcrop. They climbed from rock to rock, helping each other along. They found a path hewn from the bare rock, which led all the way up to a wall with an iron gate. They pushed the gate open to find themselves on a grass verge by a main road. Quickly, they darted back into the privacy of the beach.

Hand in hand they walked back along a completely deserted beach. Ralph mused that they must look a rather comical sight. He considered passing his observation on to Lorna, but decided against it for fear of a discourse on her unparalleled beauty.

They reached the cottage and Lorna set about cooking breakfast, clunking around the kitchen in her army boots. Life was settling into a routine. Each morning the jogging and swimming became more gruelling. Ralph felt stronger and fitter for it. They won the talent contest again with a rousing rendering of 'The Road to Mandalay', but failed with 'Minstrel Boy'. Time was slipping by. Lorna asked Ralph to take her to dinner at a very expensive restaurant off the A38 called The Smugglers. Lorna told him that he must pay if only to assuage his uncalled for guilt over not paying his way.

'I shall be provocatively dressed for our farewell dinner, Ralph. Allow me that indulgence. I am a vulgar, uninhibited woman who likes attention. You will be well rid of me.'

The words struck a chord. Ralph was suddenly stricken with overwhelming pathos. He took her in his arms. 'Well rid of you? Well rid of you? Well rid of my honey-coloured babe, my darling eccentric, my beautiful Lorna, my only ever lover? Never! Never, ever! We have named the day for our departure on our separate ways, but it will be gradual and understanding. Please never demean yourself again before me. I love you dearly, even at your haughtiest and most dominant.'

Ralph booked a table for eight that evening and told Lorna that they must leave by seven. She was busy altering one of her flimsy kaftans. She cut the front spectacularly low and chopped the bottom down to about three inches above the knee. She emerged from the bedroom and asked Ralph what he thought.

'It's the ultimate in skimpiness. It's Lorna Mark I. Only you could get away with it. Are you taking a coat?'

'It's only a short walk from the car park to the entrance. If you insist I'll wear a coat, but I'll take it off as soon as we enter.'

Lorna felt eyes upon her as she swept into the restaurant, Ralph in her wake. She slung her overcoat over her shoulder. A waitress came up to them. 'Table for two in the name of Tucker.'

'Follow me sir.' She took them to a table hidden in the corner of what seemed to be a recent extension.

'This is rather a remote location,' Lorna remarked. 'Can't we sit in the main restaurant? I saw plenty of empty tables.'

'Very well, ma'am but–'

'But what?'

'It's your dress ma'am. It's rather – er – *small*.'

'Of course it's small. It's meant to be small. It's chic. It's modern. In a few years we'll be in the sixties. It will be called the Swinging Sixties and the fashions will make my outfit look fit for a nun. We'll have this table please.'

'Very well,' the waitress sighed. 'Let me pull this chair out so that your husband can get in.'

'He's not my husband.'

Ralph buried his nose in the large à la carte menu.

'Sorry, ma'am.'

'You weren't to know. He's actually my young virile lover. Isn't he handsome? He has a superb physique.'

Lorna's voice was booming across the restaurant. Ralph was trying to remain impassive, but inwardly he was squirming with embarrassment.

Finally Lorna came to the end of her eulogy by which time the whole restaurant knew about his gentle, tender lovemaking.

Thank God little Ralph and Little Lorna didn't get a mention, Ralph thought.

'How could you Lorna?' he asked

'Are you cross with me?'

'Just embarrassed.'

'You must never be embarrassed if somebody is praising you. You must look pleased with yourself. If you analyse it, I never said anything really embarrassing. I was going to mention your massive erection, but I thought better of it.'

'I'm glad you did. Why do you have to talk so loud?'

So that everybody will know about my Beautiful Boy.

'How can I argue with that?'

'You can't. When you go out into this 'real world' that everybody has told you about and you are taking all these pretty little girls out and they'll all be talking in whispers and you'll be fumbling around in the cinema or somewhere, trying to get your hand down their knickers and having to give up, that will be the time when you think of Lorna and her commanding voice, a voice trained to address the subservient classes – the authoritative *voice* of a *wom*an to be reckoned with – Me! Me, the lady of unparalleled beauty, knickerless, braless and always ready for some jolly good fun on the bed. You've been spoilt boy! Spoilt. I rest my case.'

'You've won.'

'Yes, I've won, which of course I always will, given my debating skills, but I have to admit that though you've been spoilt, then so have I. We've spoilt each other. Shall we order coffee and liqueurs? I think we shall. I see a spare waiter. I'll grab him.'

She walked the length of the restaurant, the lights shining on her diaphanous dress. It was not just her outline that appeared, it was everything.

Suddenly there were three waiters at the table.

They drove leisurely back. It was the last night. Tomorrow they would be driving home and the day after that Ralph was off on a long overdue little family holiday to the Derbyshire Dales. After that? It did not bear thinking of – eighteen months in a little bed, in a little tent, on a little island.

'Did you enjoy your little night out, darling?'

'I was angry at first but not anymore. You're incorrigible. Your dress was disgusting, but I think everybody liked it. And in answer to your question, yes, I enjoyed our little night out and I've never been anywhere with you when I haven't been happy.'

Chapter 13

Stonyfields

Veronica looked out from her room. Ralph, looking lean and fit, a battered old suitcase in his hand, was walking across the front lawn. She rushed out to meet him and jumped on him sending the suitcase flying.

'Beloved brother, you're earlier than expected. I'll ask Mother to lay a place at the table for you and we can all eat together when Dad gets home from work. How was Devon?'

'If you let me get inside, Veronica, I'll tell you.'

He picked up his suitcase and went into the house.

'You're looking great, good brother. You really fill that shirt out. It could be Marciano in there.'

Margaret appeared and embraced him.

'My son, my *son*. I'm going upstairs to dress for dinner. I wasn't certain when you'd be here, but now you are I'll put on something alluring.'

'How was Lorna?' Veronica asked. 'Did Little Ralph pay some visits?'

'We've got a different name for it now. We call it "Having jolly good fun on the bed".'

'Oh, jolly hockey sticks! Tucker of the lower sixth and Lorna the naughty matron, eh! Tell me about Wanstock,' Veronica urged.

'We've got days to talk. I'll tell you all in due course. At the moment I'm tired from the drive. I'm parched too, I'm wondering if my little sister will make me a cup of tea?'

'Has Tommy phoned?' Ralph asked.

'Yes, he's phoned. I see him every day albeit for short periods. We've put off renting a house. I'm happier here.

We'll get ourselves sorted out when the Cyprus stint is over.'

'Did you know that he's coming over tomorrow to see us off?'

'Yes. That's another thing that I'm not supposed to know isn't it? How can I help knowing? Tommy shows the engagement ring to the four of you, tells you when he's going to propose and expects it to be a secret.'

Margaret appeared in a cocktail dress.

'Bit low isn't it, Mother?' Veronica remarked.

'Of course it is. It's solely for Ralph. He's been used to Lorna Pitt's monster mammaries. I'm demonstrating that size is not everything. I'm in proportion.'

'You certainly are, Mother,' Ralph told her.

'Whereas Lorna Pitt is top heavy, not to mention her size fourteen feet and her huge hands with fingers like pork sausages.'

'That's a bit bitchy, isn't it Mother?'

'No it's not bitchy, it's honest. Everything should be in the open as far as best friends are concerned.'

'Anyone home?' Hugh shouted, 'I can't find my housekeys.'

'Ralph let him in.'

'It's my big son! You're looking fit as a fiddle. I don't think you need a walking holiday. You're fit enough already.'

'Just try and stop me, Dad. I've been looking forward to it.'

'We all have, son. When was the last time we all went away together? I reckon it was 1947 when you're Aunt Joyce and Uncle Phil put us up in that awful boarding house. Eight years ago! Eight years which covered a dark period in the Tucker saga. I lived in the pub. Margaret smothered you kids with affection and became a stout old drudge in the process, but now look at the difference as my glamorous lady enters and sits on my lap. Look at those legs. Look at that rump. Not an ounce of flab!'

'You sound as if you're talking about a racehorse, Dad,' Veronica said.

'Well, yes. A well-bred filly,' Hugh laughed.

The table was laid. The food was served. They chattered through the meal. Ralph released snippets of information on his week in Devon. He told them about bringing Lorna home each night in a wheelbarrow.

'That's useful knowledge for the future,' Veronica told him. 'When you're chatting up a girl, you say, 'Fancy a coffee at my place? I've got the wheelbarrow outside. Wait till you see it. Chrome and green leather interior and a silver wheel.'

'Bedtime,' Hugh cut in, 'big day tomorrow.'

It was 10 o'clock. Ralph was loading luggage into the car when Tommy's van appeared, pulled up on the gravel and disgorged an eager young man, immaculate in a dark suit.'

'Ralphy!' he shouted.

'I like the whistle and flute, Tommy,' Ralph said.

'Does anybody know?' Tommy asked.

'Of course not.'

'I wanted to do things in style. Know what I mean?'

'That's the kind of man you are. I'll get Mom and Dad and Veronica out here.'

Tommy waited nervously for them to appear. He walked over to Hugh.

'Hallo Tommy. To what do we owe the pleasure of this visit?'

'I come to seek your daughter's hand in marriage.'

'Very well spoken, Tommy. I shall continue in the same mode. My daughter waits within and lo! Her face appears at the window.'

'I see it.'

'It seems that she is still in night attire.'

'And yet I see her coming down the stairs.'

'A trifle immodest,' Hugh said, 'but in the circumstances, I shall allow it.'

'Tommy, Tommy,' Veronica yelled as she ran across to him and jumped on him like a frog as was her wont.

He took the ring from his pocket. 'Now Veronica, please don't giggle. I want to do things properly. Sit in that garden chair.'

'Hurry things up, Tommy. I'm freezing.'

She sat on the cane chair. Tommy knelt down before her and said, 'Veronica, will you marry me?'

'Yes, Tommy,' she said sombrely, 'I shall marry you.'

He kissed her hand, presented the ring and rose to his feet whilst Ralph, Margaret and Hugh clapped and cheered.

'I thought it would be a nice, little going-away present' Tommy said.

'Let's hit the road,' Hugh said, and they headed for Lichfield, thence Ashbourne where they planned to stop for a drink, and on towards Buxton.

'Look for a left turn for Stonyfields,' Hugh told them. 'It should be coming up.'

'There it is, Dad,' Veronica said.

They found themselves on a narrow road for what seemed an age until they went past the Stonyfields sign. 'There's our pub!' Hugh pointed to a rambling stone building. 'Remember it, Margaret?' The Prince Harry Hotel – Bed, Breakfast and Dinner. They pulled onto the patch of ground in front of the hotel lounge. Only one car was parked there.

The Prince Harry was completely devoid of visitors.

'You've come at a very quiet time,' Mr Peverell, the owner said.

'Circumstances,' Hugh said. 'My son's due to fly out to Cyprus in the army soon. This is a little going-away present for him.'

‘And I believe you and your wife have a good reason to be here too.’

‘Yes, indeed. We spent our honeymoon here in 1936.We walked for miles. We’re going to retrace our footsteps if we can.’

‘I’m sure you can. Nothing much has changed since you were last here. I’ve got plenty of guidebooks in reception if you need them, but you look the sort of people to have worked things out. Here’s your keys – one double and two singles. Dinner’s at 7.30. Bar open from 6 pm to last drinker standing. Can you imagine any police car coming here?’

They went to their room and reappeared for pre-dinner drinks at 6 pm.

‘What a lovely little holiday this is going to be,’ Margaret enthused. ‘Your father will work out every walk and they all include a lunchtime pub call.’

‘So we don’t have to think for ourselves?’ Ralph asked. ‘Suits me. If there’s one thing I’m not interested in doing, it’s map reading.’

‘So how did you leave things with Lorna?’ Veronica asked. They had just climbed quite a steep gradient and were now on an easy track along a ridge.

‘I left things – how shall I put it? On an even keel. A status quo situation. As things stand.’

‘Try and give me an accurate answer minus the gobbledegook.’

‘Right. She’ll stay in touch by letter all through my time in Cyprus. She’s an army widow and she was an army wife. She realises the importance of men and their loved ones keeping in touch. There will be two people I shall write to. They are Lorna and you (to be passed on to Mom and Dad). There will be a long disembarkation leave after Cyprus. Lorna and I will start going our separate ways, but we shall still be in touch. We shall gradually drag ourselves away from each other. During this time, I will be trying to plan my own future. One way or another we shall have, for all intents and purposes, parted by my demob date. Lorna has said that she is not reverting to the lonely spinsterish life she had after losing Roger. She *will* have a life. She will actively seek out people – men friends, women friends, maybe lovers. She has plans in life. She will do her duty in regard to her grandchildren.

'So there it is, Veronica. On August 24th 1958, I am on my own. Lorna has told me only to get in touch in an emergency, that is to say, desperately lonely or in trouble. That won't happen. I know what I shall be doing. I'll be okay, the plan may change a little to adjust to the circumstances but there you have it.'

'It all makes good common sense, dear brother. I know you'll stick to it. You're a stubborn as a mule when you have to be. That's something I've always liked about you. If Lorna was really involved with someone else, would you be jealous?'

'There would be pangs of jealousy maybe, but I could handle it. I know I could. Here comes Mom and Dad. They look worn out.'

'Oh, to be young again,' Hugh said wearily.

Their little holiday was almost over. It had been unique. They felt stronger as a family. To use a twenty-first century expression, they had bonded. Tommy's proposal had warmed and reassured them.

The Prince Harry pub, though empty by day, was lively in the evenings with local trade. It seemed the population of Stonyfields were mainly retired. They were a varied group – farmers who had passed their farms on to the next generation and were glad to be out of it, (it was tough land to farm), ex-service men (mainly officers), schoolteachers, an old sea captain nicknamed The Ancient Mariner, all sorts of folk with one thing in common: they liked a drink and a yarn. The Prince Harry was built in 1759. The battles of a dozen wars had been fought out within its walls. Battles were won on its tables. Imagine the gruff old timers' voices.

'This pepper pot is where we were. Somewhere down by this fag packet was Piet de Wet and somewhere back round here by the ashtray were reinforcements from the Durham Light Infantry on only their third week in South Africa. You could see what a predicament we were in…'

'I remember an old boy who used to go into the Royal Oak in Walsall,' Hugh said. 'He'd been in the Crimean War. This was in the thirties. The Crimean War was eighty years before. Was it, possible? We used to debate it. He must have been a hundred. He knew what he was talking about too!' They were passing through Ashbourne. 'Yes, we've all done our time. Mine was the Russian convoys. What will your experiences be, Ralph?'

'Let's just get them all back home,' Veronica cut in. 'My Ralph, my Tommy, Stan the man, Duggie and Big Dennis.'

It was the day before embarkation leave ended. Tommy had called a meeting at the Fullbrook pub.

'We're going to try to get a few things sorted out,' he said. 'We've heard on the grapevine that B Company is short of at least five men.'

'What grapevine?' Stan asked.

'Blokes arriving home on demob and talking in the pub. We're going to see if any of us can get into the same company or better still, the same platoon or even the same tent.'

'How are we going to do that?' Dennis asked.

'We don't know,' Tommy said. 'We simply don't know how things work out over there. Let's see how and if we can swing it.'

'It's a step into the unknown, isn't it?' Ralph said. 'Remember when we did our training. The training NCOs always said that things were different in the Battalion, but they never said how. Maybe they allocate postings to platoons in a way that you can always be with your mates.'

'Well,' Dennis reasoned, 'I think that the word 'different' means that it's a hellhole compared to the Depot and it doesn't matter if you're in A.B.C.D.HQ or Support Company, it's still a hellhole.'

'I've spoken to some of these blokes coming back on demob,' Duggie said. 'They give you a load of bullshit. They make it sound like the Battle of Waterloo. Let's just get out there and do the best we can to stay together.'

'All right, lads,' Tommy said. 'Let's trust to luck. The drill is this. Be at Walsall Bus Station at twelve noon tomorrow.'

Chapter 14

Battalion

It was 0800 hrs on December 16th 1955 Draft DAQPZ of the Grey Jackets stood in three ranks, their kitbags stacked nearby. Sergeant Edwards marched over.

'Good morning lads' he shouted, 'Good leave?'

'Yes Sarnt.' They cried in unison.

'Did you exercise self-discipline or did you indulge in regular shagging?' he yelled.

'Indulged in regular shagging, Sarnt.'

'Did you retain your high level of fitness or were you in the pub every night?'

'In the pub every night, Sarnt!'

'I have come to wish you luck. There will be a regular sergeant with you – Sergeant Sam Hope. He's one of the old school. You will like him and that is an order. I told him that you were the best intake of recruits I ever had. Goodbye men!'

'Goodbye Sarnt!'

Sergeant Hope arrived. He was not the archetypal senior NCO. He was lanky and had an unsoldierly gait.

'Stand at ease, stand easy. Nobody knows what's happening yet. Get yourselves into that empty block. Take all your equipment and wait. The army's all about waiting as you must know by now.'

They trooped into Alma Block. There were mattresses on the beds which meant that they could sit down.

'Who's for a game of three card brag?' Ralph asked, holding the brand new pack that Nan Tucker had given him.

There were a few murmurings, then some okays and soon there was a school of six. Dennis and Tommy stayed out. Tommy said that it was pointless taking each other's money. Better to take some other mugs' money.

'Brand new,' Ralph announced, brandishing the cards. 'Never been used.' He shuffled them thoroughly and asked who wanted to deal. The game got under way on penny stakes. Occasionally somebody would raise it to twopence or threepence. Time drifted by. Nobody seemed to be getting decent hands. Money was being won on Jack high or a pair of twos.

Things suddenly changed. Ralph picked up his cards. He had three kings. He remained motionless. Pennies started going in. He raised it to twopence and all five players stayed with him. Another player raised it to threepence. Nobody threw their cards in. Ralph raised it to sixpence. A player raised it to a shilling. It was getting serious. There was a gathering forming around the beds. Tommy told them to disperse in case they started giving out signals. Everybody put their cards face downwards. Somebody raised the stake to two shillings, then half a crown. Ralph took out his wallet and put a ten-shilling note down. Two players stayed in. He upped it to £1. They both stayed with him. One of the last three players, Billy Matthews, threw in his hand in announcing that he was broke but for a few coppers. It was now between Ralph and the discredited braggart whom they called Barnyard. Amazingly Barnyard stayed with the game until Ralph threw down the contents of his trouser pocket and said 'I'll see you'. There was a broad grin on Barnyard's face as he threw down three queens and went to scoop up the money. The onlookers told him not to touch the kitty yet. Triumphant Ralph threw down his three kings.

A great cheer went up. Dennis came over and hugged him and whispered, 'Let me and Tommy hold that money Ralph. Everybody knows you won it. There's the best part of fifteen quid here. You don't want to be walking around with that sort of money. Let's spread it over a few weeks and have a beer or two or three or a hundred.'

'You do what's right, Dennis. One for all and all for one.'

Sergeant Hope burst in. 'Right lads, you're on your way. The vehicles are outside. Central India Squad in the front bus. Lucknow in the rear bus. By road, train, bus and plane you are off to Nicosia. And so am I! I'm ever present so behave yourselves. You're spending tonight at the Royal Artillery barracks in Woolwich. It's a horrible place and will make you wish you were in Cyprus, which is the general idea. Oh, there's something I nearly forgot to tell you. There is a card game called Regimental Rummy. That is the game that you are allowed to play in off duty periods. Gambling games are not allowed. You wouldn't gamble, would you?'

'No Sarnt!' They all roared. The news of early embarkation was like a bolt from the blue. They had all expected to be put into Holding Company and given dreary tasks like delivering coal to the married quarters. Instead they were on their way.

'What was all the bullshit about Christmas leave?' Tommy grumbled as they loaded into the buses.

'Maybe it's a good thing,' Ralph said, 'Let's get out there and get on with it. I'm going to ask Sergeant Hope if I can make a phone call. I'll tell Lorna that there'll be no Christmas leave. She'll pass it on to Nan Tucker and from then on it'll spread like wildfire. He asked Sergeant Hope if he could make the call.

'Yes, all right son. There are two phone boxes near the main road entrance. Double over there, make your call and double back. We'll wait for you but make it snappy. No conversations. Just say, 'No Christmas leave. Pass it on.'

'It looks as though we've had a bit of luck, Sarnt Major.' Major Cunningham said.

'What sort of luck, sir?'

‘Well it seems that five of the draft that arrived last week heard it on the grapevine back home that B Company were short of men. They wanted to stay together so they took the initiative of presenting themselves here at the Company Office at 0800 hrs today and asked if they could join B Company. You were on parade at the time Sarnt Major.’

‘Five new men would bring us up to strength, sir.’

‘You haven’t heard it all. One man won best recruit and two others are possibly potential officers. Anyway I’ve taken them. If I’ve broken any rules, it’s tough.’

‘Don’t forget we’ve taken one of the draft transferred in from the Worcesters, sir.’

‘Oh?’

‘Braddox ,sir’

‘The big fellow with the fearsome moustache? Yes, I’d forgotten him. So that means we’ve got six men good and true making us one over strength.’

‘It’s NCOs we need sir.’

‘We’ll get some stripes on them but not yet.’

Privates Ward, Tucker, Holmer, Compton, Jennings and Braddox appeared on muster parade next morning. Four-platoon commander, Mr McLeod arrived. Sergeant Westlake brought the platoon to attention.

‘Stand at ease, stand easy,’ Mr McLeod ordered. ‘We have some new men, have we not? Please answer ‘Sir.’ Ward

‘Sir.’

‘Tucker.’

‘Sir.’

‘Holmer.’

‘Sir.’

‘Compton.’

‘Sir.’

‘Jennings.’

‘Sir.’

‘Braddox.’

'Sir.'

Sergeant Westlake ordered the platoon to fall out except for the new men. 'You're on Police Station guards. Check on the board to see where you have to go. We leave at 0930. Go back to your tents. Get things sorted out. Draw your rifles from the armoury. These are easy little guards – a good way to start.'

Ralph decided that Yerrolakos police station was an ideal place to write a letter to Veronica

Whittington Camp Nicosia December 1955

Dearest Veronica (Please pass on to Mom and Dad),

At last I've got time to write a proper letter. I'm on a police station guard stuck out in the country – Corporal Phillips, Tommy and I plus another new man named George Braddox, one of a draft transferred in from the Worcestershire Regiment He's a huge man with a big moustache who rarely stops talking. It's like listening to Worzel Gummidge. We do two hours on and four hours off around the clock. It's actually quite peaceful. We cook for ourselves (well, in a limited way) and we swap stuff with the villagers. For a tin of oatmeal biscuits or any item of 'Compo' ration we can get maybe some watermelons or eggs. I'm no bargainer. Tommy's a natural barterer. We leave it to Tommy or Corporal Phillips. Last night at about 2300 hours when I was on 'stag', an object was thrown at us from the direction of the church. Whatever it was, it landed with a tinny sound. I could not see any movement. I called the guard out. Corporal Phillips and Tommy carried out a little patrol along the street. The object was the shell of a Mills 36 grenade – no detonator, no pin or ring. Nevertheless we reported it on the radio and the bomb disposal blokes came out next morning. Maybe it was a warning. The church was flying a Greek flag. So I have been officially 'attacked'. It occurs to me that mail may be censored – I'll have to find out but I doubt it. The only instructions we have been given on mail are to write at least weekly to our next of kin. Anyway that little incident was last night. Today's today and I am sitting on an old cane chair writing this letter. I've been trying to read a paperback – a Ngaio Marsh story – I don't like detective books much, but it's about the best of the ragged old Penguin books lying around. From this rickety chair I look out over a grassy plain to the Kyrenia range of mountains, which seem to change colour in the sun. Right now they're pink. In the corner of a field I see a solitary donkey. I wonder what he makes of it all. That's your travel brochure description. Nothing else to report or November Tango Romeo as we say in the trade.

I haven't written to Lorna yet. She has always told me that she doesn't want to hear about the army so that kind of narrows the material down a bit considering I'm in the army twenty-four hours a day. We shall probably write on other things – she's always been keen on commenting on my poetry. Between you and me, I'd like to get a really steamy letter from her – no I wouldn't. I've suddenly come over sleepy so bye little sister.

Christmas came to Cyprus. It was as cold a day as one would get back in Blighty. Sergeants followed the tradition of bringing a morning cup of tea to the rank and file in the tent lines. Ralph was woken by Sergeant Westlake.

'Hold your mug out son.'

He poured out half a cup of tea and topped it to the brim with rum. He did the same for Tommy and George.

'Merry Christmas lads.'

'And Merry Christmas to you, Sarnt,' they said as he moved on down 4 Platoon lines.

‘We’ll be pissed before we start,’ Tommy said.

‘That’s the general idea, Tommy,’ Ralph told him.

‘Some hopes of getting pissed on half a mug of rum,’ George moaned. ‘Where are we going to get more booze? The Naafi’s closed.’

Ralph pulled his soldiers’ box from under his bed and took out a brown paper package.

‘Shall we see what Uncle Ralph has got?’

He unwrapped the paper.

‘A bottle of Scotch!’ Tommy said. ‘A big one too – 40oz. Dare I ask how you got this here, Ralph?’

‘In my kitbag. It had clothes all round it. I thought it would be safe enough and it was.’

‘Just about the most idiotic thing you’ve ever done, Ralph, but we’re glad you did it. I’m going to get Dennis, Duggie and Stan in here.’

Ralph poured out six measures into their tin mugs.

‘Take it easy, chaps,’ Dennis warned. ‘This is neat whisky. We need to dilute it. I’m going down to the ablution block. I’ll take a few water bottles down with me. Don’t touch a drop before I’m back. We’ll have a civilised session.’

‘A gentlemanly piss up,’ Tommy said.

‘A squirearchical beano. Here’s to whisky but don’t take in a drop until Dennis returns,’ Ralph said.

Dennis was soon back with some full water bottles.

Ralph poured a measure into each mug. There’s a nice, modest mixture we’ve got all day in front of us.’

‘Including Christmas lunch,’ Stan said.

‘They can stick that,’ Denis said. ‘They serve up awful stuff every day. Who says they’ll get it right for Christmas? I’ve got two big tins of biscuits that my mom and my auntie sent me. We’ll eat those.’

‘So we’re all set up,’ Tommy said. ‘We’ll stay here all day and spin yarns or sing or sleep.’

Mr McLeod appeared at the bottom of the tent lines and worked his way along.'

'It's Mr McLeod,' Duggie said, 'all dressed up in battle dress, his stick under his arm. He must be Orderly Officer. I think we ought to offer him a drink.'

'You're wasting good whisky, Duggie,' George said. 'The Scots don't celebrate Christmas. They've got their own festival. It's called Mahogany.'

'Would you like a drink, sir?' Duggie shouted.

Mr McLeod came into the tent.

'Nice and cosy in, here,' he remarked. 'Thanks boys, but I'm on duty so I shouldn't drink. On the other hand, have you ever known a Scotsman refuse a whisky? I'll just have a sip from one of the mugs. Slainte.'

'And Slanjee to you sir,' Dennis said 'whatever it means.'

'It means good health, Holmer and sincerely I wish you all good health, but I must be on my way.' He took Duggie and Ralph aside and said quietly to them, 'When the day comes it will be my great pleasure to buy you both a drink in the Officers' Mess. Have a good drink today and be back tomorrow none the worse for it.'

'There goes a decent officer,' Duggie said. 'I wish they were all like that. I don't want to appear a know all, George, but the Scots celebrate Hogmanay.'

'That's right, Duggie. Mahogany's a type of wood. You spotted my deliberate mistake. Come on lads. Let's have another.'

Inevitably they began to sing beginning with The Rock n Roll waltz. The words echoed through the lines. In no time it seemed as if the whole battalion were singing.

Stanhope Hall, January 1956

Dear Beautiful Boy,

I read your letter to Veronica. You're right. If I don't want to hear about the army (which is presently your

life) then I am reducing the subject matter considerably. So write what you like. Yes, send me some poetry. My news? Sarah will be here very soon. The baby's due in February. I know! Absolutely know that it will be a boy. I'm going to be busy (I hope). Their flat is ready. I will be on call next door. Sarah insists that I do not walk around unclothed in case it confuses the child. Well, I'm going to comply for the sake of harmony in the family. However, it's going to be quite an ordeal for me. I'm so used to being able to do what I choose in my own property. When one is blessed with unparalleled beauty, one has a duty to display oneself.
I bet you had a boozy time at Christmas. Tell me about it. I was honoured to be invited to Nan Tucker's Christmas party with specific orders not to take my clothes off. Veronica has already written about the event. There's an amusing letter flying out to you. Write when you like about anything you like.
Your ever-loving Lorna.

P.S. I mean, thinking about it, Ralph, I may as well be living in a nunnery. I'm surrounded by prudishness. I'm confronted with it wherever I go. Remember the awful time I had in that dress shop in Malvern just because I refused to use that poky little changing room?
You understand me though, don't you darling? I wish Sarah did. 'Sometimes mother, I think you're on a different planet.' is what she said to me today on the phone. I wish I had you in my arms.
Love again, Lorna

Dear adorable brother,
I'm not dating my letters any more. It just reminds me of how long you and Tommy are going to be away. Tell me about Christmas, however bleak it was.

Nan Tucker's Christmas party lived up to its name. As usual Uncles Sid, Bryn and Jacob plus Granddads Rowley and Tucker got stuck into the bottled beer and played the perennial game of Newmarket. There was so much cheating going on by the two granddads that the game nearly developed into a fight. Nan Tucker intervened in her usual subtle way. She brandished the biggest frying pan in the kitchen and threatened to whack them all over the head unless they behaved themselves. Uncle Bryn told them to wind the game up, after which the usual political debate began – Lloyd George, Churchill, Eden – theory is that they were all womanising rogues if the truth were known. Aunt Lorna had been invited on the strict understanding that she did not take her clothes off. She duly arrived looking demure in her smart maroon office outfit. As the room got hotter from both Nan Tucker's coal fire and the sheer numbers crammed into the house, the men were all down to shirtsleeves. Aunt Lorna stuck it out for as long as she could but ultimately had to announce that she would have to take off her blazer. Her monster mammaries (to use Mother's expression) were literally crushed into her blouse. Uncle Sid and the two granddads were immediate fans and told Lorna so. She told them that it was reassuring to know that her unsurpassed beauty was appreciated.

In the meantime Mom and Dad arrived. Mom wore a cocktail dress and some really trashy purple high heels with straps. Nan Tucker went into action immediately. 'Trust that Maggie Rowley to lower the tone of the party. She looks as if she's been shopping in Brownhills market; Heaven knows what my boy has to put up with. He must be a saint.' More was yet to come. Aunt Lorna came in to clear away the beer bottles. As she leant over the table her huge tits fell out. Her right nipple went in

Uncle Jacob's right eye. The room was rocking with laughter.

'That's it!' Nan Tucker bawled across the room. I might have known it. I should never have invited Maggie Rowley or that Wicked Widow. They're barred. I should have known better. Christmas is over – ruined by two tarts.'

'Course it's not over,' Grandad Tucker growled. 'It's the best Christmas we've ever had. It's early yet. Lorna and Margaret, give us a song.' They sang 'White Cliffs of Dover' and 'We'll Meet Again' and 'Lily of Laguna' and got a great cheer, mainly because Aunt Lorna had finally lost the battle between bust and blouse.

Nan Tucker realised that she was in a minority of one and decided to let the party take its course. 'I'd got a little Christmas treat lined up for you, but you've behaved so badly that I'm not sure any more.'

'Go on Mother,' Dad said. Nan Tucker told them that there was a corked bottle of champagne in the cellar and that it was about time it got cracked. It was covered in dust. Dad asked if Nan was sure about opening it. She told him to go ahead; the bottle was stuck to the shelf. Dad had to get it off by prising a knife underneath it. Finally they loosened it. 'Leave this to me,' Dad said. He unwired the cork and with absolute confidence he said, 'this is how you do it!' He held the bottle upright and gradually prised the cork off with his thumbs. Suddenly there was a hell of a bang. The giant cork shot out like a cannon ball and so did the contents, like spume from a whale. The whole Methuselah (that was what it was – eight times the standard size) hit the ceiling and came down on Dad. There was the foulest stink imaginable. Dad was like a drowned rat. 'Have you got any more Christmas treats, Mom?' he asked.

I hope you enjoyed my little Christmas story, good brother. I really do miss you. I'm so glad we had that little holiday together. It marked the end of childhood. The end of teenage too, I suppose.

Love you forever and look after yourselves. I love you all.

Tommy, Ralph and their mates soon got into the swing of things. Theirs was a continuous round of guards and patrols. It was a nomadic existence. They were split into small units, sections under a corporal with a lance corporal in the Bren group. The battalion seemed to be continually under strength. Only three months had passed before Tommy and Ralph were considered responsible enough to be promoted to Lance Jacks. George, Duggie, Stan and Dennis were given stripes six weeks after that. The platoons were reorganized. Tommy, Ralph and George stayed in 4 platoon. The rest went to 5 platoon. That meant that they were sometimes split up completely for periods, but, as Dennis said, 'Let's get this Arbo Gang stuff into perspective. This is the army, not Chuckery infants. We do what we're told. We don't cry because we're separated from our little friends. Duggie and I are on the Post Office guard next week while the rest of us are at GHQ. That's the way it is.'

Ralph received a letter from Lorna to say that Sarah's baby (her grandson) had arrived, weighing in at seven pounds. She sounded so happy and enthusiastic –

Oh, how I wish, I wish, I wish that the parents were you and Sarah. That had been my dream since the first time I visited you during the war. Enough of that 'might have been' stuff. The boy will be named Jerome Ralph Pitt. Jerome after Jerome K. Jerome of course so that wherever he is in the world he will remember that he's a Walsall man. You will have to be a surrogate father to him at times. Anyway I'm deliriously happy, but that is not to say that I have forgotten you. You're about five

months into your time. I told you that time would fly. I kiss your photo each night and morning. How shall I fall out of love with you? With the long term in view I suppose I should start eyeing up some blokes, but what a damned waste of time that is likely to be with my Beautiful Boy stuck out in the heat and dust for another year. I think I'll stick with being a grandma.
I love you Lorna

Dearest Lorna.
I said I would send you a poem and here it is. It's a ballad a la Kipling. Kipling wrote of and for the common soldier, did he not? He was ever conscious of the way the common soldier was treated. How people can refer to him as a jingoist I do not know. Anyway I hope you enjoy the verse. I put quite a bit of time into it.

ROCK AND ROLL AT LAST

Remember the days when all was dust
And dirt and flies and rifle rust?
A limp flag hung from a lonely pole
In the breathless summer evening.

We heard through the haze of waning heat,
The duty bugler blow retreat.
The long sad notes hovered a while
In the velvet Cyprus evening.

The guard was still on the hard earth square.
Their khaki drill and crew cut hair
Gave them bronzed anonymity
As they stood on parade in the evening.

Beneath a hill and all around
The tent lines straddled the boot worn ground.

In the canvas gloom men dozed and dreamed
Of factory walls in the evening.

Throughout the day in Nicosia,
They had been on duty without a beer,
Weapons held at the high port,
In Ledra Street patrolling.

Others lay in the hours between guards,
Reading comics or playing cards.
Vengeance crazed men were out there somewhere.
The mares of terror were foaling.

Little we cared for political views,
While Elvis Presley sang 'Blue suede shoes'
The year was nineteen fifty-six.
The world was Rock and Rolling.

Radios blared. The guitar beat
Cut cool holes through the aching heat.
We were not sure what had begun
But we found it most consoling.

Hope to hear from you soon. I see you sometimes
through the shimmering heat, you fade and then you go.

Yes. They found it most consoling. The younger generation had taken over popular music. Thank God for that. No more would be Sinatras. No more mournful crooners. No more silly songs about 'itsy bitsy teeny weeny yellow polka dot bikinis'. No more big bands thumping out their doo wacka doo wacka doo wacka doo music. Rock and Roll had taken over. From now on youth would be revered, extremely spoilt and unjustly feared. At the outdoor camp cinema they saw 'Rock around the Clock' with Bill Haley, and stomped to the rhythm:

We're gonna rock around the clock tonight.
We're gonna rock rock rock till broad daylight.

They heard that cinema audiences back home had gone wild. Blighty now meant much more than simply home, much more than semi-detached normality. It meant a world of dance floors in a frenzy of high-swirling skirts, ponytails, waspy belts and beehive hairdos. They couldn't wait to be back home and be part of it. Some of the lads were naive and hopeful enough to think that they would have the pick of the girls when they arrived back as suntanned heroes ready to hit the dance floor. The realists were not so sure. Either way it was good to dream.

For the present and foreseeable future, they were locked into a far, far different culture from early Rock and Roll. They were the unlikely, undeserving, bewildered inheritors of the poor old redcoats of the 38th Regiment of foot. This was the 1st Battalion the Grey Jackets on active service at Whittington Camp, Nicosia. The Grey Jackets had served in half the known world. From Guadeloupe in 1759 to Martinique, Montevideo, Badajoz, Lucknow, Sebastopol, Egypt, Afghanistan, South Africa, France, Flanders, Sicily, Arnhem and on and on, with many a battle in between covering the Peninsular War, the Indian mutiny, the Crimea, the Boer War, the Great War and World War II. No doubt there would be more battle honours to come. They had fought the Dutch, the French, the Russians, the Boers, the Germans and now not fighting anybody in the true sense of the word. They were policing, looking after Internal Security. The enemy was the terrorist group EOKA who wanted independence.

Nobody knows for sure how the Grey Jackets got their name. The official reason was that they were more or less abandoned in the Caribbean for over fifty years. Their uniforms wore out and they had to replace them with home-made clothes of a hessian type material known as Holland cloth, greyish in colour. Even now in 1956, they still wear Holland patches behind their cap badges and on their collars, which incorporate a metal Staffordshire knot symbolising the fact that the majority of Grey Jackets come from the Black Country.

Ralph Tucker can still remember the layout of Whittington camp. The entrance was on a main road (Troodos Road). The first building on the right was the Guardroom, manned by the hated Regimental Police. Behind the guardroom was a jumble of buildings including the Quartermasters' store and a little sandwich shop called Pops. The road into camp bore to the left by a triangular patch of ground used for guard mounting and dismounting of the battalion Quarter Guard who manned the guardroom by night. On the opposite side of the road were the offices of the Adjutant and staff, The Orderly Room and the Paymasters set out like a three sided square.

In this complex there was also the office of the C.O. Lt Col Arthur Wood. Further along the road were the vehicles and workshops of the MT Platoon. From there the road led to the Officers' Mess and quarters. A road forked off the Troodos Road to another camp called Waynes Keep. This road bordered the square, used for football and band practice as well as the dreaded RSMs parade on Saturday mornings. Beyond the square were the ablution blocks, the Naafi, the Knot club and the tent lines of HQ Company, Support company and A, B and C Companies. On the higher ground above the tent lines stood the cookhouse and dining halls. Also in this canvas and corrugated iron jungle were the latrines, the Post Office, the Intelligence section, the medical centre, the tailor, the cobbler, the barber, the chapel, the REME, the sergeant's mess and the individual company offices with their stores and armouries.

Imagine the impact of this place of clamour and movement on each new group of raw inexperienced soldiery arriving travel worn, itchy, dirty and tired, to be marched off immediately to the cookhouse queue, not very eager to fill themselves with undercooked food, which, within weeks, they would be eating with gusto.

It was essential to learn the lingo immediately – not the dialect that consisted of variations of Black Country – but the army vocabulary. Your rifle was your 'bondook'; being 'Alakefik' meant that you were relaxed about things. It was said a lot. To some it was a way of saying they did care but pretended they did not. 'Buckshee' meant free, left over or extra but (maybe only in the Grey Jackets) buckshee meant a private soldier. 'Dhobi' meant laundry. The laundry-men were 'dhobi wallahs'. There were other 'wallahs' - office wallahs, store wallahs and cha wallahs, Indian camp followers who served tea, along the camp lines at night. Sometimes in his sleep in later years Ralph heard their wails – 'Cha wallah! Cha wallah!' It was awful tea, usually, some suspected, the remnants of the mealtime's supply, but bought it and drank it all the same.

Nobody ever lied in the Grey Jackets. They talked bullshit. If you were a continuous waffler, you talked 'a load of bullshit' or 'the biggest load of bullshit we've ever heard'. Bullshit was said to baffle brains. 'Bullshit artists' did not talk bullshit all the time. They often talked a load of crap or a load of bollocks. If you talked 'a load of bollocks' you became a 'bollockbrain'. Bollockbrains were usually 'as thick as pig shit', 'thick as oak trees', 'thick as a plank' or 'two short planks'. Quiet men were 'dozy bastards'. Complainers were 'moaning bastards', and were continually reminded that they were not on 'Daddy's Yacht.' 'Big-headed bastards' and 'Smart arses' were not tolerated and did not stay big-headed or smart for long. They were relegated to the very bottom ranks inhabited by loathsome little creatures such as frogs, grubs, worms or sprogs. A way to avoid this tiresome abuse was to get some 'gonk' in. Gonk meant sleep. The army was a great leveller. You gave as good as you got. Standard exchanges of venom had you called an ‘arsehole’ and a ‘wanker’. Whatever sort of person you were there was a name for you. A tall man was a ‘long streak of piss’, a short man was a ‘short-arsed little git’. If you came from anywhere outside the Black Country, you were a ‘Brummy bastard’, a ‘Scouse bastard’, a ‘Geordie bastard’, depending where you came from.

The most feared man in the battalion was RSM Bill Chancellor. He was on the prowl all day. If your hair was slightly longer than regulatory you were a sitting duck for the RSM. He would order you to the barbers. This Cypriot barber had a huge blown up photograph of Bill Chancellor on the canvas wall of his shop. No wonder! The RSM gave him a continuous stream of business.

If Bill Chancellor saw a man with slightly shorter than normal shorts, he would send him back to change. ‘Get out of that bikini,’ he would yell. It was not the rank and file’s fault that they often finished up with ill-fitting khaki drill. They put their dirty items into the dhobi and rarely got the same clothes back. A lot of men did their own washing especially in the summer months when they could hang clothes up in the tent lines.

Nobody was spared the wrath of the RSM on the dreaded Saturday morning RSMs parade which had to be attended by however many were in camp on that particular day. Even officers were not spared the thundering menace of his temper:

‘Get a grip of yourself, Mr Pottinger, sah! You are marching like a man with two hairs of his arse stuck together.’

So this was the Grey Jackets on active service where they were all bastards talking crap and moaning – National Servicemen or three year regulars. Officers and senior NCOs were usually time serving men. The general opinion among the men was that anybody who wanted to do more than three years was crazy. They would be back in civvies again while the professional soldiers would be in some godforsaken place getting their arses shot off.

In the meantime, bugles blew, trucks rolled in and out of camp loaded with men going God knows where on this picturesque but accursed island. Platoons marched singing the unofficial regimental song:

> How I love my mother-in-law, although she's ninety four. She's coming round today, but I wish she'd stayed away.
> I've greased all the stairs, knocked nails in all the chairs.
> How I love her, my wife's mother, how I love my mother–in-law.
> One night in gay Paree. I paid five francs to see
> her great big fat Cherie, tattooed from head to knee.
> All up and down her spine were the thirty-eighth in line, and on her lilywhite bum, bum, bum was a picture of the rising sun sun sun and under her crumpet was Harry James's trumpet, and on her back was the Union Jack, so I paid five francs more.

Singing is good for the soul. Pay night in the Naafi was a great night out by any standards, with numerous solo performances. The same man always kicked off with 'Down in the Caribbean, it's not a dream you see' closely followed by a Corporal who appeared as Al Jolson, black-faced, white lips and all. He would sing, 'Mammy, mammy! The sun shines east, the sun shines west.' Ralph sang 'Unchained Melody' and sometimes 'Save the Last Dance for Me'

Now, of course, there was the new music – 'Blue Suede Shoes', 'Heartbreak Hotel' and 'You Ain't Nothing But a Hound Dog.' Some tried to imitate Elvis's powerful raw style. They never could and they never would. Dennis got the nearest. He would really belt it out. Maybe one day he *would* be an entertainer.

Sometimes somebody was singled out and made to sing. 'Sing sing or show us your ring.' everybody would shout. All in all there was no malice, pay nights at the Naafi were genuinely times of true camaraderie, fuelled by music and beer. The tedious bickering of the tent lines was forgotten. The Naafi served one drink – a beer called Keo. You either drank from a huge bottle or the barman gave you a teacup to pour your beer into. Ralph always opted for a bottle. He felt an idiot transferring it into a teacup. Drinking to get drunk was looked down on. The pride was in 'holding your beer'.

So they drank from their huge bottles and talked of their dreams as the sky turned to indigo and for those precious moments, Cyprus was not that bad.

On one such balmy evening Duggie, Tommy, Stan and Ralph were sitting out in the open area between the Naafi and the Knot club, talking about a soldier's dearest wish – demob.

'After we get this tour over next May, it's going to be a doddle,' Tommy said. 'We get a big chunk of leave, then we're back to the depot and, except for guard duty, we can probably thumb a lift home most nights. After that, it's Germany. Germany's got to be easier than this.'

'Don't be so sure,' Duggie warned. 'I've heard that Germany's a real bastard. It's all playing soldiers. You're out on schemes in the dead of winter, freezing your balls off in some forest. The only good thing about Germany is your leisure time. You can get out in the evenings, walk round town, have a lager or two at some roadside cafe, pick up a big blonde fraulein or two, stay out all night if you want to, as long as you're back for muster parade.'

'You're dreaming, Duggie. The Germans don't like us,' Ralph cut in. 'Who can blame them? We're an occupying army. I reckon that picking up a fraulein would be nigh on impossible. Anyway, never mind all that. We're talking about demob.'

‘I can’t wait to get back,’ Tommy said. ‘Ron’s really struggling with the business. He took on a bloke who wasn’t up to scratch. That’s given us a bad name. Business has gone down. I’m stuck out here – ineffective. I tell you it’s like a house of cards.’

‘How can you expect to run a business from the army, Tommy?’ Duggie asked. ‘You’ve got one thing going for you – your determination. You know what you want to do, you’ll get there. The army’s a hiccup. It’s the same with Dennis. He knows what he wants too. He’ll get there, so will Stan the artist and George the builder. You’ll all make it. Ralph and I though, we’re the ones who don’t know where we’re going. We’ve just got this dream of bumming round Australia or Canada or somewhere.’

‘It doesn’t have to be a dream, Duggie. We can do it. Anyway, you’ve got to have a dream.’ They burst into song.

‘You’ve got to have a dream. If you don’t have a dream, how are you going to make your dream come true?’

‘I’ll tell you what, Ralph,’ Duggie said. ‘If we go to Australia together and fall out, then we go our separate ways. If a woman came on the scene, which is quite likely given my looks and charm, she comes first. Love interest is a far higher priority than mateship.’

‘You should know, Duggie. I can live with that. Let’s shake hands on it and I’ll get some more beers.’ He returned with three big bottles of Keo. As he leant over the table putting the bottles down, a photograph slipped from his top pocket.

‘Careful, Ralph,’ Tommy warned, ‘There goes your photo. Stan picked the photograph up and read out, ‘Colour Sergeant Henry Tucker, Royal Welsh Fusiliers.’

‘My granddad,’ Ralph said proudly. ‘It was taken before he went off to the Boer War. He reckons that the Boers didn’t fight fair.’

‘What did he mean by fair?’ Duggie asked.

‘Well, the Boers shot at us from behind walls and hedges. I suppose fighting fair finished with the Crimea where they fought set battles. My granddad served from 1884 to 1904. That’s what I’d call ‘getting some in’. He’s still around. He’s getting on now. He spends most of his time snoozing on the couch.’

‘A good old bloke,’ they all agreed. They drank to him before ambling back to B Company lines.

‘Another day for the Queen.’ Tommy said.

Chapter 15

The Lost Commission

Stanhope Hall July 1956

I got your poem dear Ralph. I liked it but not the title 'Rock and Roll at last'. I think you could've taken a title from the script like, 'The days when all was dust' or 'The long sad notes'. I think you should always consider your poetry (including verse and monologue) as a hobby. Have you ever read much modern poetry? A lot of it is nonsensical, even to a brilliant intellect like mine. You have to scrape off layers of verbiage before you get to the theme, which is normally totally boring in the first place. There is no resort to rhyme or rhythm to hold the words together. Rhyme seems to be 'out'. Your best chance to get some reward and fulfilment from your writing is to perform it live. Your time will come in the sixties when there will be folk clubs and poetry clubs and a whole new awakening. The time will be called the swinging sixties. I think that at some stage of your life you will be an entertainer – you and Dennis. My clairvoyance comes and goes. Some images come and go too. Some persist like the little boy Tucker with the cheeky face and the land of mountains and plantations and the ship in port called RON something. Most persistent of all is the golden-haired girl. She looks fragile but she is not. Sometimes she has a parasol. Enough of my rambling. Little Jerome is not with me today. Sarah has taken him to see one of her college friends. So I'm on my own. It's a scorching hot day and I'm dressed for the occasion. I'll leave you to guess. I'm in a deckchair on the patio. (You made a damn good job

> of the patio, darling – you really are a Jack-of-all-trades. Let's hope you become master of at least one.) How I wish I had my strong legs around you and my fingertips gripping your back. Roll on another ten months. In the meantime I have to be satisfied with admiring myself. Let's close now. I love you truly. I have been sizing a few blokes up but so far it's November Tango Romeo. Write what you like when you like. Veronica has told me that you do your duty and send Hugh and Margaret regular boring, letters.

It was a blazing hot autumn day. Major Cunningham was glad to sit in the heavy shade of his canvas-walled offices at the top of B Company lines. He puffed on his pipe and tried to think of his future, but he kept slipping into the past. His future was unknown but would be a simple choice – he stayed in the army or he did not. Of one thing he was certain. Peacetime soldiering, playing at soldiers or whatever one liked to call it, was not for him. Cyprus was classed as Active Service so technically it was *not* 'Playing at soldiers'. In reality he thought it was. He felt that the presence of large troop numbers on this rather small island added to the futility of the operation. His opinion was that the situation called for specialists to infiltrate the terrorist organization of EOKA and gain sufficient intelligence to be at the right place at the right time to thwart attacks and make arrests. He aired his views though not formally.

He had been commissioned in 1933, at the age of nineteen, and spent his early service in India. His active service began with the Burma campaign. He was with Wingates Chindits for the duration. He had a spell with the Palestine Police before transferring back to the Grey Jackets with the rank of Captain in 1949. Then followed postings to Hong Kong, Ballykinlar in Northern Ireland, Minden in Germany and the regimental depot in Lichfield where he was promoted to Major in 1954 He never thought that he would live through Burma. After Burma every day was a bonus. He felt guilty that his life had been spared when so many brave comrades had died. Fellow senior officers who had been through the war understood his depression. Though they meant well, their platitudes only served to make him ill-tempered. 'Think of yourself as a cog in a big wheel,' somebody had said to him recently. 'A cog?' he blustered, 'there's no wheel let alone a bloody cog! Everything's a shambles. The very objective of terrorism is to create a shambles. I went through it in Palestine. Now we've got it here and in Malaya and Kenya. It's here to stay. It's random, cowardly and deadly but it's here with us.'

His pipe was empty. He refilled it and went into the Company Office. He helped himself to a match from the desk of Corporal Perkins, the company clerk. He went through the pipe smoker's ritual of lighting up using twenty matches in the process.

'I'm expecting Mr Roberts, Corporal Perkins. Show him through when he arrives will you.' With that Major Cunningham returned to his office to dream.

'Supposing I stay in the army,' he mused. 'Supposing I stayed and decided to do just what was expected of me and nothing more – no flair, no innovation – just soldier on in comparative ease. I'd be Lieutenant Colonel by the age of forty-seven, followed by Staff college, War Office, Brigadier, retiree, Lord Lieutenant of Leicestershire or somewhere, boring old codger, illness, old age, help!'

'Are you all right sir?' Mr Roberts asked.

'Yes. Why?'

'You shouted help.'

'Did I? Sit down, Jules. Everything all right in 5 platoon? Don't bother to answer.'

Major Cunningham shuffled around a pile of papers on his desk. 'Right,' he said. 'Shouldn't take long. Three lads that came in on the draft in early December – Holmer, Jennings and Braddox. I want to get Jennings and Braddox up to Corporal. I'm just letting you know.' He waited for an answer. 'What's your opinion?'

'Good men sir.'

'I know they're good men. Bearing in mind that you are their platoon commander, have you got anything to add to a simple 'Good men?'

'I thought that Jennings was a potential officer sir.'

'He is, but we don't know when yet. The fact that he is potential officer material does not prevent us promoting him within the ranks. Do you agree that he has leadership qualities?'

'Yes sir.'

'Are you going to agree with everything I say?'

'You know your men, sir.'

'And so should you. Jennings is to be made Corporal.'

'Now for Braddox, the country bumpkin. Do you have an opinion on him?'

'He spins a lot of yarns about ferrets and poachers. Rural anecdotes you might say.'

Major Cunningham was getting irritated.

'What the hell have ferrets and poachers got to do with leadership qualities?'

'I was setting the scene, sir. Giving you a bit of background.'

'Well I don't need bloody scenery! I will give you my assessment and you will no doubt agree with it, as is your wont. To quote the Duke of Wellington, "I don't know what he'll do to the enemy but by God he frightens me." He's big. He's hard. He's not a fool. We'll get Braddox up to Corporal. That leaves Holmer, our budding Falstaff. No need to discuss him. He must report to the Orderly Room at 1100 hrs tomorrow. We'll make sure he knows. He's being posted to SHAPE (Suprene Headquarters Allied Powers in Europe) based in Paris. What exactly he will doing there, God knows, probably something to do with security or ceremonials. Anyway I'm sure he'll be pleased. I wish I was going. Thank you for your time, Jules. Next time we have a matter to discuss I shall expect a little more than 'yes sir, no sir, you know your men sir'. You may go.'

Major Cunningham emerged again from his gloomy office.

'Corporal Perkins, I'm expecting Mr McLeod shortly. Show him into my office when he arrives. Have you got a light? My pipe's empty.'

'You used all my matches, sir.'

'I'm sorry about that old man.'

At that moment, Colour Sergeant Willis walked in.

'Colours is here now. I'm sure he'll have some matches.'

Colour Sergeant Willis handed over his matchbox

'You might as well keep the box sir. There's only about forty matches left.'

Mr McLeod, 4 platoon commander, arrived.

'Mungo old chap! Sit down. It concerns three lads in your platoon, Ward, Tucker and Compton.'

'All good men, sir.'

'Worthy of two stripes?'

'Absolutely. No doubt about it.'

'I'm persuaded by your enthusiasm, Mungo. We'll get things moving. We've got to go further with Tucker and talk about a commission. What do you think of him?'

'I think he'd make it. I get reports that he's a bit dreamy and inept at times but I've never experienced that.'

'Neither have I.' Major Cunningham concurred. 'I've found him well-mannered and articulate. Make sure that he reports immediately after muster parade.'

Are you in there, Holmer?' Corporal Perkins shouted into the tent.

'Who is it?'

'Corporal Perkins. Come on out!'

'What have I done?' Dennis asked.

'As far as I'm aware, nothing. You're not in any trouble.

You must report to the Orderly Room at 1100 hrs tomorrow.'

'What's it all about?' Dennis asked.

'I can't tell you.'

'But you know, don't you?'

'Yes, but it's not for me to tell you.'

'What is this? The Grey Jackets or the Secret Service?'

'I've told you to be there. That's my job done.' He walked away.

Ralph reported to the Company Office immediately after muster parade. 'Come on through Lance Corporal Tucker,' Major Cunningham said as he walked past. 'Sit down. Off the record you, Ward, Braddox, Jennings and Compton will be promoted to Corporal shortly and that puts us up to strength for the first time this year.

'Now then Tucker, I've got some bumf from Lichfield via the Adjutant. It seems that you were considered potential officer material, but at your interview with Major Roade you conveyed the impression that you wanted a commission as a matter of family pride. You said it was your parents' wish. What do you say to that?'

'Major Roade is correct sir. He told me that I should have the ambition to gain success for myself rather than for my parents and relatives, however commendable my reason was. These were more or less Major Roade's words as I recall.'

'You recall correctly, Tucker. I'm sure your mother would be proud of you but the person who must be proudest of all is yourself.'

There was an awkward silence as Major Cunningham read through the data muttering to himself. He then looked up and asked, 'You would like to try for a commission, then?'

'Just give me the chance, sir.'

'Mr McLeod thinks well of you. What's this about your being dreamy and inept?'

‘I can be absent-minded and clumsy on occasions, but I don’t think that it’s my normal behaviour. We all have faults. We all have things we don’t do too well. To counter balance this there are things one does well.’

‘I think you put that very well. Now imagine that you did not have the interview with Major Roade. Imagine I am asking you for the first time. What attracts you to life as an officer?’

‘A more comfortable life, sir. The comparative privacy of life as compared to living in the tent lines. I realise that this is a very superficial reason.’

‘It’s a damn good reason. Go on!’

‘The company of other officers, sir. Civilised conversation. That sounds rather snobbish, I suppose.’

‘Yes it is but you’ve thought out your answers well. We’re not yet a classless society. Snobbishness is a fact of life. The army is based on rank. I suppose that’s snobbery. The main thing is, Tucker, you have given me your own answers, rather than tell me things that you think I should hear.

‘I like your style. Let’s sum up. You should go for a commission. There’ll be things to be sorted out. You’ll hear shortly.’

‘Sah!’

He came to attention, saluted, right turned and marched out of the Company Office. He did not know where the platoon were. He decided to lie low and write to Lorna.

Dearest Lorna

I know you don’t want to hear anything about the army but this is different. I had a long interview with our company commander only minutes ago. He’s putting me forward for a commission. I don’t know for certain what’s happening, but obviously there’ll be admin work to sort out. Anyway I’ll be hearing shortly. I don’t want to count my chickens before they're hatched, but at the moment I'm happy – really happy. As a matter of fact I'm so pleased with myself that I can't think of a single subject other than the commission. Give Veronica the news. She'll tell Mom. Mom will be pleased as Punch. She'll have me up to Colonel in no time. I'm going to close off. I cannot concentrate, I'm so chuffed. Will write later.

Love you forever, Ralph.

Tommy came back to the tent just before cookhouse call.

'Where were you?' he asked Ralph. 'We were doing some of the rotten jobs around camp including, would you believe it, putting a roof on the RSM's garage – a bit of 'own initiative' stuff. We criss-crossed wire around the trees and lay down palm fronds. It looked like a thatched roof. Old Bill Chancellor actually liked it. How come he's the only man in the battalion with a private car?'

'Tommy, you just asked me where I'd been and before I could answer, you started talking ten to the dozen.'

'Where have you been then?'

'In the company office being interviewed at length by Major Cunningham and the result is that I am being given a chance to try for a commission.'

'Congratulations. Given a chance I know you'll make it. It'll mean a trip back home to attend Eaton Hall or wherever you have to go. Maybe you'll have to go for a short service commission. You'll be informed soon, no doubt. You deserve some luck. I shall always be indebted to you. Without you, I would never have met Veronica again.'

He received a prompt reply from Lorna

Oh, Ralph you clever lad. Finally, we've heard something about this elusive commission. I don't want to put a damper on it but don't get too excited. Things can go wrong in the army and you, poor dear, are not a lucky boy. But I shall be praying for you and so, I'm sure will Margaret. Jerome is sitting next to me. What a good little boy he is. I tell him stories. He obviously doesn't understand a word, yet he laughs in the right places. By the time you see him he'll be fourteen months or so. He might be a real handful by then.

Only a day had passed since Ralph's meeting with Major Cunningham and already he was getting anxious. He told himself to be patient rather than panicky. The army was a law unto itself and within the army the Grey Jackets were also a law unto themselves. He heard loud voices in the lines and opened the tent flap. Duggie, George and Dennis were approaching. Dennis had a big grin on his face.

'Dennis has got some good news for us,' George announced

'I've been posted,' Dennis told them. 'I fly back to Blighty this week. Then I do a two week course at Pirbright. Then guess where?'

Kenya?'

'No.'

'Hong Kong?'

'No.'

'Germany?'

'No.'

Bongobongoland? Outer space? Where?' Duggie asked impatiently. 'Tell us!'

'Paris.'

'Paris?'

'Paris. SHAPE – Supreme Headquarters Allied Powers in Europe.'

'They're going to drop you behind enemy lines,' Duggie said. 'You'll be in the French Resistance.'

'No,' George cut in. 'You'll be in the French Foreign Legion.'

'I'll join the Legion, that's what I'll do.' They sang in chorus.

'It's all right you lot taking the piss, but it's me that's going to Paris and you lot that's staying here.'

'Why are they sending you to Pirbright?' Ralph asked.

'It's the Guards Depot.'

'They may give you a red tunic and a bearskin,' George suggested. 'They'll probably make you do sentry duty outside the Eiffel Tower.'

'Seriously,' Ralph sounded exasperated. 'What do you have to do?'

'It's to do with security. I can't tell you any more than that. You could be Russian spies.'

'Vod makes you zink zat, Comrade?'

'Say what you like. It's going to be the experience of a lifetime. It's the sort of place I shall feel immediately at home in. Me being an entertainer. I shall be a busker on the streets of Paris singing Maurice Chevalier songs – 'Thank heaven for little girls, for little girls get bigger every day.'

'It's the Naafi for us tonight,' Tommy said.

'Good,' Dennis said. 'I'll have a string of French songs lined up. There's plenty – 'I love Paris in the springtime,' 'Under the bridges of Paris with you.' 'Je ne regrette rien' by Edith Piaf. But for now I'm just going to lay back and dream of the wonder of all things French – Montmartre, Madame Tussauds.'

'Madame Tussauds is in London, Dennis,' Ralph told him.

'Oh! Give me a few place names to savour then.'

'Les Champs Elysees, The Louvre, The Arc de Triomphe, The Folies Bergeres, Notre Dame, the river Seine and on and on – all things French.'

'Yes of course – all things French, like French windows, French mustard, French letters, French knickers, French cricket, French kisses, French beans, French horn, French toast, French Polish and famous French people like Marie

Antoinette, Louis the 14th and for that matter Louis the 15th and all the way to Louis the twentieth, then there's De Gaulle with the big nose and Napoleon known as the little corporal, not forgetting the hunchback of Notre Dame and Esmeralda. I'm getting into a real French mood. Paris and then the world will be my lobster. I should have a mistress within weeks. I fancy a Bohemian life. I hope to make enough money to buy a bigger house for my mom and my aunty so that they can entertain their gentlemen friends.'

'We gather you're pleased with your posting, Dennis,' Tommy said.

A few more days went by. Each day Ralph expected to be summoned to the Company office. He was getting apprehensive, but one day encouragement came from an unexpected source. Duggie was called in to see Major Cunningham.

'This will be about your commission, Duggie,' Ralph told him. 'That's why there's been a delay. They're processing us together. That's what I hope.'

'Come in Corporal Jennings and sit down.' Major Cunningham was looking through a file. 'Now then, Jennings. This is about your officer potentiality; ignoring your conversation with Major Roade during basic training, tell me why you want to be an officer.'

'The comparative comfort, sir. Life in the tent lines can drive a man mad.'

'That's a similar answer to your friend and comrade Corporal Tucker. Have you been in collusion?'

'Definitely not, sir.'

'Accepted. It's a good answer from a practical aspect. What about serving Queen and country – that sort of thing?'

'That should be taken for granted, sir.'

'Quite right, Jennings. It damn well should.' Major Cunningham made some notes on the file. He then looked at Duggie and said, 'One thing that puzzles me a bit is this. Your home address is recognisable to me as a tough housing estate, yet you have absolutely no trace of a regional accent. Why is that?'

'A long story, sir. Are you sure you want to hear it?'

'Yes. Go ahead.'

'The first four years of my life, which I can barely remember, were spent at a large house in the country near Lichfield. Our family had a prosperous manufacturing business - screws, rivets, nails and all that sort of thing. The company went under in the late thirties just at a time when it should've started to improve. The damage had been done in the Great Depression, when my father lost his assets bit by bit and finally became destitute and alcoholic. He died. That was when we moved to where we live now. My brother and I were constantly reminded that fate and the slump were responsible for our poverty but that did not mean that we should accept it. We were a wealthy family going through hard times. We were not of the hoi polloi. My brother and I were gentlemen and must speak and behave as gentlemen. We found things tough and had to put up with a fair amount of name-calling and abuse but we got through. My brother is in the Hong Kong police. My mother works for a Travel Agent.'

'Thank you, Jennings. It certainly was a long story, but I was convinced by it. You'll make an officer, Jennings, I have no doubts about you or Tucker. There's some admin work to be done. Be patient. Tell Corporal Tucker to get that anxious look off his face. You'll be kept informed.'

Next day was a rare day off for 4 and 5 Platoons. They anticipated a lazy time around the tent lines, reading, writing or playing cards. Instead Mr Roberts, in his wisdom, decided that they should have a trip out towards Kyrenia and en route climb a mountain called the Pendaktilon (Five Fingers). 4 Platoon protested about being included in this unnecessary outing, pointing out that their own platoon commander, Mr McLeod, and their platoon sergeant, Sergeant Westlake, had decided to stay in camp. There was controversy over using MT Platoon vehicles for a trip to the seaside. The silly little joy ride had to have a (theoretically) 'military' objective. In the end orders, however daft, were orders and they all had to go.

They struggled over the Pendaktilon, loaded onto vehicles again and set off for Kyrenia where, under Mr Roberts' orders (and completely illegally), they commandeered a large raft made of wooden pallets and truck tyres. They floated it out a little way where, in turn, they dived off, climbed on, dived off, climbed on. Nobody had their hearts in it. Three men craftily stayed behind to look after the rifles. One by one they all trudged back without even waiting for an order.

'Who the fuck does Roberts think he is?' someone asked 'It's supposed to be a day off, but it's been harder than a day on.'

When they arrived back dirty and tired there was bad news. A bomb, planted inside a vehicle, had gone off in the MT platoon area. Amazingly there was only one casualty, of all people, Major Cunningham. He had been walking up the path towards the Officers' Mess and had been hit by flying debris. Some said it was a door that hit him. Conjecture was rife. He had lost an arm. He had lost a leg. Nobody really knew. In any event, he had been badly cut up and was losing blood before they rushed him to the British Military Hospital in Nicosia.

Ralph felt miserable. Cunningham, a man that he liked, a man who had come through the war, gets wounded on his way to lunch. What a farce!

From a selfish point of view, Ralph wondered who would be handling the paperwork on his hoped for commission. He had a foreboding that he would be on a wild goose chase. He had to start somewhere. Corporal Perkins seemed a logical choice.

‘Do you know who’s handling my possible commission?’ he asked.

‘I think the files have been sent back,’ Corporal Perkins said.

‘Sent back where?’

‘Just sent back.’

‘To Lichfield? To the Adjutant?’

‘Don’t keep on asking me questions.’

‘You’re the company clerk. You should know something.’

‘Not in this case. This was something Major Cunningham was handling.’

‘How is Major Cunningham?’

‘Stable, I believe.’

Ralph had a sinking feeling – a feeling that without Major Cunningham, his chances, and Duggie’s chances for that matter, of a commission were slim and dwindling.

He approached Mr McLeod who was more informative. He confirmed that Major Cunningham had been working on the files for corporals Tucker and Jennings on the very day that he was injured.

‘This is very frustrating, Corporal Tucker,’ he said, ‘I feel that you have been let down. I think a visit to the Adjutant is a reasonable idea. With Major Cunningham’s departure things have been thrown into chaos. I cannot go over anyone’s head and talk to the Adjutant, but I will have a word with Captain Stevens who is acting OC.’

In modern vernacular Captain Stevens would be described as ‘laid back’. He half listened to Mr McLeod before saying, ‘Sorry, Mungo old chap, I’ve got no details to hand, but as soon as I hear something I shall let you know.’

‘That’s quite a pile of files on the spare table over there, sir. Would it be out of order if I scanned through them?’

‘It certainly would. I shall let you know at the appropriate time, whenever that time will be.’

Ralph told Tommy the 'story so far' and suggested, 'Maybe I could solve things if I got to see Major Cunningham in hospital.'

'No hope, Ralph. The word is that he's been flown home to one of those places where they can rebuild you.'

'And then what?'

'I should say it's certain that he'll be out of the army altogether. The rumours are over. The fact is that his leg was sheared off just below the knee by flying debris, a vehicle door to be exact. Your dream's over, Ralph. Maybe Duggie's is too, but he's philosophical about things. Somebody didn't want you to have those pips. The Major's injury is a smoke screen. It stinks.'

'I'm not letting it drop.'

'Pursue it if you think you can get somewhere, Ralph, but don't drive yourself crazy in the process.'

He wrote to Lorna with the sorry story and, as expected, she replied immediately.

Dear Ralph,

I sometimes think you're doomed. You're getting a rough deal, but let's get things into perspective. Poor Gerard has lost a leg and a lost leg is more important than a lost commission. Gerard and I were lovers. I remember telling you not long after we met. I can remember what I said verbatim. These were my words:

There was one true lover, Ralph. I am not proud of it. He was beautiful like you. How handsome he was! He was a young second lieutenant. It was a brief affair. Roger found out. I believe he confronted Gerard and threatened him with a good thrashing if ever he spoke of the affair. His words to me were: 'I'm a bit cut up about it old gel. If it happens again I'm afraid it will mean divorce.' This was all in India where passions ran high.

To get back to the main subject, I may or may not have told you as we lay together – times, which I yearn for – that I work in a voluntary role with the Grey Jackets Regimental Association. It is my unpleasant duty to visit the loved ones of men killed or wounded. I have made two such visits since the battalion left Egypt for Cyprus. It's a harrowing duty. I shall certainly be summoned to visit Gerard. As soon as I do, I shall make the trip to see him and I'll find out just what is going on.

It's easy to theorise. For example, here is a scenario that may hold the solution. There was a young career officer of the Grey Jackets who had made rapid progress through the ranks. He was a Major at the age of twenty-six. He was my frequent escort at balls and dinners. I found him rather a cold fish. Nevertheless, despite our lukewarm relationship, he proposed to me. I turned him down. He was said to be very upset. I continued to be an outrageous flirt. That, apparently, upset him even more. I married Roger. He remained a bachelor. He is still a serving officer – a Brigadier. Just supposing information filtered through to him that the woman who once spurned him had become the mistress of one of the regiment's rank and file, namely you Ralph? Then Brigadier X will make sure that this young upstart will not be considered for a commission. Maybe this all sounds wild speculation. Who knows? I feel for you. You must be so miserable. Little Jerome has been cranky this week. It's unusual for him to be so. Maybe he knows something.

Well, my potential officer, you may have to settle for Corporal. Napoleon was a corporal wasn't he? He did quite well, didn't he? So there's some inspiration for you.

If a little French corporal could achieve so much, then a big English corporal can do even better. Please don't march your armies all over Europe.

My eternal love, Lorna

He wrote back

Nicosia 14 Aug.
Dear Lorna,
If ever I needed cheering up it was your letter. You shook me out of my misery. What right have I to be miserable? Poor Major Cunningham's the one to be miserable. He gets through the war only to be wounded on his way to lunch. I bet *he's* resigned and philosophical and trying to see the bright side of life. You make me realise that I am but a boy. I should be acting like a man.
Do you honestly think that I am the victim of sheer spite from some old boy who feels slighted from twenty odd years ago?
To revert to mundanities, Tommy has been transferred to 6 Platoon. Duggie stays in 5 Platoon. George has transferred to 4 Platoon with me. I shall have to share a tent with this enormous non-stop talker but I guess I'll get used to it.
I can almost hear you yawning from here. I look forward to a reply. Please do what you can. I'm not expecting a miracle.
Your ever-loving Ralph

Sure enough Lorna received a letter from the Grey-Jackets Regimental Association with an instruction to call on the Cunningham family at: Long Paddock, Coachdown Road. Evesham, Worcs.

There was also a telephone number, but she decided not to phone in advance in case Gerard would not see her. Why did she think that? Well, they had been kept apart after their affair and Gerard with his sense of duty might think that the instruction still applied. 'No,' she told herself, 'I'll surprise him.'

She decided to leave immediately. It was a hot late August day. She put on a skimpy dress but took it off again thinking it might be inappropriate for such an occasion. She changed her mind. She had to admit that she was dying to see him and wanted to look sensual for him. She put the dress back on. She threw her blazer onto the passenger seat as a reserve item of respectability, and set off, having said her goodbyes to Sarah and Jerome. She had no difficulty finding Long Paddock, a 1930's mock Tudor house with quite an extensive garden. She rang the bell and a voice from inside said 'coming!' Moments later Gerard came out on crutches. He stared for a while.

'I'm speechless! Is it Lorna? Is it you Lorna? They took you away from me. You're back. I cannot believe what I see before me. You're still the girl I fell in love with. You're actually more curvaceous. Your beauty must be ageless. I reckon you'd be forty-three years old.'

'Correct. Oh Gerard, Gerard, Gerard.' She clutched him in her powerful arms. 'You're still a gorgeous handsome man. Are you here on your own?'

'Yes, for a few days. My wife and my little girl are at my mother-in-law's in Bristol for a week.'

'What? That's a bit off, isn't it? So soon after your injury.'

'I asked to be alone for a while so that I can think things over. I can get by all right. A cleaner comes once a day.'

'Shall we go inside?' Lorna asked.

'I'm easy. We can sit out on the lawn if you like. Shall I bring us out a drink? Wine? Red? White? A snack? Chicken drumsticks, tomatoes, lettuce, fresh bread and butter?'

'Tell me where everything is and I'll get lunch set up,' Lorna volunteered.

'No you won't. I have to keep active. It's hell, but I'm not going to be beaten. As the years go by and medicine advances, I shall get better and better aids. I'll have a replacement leg so good that you won't be able to tell it from a real one.'

He limped away to prepare lunch, returning minutes later.

'Here we are. I've loaded it all on the trolley. Sit down and tell me why you're here. D'you know, many is the time when I've been unhappy because my wife (Linda) has stormed out. I've thought to myself 'Oh, Lord! Please send Lorna to me.' Then I open the door and you are there in all your wondrous beauty and you have come to take me away.'

'Gerard, you asked me why I am here before you went into raptures about me, for which I thank you. I'm here on behalf of the Regimental Association. I work for them in a voluntary capacity as a visitor to the relatives of killed or wounded men. It's not very pleasant. I have to ask you if you require any help financially or medical help.'

'Tell the old comrades association, which is what I call it, that if I ever need any help, I shall ask them. That's a bit curt I suppose, but I don't want to be a burden on anybody. The truth is that for many months before my injury, I was ready to resign my commission anyway. I'd just about had the army up to here.' He put his palm to his throat.

'And now the terrorists have made your mind up for you,' Lorna said with no small amount of venom. 'Those bastards! Blowing up vehicles, maiming good men doing their duty. To see you like this, Gerard, it makes me feel angry.'

'I feel like half a man sometimes.'

'Half a man? You're twice more a man than any man I know. I need some help from you.'

'For you, dear Lorna, anything.'

'I have a young friend who serves in the Grey Jackets. He had his mind set on becoming an officer and until recent events it seemed that his dream was about to come true.

However, now that you have departed, he tells me that there is a wall of silence. He is simply trying to find out what is happening regarding his commission. He surely deserves more than blatant deception.'

'There are two potential officers in B Company, Corporals Tucker and Jennings and I guess that your young friend is Ralph Tucker. Lorna, apart from the joy your very presence has brought me, I'm damned glad you've brought all this to my attention. Both these lads were highly thought of. Both were leaders. Both were charming, well-spoken and polite. All the relevant data was on my desk the morning that I got injured. Everything was in order. It was simply a matter of a few signatures. If somebody has countermanded my orders it's an absolute disgrace.'

'What can you do about it, Gerard?'

'I can write to the C.O. for a start. Let's draft a letter. I'll go inside to get a pad.'

'Can't I get it for you, Gerard? I hate to see you hobbling everywhere on crutches.'

'I've got to get used to it. Let's make a start. We send it to Lt Colonel Arthur Wood M.C. 1st Grey Jackets, Whittington Camp, Nicosia, M E L F 26.

This is what I'll say:

Sir,

As you know I am currently resting after my injury. Because of my condition at the time of the incident, (I was losing a lot of blood) and the need to get straight into BMH Nicosia and thence the UK, there was no formal handover of my duties. I am most perturbed that important data that was on my desk on the day of my injury has gone astray. The data concerns two potential officers from B Company, viz, Corporals Tucker and Jennings. Corporal Tucker has been attempting to find out what is happening concerning his commission. Nobody can tell him anything. He is being treated off handedly by the very people who should be helping him. Surely somebody knows something? It's a crazy situation. If it is not resolved, the army will have been deprived of the services of two good officers. I know them well as I try to know all my men. Or should I say *knew* for I do not think that I shall be a Grey Jacket for long unless they can gainfully employ a one-legged major.

Please pass on my regards to my men and my brother officers. I may not see them again. Let me therefore address you in civilian terms:

Arthur, you're a good brave and true man. Do your best for two lads who deserve a better life than the tent lines. I was a Grey Jacket for twenty years and I never, until now came across any jiggery-pokery. Please let me know what the hell is going on.

Regards

Gerard Cunningham.

He took the rough draft from Lorna and read it out.

'How does it sound?'

'Brilliant!' Lorna enthused.

'Good. I'll get my wife Linda to type it up for me as soon as she gets back home. I'll send you a copy. I see from the letter you have that your address is Stanhope Hall, Gorway, Walsall. Sounds very grand but there again you're a grand lady.'

'Yes, I'm grand and haughty and a snob and with the years I have become conceited and vulgar. Had we happened to have married, Gerard, I would have given you a dog's life.'

'I'm sure you would not have and we shall never know.'

'I can't thank you enough, Gerard,' she said.

'Let's hope we get somewhere. Maybe they'll close ranks. We'll have to wait. Tell young Tucker that it's not the end of the world. I'll walk with you to your car.'

They reached the car and she kissed him farewell.

'I should maybe have asked you sooner, Gerard, but is your marriage suffering?'

'It was suffering before all this. It's sort of fizzled out. Linda's a good woman. She's put up with service life. She was looking forward to being back in civilian life and starting again. We'll be starting again, for sure, but not the sort of start we would have liked.'

'I'm sorry. I hope you'll have a good life. They'll get your legs going again – the medical boffins. If you're ever really down, phone me. Well dammit, phone me anyway.

She flung her arms around him.

'Those bastards!'

She drove away. On her way back home she wondered if it would be a good idea to tell Ralph what had transpired. Maybe, it would be better to do nothing until there was some positive news. It would be no good lifting his spirits only to have them drop again. If the quest became like a detective story with multiple theories and contradictions, then best to pack up. Let the guilty parties rot in hell.

Duggie did not seem much perturbed. 'Que sera sera' was a popular song at that time and it summed up his feelings. For Ralph, it was a miserable time. He was 'soldiering on'. He said it through gritted teeth as he plodded his weary way. Like the proverbial ploughman across the hard-baked earth to the ablutions with all the other zombie-like silent men.

He shaved in freezing cold water, which in his case meant going over the same patch of stubble six or seven times to achieve the required baby's bottom smoothness. He toyed with the idea of reporting sick, but sick in the army did not include feelings of emptiness and frustration. Coughs, colds or 'gippy' tummy did not count as 'sick' either. Being sick in the Grey Jackets meant having a carbuncle the size of a tennis ball up your bum or your toes rotting and dropping off or your cock turning green. He resigned himself to purgatory. The ‘commission that never was’ was constantly in his thoughts.

One evening in the Naafi, Duggie remonstrated with Ralph.

‘Ralph, I’ve got to tell you this as a friend. Stop moping around with a hangdog expression. Your miserable face is making everybody else miserable. Face facts. The commissions are dead. You’ve got to start acting like an NCO again. You’ve got a section. We’re on active service. Whatever’s happened about these commissions – God knows. I know it’s an injustice but that, my friend, is life. Life is unfair. Look at it this way. We’re over halfway through our time. Just supposing the wheels of bureaucracy start moving. We’ve got to get through the training. By the time we’re ready to get our pips sown on, it would be demob day. I reckon we’d be bound to go for short service commissions. Who knows which regiments we’d be sent to? Not the Grey Jackets I’ll bet. We’d probably be in some rural county regiment in charge of blokes with impossible accents. I know that last Christmas Mr McLeod said he was looking forward to buying us a drink in the Officers’ Mess. That was wishful thinking.’

‘I hear you loud and clear Duggie. There’s a bit of correspondence on between Major Cunningham and Colonel Wood via the Regimental Association so I’ve heard. If it comes to nothing, I shall consider it all as ‘subject closed’.’

‘Good for you Ralph. We all like the old Ralph Tucker, the lad with a smile. Let’s get a drink.’

October came and the temperature dropped. George Braddox was transferred to an empty tent. Ralph moved in there too.

B Company were once more short of men. This was a blessing in disguise when it came to accommodation. Two men to a tent was a luxury, even though he had to tolerate the enormous, verbose presence of George Braddox. In the long term it did not matter too much because B Company seemed to be spending more time away from camp that than in it. They were out on the Post Office guard in Metaxas Square or Police Station guards or roadblocks. It was a semi-nomadic existence. Right now George was in the tent supping his tasteless tea from the Cha Wallah and telling a long rigmarole of a rural yarn.

'So what do you think of that?' George concluded.

'Er, well it's er, well it's obvious I should say.'

'You haven't heard a word I've said, have you? Still thinking about that commission? You've got to do what Duggie tells you. Forget it. As I see it though you could pursue things when you're out of the services. You could sue the War Office. You could say that you have been dispossessed.'

'Dispossessed is a bit strong isn't it?'

'I don't think so. It's the Queen's Commission isn't it? You can't get any higher than that. You could say that, because of corruption in the army you are unable to live like a toff. You are forced to live with humble pheasants.'

'I've never thought of myself as a toff, George.'

'You're not a toffee-nosed, hoity-toity toff. You're a nice toff, but the fact is that you're a toff. There's a toff inside you begging to be let out. It's the same with me.'

'I'm astounded, George. You are the absolute ultimate anti-toff. Are you saying that your rough interior hides a toff?'

'More than a toff, boy, a nobleman. Do you want to hear more? Yes, I know you do. I am the direct descendant of Gilbert de Bradac, a trusted courtier of Edward III. The great, great, great and six more greats, grandson of Gilbert de Bradac was Giles Braddock, Lord of the Manor of Penny Mortimer and Acornbridge at the time of the Civil War. He fought the Royalist cause and took the rank of Colonel.

'Giles Braddock led a raiding party on Acornbridge Tavern where parliamentary forces were encamped and was successful in driving them off his land. For this action he was severely punished. Cromwell called in reinforcements of over two hundred men. They were ruthless. They destroyed all the farm buildings and dwellings of Acornbridge and Penny Mortimer. They set fire to Braddock Hall, a fine mansion at that time. Those bastards burnt it to the ground. Giles was killed along with most of his servants. By all accounts some were burnt alive. His sons, Miles and Henry, had been twenty miles away in another skirmish. Word got to them and they rode back with a band of ruffians recruited on the spot. Imagine their feelings when they saw their house a pile of embers with the charred bodies of the occupants part of the smouldering heap. Cromwell's men had gone. There was nobody to fight. Miles and Henry had no home to return to so they fought on for the Royalists, hoping for some justice after the war but there never was any justice. The Braddocks and their kin became labourers, ploughmen grooms and menservants, their ranks and titles gone. Their land seized and divided up for Cromwell's cronies. Now that is what you might call injustice, Ralph. My grandfather passed it down to my brothers and me. Most people think that three hundred years or so is too long to hold a grudge, but we don't see it that way. Over the years some of our enemies have tried to rewrite history. They claim that the raid on Acornbridge tavern was one of the most dreadful actions of the Civil War. Men were shot or stabbed in their sleep. It's easy to say that well after the events. It was a brutal war. We stick by our version.'

'What a story, George. You could build a book around it. It makes my lost commission seem like a storm in a teacup.'

'Which it is, Ralph.' He turned over in bed and was soon snoring fit to bring the tent down.

Gerard Cunningham received a reply from Colonel Wood. It was completely informal and read:

My dear Gerard,

You have the sincere sympathies of all who knew you. What can I say that does not sound maudlin? Let me be objective and say that I hope you will at some stage be able to lead an active life again.

Now about these commissions for Tucker and Jennings. We're stretched for personnel and do not have the time to carry out an enquiry. Yes, we know that something underhand has happened and we know that there are people capable of chicanery within the echelons of the Grey Jackets. It's an awful thing to have to admit but it is so. As I may have advised you recently, I shall be a civilian by the end of the year. Yes, my time is up. This would be the time for me to make a few calls at the Officers' Mess in Lichfield, have a few drinks with old friends and hope that the drink may loosen a few tongues. As for Tucker and Jennings I'm sure that they will be stoic. They will certainly get commissions in the T.A. if they still have an appetite for soldiering after demob. In the meantime, I'll keep eyes and ears open. Does that sound like an empty promise? I expect it does.

My regards to your wife and daughter,

Arthur Wood

Gerard Cunningham decided to phone Lorna.

'Lorna? It's Gerard.'

'Gerard!' She boomed. 'Can you wait a few seconds? I've just got out of the bath. I'm drying myself. I won't be much longer. Right. Finished. Have you any news?'

'I received a letter from the Colonel. It was very nice but negative. I'll send you a copy. To cut a long story short, The Grey Jackets have not got the resources or time to carry out an enquiry, even though it is obvious that something underhand has happened. Arthur Wood becomes a civilian in the New Year. He is willing to do a bit of detective work by visiting the Officers' Mess in Lichfield but that's a long-term thing. Tucker and Jennings will have to be stoic. It's not really worth your going into much detail with Ralph about seeing me or anything. It's an injustice. It's happened. It's over.'

'Okay Gerard. You did your best. Keep in touch. I mean that. I loved meeting you again. You're a very handsome man.'

She put the phone down.

Chapter 16

Sent to Petty Fights

George Braddox was summoned to the Company Office to see Captain Stevens.

'Braddox, old chap. How are you?'

'Fine thank you, sir.'

'Braddox, we have the Middle East Land Forces Boxing Championships coming up. You fit the bill for a heavyweight. Six feet four, fourteen stone. You look to be my man.'

'Your man, sir?'

'Yes. I'm in charge of training.'

'Bloody Hell!' George thought to himself, if he's in charge, we'll never get going.

'I'm not sure I'm your man, sir. I'm not the biggest man in the Battalion.'

'I know you're not,' Captain Stevens replied. 'We've done our research. There are four bigger than you. One is a bandsman who is well overweight. One is going on demob next week. The other two, by all accounts, couldn't punch their way out of a paper bag.'

'That's the same with me, sir. I'm a gentle giant.'

'Be as gentle as you like until you get in that ring. That's all, Braddox. Colour Sergeant Harper will be in touch with you in a few days' time.'

George saluted and marched out.

He returned to the tent.

'You look all excited.'

'I am. I'm in for a skive. I'm in the boxing team as a heavyweight.'

'I know that you're no lightweight,' Ralph said.

'I'm the fourth biggest man in the battalion.'

'I can believe it. What makes you think it's going to be a good skive?'

'Training every day – no regimental duties.'

'What sort of training?'

'I haven't thought about it yet. There's a boxing ring all set up on the square, isn't there? That's where we do our sparring. Mind you, come to think of it, we can't spar against each other can we? We're all different weights.'

'Exactly George, and there's no gym and no equipment. I'll tell you what training you'll be doing – running, running and running. Who's in charge of it?'

'Captain Stevens and Colours Harper.'

'Then you really *could* be in for a skive. They're about the laziest men you could wish for. Can you imagine Stevens giving you instructions? "Hold your gloves up higher old chap." "Try and put a bit more power behind it, old boy".'

'It's all right you being sarky about it. Let's see how it goes. You got my back up a bit there, Ralph. You watch me go when I get in that ring. You'll think you're watching Marciano.'

George trained hard. They did a lot of exercises that required no equipment like pull-ups and press-ups. Three mattresses hung up inside the Knot Club acted as punch bags. Some climbing ropes were suspended from the Knot Club rafters. Against all predictions, Stevens and Harper put them through it. In the end, they had a solid squad with reserves. What they lacked in skill, they made up for in stamina. George had put on muscle and looked fit. He had something more than determination. He seemed to be able to work himself into a venomous mood, changing back suddenly to his crafty country boy ways. Perhaps the centuries of bitterness that the dispossessed Braddocks had suffered was what drove him on.

The day of the first round of the MELF (Middle East Land Forces) boxing championships arrived; the Grey Jackets had won the bantamweight and middleweight divisions. Their opponents, the Bedfords, had won the lightweight and flyweight divisions. The result now hinged on the heavyweights.

There was a sudden silence when the Bedfords heavyweight stepped into the ring. He was gigantic. His arms seemed to end somewhere below his knees. He shuffled round the ring shouting, 'Where is he? Let me get at him!' A full three minutes passed with no sign of George. Finally he appeared at the top of the tent lines, flanked by his seconds.

'He's mouthing off at you, George,' Colours said. 'Give him what for! He's been calling you the village idiot. Whack him! He's been saying that Oliver Cromwell was the greatest man who ever lived. Give him a haymaker!' They reached the ring amongst raucous cries. 'Stick your pitchfork up his arse! Plough him under!'

George was truly scared. Wisecracks of encouragement were all very well, but this opponent was a colossus. Colours continued to try and whip George into a ferocious mood. 'Remember that you are a yeoman of England, George, a true son of the soil, a sleeping giant, finally aroused. This punk from the Bedfords is a layabout. He's all fat. He's a big tub of lard. You're big where it counts – in your heart.'

The referee looked over to George's corner and snapped, 'Seconds out of the ring,' the bell went. The man from the Bedfords, inaptly named Corporal Little, lumbered around the ring. George Braddox took up a pose, his gloves covering his face, his left ready to jab. He was almost motionless. Little threw a mighty right that would have taken George's head off had it connected. Little was giving George far too much time to work things out. He threw a left. George ducked. He tried some jabs but only hit fresh air. That was to be the pattern of the fight for the whole first round. Little was pleased to hear the bell and sit down.

In George's corner there was anxiety. 'George!' Colours implored, 'you've been in there for three minutes. You haven't thrown a single punch.'

'And he hasn't landed one, either.'

'Get in close and rough him up. Keep your jabs going.'

'And remember,' Captain Stevens added, 'if you win this you'll be a regimental hero. Concentrate. Watch him because if ever one of those big punches land, you'll be down and out. Out for the count.'

The bell went for round two. It followed the same pattern. The crowd were restless. 'Come on George!' someone shouted wearily. Others took up the words and chanted 'Come on George.' Soon there was a chorus. 'Come on George, Come on George, Come on George.'

Little lumbered forward menacingly. This time George held him and got inside with two or three punches which actually landed. The crowd went wild having watched the only punches in the contest. Little, having been forced to chase George, was tiring. He had slowed down, but he was still dangerous. The crowd urged George on. He started to move around the ring more. He relaxed and lost concentration for a second. Little landed a punch bang on George's neck. It knocked the stuffing out of him. He hung onto Little for dear life, recovered, and landed a body punch. The ref ordered him not to hold. The bell went for the end of round two.

'He's tiring,' Colours said. 'He's tiring George. He's not fit. D'you see what fitness can do for you? You can win this fight. All you've got to do is score points. Don't try and mix it with him. Wait for your opportunity. It'll come.'

The bell went for the third and final round. Little looked refreshed. He was moving better. He knew that he could afford to have a different outlook in the last round. If he exhausted himself in the process then so what? He would land a sledgehammer blow on George Braddox, however many punches he took on the way. Little let loose all his pent up frustration and began flailing his arms around like a street fighter. He was slowing down. He dropped his guard. Then everything seemed to slow down for George. He had time to set up a 'one two'. He let loose a straight right with fourteen stone behind it and all the hatred he could muster. The punch went through flush on Little's nose. Little actually smiled through the crimson mask of his face. He slumped to the floor and George caught him with a vicious left to the body on his way down. He was up again at the count of five. He summoned up all his reserves, forced George into a corner and began raining punches but they all landed on George's gloves. The bell had gone anyway, unheard by the delirious crowd. The ref came across and held George's arm up. Amazingly, through his cunning, he had won.

After the fight, George was modest enough to say that if he had been up against a boxer rather than a scrapper and mauler, he would have lost. It was only Little's poor mobility that gave him his chance. He told Little after the fight, that he had fought bravely.

In the next bout against the King's Own Yorkshire Light Infantry (the KOYLIS) he was up against a good all-rounder, a product of the mean streets of Bradford. Lance Corporal Danny Edmonds was his name – tough, fast and immensely strong. George fought at his best. Unfortunately his 'best' was not enough to beat Edmonds. He did not go down, but he was outclassed.

The Grey Jackets were out of the competition. George Braddox had earned himself a place in Grey Jacket folklore, for it seemed that Corporal Little, at six foot seven and eighteen stone, was the biggest man in the British Army. The fight against Little took place of honour in George's compendium of anecdotes for the next five decades.

Corporal Little would grow to seven foot three and swell to twenty-one stone.

Dearest Lorna

It seems incredible that Christmas 1956 will soon be here. That's over a year served, and contrary to the popular opinion that army time drags, it seems to have flown by. I have been posted to the Battalion Orderly Room to commence in February 1957. I'm quite pleased. It'll be a fresh start. I'm replacing Corporal Chivers who is the Part II orders clerk. That's going to be quite an important duty as the Battalion prepares to come home in May. I shall have new friends and colleagues. (Not that I would ever sever the link with Tommy, Stan, Duggie or George.)
I've put the commission business to the back of my mind. No good moping about it. I'm eternally indebted to you for the work you've put in, but Duggie and I have decided that it's all over. Whatever underhand dealings there have been, whatever the injustice, it's dead.

Eternal love Ralph

Christmas came to Nicosia. It was a crisp cold day, almost English. They gathered in one tent. Sergeant Westlake had already distributed rum-laden tea to the tent lines. They were wondering what to do next when Ralph said, 'Let's see what I've got in my soldiers' box. He opened the lid, took out a rolled up towel, laid it on a bed, opened the towel to reveal a large bottle of Johnny Walker Black Label whisky, two bottles of dry ginger and six plastic beakers.

'Where did this all come from?' Tommy asked.

'I jammed it into my kitbag when we came out last year.'

'Are you saying we could have drunk this last year?'

'Yes, but aren't you glad we didn't?'

'Glad's not the word for it. We're elated,' Tommy said, 'but what I can't understand is how did you manage to get last year's and this year's booze in your kitbag?'

'I cheated. I left out a few items of clothing to make room for the booze, and my mother mailed them on in a parcel describing the contents as biscuits. Anyway, the booze is here and that's the main thing. Let's set up our little bar, shall we? Five scotch and dry gingers coming up.'

'You're a good lad,' Duggie said.

'Am I your best friend?'

'Why do you keep asking me that? I'm going to travel the world with you aren't I. We're going to write a book about it together aren't we? I'll drink to you. I'll drink to everybody. If there were any justice in the world Ralph and I would be drinking a health to the Queen in the Officers' Mess.'

'We can still drink to the Queen, can't we?' George said. 'We're all Loyalists, aren't we?'

'If there's a drink in it, I'm a Loyalist,' Stan said.

'I'm half-Irish,' Tommy said.

'All right,' George said. 'You can drink a toast to the Queen and one to – who?'

'Old Mother Reilly,' Stan suggested.

'No. It's Devalera,' Tommy said.

'Let's cut down on these toasts shall we?' Ralph suggested, 'We're going through the whisky too fast.'

'It's here to be drunk,' George said. 'It tastes all the better for being free.'

'Free for you,' Ralph cut in, 'but not free for me. I've never had a free drink in my life. Even at Christmas time at my Nan's, the menfolk have to chip in to cover the cost of the beer.'

'There's an old man in our village who's never paid for a beer in his life,' George said.

'What's his name? George Braddox?' Stan asked.

'His name is Horace Bradnack. This is how he does it. He stands at the bar waiting for a townie to come in. Sure enough one appears sooner or later. Then old Horace says to him, "Good morning" and the townie says "Good morning" and starts a little conversation. Then he says to the townie, "What's your name young man?" and the townie says "Martin. What's yours?" "I'll have a pint of bitter sir, thank you very much."'

'I don't get that,' Stan said.'

'I might have known,' George sighed. 'What's yours means what are you drinking.'

'Don't go through an explanation, George,' Duggie said. 'It spoils it. Just tell us the name of the pub, and we'll all make sure that we avoid it.'

'I hope you don't avoid it. You'll all be there next June partaking of buffet and booze and a pig roast and entertainment when I wed my lovely Betty at Saint Luke's Church. The name of the pub is the Royal George.'

'So we're all invited?' Tommy asked. 'That's something we can look forward to.'

'You're my mates,' George was slurring his words. 'Best mates I ever had. The invite includes lady-friends.'

'Since we're on the subject,' Tommy said, 'You're all invited to my wedding too. Also in June. Probably at Saint Matthew's Church. Reception 'chez Tucker'.

'Who's Shay Tucker?' Stan asked.

'At the house of Tucker,' Duggie explained. 'Don't let him have any more scotch, Ralph.'

'The scotch is fast disappearing. We've given it a real hammering,' Ralph told them. 'One round of small measures will see it off.'

They swilled down their final drinks. They were all decidedly wobbly. Man by man they slumped on the nearest bed or, in Stan and George's case, lay sprawled out on the duck boards.

‘Next Christmas in Germany lads,’ Ralph slurred, but he was answered by the deafening snores of men in drink. He looked forward to Veronica’s letter about Nan Tucker’s annual Christmas gathering. That was the last thing he remembered before falling into a deep sleep.

Veronica’s letter arrived in the New Year. Ralph opened it eagerly.

Dear brother,

No! That’s not loving enough. Dear adorable, good, kind brother. How I miss you and love you. So does mother. She pines for you. Keep sending those mundane letters. We realise that apart from the army there’s nothing to tell us about but that’s okay.

Did you get drunk at Christmas? I bet you did. Mother told me about the big bottle of whisky you smuggled in. We were all at Nan Tuckers as usual. All the same people were there. Uncles Sid and Jacob and Bryn, Granddads Tucker and Rowley. The addition this year was Sarah with little Jerome – poor little fellow! He was so overawed he cried and cried until Lorna took him on her lap. He was silent almost immediately. She whispered something in his ear and he smiled. She has a wonderful way with that little boy. She dotes on him. This fact is not unnoticed by Nan Tucker, who said, ‘Vulgar woman she well may be, but anybody who could calm a child that quickly must be full of love and understanding’. Lorna and Nan Tucker are supposedly bosom pals, but you know how Nan Tucker can suddenly turn. Lorna upstaged everybody. She wore a kaftan that she had bought in a charity shop. It had worn rather thin – almost transparent in fact. She is simply the most provocative woman on earth. She oozes sex. Oh, dear brother, can’t you marry a little Brummy typist and have Lorna on the side as your mistress? Anyway,

Lorna, in her shortened low-necked kaftan, sat herself down between Uncle Sid and Uncle Jacob. It was a tight fit. Both the uncles were ecstatic. Nan Tucker already had her eye on Lorna. This was normally the time for the annual political debate.

'What d' you think about this new bloke who's taking over from Eden?' Uncle Bryn asked.

'Do you mean Macmillan?' Sid asked. 'He's a toff.'

'Nothing wrong with being a toff,' Jacob said, 'in my business I rely on toffs. Toffs dress well. Toffs understand quality. They know a good suit. They don't quibble over price.'

'It didn't take us long to get back to suits did it?' Sid commented.

'Suits are a political subject. Tailoring is big business, but we've hit hard times. I'm on the brink of ruin. Attlee, Churchill, Eden, MacMillan – none of them have done anything for me. MacMillan's got a face like a walrus anyway.'

'What's that got to do with anything?' Sid asked. 'Everything,' Uncle Bryn said. 'At one time it didn't matter, but now we've got the growing influence of television. The Prime Minister is in the public eye. His appearance is important. The ladies have got to like him. They're more than half the voters and they don't want some ugly geezer running the country.'

'I think all prime ministers should have a medical,' Lorna said, 'and they would have to meet certain criteria. We want a man at least six feet four not including his top hat. He should have a good physique, big chest, footballer's legs broad shoulders, the stamina to run a hundred yards, piggybacking a twelve stone woman. That's just the fitness part. He should be tested in English history from 1485 to 1957. He should be a happily married man with two children. His wife should have one leg slightly longer than the other to make sure of the sympathy vote. Basically, it's just a matter of sorting the wheat from the chaff.'

'And he must have a big cock,' Granddad Tucker added. They all thought he had gone to sleep. There was uproar. Nan Tucker looked daggers at Granddad Tucker. Lorna, completely unaffected said, 'Ah, yes. I was coming to that. He should be able to achieve an erection of at least seven inches. His trousers should be made specifically to emphasise a bulge in the crutch.'

'That was well composed, Lorna,' Bryn said. 'I think we should make you an honorary member of the Christmas Debating Society.'

Nan Tucker came in with the cold meat, bread, butter, biscuits and cheese and replenished all the menfolk's glasses of stout or beer. She was getting dangerously moody and everybody could sense it.

'I'll decide who comes here at Christmas, my lad – not you! That Merry widow of Walsall was invited on strict instructions that she did not take her clothes off and look at her now, the brazen hussy, her dress has all but fallen off her.' Just then Mom and Dad arrived. Mom was the height of respectability in her office clothes. They were surprised to walk straight into a slanging match with Nan Tucker, as always, at the forefront.

'So you finally decided to put in an appearance did you,' she shouted at Mom.'Just what I'd expect from a common family like the Rowley's. My boy Hugh must be a saint to put up with you.'

'We thought we'd come a bit later to give the party the chance to liven up,' Mom explained.

'It's livened up all right. We're not having another one like this. Certain people are banned next year, namely the brazen widow Stanhope, and her friend Maggie Rowley.'

'We don't have to be that serious do we?' Uncle Jacob pleaded.

'Yes we do,' Nan Tucker snapped. 'Every year I put on a party for a lot of ungrateful families including your lot – the Greenbergs a load of skinflints and swindlers.'
Thank heavens Uncle Sid intervened. 'It's Christmas, Amy,' he said to Nan Tucker. 'Let's quieten down shall we? We should be starting the entertainment by now. Let sleeping dogs lie. Let's get the entertainment going. I'd like to recite a short poem which I dedicate to my great niece, Veronica, with wishes for a happy married life with Tommy who cannot be here. I know that they plan to wed come June time and good luck to them. The poem is called 'Carry her over the water.' It's by W. H. Auden.
Oh, dear brother, I was so touched by it all I burst into tears but remember the two first two lines of the second verse which read:

Put a gold ring on her finger,
And press her close to your heart.

I thought of you and Tommy out there in the bleak tent lines. What a strange family we are! Bad tempered one minute, bawdy the next, loving the next. The atmosphere changed thanks to Uncle Sid. Uncle Jacob sang. It was all in Hebrew and very mournful. There were tears in his eyes. We would have all cried too, had we known what we were crying about. Lorna read a poem that you had sent her once. It was called, 'In Russian there are forty words for love.' She read it so well in that deep and rhythmical voice. Her dress was near to transparent. She knew it. She's a complete show-off. She looked wonderful. I swear she's ageless. Mother's 'White Cliffs of Dover' and 'Oh for the wings of a dove' closed the show.
Well, that was our wonderful Christmas at Nan's. I hope you enjoyed it. When you come home, which I'm told is May, Mom and Dad want us to have a final family holiday. It brings our teens more or less to an end. You'll

be twenty. I expect it will be on the south coast somewhere. Probably boring, but I think we should go. We can lounge around and walk and talk. Tommy will be working. It will be my last holiday as a single woman. Thank God! Keep in touch. Your adoring sister,
Veronica.
P.S. Mother's going to write to you – a special letter – not a 'Mom and Dad' letter.

Said letter duly arrived.

Darling Ralph,
my only son and once my little scamp. I should have written before now. I know that we have sent you regular boring letters from Mom and Dad, but I owe you a special mother to son letter as befits our special relationship. I hope that you are attempting to put the 'lost commission' to the back of your mind. The whole affair was unacceptable and I imagine that heads will roll at the highest level. How I miss you. I can't wait for your disembarkation leave in May.
I know that you'll look handsome, sturdy and bronzed. Veronica will have told you that we plan to take possibly our last ever family holiday in May/June somewhere on the south coast. We haven't decided exactly where yet. It will be wonderful to have my adult scamps with me. I'm going to buy a bikini. Is forty-four a bit old for a bikini? It is for most women but not for me. I've got my figure back and I believe that I am a very attractive woman. Let's face it, I'm in proportion whereas Lorna Pitt is top heavy, that's why she's got huge feet to counter balance the weight of her torso. Otherwise she has a reasonable figure, except for her big hands with fingers like pork sausages. However, far be it from me to be scathing about my best friend, however vulgar and show-offy she is and I didn't want this to be a gossipy letter. I get

enough gossip at work and I have the feeling that my second best friend Beryl and my third best friend Shirley are talking about me behind my back. When and if I catch them at it, the sparks are going to fly. I shall tell them that my son is fighting in a foreign field to make Britain a better place for common, ungrateful people like them to live in.

Time goes on, my loving son. You've taken what the army can throw at you. Germany should be no problem. Please don't come home with a fat fraulein with blonde plaits and fur boots. In fact, I should avoid them altogether. They could be East German spies. I'll have to close off now. Your Dad's just pulled into the drive.

Bye son xxxxxxxxxxxxxxxxxx

Chapter 17

The Unspeakable

February came and Ralph was preparing for his transfer to the Orderly Room. He stayed in B Company lines but was seconded to the Orderly Room for three days a week to sit in with Corporal Chivers. As soon as Chivers was demobbed, then Ralph would have to move to HQ Company lines, lock, stock and barrel. In the meantime, he stayed in B Company and shared a tent with George.

One day, he arrived back at his tent to see George sitting on the edge of his bed with his head in his hands.

'What's the matter, George?'

'Oh. Ralph! Life's a bastard. Do you know what happened today out at a road block?'

'Tell me. I'm dreading what I have to hear.'

'Duggie's been killed.' Looking back on it in his later years, Ralph was never able to put events into sequence. He could not remember what he said. He thought he said something banal like:

'Has it just happened?'

'Word's just got through.'

'I don't know what to say or what to do,' Ralph held back a tear. 'Duggie was my best friend.'

'He was everybody's friend,' George muttered.'He was a prince.'

'Does Tommy know yet?'

'Tommy's gone sick today. He's in bed. I haven't got the stomach to tell him, nor Stan either. Stan was his cousin.'

'I'll tell him,' Ralph said. 'Was it a bullet or an explosion?'

'An explosion I think. I can't think straight, Ralphy. Everything seems to have drained out of me. He's gone. That's all I can think of. He's gone.'

'It hasn't hit me yet,' Ralph said. 'I'm okay for now. What a fucking thing to happen! What a bastard! I'm off to Tommy's bedside.'

'It's me Tommy,' he shook him. 'What's the problem?'

'Some sort of fever. I'm sweating like a pig. I feel like death.'

'Tommy,' Ralph croaked. 'I've got some bad news.'

'Save it until tomorrow.'

'I can't Tommy. Duggie's been killed. There was an explosion at a road block and Duggie was—'

'Don't say it again, Ralphy.'

That was as far as anybody remembered. There must have been a funeral somewhere. There must have been a body bag flown home. The Padre must have spoken to them. Memory was a blank. Duggie was dead and the thought of that was agonising. The realisation came to them of how horrific 'real wars' must be. They imagined the helplessness of losing comrades in large numbers. How ghastly, depressing, shocking and harrowing it must have been.

Cyprus, in the words of Granddad Tucker, was a penny fight. Maybe, but death in a penny fight was as final as death on the Somme or the Crimea, or South Africa where Granddad Tucker no doubt lost comrades, though he never talked about it. He had probably carried the sadness around with him all his life, as many must do, as many millions must do.

After some days the numbness had left them but the sting was still there. Tommy brought them all together one evening and said:

'Listen, lads. We've grieved, we've moaned, wailed and sworn. Duggie won't come back. We're never going to see him walking up the company lines again. We've got to get back to being good soldiers and doing the job we were sent here to do. We're not the only sad lads in the world. Let's get on with things.'

'I had a dream,' Ralph said. 'There was a file of men – red coats – marching across a dusty plain. They were dirty, tired and hungry except for one man bringing up the rear. He was turned out immaculately as if for guard duty, his coat as scarlet as new, spotless white belt, boots shining, beard shaved clean. He smiled as he marched. I swear he touched me as I slept. It was Duggie.'

'That dream means that his soul has passed on,' George said. 'That's good enough for me. He's at rest. God bless him.'

'But God damn the bastards who killed him,' Stan said.

It was Colonel Wood, now a civilian, who took it on himself to act as a spokesman for the Grey Jackets until such times as his replacement, Colonel Irons, had a 'feeling' for certain aspects of the command of the Battalion.

On the death of Corporal Jennings he said to the press:

> Corporal Douglas Jennings will be sadly missed by his comrades and, indeed, the regiment. He had leadership qualities and was considered as officer material. He would have made a good officer. Now, tragically, that will never be. He was intelligent, articulate and polite. Our deepest sympathies go out to his family.

Lorna, having read the report in the newspapers under a bleak heading: 'MIDLAND SOLDIER KILLED IN CYPRUS' was both upset and angry. She was upset by the news and angry that young men were being killed in a skirmish that was not entirely necessary for Britain to be involved in. On the latter she wrote to *The Times*. She received the letter that she had been expecting from the Regimental Association. She wrote straightaway to Mrs

Jennings asking her for a suitable date and time for a visit. Mrs Jennings wrote back immediately and a firm date was fixed.

She informed Sarah that she had to make the visit.

'Are you all right to drive mother?'

'I shall be fine. I have to go. It's a duty that makes me proud and depressed at the same time, a strange mixture of emotions. I'm probably not the right sort of person to visit the bereaved, but I volunteered and could not possibly let the dear old Grey Jackets down.'

She put on a sombre office outfit and drove off for the Jennings home in Friar Park. She found the house easily and knocked on the door. Mrs Jennings ushered her in. Lorna was surprised. She had been expecting to see the archetypal squaddy's mum – careworn, stout, dowdy and lost for words. Mrs Jennings fitted none of these descriptions. She was well dressed, trim and attractive.

'My name is Edna,' she announced.'

'And I'm Lorna. I had a vision of you which does not fit the rather elegant lady that I see before me.'

'You flatter me, but I appreciate your praise when it is needed, such as now. Nothing boosts a woman's well-being like genuine praise. Don't you think?'

'As a conceited woman I agree with you. I thrive on admiration. Can I get down to basics please Edna and then we can talk. I'm here in a voluntary capacity for the Regimental Association. It is my duty to visit the loved ones of those men, injured or killed whilst on active service with the GreyJackets. We are here to offer you any help we can – financially, spiritually, emotionally or any other way.

'Good heavens! All that? Financially things should be satisfactory. My eldest son is in the Hong Kong police. He thinks that he can get me an administrative job out there, and I could live with him. He's a bachelor. I shall consider the offer seriously. Emotionally I am a wreck. I'm holding myself together for the length of this meeting. I was determined not to become a weepy woman. Spiritually, what is to be done? Am I to pray that Douglas will come back?'

'It's hardly the right occasion for such a comment, Edna, but I like your style. Yes, I have spoken to my share of weepy women, especially those who say in a tearful voice, "You don't know what it's like". I tell them I do. I tell them that I lost my husband in Holland in 1944 – Captain Roger Pitt was his name. He was a Grey Jacket hero.'

'I would rather have lost my man honourably than the way it *did* happen. The family business went under in the Depression years. My husband died a debt-ridden alcoholic in 1938 – ironically just when things had started to pick up. Shall I tell you about Douglas? He was the apple of my eye. Thank God I've got another son. Douglas had pride. He understood completely my stance on correct behaviour. I taught him that though we were no longer wealthy, he and Robin (my other son) should act and speak like gentlemen. They did. They were articulate, well mannered and well spoken, but now Douglas has gone and it was all a waste of time.' She broke down and sobbed uncontrollably.

Lorna sensed that Edna was not the sort of woman who would want to be hugged or soothed. She was stoical and independent. It was time to leave silently.

'How did it go, mother?' Sarah asked.

'Not too well.'

'You seem down in the dumps.'

'I am.'

'What happened?'

'I left her in tears. I'm not a very good counsellor, am I?'

'I'm sure you are. The Regimental Association are lucky to have you. You're a volunteer, not a trained professional.'

'Will you bring Jerome in for me, please?'

She brought Jerome in and sat him on her mother's lap.

'Ganny,' he said.

'I don't know if we're ever going to track down this little fellow's father, and I don't think you care, but I'll tell you what. He must be a handsome devil. Can you give me another four like this?'

'I hope so. It depends on finding a good father. You always wanted me to marry Ralph. You chose to take him for yourself.'

'He was so beautiful. I don't want to talk about things that have been debated over and over again. It's not the best day. I don't get depressed much, but I am now. It will pass. There will be a man for you, Sarah, a good kind man. Wait until the battalion comes home. You'll fall in love in a flash.'

'If you say so, Mom.'

The telephone rang. Lorna picked it up.

'Hallo.'

'Is that Lorna Pitt?'

'It is indeed. To whom am I speaking?'

'Arthur Wood.'

'Arthur! How wonderful to speak to you after so long. What can I do for you?'

'Well nothing really. I just wanted to let you know that I've received a phone call from Mrs Jennings. She thanked me profusely for arranging your visit. She said that you helped her to look to the future. She was grateful for your true understanding. She had been dreading a 'there, there, don't cry' drama and platitudes like 'he's gone to a better place.' She's a stiff upper lip type. She apologises for breaking down and crying. Can you imagine that? She's one of a dying breed.'

'I'm so glad you phoned, Arthur. I had left her in tears and I was wondering if I should have stayed. I was down and depressed and that's a rare thing with me. Now I'm no longer depressed.'

'Nor should you ever be, Lorna. Your work with the Grey Jackets has always been appreciated. You've got my number. Phone me any time. I'm a lazy civilian at the moment, taking a long overdue rest. I've been for a few job interviews for security work, but the title 'Colonel' puts people off a bit. They think I'm going to be bossing people about all day. I'll find something to suit me I suppose.'

'I'm sure you will, Arthur. We'll keep in touch. I look forward to seeing that upright, gallant, fine figure of a man. Goodbye dear Arthur.'

'Well, you probably heard that conversation. Mrs Jennings has expressed her appreciation for my visit. I'm happy again. I feel like celebrating.'

'Not by taking your clothes off, I hope,' Sarah said wearily.

March 1957 was halfway through. Ralph had taken over from Corporal Chivers as Part II orders clerk. He banged away at a rickety old typewriter much of the day. The basis of the job was to report on movement of troops, conduct, promotions and demotions, arrivals and departures and all manner of things set out in the correct way. Other duties were supervisory, but in reality everybody knew what they were doing. Orders were rarely given. Discipline was assumed. They were expected to set a high standard. Headquarter Company, to which the Orderly Room belonged, were compelled to provide personnel for the Battalion Quarter Guard, which was regarded as a 'Bullshit parade' where only immaculacy was acceptable. If you were on this guard you had the whole afternoon off to clean your kit. The orderly Officer always seemed intent on finding something wrong, so that the guard commander could roar at the man concerned. A speck of dust in your rifle barrel, speck of dirt in a fingernail, a minute speck of metal polish on your web belt – all the aforesaid warranted a bollocking. Ralph found himself on guard almost one night in three.

He still went down to B Company lines to see his old mates whenever they were in camp. The Arbo Gang, though, were breaking up. Dennis in Paris, Ralph in the Orderly Room, Tommy as Platoon Sergeant of 1 Platoon in A Company. That left only George, who would certainly be transferred back to the Worcesters after disembarkation and Stan who had been summoned to the Adjutant's office – so maybe he was off somewhere too.

'Sit down, Corporal Compton,' Major Le Breton, the Adjutant, ordered.

Stan sat on the only available chair next to the assistant Adjutant, Mr Benson.

'I'll explain the reason you're here,' the Adjutant told him. 'You may recall your meeting with Major Roade very early in your service. You were asked the standard question concerning your ambitions. You mentioned your GCE in art and said that you would like to develop that particular talent. Do you remember that?'

I certainly do, sir. There was mention of the possibility of taking on a war artist.'

'Well recalled, Compton. We want the activities of the regiment recorded in a volume entitled simply 'The Grey Jackets 1954 to 1957'. This would cover the Battalion's posting in Egypt and Cyprus. We could have used photographs but we think that illustrations by an artist who is a member of the Grey Jackets would have more impact. To cover our time in Egypt we'll give you some photos to use as a basis.'

'I shall be able to do most of the work without any aids, sir. I seem to have a photographic memory.'

'What medium would you use?' Mr Benson asked.

'Pencil, ink and coloured pencils mainly. Sometimes water colours or pastels.'

'Have you got any materials with you?'

'A limited supply. The thing I'm really short of is cartridge paper.'

‘As soon as we’ve set you up with a studio, we’ll get you all the materials you’ll need. Now then, Corporal Compton,’ the Adjutant said, ‘I’ll tell you what I want. I want a portfolio from you covering as many aspects of camp life and outside duties as possible. To give you an idea – spud-bashing, guards, patrols, sport, eating, drinking, merrymaking, RSM’s parade, Christmas in the ranks – I could go on. Put yourself on a roving commission. Come up to the Officers’ Mess, See me first. Ditto the sergeants’ mess. Speak to the RSM first. In fact, get a sketch of him. One of the Colonel too. I’m sure that as you go on you’ll think of more and more ideas. Mr Benson and I will visit you periodically. You’ll be transferred to the Intelligence section. You’ll have to move into HQ lines. They have a spare office, which will do as a studio. Corporal Tucker presently has the luxury of a tent to himself. Move in with him. I understand you’re good friends. You’ve got until June 9th to finish the project. The battalion will be back in UK by then. We’ll probably call you in. We’ll readjust your leave. See Mr Benson at 0800hrs. He’ll show you where you’ll be working. That’s all Corporal Compton. Feeling confident?’

‘Yes sir! Just give me the chance and I’ll do the job.’

Ralph got a shock when he got back to his tent that evening.

‘Stan the man! What are you doing here?’

Stan gave him the whole story.

‘That’s brilliant, Stan. War Artist eh? I’m amazed that I didn’t know anything about your hidden talent. All those months at QBS and you never said anything.’

‘I was a shy sort of lad then. Still am I guess. I’d told you and Jeff a few stories about this and that and you’d never believe me. So I didn’t ever mention my artistic ability. I did get you and Jeff on paper though. When I get things all set up, I’ll show you.’

‘This could be the start of a brilliant career for you, Stan. I mean commercially – not in the army. We’ll talk about it as the weeks pass by before we go back to dear old Blighty. I’m chuffed you’re moving in here too. At least I know we’ll get on with each other like we did at QBS.’

‘But you were always taking the piss out of me at QBS.’

‘That’s what I mean, Stan. We got on well. ‘Larking about’ as Jeff called it.’

‘Great days,’ Stan agreed.

The next morning, Major Le Breton and Mr Benson called Ralph into their office.

‘The ORS (Orderly Room Sergeant), Sergeant Kennedy, is most impressed by the way you’ve settled in Corporal Tucker, and so are Mr Benson and I. You have the attributes necessary for an officer. Would you consider extending your service?’

‘Yes sir, I would if I could be commissioned.’

‘I see no reason why not,’ Major Le Breton said.

‘I’m afraid you are wrong, sir.’

‘I don’t understand.’

‘It’s a long story, sir. Are you sure you want to hear it?’

‘Yes, we’ll hear it.’

Rather wearily (though he tried not to show it), Ralph reiterated the events surrounding the commission that never was. He was glad to reach the conclusion.

‘I imagine that you are no longer interested in being an officer,’ Major Le Breton said.

‘Not any more, sir.’

Chapter 18

Homeward Bound

The news was official. The Battalion would ship out on the troopship EMPIRE KEN on May 14th 1957. Suddenly everybody seemed to be in a good mood. The banter was still there, but the angry swearing had ceased. There was a lull in terrorist activity. The walled city of Nicosia was in bounds again to off duty troops. Only the diehards who felt the need to visit the brothels of Tanzimat Street, bothered to put civvies on and visit Nicosia, a town that everybody was overwhelmingly bored with anyway.

Soon, Ralph knew Cyprus would be a strange memory for him; the sort of memory that broke into a hundred pieces and died piece by piece. The sort of memory that old men have of long gone wars. They find it hard to believe that they were ever there. Ralph would remember the sun setting on the Kyrenia Ranges. They changed colour according to the light. He would remember the 'leaking tents' saga. Somebody wrote to the newspapers in UK and complained of the awful conditions during a period of heavy rain. The war minister, Sir Anthony Head, came out to see for himself. What was the outcome? Nobody knew. Nor did anybody know why, at the time of the Suez crisis, the order went out to deepen the monsoon trenches along the tent lines. Did the powers that be anticipate trench warfare? Ralph would remember the mournful cries of 'Cha Wallah' as the Indian Tea sellers moved along the lines. He would remember the eternal gabble of conversation and argument throughout the lines and the blare of early rock and roll. Most of all he would remember pay nights at the Naafi and singing loud enough to shake the buildings down. He would remember the colour of everything, the smell of everything.

If an artist were to paint a Cyprus scene, he would not have to use many colours. He would start with a base of yellow ochre, add a small amount of red for the orange groves, touch of grey for the hard-baked earth, deep blue for the sky and turquoise for the sea. As for the smells, he hoped he could soon forget them – the cookhouse, the latrines and the musty stores.

'Will you miss anything, Ralph?' Stan asked.

'I don't think so. The camaraderie perhaps.'

Dismantling Whittington Camp was a major operation. Every last square inch of canvas, every tent pole, duck board, sign board, quartermasters' stores, empty soldiers' boxes, weapons, company stores, beds, mattresses, blankets, vehicles, timbers, cookhouse equipment. It all had to go. The Orderly Room had to keep going until departure. Every piece of office equipment, stationery, chairs, trestle tables which acted as desks, were packed into crates. Everything that could be dismantled was dismantled.

The end result of their labour was a stark expanse of land. Only the permanent buildings remained. The quarters of officers, sergeants and other ranks were gone. What had once been home of a sort was consigned to history in a period of days. Senior officers and NCOs had vacated their married quarters. Wives and children were all to board the Empire Ken, as were all the attached personnel – REME, the ACC cooks, the Pay Corps, and 'Uncle Tom Cobbley' and all were going back to Blighty.

The ship was waiting at Limassol. Everybody was ferried out in launches. Bunks were allocated, lifeboat drill was given. They were on the high seas. A great cheer went up. A group of men started singing the Maori Farewell – 'Now is the Hour.' Not to be outdone the men of A Company burst into song with, 'Last Train to San Fernando, Last trayeeeen to San Fernando'. Suddenly the whole battalion was singing it. What it had to do with leaving Limassol nobody knew, but they sang it anyway. 'If you miss this one, you'll never get another one. Beady beady bom bom to San Fernando.'

The Orderly Room was accommodated within the Purser's Office, a spacious, clean and shiny place. There was very little for them to do. The work had been done. Ralph had prepared the complete personnel manifest, which had to be in strict alphabetical order – number, rank and name for all personnel on board. Every single name had been checked off with no queries. Ralph was pleased and proud about that. It meant that when they got to Liverpool, the identical copy manifest would check out too.

The Empire Ken had been a passenger ship before the war. The bars and restaurants were well furnished. There was a sense of being on a cruise ship, even though the vast majority of the passengers had never been on a cruise. It was pleasant to sit with a beer in front of you and imagine that you were somewhere else. There was a rumour that this trip from Limassol to Liverpool was the Empire Ken's last voyage.

Ralph and Stan stood leaning on the ship's rail, pints of beer in their hands. They were passing a long piece of land.

'Would that be an island?' Stan asked.

'Crete,' Ralph said.

'We're seeing a few places, Ralphy.'

'It's Malta next but I'm duty clerk. I can't go ashore. I'm not too bothered. Valetta's just a big naval base.

The summons went out for the Royal Navy to muster for rum.

'Why can't the army have a tradition like that?' Stan asked.

'You know what Churchill thought about naval traditions don't you?' He said it in parliament to a backbencher who pompously referred to those traditions. He said, "I'll tell you what the great traditions of the Royal Navy are, sir – rum, sodomy and the lash".'

‘Sodomy? That’s a bit of a slur isn’t it? We never met any in the army did we?’ Stan asked.

‘Any what?’ Ralph said.

‘Bumboys.’

‘There must have been some – law of averages. I only knew one. He was an Officers’ mess waiter. What got us on to this subject?’

The Empire Ken duly sailed from Valetta to Algiers where there was ‘some shooting going on’. Neither did they stop at Gibraltar. They saw it from the ship. ‘A big rock’ was the general opinion. Nobody was thinking about scenery any more. They just wanted to see Liverpool, which they did on May 26th. No one was allowed ashore until the next morning. Their sea kitbags, which carried their khaki drill and any other items of tropical rig, were taken from them and put in storage, presumably to reappear at Lichfield when they returned from disembarkation leave. Next morning they marched onto Water Street station where WVS volunteers served up free hot tea. Rail warrants were handed out. Ralph had a warrant for three hundred men to Walsall on a train leaving in ninety minutes. He found a call box and phoned Stanhope Hall.

‘Lorna?’

‘Yes?’

‘It’s Ralph.’

‘My little Corporal,’ she boomed. ‘Listen very carefully. Come straight here. I’ve locked the connecting door. You won’t see Jerome and Sarah until tomorrow. Don’t go home. There’s only Veronica there. Tommy’s going to stay there a couple of nights. Margaret and Hugh are already down at Rockingham on Sea or somewhere. Veronica’s got all the details. You and Veronica have got to travel down on the train.’

‘Sounds a bit complicated.’

‘Not for us it’s not. We’re in our own little nest. I’m terribly excited. I just can’t wait. I’ve already taken my clothes off. I've worked out a little programme. I want it to be a wonderful experience and then we'll have a candlelight dinner and wine. I've bought some very high-heeled shoes because now you're my little Corporal I need to be slightly taller than you. What time are you in Walsall?'

'About two o'clock.'

'I'll be ready for some jolly good fun. It's been eighteen months. I must sit down. I'm overcome with excitement. Bye darling.'

The train drew into Walsall dead on two o'clock and over three hundred of the First Grey Jackets alighted in best battledress, kitbags and suitcases. There was nobody to greet them save a little man in a dark suit who put his hand out to as many men as he could saying, 'Welcome home son.' Tommy, Stan and Ralph walked together. They asked him who he was.

'I'm the Mayor of Walsall and I'm very embarrassed.'

'Don't be,' Tommy said. 'We never expected a brass band and neither did we expect a horde of screaming womenfolk squealing and sobbing for joy. We're Walsall men aren't we? We don't say much and we don't ask for much.'

'I appreciate what you're saying, sergeant. It's just that when the Territorials go to annual camp there's always a four-page spread in the *Walsall Observer*. It means that the ragamuffin reserves get royal treatment and the smart regulars get nothing. I'm only here by chance. My neighbour's got a son with the Grey Jackets, otherwise I would have known nothing.'

'It's been nice talking to you sir,' Tommy said, 'but we must be on our way.'

They walked on.

'I bet he's an old soldier,' Ralph said.

'Maybe,' Tommy said, 'but there's a bit of pageantry to come. We've got the freedom of Walsall, freedom of Wolverhampton, West Bromwich, Bilston and just about everywhere and we'll be marching through every one of those towns plus the regimental band.'

'Let's forget about it for now,' Stan said. 'We've got five weeks disembarkation leave. Let's make the best of it. I've still got my portfolio to finish off. So I'm not completely on leave.'

Just then a taxi pulled up and one of Stan's cronies yelled out, 'Stan! We're going to Friar Park. Jump in. You can share the fare.'

Stan said hurried goodbyes and squeezed into the cab, kitbag, suitcase and huge folder of sketches to boot.

'So that leaves you and I, Ralphy, and I reckon we're going to be lucky lads today.

'That we are. Tommy. That we are.'

When Ralph arrived at Stanhope Hall he made for the kitchen door which was usually open. It was locked. He knocked and waited. Soon he heard the clunk of high heels on the tiles.

Lorna opened the door. He tried to speak. He was as tongue-tied as he had been the very first time that she had revealed her pale golden body to him at the garden party all that time ago. She had let her hair grow back past her shoulders. The light from the kitchen window picked out the lustre of it. Her skin shone. Everything about her was as wondrous to him as had been the first time, her enormous breasts, her total curvaceousness, and her great strong yet shapely limbs. She had shaved off her forest of wiry pubic hair. She stood before him, brazen, haughty and with no secrets.

'Are you going to say something?' she asked. 'Or are you overwhelmed by my unsurpassable beauty?'

'The latter,' he croaked.

'Oh, my poor tired overawed Ralph.' She took him in her arms, almost crushing him. 'Have I missed you? Have I longed to have you in my bed? You're looking well. You certainly fill out that uniform. How tired you must be. Let's get this uniform off you.' She commenced to undress him. 'I'd forgotten just how much a soldier wears.'

She removed gaiters, boots, socks, battledress, shirt, tie and pants.

'Stand up!' she ordered. 'You've put on a little weight, not much though. You've still got a good physique. You're still bronzed. You're hairier than ever, your back and chest particularly, but I like it.'

She hung his clothing neatly in the wardrobe.

'I think Veronica and Nan Tucker want a photo of you in uniform so you'll have to dress up again tomorrow. What a pain for you, but it's your fault for being so handsome. Stand in front of the mirror with me, Ralph. Don't we make a beautiful couple? This is about as narcissistic as it gets. I think you're getting excited. Little Ralph is making a move. You must be excited Ralph. I am. I've been thinking about you all night. I cannot ever remember being so excited. I think it's time for us to go into the bedroom. I think your tiredness will go. Let's go and have a look at my big new bed and while we're there we can have some jolly good fun. I've got you going, haven't I?' Little Ralph is huge isn't he? And look Ralph. I'm in position. I'm so so looking forward to this.'

Ralph turned over in his sleep. He felt for his pillow to pull it under his head. It seemed firm rather than soft. He ran his hand over it and reached a… 'A what?' he asked himself in his half sleep. A nipple! He knew where he was. Lorna stirred and said, 'You've woken me up.'

'I reached out for my pillow but found a nipple instead. Making love is full of surprises.'

'Is that all my nipple is to you? A surprise? I think it deserves a better description.'

'What time is it? I can see its still daylight, but I've lost track of time.'

'It's late evening. I'm very pleased with you, Little Corporal. You made love to me twice and you were so gentle and tender. I had worked out a little programme for us introducing alternative positions but you fell asleep and I hadn't the heart to wake you. You've had a busy day.'

'I'm glad you're pleased with me. It had been so long. It sounds ridiculous, but I was nervous. I thought back to the very first time and how frantic it was.'

'You must never take things seriously when it comes to pleasure, Ralph. Otherwise it ceases to be pleasure. There are enough serious things to be serious about. You and I are fun for each other. You're on leave – time to relax.'

Chapter 19

The Suit

'I shall be calling you in for dinner soon, Ralph. It's a celebratory dinner for your return. You know from past experience that I'm no gourmet cook. In fact, I'm no cook at all. My poor Roger always said to me. 'I'm either going to die in battle or die from your sausage and mash old gel.'

She had laid out the kitchen table with a bright white tablecloth and napkins. She had polished up her silver cutlery. Three candles burnt in the holder. It looked like a table at a five-star hotel. She brought in two large plates of her speciality – chicken salad. 'It's very hard to spoil a salad,' she always said but this was a monster salad to end all salads. It consisted of two drumsticks each, fresh lettuce, tomatoes, spring onions, cheese, pickle, hard boiled eggs and just about everything one could put in a salad. She put out two large wine glasses and poured out enough of her private stock of red wine to fill each glass.

'This is dinner at the Ritz, Lorna. I can see what trouble you've gone to. I don't know what to say. I'm overwhelmed.'

'Don't say anything. I did it because I love you and have missed you and don't want to lose you, even though it's certain that I will. Anyway, when did you last eat?'

'A biscuit and cup of tea on Water Street station. I'm ravenous. I've had to eat vile food for eighteen months. To sit down to a feast like this is a soldier's dream. Should we dress for dinner?'

'Certainly not. I wear no clothes at every opportunity and this is one.'

Ralph was conscious of the fact that he had grown used to wolfing down his food with the mannerless soldiery. He made an effort to be civilised again.

'This is unique, Lorna – a nude candlelit dinner.'

'Enjoy it, darling. It's for you. I've been thinking about this night and getting more and more excited about it.'

She poured out two glasses of wine.

'Here's to us and an utterly decadent celebration.'

They adjourned to the lounge. She smiled lasciviously and sprawled lewdly on the sofa.

'For no other man would I do this.'

'For my part I cannot counter that. You are the only woman I've ever known – known, carnally that is.'

'There will be other women, not many but some, just as there will be men for me. It's something we will talk about but not now. Now is for us. Do you like me now that little Lorna's forest has gone? It'll grow again. Feel the stubble. I had it done for you. One of my office colleagues did it. Does it entice you? I hope so Ralph because I've been looking forward to our jolly good fun. Maybe you should slow down on the wine.'

'Maybe, but everything's under control at the moment. Look!'

'Oh, my little Corporal! What a fantastic sight do I see before me. No wonder you conquered Europe. That is one huge erection and I'm already in an alternative position.'

It was dark outside. Ralph lay in the proscribed manner, his head resting on her 'ample bosom' as she insisted it should be called. Her hands were placed upon his forehead. 'Oh, Ralph,' she sighed. 'You are the love of my life. How I wish that we could always be together but…' she shrugged, 'we cannot and that's that. Savour the precious moment. Empty your head of all the harrowing stuff about the commission. Try not to think too much about Duggie. I know you've got this 'great adventure' to Australia in your head. Well, you can still go, in fact you will go.'

'How do you know all these things?'

'I just do.'

He knew that the subject was closed, but he still had the premonitions in his mind – the ship in port and the letters RON, the son on an island, the land of mountains and plantations and the golden-haired lady with a parasol.

Jumbled images filled his head and twirled in front of him in the darkness. Lorna's hands pressed a little on his head. Why did she have such big hands? 'Fingers like pork sausages' his mother had said and she was right.

'Empty your mind, dear Ralph,' she ordered. 'I sense a lot of nonsensical theorising going on inside you. Think immediately of something near you. Tell me what it is.

'Your torso.'

'Good choice. Think what joy my magnificent torso has brought you. Now you should have a wondrous image, which will blot out all others. I shall slowly remove my hands and you will sleep.'

He slept deeply until seven o'clock the next morning. He turned over in bed and slept briefly again. He had a nightmare. He was still on the Empire Ken. The ship was going down. He tried to move but he was crushed and he shouted, 'Help!'. Lorna's hand was on his forehead and the whole weight of her was on top of him – twelve stone ten pounds of honey-coloured woman.

'You're crushing me,' he protested.

'But you love it. I'll sit up if you like. Little Ralph is up with the lark and ready to go. There! Up he goes! Oh, Ralph. Hasn't it been an exciting time for us? I'll get you breakfast,' she told him. 'Remember the gardener's breakfast I used to get you? I'll cut the size down because I won't be needing you to do any manual work – well not just yet anyway. Your main job is to make me happy and you do that by being in my bed. I had a lovely dream. You and I were in a different place in a different time. We were both young and carefree. You wore uniform and I wore not a thing, but it did not matter. Everybody knew me and complimented me for being so daring and starting a new fashion. We had a little boy with curly hair like yours. He had a cheeky face. He was called Michael.'

Ralph ate his breakfast with relish. Everything on this leave seemed new and refreshing. Previous leaves had been enjoyable but full of foreboding – the weeks of gardening at Stanhope or embarkation leave with the dread of Cyprus.

Now things were different. Germany caused no fears. Even when disembarkation leave was over, the battalion would be reporting to Lichfield depot in dribs and drabs. Time was not precious. Most of the men admitted that they would spend their leave lounging around and drinking.'

There was a knock on the partition door.

'That will be Sarah and little Jerome,' Lorna said. 'They're earlier than expected.'

'But we've got no clothes on.'

'Too late now, Ralph. I'll go and let them in.'

She unlocked the door, and let them in.

'Ralph,' Lorna ordered, 'come and meet my beautiful daughter and my handsome little grandson. This is Ralph' Lorna told Jerome. 'Raf,' he said. 'Raf, Raf Raf.'

'And this, Sarah, is my virile young lover Ralph.'

'Hallo, Ralph. You're just as mother described.'

'I apologise for my state of undress,' Ralph said. 'I understand that nakedness could be confusing for Jerome.'

'Well, I'm not sure about that. He's only fifteen months old. I'm not sure that he would understand. Anyway, I'm glad I've seen you in your natural state as it were.'

'Hasn't he got a good physique, Sarah?'

'I'll say! Bronzed and muscular. I'm told you did a Herculean rescue job on the Stanhope grounds and that was what started off your fitness. When mother showed me what you had done, I couldn't believe it. I bet she was a slave driver.'

‘I *was* a slave driver. He loved it. I embarrass him in company. He loves it. When we went to Wanstock I used to make him run and swim every morning at six o’clock, longer and longer distances each day. He used to take me to the pub in a wheelbarrow.’

‘I’m glad you’re making my mother happy, Ralph. There’s no long-term benefit from it, as I think we all know, but my mother’s deliriously happy. I know when she’s happy and when she’s down in the dumps. When she’s miserable her skin looks dull, but when she’s happy it shines like a polished table. I’m glad I’ve seen you. Mother wanted that. Maybe you can help me out with a bit of baby-minding like mother does. I’m out looking for a job at the moment. I’ll see you around Ralph. We’ll be in and out of each other’s flats, no doubt. Don’t worry about what to wear. We all know each other, don’t we?’

‘I don’t know what you look like,’ Ralph said.

‘Ralph doesn’t know what I look like, Mother.’

‘Well show him, darling.’

‘Let’s get this dress off then. Ready for this? Voila! What do you think, Ralph?’

‘Great figure.’

‘Yes it is, isn’t it? So now we all know each other. What are you laughing at Jerome, you naughty little boy!’

Ralph decided to phone Veronica.

‘Good brother! I’m off work until the end of our family holiday. Are you coming round?’

‘Yes of course. I understand you want a photograph of me in uniform.’

‘Yes I did. Is it a nuisance?’

‘Well, it is actually, but I’ll get my uniform back on. You realise that you are the only person in the family that I’d do this for. You’ll have to take two photos – one for you and one for Nan Tucker.’

‘Why can’t you go to Nan Tucker’s yourself?’

'Because I'm not walking through the streets of Caldmore in uniform. It would look as if I was posing. Every Grey Jacket in the world will be in civvies today.'

'Message received loud and clear. I'll see you in twenty minutes.'

Veronica was at the door. She threw her arms around him.

'My darling, darling brother. Eighteen months without you is too long. You look great. You're a bigger man, I swear it. I'll take four photos of you, one for me, one for Nan and one each for Mom and Dad.'

'I'll stand at ease shall I?'

'If you like. Now smile. No, not a grin like a Cheshire cat. A normal smile. That's it. I've finished the film. I'll go down town and put it in to be developed this afternoon.'

'That's one matter out of the way. Next subject – is Tommy making you happy? I mean really happy?'

'Yes he will be, but he's only been on leave a day and he's spent most of that helping Ron out. To be honest, I'm getting a bit worried about things. Ron just thinks of the next job. Tommy wants the business to be on a sounder footing, but he's got fourteen months service left. He needs advice.'

'How about Lorna? She's rolling in it.'

'He's too proud to take money.'

'It would be a loan with interest. There's no shame involved. It would be a commercial transaction. Just leave it to me. Don't tell him that we've had this conversation. He'll think I'm interfering but I'm not. Tommy's like a brother. I'd never let him down.'

'Tommy would do anything for you, Ralph. If you help him out, find something genuine that *you* need help on, then his pride won't have been hurt. He's a very proud man. Let's change the subject shall we? I saw Lorna this morning at about five to nine, striding into Walsall in her blue office outfit with a rather short skirt. She looked great. She looked like a career woman – secretary to the Managing Director of ICI or somewhere. I thought to myself, my darling brother's been busy. So tell me, good brother, am I right?'

'You are right, my angel Veronica. You are so right. Conscious of the fact that we have decided to part once I come home on demob, it seems that Lorna is hell bent on making our time together a time to be remembered. I'm right back hopelessly and completely bewitched. I cannot believe that I've only been back a day. It's been so… er…'

'Active?'

'Hyperactive.'

'So I imagine spending a few days with Mom and Dad doesn't appeal much, I bet.'

'Not really but we couldn't possibly not go, could we? I know it's symbolic for them. I'm twenty at the end of this month. That ends our teenage – well mine anyway.'

'So, when can we go? Two more nights here means five nights at Rockingham. Three more nights here means four nights at Rockingham. Let's go for two here and five there, shall we? I'll phone Mom. It'll be fun, what with Mom in her bikini showing off for her little scamps. It's a bit of a blow having to go by train, but I've got the route worked out!'

'So it's Rockingham on Sea here we come. I wonder what it's like. Bye little sister. I'm off to Nan Tucker, but I'm going back to change first. Then this uniform goes into the wardrobe at Stanhope Hall and it doesn't come out until the day I report back.'

Ralph arrived at Nan Tucker's late in the morning.

'You should have come in uniform so your Granddad could have seen you.'

'I've put my uniform away for five weeks, Nan. I want to forget all about it for a while. Veronica's taken some photos and she'll let you have one as soon as possible.'

'And I hear you're off to join your Dad and Maggie Rowley at the seaside and she's bought herself a little bikini. I ask you! A woman in her forties parading around like a little floozy. My boy Hugh must be a saint to put up with all these shenanigans.'

'Well the last thing that I want to do is argue with you, Nan, but my father, much as I love him, is no saint. He used to spend most of his time in the pub. It was my mother who dragged him back into the fold and got us back as a family again. My mother is Margaret Tucker not Maggie Rowley and I love and adore her and I know she'll look wonderful in a bikini. I'm going to see Granddad.'

Harry Tucker was reading his newspaper. He was using a magnifying glass.

'Dammit,' he said, 'my eyes are getting worse and worse. I can't make out a thing.'

'You've got the paper upside down, Granddad.'

He looked up.

'Why if it isn't young Ralph. Did you shoot any of them EOKAs?'

'No, Granddad.'

'Why not? They killed your best friend, didn't they?'

'It's all regulated Granddad. You can only fire if you have shouted 'Halt Stamata Dur', which is 'stop', in English, Greek and Turkish. If they don't stop you can open fire.'

'When it's too bloody late! What are you now? Corporal?'

'Corporal now. Maybe Sergeant next year. I'll have done three years.'

'I did twenty – 1884 to 1904 – Ireland, Egypt, India, Burma and the big one – South Africa. All fading memories and I'm certain you've heard it all before. I'm a boring old man.'

'No, you're not Granddad.'

'Yes I am. I'll try to stay alive until August 58.'

'That's decent of you.'

He fell asleep.

Ralph went back into the kitchen.

'There's a nice cold Guinness there for you, boy's boy, and I'm sorry for what I said. It's gossipy old age creeping up on me.'

'I was only sticking up for my mother. I know I'm a mummy's boy. I don't care. I haven't turned out that unmanly, have I?'

'You've turned out a credit to us all, but you wouldn't have done if your mother had kept on namby-pambying you. Let's forget it. Where are you off to now?'

'Uncle Jacob's, I want him to make me a suit. I don't want a suit off the peg. I want the best. A dark suit, made to measure. It's for a wedding.'

'Well it must be a very important wedding that's all I can say, to go to that shyster skinflint Jacob Greenberg.'

'Now, now Nan. You're in a critical mood today, aren't you?'

'He's my brother-in-law. I know him. He'll overcharge.'

'I'll bargain with him. As for it being an important wedding, yes it is. It's one of my best mates from the army. George Braddox is his name. The wedding's at some place at the back of beyond down in Worcestershire.'

'Acornbridge,' Nan Tucker said casually.

'Yes. That's the place. How did you know that, Nan?'

'Surely you knew that Braddock was my maiden name?'

'No and it never occurred to me to ask. You were Nan Tucker.'

'Before I married I was Amy Braddock. I was raised in Acornbridge.'

'Not Braddox – Braddock. That's right. Braddock, Braddox and Bradnack are all the same family. The names got spelt differently in Parish Records. My father was Walter Braddock. He had four brothers who went on to have families. There are Braddocks all over the place, but the clannish Braddocks are still in and around Acornbridge and Penny Mortimer.'

‘Wait till I tell George about this. We’ll be blood brothers for life or maybe not as close as that – blood cousins. You should come to the wedding with me Nan. You’re a Braddock. You’d see people you’ve not seen for years.’

‘I’m not going to any country wedding at my age. You should take the Gorway widow with you. It’ll be a wild old do. She’d be in her element – dancing naked on the tables. Now be off with you to Jacob’s and don’t let him put one across you.’

Jacob Greenberg’s tailor’s shop was a short walk to Caldmore Green. It stood on a corner. The shop sign had almost faded away. Jacob told Ralph that having no sign had its advantages. It meant that he would get none of the sort of callers who simply waste time. They hum and haw and change their minds every few seconds and finally walk out with nothing.

‘We call them wankers in the trade,’ Jacob concluded.

The inside of the shop was like a rabbit warren. Bolts of cloth, suits in progress, sewing machines and all manner of equipment strewn haphazardly around. Only Jacob knew where everything was. Only Jacob knew how to get in and out of the premises.

‘Now then, young Ralph. I think I know what you’re here for. You’ve got until the August after this in the army and you want a nice sharp suit to step into for demob.’

‘It’s a bit more urgent than that, Uncle. I want to pick it up from you by mid-June at the latest. It’s for a wedding on the 19th.’

‘So there’s a time limit. Sometimes a time limit can affect the price, but I’m sure we can work something out. You’ve come to the right place. In a Greenberg suit you will certainly be the best-dressed man at the wedding. In fact you’ll be amongst the best-dressed men in Walsall. The Mayor wears one of my suits, so does Jolyon Noble, Tory

MP for Walsall South. So does Wilf Workman, Labour MP for Walsall North.'

Jacob had already got out his tape measure and was running it over Ralph rapidly, jotting figures on a scrap pad.

'Can you give me some idea of price,' Ralph asked.

'Do you want a waistcoat?'

'Yes, I'd like a waistcoat with a pocket for my gold watch. Can you give me an idea of the price?'

'Do you want flaps on your pockets?'

'No. Can you give me an idea of the price?'

'Do you want turn-ups?'

'No. Turn-ups are going out of fashion Can you—'

'Do you want wide lapels or narrow lapels? Narrow is 'in'.'

'Narrow it is then.'

'That's everything,' Jacob said. 'Now let's have a look at my pad and work out a special price for family.'

'Jacob tapped his pencil of the pad muttered for a while before saying. 'Price including administration and customer service and family discount and extras, with a deduction for soldiers on active service. Forty quid.'

'I was thinking of fifteen.'

'Ridiculous! Go down to Walsall market if you're looking for a £15 suit. Thirty two.'

'The other way round. Twenty-three.'

'Thirty.'

'Twenty-five.'

'Twenty seven pounds, ten shillings. Special price for relatives. I'd be ruined if I did this every time, but I'm a generous man. I can't help that. I've done so many favours for people that I'm on the brink of ruin. Call in ten days' time, Ralph.'

Ralph walked back to Stanhope Hall, weary from conversation. Sarah and Jerome were sitting on a deckchair on the patio. Jerome looked up and said 'Raf'. She passed the child over. He smiled again and said, 'Raf'.

'He's taken to you in such a short time,' Sarah said. 'You'll make a good father one day, Ralph.'

'Hope so.'

'You will. Mother says you will and she's almost clairvoyant. It will be some years yet, but it will happen.'

'The plan was for you and I, wasn't it?' Ralph said.

'That was mother's plan from the time we were seven.'

'What happened?'

'What happened? I went to a party at college, got drunk, and you know the rest. Mother made a big show of tracking down the father, but the fact is, it could have been any one of six.'

Chapter 20

Rockingham on Sea

Ralph told Lorna that he was travelling down to Rockingham on Sea with Veronica, Hugh and Margaret in two days' time.

'It will only be for five days,' he explained, 'but it is something that we cannot possibly duck out of, not that we would want to do so anyway. It's a little family break. It's a farewell to our teens. Veronica's nineteen now and I'm twenty. My mother's thrilled about it.'

'It may sound a little peevish, Ralph, but I shall miss you.'

'Come on Lorna, five days! You went eighteen months without me. I owe this to my parents. Veronica and I are mother's little scamps!'

'And that's what she'd love you both to be and never to grow up.'

'Well if we're talking about growing up, a big part of it is acceptance of reality. As time goes by and the battalion gets ever nearer to getting back to strength and preparing for Germany, our affair will be over.'

With that he walked out and into the gloom of the uninhabited area of Stanhope Hall. He felt unaccountably tired. He put it down to delayed reaction after all the activity of the Grey Jackets' move from Cyprus. He found himself an armchair and immediately fell asleep. He did not wake until two hours later. Nobody had tried to find him. Maybe they were all annoyed with him. Maybe they thought him stroppy. Maybe they were right.

He remembered that the evening was booked for day two at the Ritz with candles, whiter than white table linen and a basic meal a la Lorna. Odds on favourite would be corned beef with vegetables washed down with red wine. He wondered if he could face it. He felt more like going down to the Fish & Chip shop and eating a huge plate of plaice and chips with a mug of tea, thence a visit to the Windmill or wherever the lads were, and sinking a few pints.

Having undergone what seemed a decade in a totally male world, why should he wish to continue it? Was it the camaraderie? It was, he decided, an outpouring of relief. He had done his Active Service, something to be proud of, and marked by the bizarrely coloured purple and green General Service Medal.

He decided that he could not possibly absent himself from day two at the Ritz. Lorna would be terribly upset. 'Ralph,' she shouted as she walked through the eerie emptiness of the Hall.

'I'm here,' he shouted, 'and I'm sorry if I got stroppy. I felt suddenly and unaccountably tired and found myself an armchair. I haven't forgotten day two at the Ritz.'

'Good. Let's go back to the kitchen shall we? It will come as no surprise to you that we shall feast on corned beef salad and red wine. I know it's boring, but it's the least important item on our agenda. The most important is some jolly good fun on my big bed.'

'What's the dress for this evening?' he asked. 'Is it formal, casual or zero?'

'Zero. There will not be many more times. Zero is essential. To envelope my sensational body with clothes is a sin. Swear to me that, wherever you are in this world, you will constantly ache for Lorna's heavenly body.'

'Isn't a heavenly body a planet or something?'

'How would I know? Come along, Beautiful Boy. Let's get to the important part of the evening and do a bit of zeroing.'

'It's a long time since you called me Beautiful Boy.'

'That is because you no longer fit the description. You graduated to become My Handsome Man. I hope that you're now refreshed after your sleep because I want you to be my Virile Young Lover. Do you remember that? Do you remember your embarrassment when I used to call you that in public? It was such fun.'

'Fun for you. Not for me. I never quite got used to it.'

'But you complied. You were putty in my hands. I made a man of you physically, but in other respects you were often like a little boy lost. You're still naive, lovably naive. There are so many things I shall miss about you.'

'Vice versa for me. What shall you do?'

'What shall I do when?'

'When I'm not here.'

'I thought that *I* was the one to be conceited. Life without Ralph Tucker will no doubt be interesting. It will certainly not be a moping time. What shall I do, you ask? I shall keep my little house in Chelsea. I shall continue my column in the *Express* – The Stanhope Widow. People like it.'

'I'm one of them. I read the one about Wimbledon. It was on the ball.'

'I've done several about Wimbledon over the months. I make a good living from The Stanhope Widow. That and my property interests make me a wealthy woman. I shall continue to be content and comfortable. I go to the local pub. They're a rough and ready lot. I play the concertina. I'm happy enough. As far as my love life is concerned, living in a literary environment will no doubt give me scores of opportunities, but I shall spurn them all. Men are unpredictable, fat, pompous, presumptuous, dishonest, callous and vain. I cannot and will not put up with any man who fits into these categories. I shall have boys. They must be between the ages of seventeen and twenty, single, well built and intelligent. I shall have them one at a time. When we are mutually bored, we part. I then move on to the next one. Oh, how I'm looking forward to it. To have a charming strong boy in my bed. So there you have it dear Ralph. Are you jealous?'

'I've every reason to be, but I'm not.'

'Good. You're a man now. Let us adjourn to my big bed and you can climb on for the trip of a lifetime. Remember that silly expression, Ralph. You will hear it again from another woman.

'You are proof of my theory, Ralph – my theory that boys are best. I'm not going to list your qualities. You seem to be conceited enough already – maybe rightly.

'Some people say 'never look back'; it's a shallow expression favoured by those who have much to be ashamed of. I hope, dear Ralph, that you will look back at our times together. I have never been so happy.'

Veronica was already waiting outside the house when Ralph appeared with his battered suitcase. She only had a small holdall.

'I've ordered a taxi to New Street station. He should be here any time now.'

The taxi arrived and they bundled themselves in. Half an hour later they were on their way.

'We're in a carriage of our own, good brother. We can have a nice little chat.'

'It'll be more than a little chat once you get going little chatterbox.'

'There's something I'm dying to ask. What happened on day 2 at the Ritz?'

'Why should I tell you? It's private. Just supposing I asked about you and Tommy?'

'I'm not stopping you. Tommy believes in getting the job done. Get in, do it, get out. Just like a plumber. I know it doesn't sound very romantic, but we love each other. Work wise, as you know, things aren't going all that well, but I shall always, always, always be behind Tommy and he'll make it.'

'I admire you, good sister. Of course he'll make it. Sergeant Tommy Ward, founding member of the Arbo Gang! He'll make it.'

'Don't try to deviate from the main issue, Ralph. What happened on day 2 at the Ritz? I want to know every lurid detail.'

'All right, you dirty-minded little madam. You asked for it. Lorna set a table up in the kitchen with dazzling white linen and polished cutlery. Hence my definition 'like a table at the Ritz'.'

'That's not very sexy. I want to hear some real juicy stuff.'

'Okay. How far had we got?'

'As far as the table cloth,' Veronica moaned. 'It's boring.'

'All right, I'll shut up then if you're bored.'

'Just tell me something you did.'

'Something we did? I'm thinking. It's difficult to remember specific things. I shall need a little time to ponder.'

'Forget it, you mean swine! I'm not interested any more, you nasty, teasing, pretty-faced little mummy's boy.'

'Fine. I shall read my paper and admire the scenery as green field after green field flashes by. I might even have a little sleep.'

'Good idea! Don't wake up. I'm looking forward to the day when you're reincarnated as a cockroach and I shall be waiting for you in a pair of big boots.'

The train rattled through the countryside. Ralph and Veronica sat in moody silence for another half hour. Finally Veronica broke the silence.

'Please Ralph. Tell me one thing.'

'Little sister, I'm not going to tell you anything. To be absolutely honest – in other words repeat to nobody – I'm well prepared for the day that Lorna and I part. When it started it was a sensational experience for me, I was readily seduced. Now I want to get back to sanity and there's nothing saner than the Tucker family off to the seaside. I've been looking forward to this trip. Nobody knows how much.'

'I understand, good brother. Yes, she was a dominant force in your life. Now it's time to be Ralph Tucker again.'

They chatted and soon they were at London Euston to change trains.

'Do you remember Mom getting us across London when we went to stay at Pembroke? She seemed to know exactly where to go with a five and six year old tugging her coat tails. I was in awe of her,' Ralph recalled.

'And do you know what, Ralph, you still are – and she's in awe of you. Here's the Brighton train. Don't forget your famous battered suitcase. If that case could tell a story!'

'Half a story,' Ralph replied. 'I shall be taking it to Australia for starters.'

Hugh collected them from Brighton and drove them the twenty miles to Rockingham on Sea.

'This is where we're staying.' He pointed to a large white hotel called The Rockingham. 'You're sharing a room, which is not normal for a twenty year old and a nineteen year old, but that's all they'd got.'

They pulled into the car park and carried their luggage in. Margaret was waiting in the foyer. She was uncontrollably excited to see Ralph. She pressed herself hard against him.

'My son, my son, my wonderful son. Those eighteen months were eighteen years for me. Let me look at you. What a physique! And bronzed too. Have you brought your trunks? We'll be down on the beach first thing tomorrow. Wait till you see me in my bikini. I was going to buy one, but then I saw a pattern in a magazine so I made it myself. I cut it down a bit. It's a bit daring. Your father says it's disgusting, but he's not too well up on fashion.'

Hugh suggested that Ralph and Veronica got settled in and that they all meet up for a drink at six thirty. Ralph and Veronica took a walk along the beach. It was almost deserted. The sunbathers and swimmers, having endured a scorching day on the beach, had found themselves a cool bar somewhere to enjoy a cold beer.

'Well, it doesn't look much,' Veronica said, 'but I quite like it already. There are some rocks over there that we can explore. Let's take a walk over there.' They walked by the rocks and found a secluded little inlet.

'This is a nice little beach,' Ralph said.

'It is,' Veronica agreed, 'but do you see the sign?'

'Naturists beach! I wonder if Mom knows about it.'

'Don't tell her for lord's sake.'

They arrived back at the Hotel dead on six thirty.

Ralph bought the beers.

'Cheers,' all said.

'We appear to be one chair short,' Hugh said.

'That's no problem,' Margaret said. 'Ralph, you sit in this armchair and I'll sit on your lap.'

The five day break at Rockingham on Sea passed peacefully and pleasantly. Most days they played cricket on the beach using the same improvised equipment that Hugh had put together for Ralph when he was a boy – a second-hand bat bought from a junk shop, wickets and bales made from old mop handles and a hard rubber ball.

Veronica excelled at cricket. She wielded the bat with strength and accuracy. She kept whacking the ball for six straight out to sea. Ralph, Margaret and Hugh were running non-stop in their attempts to field the ball. Hugh was the first to wilt. He lay flat on the beach exhausted moaning, 'Enough is enough'.

Ralph asked Veronica to walk along the beach with him.

'Would you like to come too, Mother?' he asked.

'Not really darling. It reminds me too much of you and that brazen hussy walking nude along the beach at Wanstock. You two go ahead. Your father and I can stay here and soak in the sun.'

Ralph and Veronica walked past an outcrop of rocks as far as the inlet where a sign said, 'NATURIST'S BEACH.'

'I suppose that we shouldn't be here,' Ralph said.

'There's nothing that they can do about it, good brother. They can't send somebody out to order us to take our clothes off can they?'

'I don't know about that,' Ralph replied. 'There's somebody coming over to us now.'

A rather wizened old man with an all over suntan approached them and asked, 'You do realise that you are on a naturists' beach, don't you?'

'Of course,' Veronica told him. 'Have you any objection?'

'Well, we like people to comply.'

'Are you asking us to take our clothes off?' Veronica challenged with mock disgust.

'Yes we are,' the wizened old man confirmed.

'I'm afraid that ordering people to undress contravenes Bye Law 67,' Veronica informed him.

'How did you know that?'

'We're from the National Beach Inspectorate. We have no objection to your nudity. Therefore you should have no objection to our being suitably attired for the beach.'

'You soon told *him*,' Ralph said admiringly. 'Let's get to the caves and then back to Mom and Dad. We'll have a few beers tonight to cap it all off and a good time will have been had by all.'

Hugh started out at the crack of dawn from Rockingham and reached home by mid-afternoon. Veronica and Margaret alighted and Hugh drove Ralph to Stanhope Hall.

‘She’s there!’ Hugh shouted, ‘Waiting for you. My God! Lorna in nothing but her wide brimmed hat. What a sight! There’s something about that woman, apart from her oozing sex appeal. I have to go straight to work. I was dreading it but now I’m happy.’

‘That’s what she likes – making people happy.’

Hugh pulled up onto the grass verge and opened the car window.

‘Nice holiday?’ Lorna asked.

‘Great. Right up your street actually. There was a nudist beach there.’

‘Full of pear shaped cretins, I’ll bet. Have you got me the photo of Margaret in her bikini?’

‘Veronica’s sorting all that out. I’ve got to get back to the office for two hours. Nice to have seen you, ‘seen’ being the operative word.’ He drove away.

She took Ralph’s hand and they walked back through the avenue of cedar trees to the house.

As soon as they had reached the kitchen the phone rang and Ralph answered it.

‘Hallo.’

‘Can I get Corporal Tucker on this number?’

‘This is Ralph Tucker speaking.’

‘It’s Major Le Breton. Enjoying your leave?’

‘Immensely, sir.’

‘I need to get hold of Corporal Compton urgently. It seems that he’s not on the phone.’

‘I can get hold of him, sir. I’ll go down to his house and get him to contact you.’

‘I was wondering if you could go one better. Have you got use of a car?’

‘Please bear with me a minute sir.’ Hurriedly he explained things to Lorna. ‘Of course you can use the car,’ she affirmed.

‘Yes, sir. I’ve got use of a car.’

'Good man. Will you do this for me? Collect Compton tomorrow and get him here at Lichfield by 0900 hours. I've got his portfolio of sketches here. The publisher is coming here tomorrow and we need him at the meeting.'

'I'll get him there sir. In civvies?'

'Smart civvies – collar and tie. You should both bring your pay books for identification at the guardroom.'

'May I ask a question, sir?'

'Of course.'

'Are the sketches up to standard?'

'They're of a very high standard. In fact, they are excellent. He's put a tremendous amount of work in. He's got a future.'

'I'll deliver him. If there are any hitches I'll contact you sir.'

'Good man.' He gave Ralph a phone number, thanked him profusely and rang off.

'You'd better get straight down to see Stanley,' Lorna ordered.

Ralph reached Stan's house and knocked on the door He heard a voice say 'coming'. The door opened and a decidedly hung-over young man appeared.

'Ralphy!'

'We've got him, James, We've got him,' Major Le Breton shouted across the office to Mr Benson. Our trusty man, Tucker will get him here by 0900 hours. Let's have another look at those sketches. Even the ones, which are copies of photographs, are brilliant. I like his colouring too.'

'How do you like this one sir?'

It was of George Braddox sitting on his bed with his head in his hands having just heard of his comrade's death.

'Or this one?' It was Ralph's dream of a file of redcoats on a dusty plain, dirty and weary save for Duggie at the rear, happy and smiling.

‘Their uniforms are accurate too,’ Major Le Breton said ‘This bloke Compton’s got a photographic memory. His work has amazed me. I have to admit it.’

‘So that’s the story so far, Stan,’ Ralph said. They were sitting in a nondescript pub in West Bromwich. ‘This is a celebration.’

‘What’s there to celebrate? You’re going a bit over the top, Ralphy. It depends on what happens tomorrow. They may reject the idea.’

‘Talk about pessimism! They will not reject anything. Major Le Breton told me that the sketches were excellent and that’s good enough for me. This will be the start of a career for you. It’s a specialised type of art. Do you want to spend your life humping rocks while Jeff Pyke’s wallet gets thicker and thicker?’

‘You’re the last person to be lecturing me on grabbing career chances. Tommy knows what he’s going to do in life, so does Dennis, so does George. What are *you* going to do?’

‘Damned if I know. I hate to bring the subject up but before Duggie was killed I knew what I’d be doing too.’

‘I’m sorry Ralph,’ Stan said,‘I appreciate what you’re trying to do for me.’

‘Be ready at 0800 hours tomorrow. No, be on the safe side, 0745. Smart civvies, collar and tie.

Chapter 21

The War Artist

'This is an old motor.'

'What did you want? A Rolls? A Jag? This will get us to Whittington. I've driven down to Devon and back in this.'

'Yeah, well you can thank me for that. I taught you how to drive in the van.'

'I knew before that. I drove my dad's car.'

'What are we arguing for?'

'Nothing really. We can have a bit of rock and roll if you like.'

'Don't tell me this car's got a radio.'

'No, dummy. We provide the music.'

They sang 'Heartbreak Hotel', 'Blue Suede Shoes' and 'Hound Dog'.

'What's your favourite of those three, Ralph?'

''Hound Dog' – You ain't never caught a rabbit and you ain't no friend of mine'.'

'Have you ever caught a rabbit?'

'Yes. A long time ago at a farm in West Wales – me and Uncle Bill. As a matter of fact we shot ten. He carried eight on a pole across his shoulder and I carried two. I was only six.'

'I can imagine you when you were six – curly haired pretty little mummy's boy.'

'Yes I was. You didn't expect that, did you? You thought you'd start another argument, didn't you? Don't start arguing at this meeting will you.'

'Credit me with some common sense. I wasn't arguing anyway. It was just a bit of banter.'

'Banter? We've just had eighteen months of that. I'll tell you something I've been meaning to ask. How come Jeff and I knew nothing of your talents?'

'I'd be sitting there in the half-light sketching away unnoticed. Only when we had a quiet period of course.'

'Of course. We're nearly there.'

They booked in at the guardroom. Stan was directed to Major Le Breton's office. Ralph was ordered to leave the barracks and return to collect Stan at 1130 hours. He decided to go into Lichfield and have a stroll round.

Major Le Breton, Mr Benson and Mr Turnbull, the publisher, were already there. Stan was called in and introduced. Coffee and biscuits were already on the table. Stan took his notebook from his huge sketch wallet and sat in the empty chair.

'Corporal Compton,' Major Le Breton began.

'Can I just cut in here?' Mr Turnbull asked. 'I'd like to be on first name terms with this talented young man, Stanley Compton. A combination of Stanley Matthews and Denis Compton, eh? I'm Malcolm Turnbull, Sales Director of Lionel Street & Sons. We're publishers of military literature. We were established in 1860.'

Major Le Breton looked slightly irritated as he asked if a start could be made. He went on to explain that a hardback book would be produced with a narrative and sold initially through the regimental museum, though other outlets would be found, and the whole effort would be backed by newspaper advertising and publicity. They went on to discuss other facets of the operation – the form of narrative, the chronology, an exhibition of the original sketches. Stan felt well out of his depth. Every time he had something intelligent to say he found that by the time he was ready to speak they had moved on to another subject. Eventually he was confident enough to interject and put some ideas forward. He had been overawed, but he felt a lot of pride too for the job he'd done. Ralph would have handled it well in that articulate and charming way he had.

The class divide was still strong in the fifties. It was still a very much 'them and us' world. Stan was determined to be at least a suburbanite. He would try his utmost to rid himself of his gaucheness and shyness. The newly reconstructed Stanley Compton would be a career artist/journalist on a level with Dennis, star of screen and stage, Ralph, traveller and writer, Tommy, tycoon, owner of a chain of plumbers and builders suppliers, George, landowner, squire of Acornbridge after a break of three hundred years.

Ralph was waiting in the car just outside the main gates. Stan got in.

'I watched you as you walked back to the car. You looked to be in a dream. How did the meeting go?'

'The meeting was an experience. I just wish that I could have contributed more. You would have handled it fine, Ralph. You've got the ability to converse with the officer class.'

'Somebody didn't think so,' he said wryly. 'Let's stop off at the Horse and Jockey pub for a swift drink!'

When they were in the pub Stan took some sketches from his folder.

'There's you.'

'Yes, that's me all right amongst the owls and kestrels.'

'And who's this?' Stan passed over another sketch.

'Jeff!' Ralph laughed. 'Jeff loading some bricks into the van. This sketch could be valuable one day – Jeff actually doing some work.'

'I did those two at home.'

'You must have a photographic memory.'

'That's what the Adjutant said.'

'It's a talent, boy. It's a god given talent. Come on, let's hit the road. Whittington's not my favourite place.'

'You can have that picture of you, Ralph. It's a gift from me. You were the best workmate I ever had.'

'Likewise, my old friend. How did Jeff describe the working day?'

'Larking about.'

'I'm going to do something for you now, Stan, which may change your life. Do you remember telling me a story about your window cleaning days and the curvaceous naked lady of Stanhope Hall?'

'Yes I do. Nobody has ever believed me though. I've put it to the back of my mind. It was a dream.'

'No, it was not a dream, Stan. We've got a way to go yet. When we get back to Walsall I'm going to take you to Stanhope Hall.'

'Here we are, Stan. We're near the avenue of Cedar trees. He pulled up. Follow me. Bring your portfolio. They reached the patio outside the kitchen and there she stood. Lorna in her favourite attire – none.

'There Stanley, is your glorious ageless perfect specimen of womanhood. My wonderful mistress.'

'Yes, I remember you Stanley. The good-looking young window cleaner. The impatient young man who got me from my bath to collect his money. I expect you remember that day very well,' she said. 'I'm certain that you were dazzled by my indescribable beauty. Come here and let me hold you for a while. You're trembling.'

'There is a reason that you are here, Stanley.'

Sarah appeared.

'This is my daughter, Sarah. She's such an obedient girl. Take that skimpy little dress off, Sarah and let Stanley see you.'

'Of course mother.' She pulled the dress over her head.

'What do you think of her Stanley? Don't compare her with me. I'm on a different level.'

Stanley was frantically trying to think of suitable adjectives but finally said, 'There are no adjectives to describe you. If I wasn't so overwhelmed, I'd find one.'

'He's very natural, isn't he mother? He's good-looking too with his curly hair and broad shoulders. Take your shirt off, Stanley.'

He felt as if he was playing a part in an X-rated French film. He was convinced that everybody was mad. He took his shirt off.

Sarah came over to him and ran her hands over his chest. 'He's hard and hairy mother. I think he'll do.'

'What do you mean – I'll do?'

'You'll do as a husband. I've been going out with a lot of slimy blokes in suits – sales reps and the like. Under the suits they're pot-bellied and flabby. You're a fine looking well-built man, Stanley. You're a bit timid at the moment, but that's because you probably think you're in a madhouse.'

'My mother is almost clairvoyant. When I despaired that I would never ever find a man – a real man, she used all her powers of prediction and today was the day for something to happen. We didn't know quite what, but as soon as we saw you we knew you were the man.'

'Do I get a say in all this?'

'You'll be given a little time to think things over because there is one important factor to be considered.'

Lorna appeared with a peacefully sleeping Jerome in her arms.

'This,' she announced, 'is Jerome, my lovely little grandson and son of my beautiful daughter. He has no father. He is the product of a college romance, which failed as soon as the cowardly swine broke his promise and disappeared. Whoever marries my daughter must take on this child. He must love him as his own which is normally too much for a man's pride. You've got a little time to think about it. Let me just pass Jerome over to you, Stanley. We shall know if he likes you. Stanley took the child. He smiled and looked up at Stanley saying, 'Raf Raf.'

'He thinks you're Ralph.'

'I don't think so,' Stan said. 'He thinks I *look* like Ralph, which I do a bit.'

'Yes, I think you might be right there, Stanley. By the way, you will always be known in this house as Stanley – not Stan or Stan the man or any of that nonsense. Now the thing is, Stanley, do you feel confident with Jerome?'

'I do. I really do. I think he's a grand little fellow. Anyway, I'd hope that he would soon have a little brother or sister.'

'That's the spirit, Stanley,' Lorna enthused. 'I know that this will work out well. Let's put little Jerome back.'

'We hope to see you very soon. *Very* soon. Ralph will drive you home.'

'Ralphy,' he said on his way home. 'What a day! Emotional! My head's in a whirl. I begin the day at a meeting with toffs who actually treat me like a human being. I end the day at a Gothic mansion where Dracula would have been at home. Nobody has any clothes on. I meet a grandmother who looks like a beauty queen. I am introduced to my naked future wife and I'm asked to be a stepfather.'

'What are you going to do, Stanley?'

'It may be best if I don't tell you yet. You may spill the beans. I presume you sleep with Lorna and she'd soon wheedle it out of you, wouldn't she?'

'Yes, she'd wheedle it out of me and I know how, but couldn't you give me a little clue?'

'A little clue. Okay, here's a little clue, only a few hints mind you. I'm going to Walsall to buy an engagement ring. I'm going to arrive at Stanhope Hall with said ring in my pocket. Firstly I shall present her with a sketch of herself which I shall complete at home tonight. The sketch will be an extremely vulgar one in keeping with the mood at

Stanhope Hall. I shall then get down on my knees, propose to her and promise that the first time we will make love will be on a four-poster bed at the Royal George Hotel when we go to George's wedding. Finally, I shall produce the ring. Tell me, Ralphy, can you work anything out from the little clues I've given you?'

'Yes, Stanley, I think there's enough there for me to get the general idea. This is where I drop you off isn't it? I may run into you tomorrow. I think she'll like your style. I think you're the right man for Sarah. Lorna had always hoped that it would be Sarah and I. I suppose that would have been logical, but life's not logical is it? Good night Stanley.'

Ralph arrived back at Stanhope Hall, physically tired and emotionally drained. Sarah and Jerome were back in their flat. Lorna lay on her stomach on her bed. He undressed and hung his clothes in the wardrobe. He had intended showering but was so fatigued that he decided to join Lorna in sleep. He slept for an hour. He awoke to find that Lorna had not stirred. He ran his hand along her backbone, down to her buttocks, then her legs. She looked up at him and asked, 'What's happening with Sarah and Stanley?'

'I'll tell you if you're nice to me.'

'Come on, Ralph. I kept my side of the bargain. Tell me what is happening.'

He told her the full story. 'That's wonderful! You were the matchmaker. You're a wonderful man. It's a wonderful world. Oh, what a wonderful morning.' They burst into song. 'Oh what a wonderful day. I've got a wonderful feeling everything's going my way. I'm so excited. I bet even you are excited Ralph. You were the instigator. I'm yours – all twelve stone seven of my honey gold resilient flesh is yours. It's a special occasion so I'm climbing on top and whoops! Up it goes. I'm in heaven!'

They all estimated that Stanley would be at Stanhope Hall by mid-morning, bearing in mind that he was going into Walsall to buy an engagement ring. In reality, his Nan – very excited and sworn to secrecy – gave him an old ring assuring him that it was pure gold.

'Even if it isn't, it doesn't matter, Nan. She's not the type to be demanding expensive things. I wouldn't marry her if she were.'

He put on the best clothes that he possessed, picked up his portfolio and set out for Stanhope Hall.

It was seven o'clock. He reckoned to be there by eight. Hopefully they would be having breakfast. He fancied egg, bacon and fried bread. He felt a little apprehensive after his euphoria of the day before. Supposing that they were part of a strange clothes-less cult. They could be devil worshippers. They would entice him into their pagan den and would lure him into their satanic world and pretend to be his friends, until the day they ceremonially chopped off his penis as a sacrifice to the Goddess Barebum, Queen of all the nudes.

But surely Ralph wouldn't be involved in something like that, would he? What about if Lorna kept him as a slave or a eunuch? He might live in a dungeon and be released periodically to pleasure all the witches in Goddess Barebum's castle, which is, of course, Stanhope Hall. It was all beginning to piece together now.

'Watch where you're walking, you dreamy bugger,' a voice shouted from a passing car. He then realised that he had wandered into the middle of the road.

'Pull yourself together,' he told himself. 'Your fantasising will be the death of you.' He had nearly reached Stanhope Hall. Lorna was waiting for him in nothing but a sunhat. 'What a vision! Why did everybody say that Ralph Tucker was unlucky?' He asked himself. She walked over to him and hugged him tight. He felt his penis stiffening and so did she.

'Nothing lacking in the reproduction department, Stanley. Sarah and I will have a little private viewing later on today. In the meantime, we've put a few snacks and drinks out for our little engagement ceremony.'

'Let us amble back through the cedar trees, Stanley. Sarah will be waiting for you. To say that she's excited is an understatement. Take my hand, Stanley.'

They reached the kitchen patio. Sarah sat with Jerome on her lap. She had a flowery summer dress on. It was low necked and a mere inch shorter than normal.

'You look like an English rose,' Stanley told her.

'Thank you Stanley. To what do I owe this visit?'

'You will be informed in due course, but firstly I must talk to your mother.'

Lorna was sprawled on a cane chair. Stanley knelt before her.

'What a breathtaking view,' he said.

'Now, now. Stop being a silly boy and ask what you have to ask.'

'Mrs Pitt. It is with humility that I kneel before you this day to ask for the hand of your beautiful daughter in marriage. I think I got the words mixed up a bit.'

'No you didn't Stanley. That was excellent. I will not put you through the ordeal of an interview. I know you are the man. I foresaw it. Now rise and kneel before Sarah and no more smart alec wisecracks.'

He did as he was bid and asked, 'Sarah, will you marry me?' He took the ring from his pocket.

'Of course I will. Oh, yes! Dear dear Stanley.'

He gave her the ring. She put it on her finger.

'That's a temporary ring. My Nan gave it to me. She says it's solid gold, but she might be wrong. As soon as I'm in funds I'll give you a nicer one.'

'Stanley. Please don't spoil it. I don't care if it's a curtain ring. I shall wear it for ever.' She sat on his lap and kissed him.

'Now we must have our little celebratory drink.' Lorna poured out four glasses of red wine. The milkman had just arrived. He parked at the top of the drive and walked through the shade of the cedar trees with a crate of milk.

'Pour out another glass of wine, Ralph. The milkman's here.'

'This is Bazzer, my weekly milkman,' Lorna announced. 'Would you like a drink of wine, Bazzer?'

'Better not.'

'Fair enough. We can't have you drunk in charge of a milk float, can we?'

'Whatever it is you're drinking to,' Bazzer said, 'I wish you all the luck in the world.'

'We're drinking to the engagement of my precious daughter Sarah and her fiancé Stanley – a budding artist.'

'I wish you all the happiness in the world,' Bazzer said, and walked back to his milk float.

'He's ever such a nice man,' Lorna told them. 'He's divorced and lonely or so he tells me. He says that whenever he sees me, it makes his day. I tell him that I love making people happy.'

'And that you do, Mother,' Sarah said, 'that you do.'

'There's just one more thing,' Stanley said. He picked up a single large sheet from his pack of sketches. 'Before I give you this, Sarah, I should tell you that it's not quite finished. There's still a bit of colouring and light and shade to put in. What do you think Sarah?' He handed her the large sheet of cartridge paper.

'Stanley!' she shrieked. 'It's brilliant! It's me. I thought you said it was vulgar. What is vulgar about it? Look mother.' Lorna took the picture.

'It's a wonderful likeness. It's very natural. Your dress has risen up and your pussy becomes the focal point. Just wait until you produce the likeness of me, Stanley. It'll be far more provocative and not an item of clothing in sight except my size fourteen high heels.'

Lorna disappeared inside the house to make a telephone call 'Mr Jacob Greenberg please?'

'This is Jacob Greenberg himself. Master tailor and maker of suits for the gentry, the nobility, and the giants of industry and commerce.'

'Have you finished? I was getting bored. This is Lorna.'

'Lorna! I have a vision of a beautiful shapely lady and a good sport too. What can I do for you?'

'Tomorrow Ralph collects his suit. A suit not only for his friend's wedding but also the suit which he will wear when he is consigned to the cruel world of Civvy Street.'

'The suit is ready and waiting for him. He'll love it.'

'I hope so. Ralph will be accompanied by a young man named Stanley Compton who is engaged to my daughter. He also needs a good suit for the same wedding. Measure him, make it and have it ready before June 19th. I'll pay extra.'

Chapter 22

Lady Lorna of Acornbridge

'This is what is called a 'special', which affects the price considerably.'

'Jacob, I've already told you I'll pay extra. I want a price now and an assurance that you can do it. I'm not doing any bargaining. If you don't give me an immediate answer I shall get him fixed up with an off the peg suit. So, Jacob, I don't want to hear any bull about being on the verge of ruin any more if you don't make this suit, a suit that could save you from ruin. I'm waiting. Yes or no and price or this phone goes down.'

'Yes I'll do it within the time. Price Forty.'

'Probably too high but accepted.' She put the phone down.

Ralph collected Stanley early next morning and they drove to Jacob Greenberg's.

'Is he Jewish?' Stanley asked. 'Yes. He married my great aunt Alice.'

'Has he got a long grey beard? Is he a miser like Shylock?'

'Well some people might think that, but he's a good old boy really. His accent's unique – Walsall Jewish. He'll tell you who he's made suits for.'

'Let me guess. Kirk Douglas and Robert Mitchum. They always look good in suits.'

'No. He's never made a suit for a Hollywood star to the best of my knowledge.'

'Who then? English stars like Dirk Bogarde and Jack Hawkins?'

'I don't think so.'

'I'm going to run out of famous people.'

‘He’s made suits for the Mayor of Walsall, the MP for Walsall South, the MP for Walsall North and—’

‘I’ve heard enough. The Mayor of Walsall! So I’m going to finish up looking like the Mayor of Walsall?’

‘Don’t be ungrateful. Lorna is buying you a suit. She’s your future mother-in-law. Have you ever heard of a mother-in-law buying her son-in-law a suit? Your mother-in-law’s supposed to be your enemy, hence all the jokes about mother-in-laws.’

‘You’re right there Ralph - the Grey Jackets’ song:

How I love my mother-in-law

Although she’s ninety-four.

She’s coming round today,

but I wish she’d stayed away.’

‘That’ll do Stan,’ Ralph cut in. ‘I want to put the army out of my mind for a while. We’re here anyway.’

Jacob came out into the street to greet them. ‘Ralph my boy!’ he exclaimed, ‘And this will be young Stanley.’

‘What’s that awful suit you have on, Stanley. It’s a Teddy boy suit isn’t it? When you get your new Greenberg suit, I suggest that you take your horrible Teddy boy suit to the bottom of the garden and burn it. Life starts again for you today, young Stanley. I’ll have you looking the business.’

He got out his tape measure and note pad and darted around Stanley taking measurements.

‘That’s you sorted out, Stanley. Do you want a waistcoat?’

‘Yes I fancy a waistcoat.’

‘What about turn-ups. They’re going out, unfashionable?’

‘No turn-ups then.’

‘Narrow lapels? They’re in.’

‘I’ll have them then.’

‘Collection date 17th June?

‘I’ll be here with the money.’

'Forty guineas.'

'Lorna told me £40, but I'm not arguing.'

Jacob turned to Ralph. 'Let's get *you* sorted out. The suit's ready. Here it is. Try it on, try it on. I'm dying to see what it looks like on you.'

Ralph put the suit on.

'How does it feel?'

'It fits great.'

He asked Ralph numerous questions. 'Does it fit here? Is that snug?'

He went on asking questions until Ralph said, 'Uncle Jacob, no more questions. It's perfect in every detail. I just have to look in the mirror to see that it's quality. It hangs well. It won't crease. It will last a lifetime. It's a bargain.'

'What did we agree? Thirty two pounds?'

'Twenty seven pounds ten shillings.'

'I must have been drunk that's all I can say. I'd be ruined if I charged everybody special low rates.'

Ralph counted the money into Jacob's hand.

'Five, ten, fifteen, twenty, twenty-five, six, seven and ten bob. I hope that will save you from the brink of ruin.'

The days passed by. Lorna went back to work from nine until two. It was strange to see her dressed. Stan went back home to stay with his grandmother but made the trek to Stanhope each day to be with Sarah. She told him how much she was looking forward to consummating her betrothal on a four-poster bed in the Royal George Inn at Acornbridge. Lorna was still ecstatically happy to have brought Stanley and Sarah together though she always gave her golden boy Ralph the credit. Tommy was down in the dumps about his business and had arranged for a meeting with Lorna and her accountant about a business plan to commence the day after his demob date. He resigned himself to starting again, with or without his brother, Ron, who had worn himself out to little avail. Veronica was melancholy. She knew that Tommy would succeed, but she hated the idea of another long wait for him. Ralph owed Hugh and Margaret a visit. Hugh seemed to be on his way back to his pub philosopher days. Margaret seemed to be going a little bit dotty in a loving, eccentric way. Nobody had heard from Dennis. Maybe he'd send a congratulatory message to George on his wedding day. On that subject, Ralph decided to go ahead and book rooms at the Royal George.

He informed the Royal George that he would be requiring three double rooms for the night before the wedding and the actual wedding night. That meant that they could travel there and back in casual clothes.

'Are you here for the Braddox wedding?' the hotelier asked.

'Yes we are,' Ralph answered.

'Are you family?'

'My grandmother is Amy Braddock – Amy Tucker is her married name.'

'Tucker – that name rings a bell. Yes. I've got you on my list. You're one of George's best mates from the army. Ralph Tucker and his lady Lorna. You'll be in the Cavalier Suite. Your comrade Mr Tommy Ward and his fiancée Veronica are booked into the Loyalist Suite. Your comrade Mr Compton known as Stan the man and his fiancée Sarah are booked into the Prince Rupert Suite.'

'Thanks a lot. You've been very helpful Mr… er…?'

'Braddock. Phil Braddock.'

'Could you give me an idea of the cost, Phil?'

'That will all be sorted out within the family. George would be furious if he thought that I was charging you.'

The day arrived for travelling down to Acornbridge Tommy and Veronica left early. The remainder left around midday. Stanley had collected his suit from Jacob. He lay it down very carefully in the car boot along with his white shirt and silver grey tie. Ralph laid his identical clothes neatly on top. Sarah and Lorna wore summer dresses and had already handed over their wedding outfits to Veronica who loaded them into Tommy's van.

Stanley volunteered to drive. Lorna sat in the front passenger seat with Ralph and Sarah in the back.

'I've arranged it like this to avoid any snogging on the back seat. Kissing and canoodling in public is something that I cannot abide.'

'It wouldn't have been in public,' Sarah said.

'Of course it would – in a car on the open road. Anyway those are my instructions which you will obey.'

'You are an enigma, Mother, that's all I can say,' Sarah protested. 'It's all right for you to go for nearly two weeks with no clothes on, but a harmless cuddle in a car is forbidden.'

'All right, I'm an enigma. I don't want to argue on what should be a joyous occasion, save to say that I am a woman of incredible beauty with an obligation to display myself.'

'Understood Mother,' Sarah sighed.

Worcestershire, most beloved of all counties, flashed by them in a blur of ochre and green, meadows and woodland, sheep and cattle, cottages, farms, inns, oaks and elms. They reached Worcester and threaded their way through a tangle of streets, picked up the sign for Malvern and reached the main road.

'Watch for signs for Penny Mortimer and Acornbridge,' Ralph told Stan. 'There it is look. Left turn and three miles on and you'll come directly to the church. Here we are. The pub and the church are next door to each other.'

They took their small amount of luggage from the car and booked into the Royal George. Phil Braddock showed them to their room.

'This is a special room' he said, opening the door of the Cavalier Suite. King Charles stayed here. If you are a virgin, King Charles I's ghost may come on top of you at midnight and have his way with you. A lot of women have had that experience, it seems. They keep coming back every September.'

'Why September?' Ralph asked.

'I don't know. It's a legend lost in the mists of time. Here's your key, Mr Tucker. I hope you enjoy your stay. Now then, Mr Compton, I'll take you to your room. It's a very special room – the Prince Rupert Suite. Prince Rupert once stayed here, having ridden many miles. He was hungry and thirsty. He rang that gong over there to order food and wine. Periodically the gong rings of its own accord, usually just after midnight. That is a portent that a child will be conceived here. Here's your key. Enjoy your stay. By the way, if you have brought any wedding presents, which I see you all have, please leave them in reception. I'll see you later.

'Oh, I forgot to tell you that there will be a gathering of the Braddocks and guests at six thirty. Beer is free.'

'Isn't this lovely, Stanley?' Sarah said excitedly. 'How do you like our four-poster bed? The Prince Rupert Suite. How romantic! I wonder who Prince Rupert was. The only Rupert I know is Rupert Bear.'

'Ralph will know,' Stanley said.

'I'll be back shortly, Stanley. I have to phone Nan Tucker. There's a phone in reception. While I'm out, you can get our stuff unpacked.'

'Hello.'

'Is that Nan Tucker?'

'Yes. Is that Sarah?'

'Yes. How's little Jerome?'

'Good as gold. What a lovely little fellow. He's hardly cried.'

'I can't thank you enough for looking after him. We'll be back by midday Sunday. We've got a lovely room. The whole of the pub seems to be haunted. There's a gong in the room. If it rings of its own accord just after midnight, it is a portent that a child will be conceived.'

'That sounds like a typical load of Braddock cobblers. There's only one way that a child will be conceived and it's got nothing to do with a gong but far be it from me to interfere. See you on Sunday.'

Sarah went back to the Prince Rupert suite.

'Trust Nan Tucker to put a damper on it. She said that gong story is rubbish.'

'Maybe it is. We could pretend it was true just for this afternoon though couldn't we. We could have a real good go at getting the gong to ring.'

'That we could, Stanley. How many times in our life are we to have the use of a four-poster? I think we should be doing what lovers should do on a four-poster bed. My mother calls it jolly good fun.'

Sarah and Stanley were noticeable by their absence at the gathering.

'Here they are,' Tommy said suddenly. 'They've got big smug grins on their faces.'

'Where have you two been?' Veronica asked.

'We had a quiet afternoon. I did a bit of sketching,' Stanley told them.

'Did you use your long thick pencil?' Veronica asked.

'I get it,' Stanley said, 'double talk. We had a good time on our four-poster and if the ghost of Prince Rupert had seen us he would have said "Gadzooks – a pretty maid and her manly swain. I'd give them the gong for their energy alone Booooooiiiinnnng!" Who was Prince Rupert?'

'Prince Rupert of the Palatine, I think,' said Ralph. 'He was a German cousin of Charles I and he came over to support the Cavaliers.'

'I knew you'd know, Ralph,' Stan said.

'So this place is haunted,' Sarah said.

'I don't believe it is,' Ralph replied. 'I think it's made up by Phil Braddock. Gongs, ghosts of Charles I – bullshit! What's special about your room, Tommy?'

'Some stuff about a gold sovereign falling out of Charles I's pocket and whosever finds the sovereign will inherit enormous wealth, The gold sovereign, if found, should be handed in at reception.'

'That just about sums it up,' Ralph laughed.

The gathering had swollen to over a hundred and fifty people. It had become a handshaking session, Braddock after Bradnack after Braddox introducing themselves. Ralph's head was in a whirl as he tried to remember names. To make life even more confusing, a yob element of outsiders had gatecrashed the party. Russell "Iron bar" Bradnack and Norman "Red dog" Braddock, two hard men, had begun politely removing the unwanted guests. Police Sergeant Geoff Bradnack and Marlon Braddock the hairy biker had joined in. The bar was closed immediately. The Royal George and its environs were suddenly empty.

Phil Braddock told Ralph that he and all his party were welcome to stay for dinner. They sat themselves around a large table and Phil Braddock handed out menus.

'Ignore the prices. It's free of charge.'

'That's very decent,' Ralph said. 'The Braddocks were reduced to penury, were they not and forced to work as maids, menials and skivvies, labourers, ploughmen and grooms? Now it seems, they own the village and can afford to provide free bed and board.'

'I'm a practical man,' Phil Braddock said. 'The destruction of the Manor of Acornbridge and the dispossession of our family is true enough, but I'm not one of the Braddocks who bear a centuries old grudge. I think we should be using our Civil War connection to make some tourist money. One idea is to enact the battle on a regular basis. There is a society called 'The Sealed Knot' who fight out mock battles all over the country. Their costumes and weapons, like halberds, are authentic. In fact, most of them are Civil War fanatics. Nutters in my opinion but they're a big draw.'

They ate their meal in semi silence. The truth was that they were worn out. They had shaken hands with Nola Bradnack, exotic dancer, Irene Potts née Braddock, retired circus performer, Scott Braddock, guitarist, Greville Braddock, rat catcher, Wayne Braddox, builder's labourer and George's younger brother. The list went on.

'Tomorrow will be a boozy old day,' Ralph told them. 'Lorna and I are going to have an early night.' On their way out they heard Phil Braddock talking quietly with the ferret-faced rat catcher, Greville Braddox. 'Here's the key Greville. Straight in one almighty bang on the gong and out in a flash. Usual drill. There's three pints of free beer in it for you tomorrow.'

'Yes, but *everybody's* got free beer up to three pm.'

'I know but you'll be getting your free beer at five past three when everybody else is paying.'

'Fair enough. Thanks a lot Phil.'

Lorna and Ralph were glad to get back to the lavishly furnished Cavalier Suite. Lorna immediately pulled off her summer dress and held the pose for a few seconds. It had become a ritual. Ralph sunk down in a big armchair and Lorna plonked herself unceremoniously on his lap.

'I'm seldom bored am I darling? We enjoy simple things, don't we? Well, on this occasion, I'm bored. I suppose I've become a bit selfish and indulgent. I love our little 'dinners at the Ritz'. I just know what tomorrow will be like, not including the church service and the speechmaking, which I'm sure will be dignified and humorous. No, it's after that when the party could deteriorate. Free beer and buffet from mid-morning to three in the afternoon!'

'Phil's got a few hard men to keep things in order, plus some off duty police. I'm sure he must be used to these occasions. We've got to stick it out. If George ever found out that we'd sneaked out it would break his heart. He's a very emotional man. When Duggie got killed we all managed to keep a stiff upper lip, but George wept.'

'I would never even dream of sneaking out. I'm hoping that I'm wrong and that we can have an entertaining afternoon. Anyway, as well as feeling bored I'm tired, so let's go to bed.'

Sarah and Stanley were the first to wake. Sarah knocked on the door of the Cavalier Suite and a rather sleepy Lorna came to the door.

'Guess what?'

'What?'

'The gong went last night just after midnight.'

'Well that's nice darling.'

'It means that you're going to become a grandmother for a second time.'

Lorna ushered Sarah inside.

'You know only too well that this ludicrous folklore about a gong signalling a conception is a roguish Braddock ruse. However, you may be able to pull one on the doubters.'

'How shall I do that?'

'By listening to your mother who has true powers of clairvoyance. I shall know to within a month when you will become pregnant. I shall know about Veronica too. We'll meet up at breakfast. Don't mention gongs or any such nonsense to anybody.'

Ralph and Lorna decided on a light breakfast to leave room for the buffet and (apparently) the pig roast. They changed into their wedding clothes back at the Cavalier Suite.

‘Yes,’ Lorna said decisively when Ralph was dressed, ‘neatly trimmed hair, clean at the neck, spotless white shirt, plain silver tie, new dark suit, highly polished black shoes, white handkerchief in top pocket. Absolutely perfect, as befits the man I love with all my heart.’ There was the slightest sign of a tear in her eye.

Lorna dressed quickly in her maroon outfit and hat to match. The ensemble normally comprised a jacket, long skirt and blouse but she dispensed with the blouse. Apart from her size fourteen high heels she wore nothing else. Her copper hair had grown a little and hung around her shoulders.

‘As usual, Lorna, you’ll steal the show,’ Ralph said, and not without a hint of pride.

The whole party walked together the short way to the church, which was filling fast. ‘Braddox on the right,’ the usher whispered.

The vicar, the Reverend Neville Braddock DD MA (Oxon) had some praiseworthy comments on George in his sermon.

‘George left home early,’ the vicar said, ‘to ease the economic burden on his family. He joined the Grey Jackets, a famous infantry regiment as a boy soldier and served for seven years reaching the rank of Colour Sergeant.’ Tommy looked at Ralph and Stan with a grin. ‘He was recommended for a military medal for his action in diffusing an unexploded bomb in Cyprus, but was too modest to accept an honour. He fought for his battalion boxing team in the Middle East Land Forces tournament and succeeded in knocking out the biggest man in the British Army – Corporal Little who stood at seven feet three inches.’

The vicar went on to talk of the romance of George and Betty who worked at the cake shop. It seemed that George never paid for his doughnut. Eventually she put an ultimatum to him, ‘No more free doughnuts until you ask me to wed you.' It had been an enjoyable service in a packed church. George and Betty greeted everybody as they filed out. Tommy and Ralph congratulated George on being promoted to Colour Sergeant. Stan's comment was rather less than congratulatory; he simply called George a lying bastard. 'All a joke, all a joke, Stan the man,' was George's reply.

The buffet that followed also included speeches.

Ralph was pleased to announce that he had recently learnt that he was a quarter Braddock, but the main content of his very short speech was the confirmation of a lifelong friendship with George from all his army mates.

Lorna found herself talking to Nola Bradnack, exotic dancer and Irene Potts née Braddock, retired circus performer.

'Us ladies usually put on a little show on these occasions,' Irene said.

'What sort of show?' Lorna asked. 'A few sketches and songs?'

'No. A striptease. Interested?'

'Count me in. I love taking my clothes off. I'd need to get familiar with the routine though.'

'Come on last then,' Nola suggested, 'and watch what we do.'

'Is there a prize?' Lorna asked.

'Sort of. The winner's judged on audience reaction. The winner's prize is to be Lady Godiva.'

'I thought that was Coventry.'

'Coventry copied our ideas,' Irene said. 'Anyway, the prize is to ride naked on a horse – that horse over there in fact, the one tethered to the fence. He's a docile old boy now, but he used to be a good hurdler. Silver Warrior is his name and that bloke with him is Monk Braddock, George's older brother. He's a racehorse trainer.'

'I'm looking forward to it,' Lorna said. 'It should be fun.'

‘Won’t your young fellow mind?’ Irene asked.

‘He won’t mind. He adores me. I can make him do anything. He’s my virile young lover.’

‘He’s a gorgeous boy. Where did you get him?’

‘It’s a long story.’

The pig roast was in full swing. The folk singer sang. The fiddler fiddled. The guitarist twanged away. Everybody went their separate way though not intentionally. They were simply carried by the heaving throng. It was impossible to move at times. The ‘biergarten’ and the field beyond were full of revellers.

Ron Braddock, the butcher, supervised the pig roast. Plates were pieces of cardboard ripped from cartons. Forks were pointed sticks. Guests queued with their cardboard plates ready for Ron, the butcher, to hack off a good portion of pork and crackling and bang it down.

The powerful voice of Wayne Braddox cut through the air. ‘May I have your attention, folks? George and Betty have been collected by taxi. They’ll be off on their honeymoon in Paignton soon and I’m sure you’ll all wish them well.

‘We will shortly be putting on our traditional centuries old striptease show. It’s seven o’clock and still light so we’re moving the stage outside. Ladies will you please gather together and prepare yourselves.’

Wayne Braddox was frantically waving for the ladies to come forward. Finally, all three arrived and positioned themselves by the stage.

‘Our first act tonight,’ he roared over the noise of the crowd, ‘is the lovely Irene. She flounced onto the stage and commenced a painfully slow routine to the rather strange twanging version of the Stripper. She overdid everything, taking five minutes simply to get her bra off; the crowd were bored and booed. When she had got as far as she intended to, she ignored the cries of ‘Get 'em off’ and walked off the stage. There was hardly a clap. 'It's murder out there,' she told the others.

Nola came on next. She described herself as an exotic dancer and indeed there was a lot of shimmying and wriggling in her act. She got a good rhythm going and took off garment after garment at a pace, earning herself some applause. In the end though, the crowd felt badly let down when it turned out that she was wearing a flesh-coloured body stocking. They booed as she walked off the stage.

Lorna had been watching in order to pick up some hints. She was totally unimpressed. She would show them what a real woman looked like she vowed.

As soon as she walked onto the stage there were cries of 'Get 'em off'. She shook her mighty fist and shouted, 'I'll decide when to get 'em off. Behave yourself before I get yours off and give you a good smacking.'

A great cheer went up. The ruffians were quiet. Lorna unzipped her long skirt and let it fall to the ground. She then kicked it to Ralph. She unbuttoned her jacket and flung it to Ralph too. The crowd gasped at the sheer brazenness of it all. They were numb. There was what seemed like a long silence before the packed crowd of visitors let out a chorus of screams, whistles and cries of 'More'. She bowed, waved her hat and walked slowly off to endless applause.

It was immediately announced that Lorna would be Lady Godiva, and that any contributions in support of the event should be put in the carton marked 'Lady Godiva handicapped children's fund.' Monk Braddox led the horse to a patch of ground near the marquee and helped Lorna mount. She was conscious of his presence – his raven hair, moustache, sideburns and fierce blue eyes, his very size – only two inches short of his gigantic brother George. To represent his position as an elder of the Braddox's he wore a cavalier hat with a feather in it. He cut a dashing figure.

'You're a handsome devil, Monk.'

'You're not bad yourself, Lorna.'

‘Not bad? Not *bad*? I’m a woman of unparalleled beauty.’

‘Shall I walk him round?’ Monk asked. ‘We can go as far as the village and back.’

‘Pass me those reins. I’ll ride him round. If I ever do this stunt for you again, Monk, I shall demand a saddle. I rather like the sensation of bare flesh on leather.’ She grinned.

‘You shall have what you desire, Lorna.’

To loud cheers she rode the grey out along the road into the village. Word must have got around. People were in their front gardens and out on the street to see her. Silver Warrior clip-clopped steadily along. She rode around the village square where there was another pub, The Crown. All the drinkers were already outside to cheer her on.

‘That’s a real woman as nature intended,’ she heard one old boy say. ‘No pink body stocking or whatever it was the other ones had on.’

‘This’n ‘ll get the job in future,’ another said.

She got back onto the main road and reached the T-junction where the sign indicated left back to Acornbridge and right to Penny Mortimer.

‘To hell with it!’ she told herself ‘I’ll take a ride to Penny Mortimer.’ The grass verge was wide so she rode on it. She felt like some ancient tribal leader, an ancient Briton. She was tempted to break into a gallop but instead she settled for a trot. Passing motorists blew their horns. She was in her element – the focus of attention. Finally, she decided to turn back to the Royal George. She stayed at a trot, took the old grey up to the fence and dismounted with the help of the rails.

‘So you’re back,’ Monk sounded annoyed, ‘you weren’t supposed to do that.’

‘Are you cross with me?’

‘Yes. Well no. You had the urge to ride him. He’s a wonderful old horse. He liked it. Just look at him nuzzling up against you. Maybe you’ll get to ride him again. We have a lot of fetes and pageants. You'd be a perfect permanent Lady Godiva. We may call you our Lady Lorna. I've got your address in the hotel register. I'll drop you a line.'

Lorna walked away to where Ralph stood with her clothes.

'You've been a long time,' he said.

'Are you cross with me?'

'I don't know about 'cross'. Up to the time you vanished, we were all very proud of you. You put those other two women to shame. I was annoyed that I had to stand around with your clothes while you were away, and to cap it all, you stopped to talk with that Monk bloke.'

'Monk is a handsome devil, but he's got womaniser and rogue written all over him. We can't stay out here arguing. Let's go to our room.'

They put the 'Do not disturb' sign on the door. Lorna threw herself onto the four-poster.

'Ralph. Get out of that wedding suit. You must have felt sweaty and itchy in it if you've been in it all day. Get yourself onto this bed with me immediately you're stripped down to the hairy he man that you are. Come on, climb on. Now lie with your head on my bosom like you used to.

'I'm glad you were jealous of Monk Braddock. It shows how deeply you love your Lorna. I may well have male friends when we have parted, but I am not naive enough anymore to entertain the likes of Monk, fine figure of a man that he is. He trains horses for several upper-class ladies, three of whom I vaguely know. He probably takes them all to bed.'

'What? All at once?'

'Of course not, you stupid boy. They probably think – each one of them that is – that they are the one. One of them, in particular, is an archetypal snooty, horse-faced miss bossy boots.'

'Who would that be?'

'I'm surprised you're interested. She is Penelope, Marchioness of Uttoxeter.'

'Nor should you be. We have to look upon our enforced estrangement in a practical manner. We do not talk. We do not write, and then as things settle down we may meet occasionally, according to our separate situations.'

'It all sounds very formal.'

'Well it has to be. Ralph, much as I absolutely and deeply love you, I do not want to receive lovelorn letters or phone calls. You'll have your ups and downs. Be a man. Put the thought of women to the back of your mind. Choose your profession, work hard, go on your trip to Australia or wherever. Do it all. There's a woman waiting for you at the end of it all. I call her your golden girl. She's still a teenager. She's angelic on the outside but a tough nut inside. But enough of that.'

'Why? I like to hear your portents. They reassure me.'

Ralph looked through the window.

'People are starting to leave. It looks as if there's been a fight – or two. There are two police cars here,'

Lorna shrugged, 'It was bound to happen. Put free booze on all afternoon and let gatecrashers sneak in and this is the result.'

'I had no intention of going back down there any way,' Ralph said.

'Nor me. Have a look in that fridge, Ralph. Let's see what drinks they've got.'

He opened the door. 'No red wine, miniatures of scotch, gin, vodka, bottled beer.'

'Two beers are okay for a start. Here's a toast to George,' Lorna said. 'Thanks George for inviting us to your wedding and reception. We wish you every happiness for the future. If you're ever our way, call in for a drink.'

'That was a good toast, Lorna, leave it in reception.' She wrote it out on a hotel letterhead. 'It's an early breakfast for us tomorrow and then we'll hit the road.'

Chapter 23

Uncle Bryn's Offer

Ralph and Lorna rose early. He looked through the window. An army of helpers were taking down the marquee and clearing the debris.

They washed and dressed and went down to breakfast. Stan and Sarah were already there, drinking their coffee and looking adorably into each other's eyes.

Tommy's van was not in the car park so it was assumed that he and Veronica were on their way.

After breakfast they loaded their wedding clothes carefully into the car and then went to reception to hand in their keys. 'Lorna,' Phil Braddock said, 'We can't thank, you enough. You were an important part of the entertainment. You are real class – classy when dressed, classy undressed. Do you want to take some food back? There's stacks left over from the buffet. The more you can take, the better. I hate the idea of having to throw food away. Here's a nice big carton. Take as much as you can pack into it.'

They were happy to be on their way. Stan drove again. He loved driving. Lorna sat in the front with him with the carton of food on her lap. 'I don't want to be mean boys and girls,' Lorna said, 'but I am commandeering this carton of buffet food. It's a reward for taking my clothes off in front of a crowd of foulmouthed roughs and riding a horse bareback – not only bareback but bare bum. If anybody is really hungry though, we can always pull up at a lay by, find a grassy bank and eat a few sandwiches and sausage rolls.'

They took her up on the offer and helped themselves from the carton of leftovers. Lorna insisted on showing everybody where she felt sore. Stan lay back on the grass, closed his eyes and wondered if he was in heaven or an asylum or somewhere in between.

No sooner had they arrived back at Stanhope than the phone rang. Ralph picked it up. 'Hello'

'Ralph?'

'Dad, how are you?'

'Dog and Partridge tonight. Seven thirty. Any problems?'

'No problems. I'll be there. Bye.'

When Ralph entered the Dog and Partridge dead on seven thirty, Hugh was already sat at a corner table with two pints in front of him. Ralph grabbed his drink and sat down.

'Cheers.'

'How did the party go? How many fights were there?'

'There were a few. We watched from the window in our room. By that time we'd had enough.'

'Did they have folk singers and fiddlers and all that stuff?'

'They had everything, buffet, booze, a pig roast and they even had a striptease.'

'Don't tell me. Lorna won the striptease.'

'You've guessed right, Dad but she also rode naked through the village like Lady Godiva. She was away ages because she decided to take the horse on a little run. Then when she got back, she spent time chatting with this flash geezer named Monk.'

'Monk Braddox, the racehorse trainer? Were you jealous?'

'I was a bit until I found out that he was a womaniser. Lorna knew all about him.'

Ralph went up to the bar and ordered two more pints.

'Now, my son,' Hugh commenced. 'I've been talking to Uncle Bryn about you. If you think we're interfering, we understand. However, hear me out. Bryn has a fairly big detached house in Great Barr. He's on his own there, except for two medical students from Singapore. They occupy one of the flats. The other flat is being built now. Guess when it'll be ready for occupancy? Late July 1958 – just a few weeks before your demob. Bryn tells me it's going to be a nice roomy, light flat with its own bathroom and toilet and entrance from the street, so it's private. It's in a pleasant road. He wants to have a chat with you. I think he'll be asking about £2/10 a week. That's a bit high, but it's going to be fully furnished, with a little kitchen and a nice big TV. Oh, and a fridge. So, what do you think?'

Hugh was anticipating a negative response from his notoriously stubborn son, implicating that he was perfectly capable of making his own decisions. To Hugh's surprise Ralph said, 'Sounds great Dad.'

'You'll go for it, then?'

'Of course. Who am I to look a gift horse in the mouth?'

'Here's Bryn's business card. Give him a ring. I think you'll find that he's got a few other things to discuss. Quite exciting things actually.'

'Like what?'

'I wasn't going to tell you. I was going to leave it to Bryn. Since you *have* asked, I'll give you a few ideas. Bryn runs his business from home. It's a good business; for want of alternatives you could call his business an Export Merchant or a Confirming House or perhaps a Trading Company. He buys and sells, imports and exports to Latin America, the Far East, Australia and New Zealand and some African countries. In other words, all over the world. He's thinking of early retirement in a few years' time, though knowing Bryn that won't happen. He'll work till he drops like your Uncle Jacob.

He's got nobody to leave the business to – no sons, two daughters. Nobody interested but *you* might be – a nephew. That's all I'm telling you. Bryn will do the rest. I've explained that hell or high water won't stop you from going to Australia but you never know. I think he may have ideas of you setting up something up for him, but I'll say no more on it. One more pint for the road then. I'll get it!

'I'm glad that you're interested,' Hugh told him. 'I like to think I've given you good advice. I feel that I let you down in the past.'

'No, you didn't Dad.'

'What about Oxford? I led you to think that a classical education was impractical. I was wrong. You could have come away from Oxford with a degree, begun a career in, say, the law. Instead, I let you take on a labouring job that any lad could have done.'

'I made my own decision, Dad. I never regretted it.'

He walked back to Stanhope. Lorna had the remainder of the buffet leftovers arranged on plates with an opened bottle of red wine. 'Not exactly dinner at the Ritz but good enough,' she said.

Disembarkation leave had fifteen days to run. Conscious of the limited time Lorna and Ralph had left together, they insisted on being just a little bit selfish. Sarah was sympathetic. 'Don't worry about Jerome, mother. You do enough already. Lock the connecting door. You and Ralph have maximum time together.'

'Fifteen days is enough time to get you fit again,' Lorna told Ralph. 'Walk everywhere and put in a few laps round the Oval each day.

'The gardener has gone missing for a week. That means that I shall need my virile young lover to make a start on the lawns. I'm not going back to the office until your leave is up, Ralph. No doubt there'll be some moans, but it will not drag me back. I've been there since the year dot. I work flexible hours at an hourly rate and that's the end of it. I'm here to be your full time gym mistress and I shall be expecting some athletic performances in the bedroom. The result of all this will be to have you fit, strong and enthusiastic.'

'I don't know why it's got to be so rigorous,' Ralph complained. 'I'm only going to the Orderly Room.'

'You'll still have some hard playing at soldiers to do and I'm told that there is a cross-country run every Saturday morning. Anyway irrespective of anything else, it's for my own pride that I want to see your development from a pretty boy to a tough, hard young man. I want to see you in your raggedy old trousers and run my hands over your firm body and get you excited and drag you into bed. Each time more thrilling than the last.'

'Won't this feverish activity make parting even harder?'

'Yes it will. We're going down with all guns blazing.'

'You are incredible, Lorna. If I live to be a doddery old octogenarian who's forgotten who he is, I shall never ever, ever forget my Guarani warrior, my Lady Lorna of Acornbridge.'

'I know how you feel, Ralph. You think that I'm wonderful, how accurate you are.'

The sun was up. It would be another hot day. Lorna lay on her back. He gloried at the sight of her. He knew he always would. He knew that if he so much as touched her, so much as one fingertip anywhere on this honey-coloured mountain of flesh, she would open her beautiful blue-green eyes and smile at him and pull him down upon her and whisper, 'My handsome man!'

'Is this your first morning as my gym mistress?' Ralph asked.

'Yes, and I'm going to break the rules. Climb aboard. We can get onto the serious stuff later.'

'Gym was never like this at school,' Ralph said later. 'We had a grizzled old Geordie ex-Sergeant Major.'

'Well, I'm sure that's very interesting, darling. Would you like a nice big 'gardener's breakfast?' She rose and walked into the kitchen.

‘Another glorious day,’ she said. ‘How I’ve loved this long summer. I’m told that I’m looking radiant. That’s due to my virile young lover, I always say, but there’s another reason for my radiance. It’s the sight of my Sarah and Stanley totally in love. That’s your doing, Ralph. That’s twice you’ve been the matchmaker and I predict a third time. It’s a bit vague at present, but I see a fat man.’

‘Ralph ate his big breakfast and told Lorna that he was going to see his Uncle Bryn. ‘It won’t upset the fitness programme,’ he said. ‘I shall walk to Great Barr and back and start the lawns whenever I get back.’

He phoned the number on Bryn’s business card.

‘Uncle Bryn?’

‘Speaking.’

‘It’s Ralph.’

‘Ralph, my dear boy. I presume you’ve spoken to your dad and you’d like to come and see me.’

‘Exactly. I will walk it. I’m starting a fitness programme this morning. I should be there within two hours if that’s all right with you?’

‘Of course it’s all right. I’ll see you at about eleven.’

He set off along the Birmingham road, striding out despite the heat. He estimated that the total distance for the round trip was nine miles. It felt good to be walking a long distance. He felt more relaxed than he had been for some time. He felt optimistic about his future, to the extent that he often forgot that he still had a year’s service in Germany to complete. He felt happy that Stan and Sarah had hit it off thanks to him. He dreaded the day when he must say a long goodbye to Lorna, but he knew that they were both strong enough to live their lives. He knew that Lorna had a lot of ideas on her future. Just supposing things began to go wrong love-wise, health-wise, job-wise, money-wise. He would handle it. This was why he liked walking. It gave one time to think positively. Sulk in an armchair and you’ll think of morbid things. Take a brisk walk and you'll shake off the blues.

He finally arrived at the house-cum-office-cum-flats wherein dwelt and worked Uncle Bryn.

'Come in, Ralph. You made good time. Marching pace – four miles an hour eh? I'm just about to put some coffee on.'

'Nice cosy little office, Uncle Bryn.'

'Cut the 'uncle'. It's not that I'm not proud to be your uncle but I prefer just 'Bryn'. You're right, however – it *is* a cosy little office. I have to spend a lot of my time here and I might as well do it in pleasant surroundings.'

There were large maps on all of the walls – North America, France, Brazil, the Middle East, New York harbour and Birmingham street index.

'The maps are in no particular order and have no particular significance,' Bryn admitted. 'Your dad will have told you the sort of business I run. The time will come when I simply have to take on an extra person. I need to get out 'on the road' as it were. I owe nearly all my agents a visit. It'll be expensive but necessary. Britannia doesn't rule the waves anymore, as far as trading is concerned.

'There's growing competition. The extra person would either make the courtesy calls while I looked after the office or vice versa or maybe we split the operation.'

'When does all this happen, Bryn? I'm not out of the army until August '58.'

'It doesn't happen yet awhile. It's something for you to think about. I'll just give you some ideas. You can take them up or reject them, as you will. I know that you've got your Australia adventure to look forward to. My question is this. Do you want to thumb your way around, work your way around or do you want to see as much of the country as you can whilst holding down reasonably paid jobs? Do you want to be a bum or a drifter or do you want to be a happy, relatively secure young man?'

‘I should say the latter,’ Ralph replied, ‘with maybe one or two incongruities.’

‘Exactly. Who are the young lads who become drifters? They’re the ones with no qualifications. Get yourself qualified, boy. Chartered Accountant. Chartered Secretary, or nearer to home, Institute of Export or Institute of Freight Forwarders. It would take you three years – Preliminary, Intermediate and Finals part one and two. Get yourself a job as quickly as you can when you leave the service, study at night, either at home or Birmingham College of Commerce. Get letters after your name, then give Australia a try. You’ll only be twenty-five or so. Think about it.’

‘I will, Bryn, I surely will. I appreciate it.’

‘Would you like to come across the road for a beer and a snack?’

‘I can’t. I’ve got to walk home. Then I’ve got to mow the lawns at Stanhope. But I’ll see you again about the flat.’

‘That’s yours Ralph. Two pounds ten a week. Come and see it when it’s more than just a hole, which it is now.’

Ralph walked home in good heart. Lorna was waiting for him at the top of the drive in her sun hat and threadbare kaftan.

‘I swear you look sexier in that kaftan than in nothing at all.’

‘Do you, my handsome man? Whatever I wear, it seems that I look sensational. That’s just a fact of life.’

Ralph set about cutting the lawns as soon as he got back to Stanhope. He was rather annoyed that they had been left for so long, but it was no good dwelling on that. The grass was short enough to take the hand mower. There was no scything to be done. He oiled the mower and began. It was hard going at first, but on the second cutting he was able to put the lines on. He packed up at about seven o’clock leaving himself half a day’s work for tomorrow. Lorna sat on a deck chair. He walked over to her.

‘My handsome man,’ she put her hand out and he took it.

She had not done that for a while. She smiled at him, but there was some sadness in her eyes.

'Bring the other deckchair over and sit next to me. You've had a full day. I think we shall have one of our special little dinners at the Ritz. Would you like that darling? I'm afraid that it's only a ham salad. If the way to a man's heart is through his stomach then I'd never have won a man.'

'Ham salad's fine.'

'Everything's fine for you, you never complain.'

'What we eat is not important,' Ralph said. 'Our little dinners are part of our temporary fantasy world which will soon be over.'

'Yes, I suppose they are. Are we childish? Yes, but what the hell!'

The table cloth was already down, so was the cutlery, two bottles of wine were already opened.

Ralph was ordered to get out of his raggedy shorts and wash himself.

'I want you ready for inspection,' Lorna demanded. He came out minutes later.

'What a man. What a beautiful man! Let's go into the bedroom. I need to inspect you properly and the light's better in there.'

She took his hand.

'What a body! It won't take you long to get back in trim. You're nearly there. You're nearly my iron-hard shapely man.'

Chapter 24

Tommy Overjoyed

The days drifted by. Ralph completed the lawns. He did the rounds of visits. Nan Tucker was her usual chatty self, though stroppy at times. Now and then she lapsed into completely unfounded gossip involving Maggie Rowley and the merry widow of Stanhope. She was glad that Ralph would be renting a flat from 'her boy'. Granddad Tucker read his newspaper from cover to cover with the aid of a powerful magnifying glass. He read between bouts of snoozing or should one say he snoozed between bouts of reading. He promised Ralph that he would hang onto life until demob day. Stanley had moved into Stanhope with orders from Lorna to marry Sarah by September 1958.They were still lovesick and calling each other doves and angels in the style of Margaret Tucker in the childhood days of Ralph and Veronica. Veronica still lived at home. Tommy still lived with his mother and brother. The whole of his business was 'on ice' until demob day, after which Tommy would set up the business properly and work to Lorna's business plan. They would be marrying no later than September 1958.

Inevitably the day came for reporting back to Lichfield. Tommy, Ralph and Stan rendezvoused in Walsall. They all found it strange to be back in uniform again. In the style of the Grey Jackets they had dressed as if for guard duty, with brightly polished brasses and smoothly Blancoed webbing. On arrival at the depot they found everybody milling round, nobody knowing where they had to report. Tommy and a few other NCOs got things in order by splitting the mob into companies. By that time a warrant officer arrived with a list, ticked names off, and got everybody to their quarters.

Tommy reported reluctantly to the Sergeants' Mess. Ralph and Stan found their bed spaces in HQ Company. It seemed that Stan was still in the Intelligence section.

'I wonder what I'll be doing?' Stan asked.

'Nothing. You just have to walk round looking intelligent.'

'I might get a good skive,' Stan said. 'I might be sent on a course where they teach you to look intelligent.'

'You'd fail.'

Tommy was on his way to the Naafi to replenish his stock of Brasso and Blanco when Sergeant Edwards confronted him.

'As I live and breathe its Sergeant Ward,' he roared and shook Tommy's hand. 'You're looking fit, Tommy. It *is* Tommy isn't it? Your turnout is immaculate. Come and have a swift half in the Mess and call me Alan.'

They sat in a gloomy corner and Ralph said, 'Cheers'.

'Cheers, lad. Looking forward to Germany?'

'Not really. A lot of us think that it won't be the sort of soldiering that we've been used to.'

'I shouldn't worry too much,' Alan said.

'I try not to but the army's the army and a man can moan and groan all he likes it won't make any difference. Most of us want to get out there, do our duty and come back. In my case that means dear old demob on August 1958.'

'Ever thought about signing on?' Alan asked.

'Many a time. It's then I'm thinking about what happens to my plumbing business.'

'You want to think about it. You'd do well. You're just right for the services. You were the best recruit of the best squad I ever had and by the way, when I said to you that you shouldn't worry about it too much I really meant it. Do you understand what I'm saying? Don't worry about Germany because you're not going there. You're staying here at the Depot as a training sergeant. Report to the new training officer, Major Gill at 1000 hrs tomorrow. I'll be there. So will all the team. We're going to be in competition. I'll be with Bushire Squad. You'll be with Alma Squad.'

'Can I ask you a question off the record, Alan?'

'Just ask it. Never mind about off the record.'

'Has there been any outside influence in getting me this posting?'

'God forbid that such an underhand trick be played!'

'Okay. I won't pursue it. I'll assume that I got the job on merit.'

'Exactly Tommy.'

Tommy was overjoyed. He hurried out of the depot to the phone box on the main road and made his phone call.

'Veronica?'

'Tommy!' she cried. 'My wonderful, lovely Tommy. Have you settled in yet?'

'And how! Guess what. I'm not going to Germany. I'm posted here as a training sergeant. It's a great job but it's strenuous. I don't mind that. It's the sort of job I enjoy. A mob of misfits arrives at the depot and twelve weeks later they're a crack squad. I should be able to get home fairly regularly.'

'Slow down, Tommy. It's wonderful news. You'll be running these new recruits around from dawn to dusk. You won't have time to think of anything else. You should do as planned. Start your business up in September 58 after our honeymoon. Don't think of anything in between. Let Ron do what he wants. He could work as a one-man band but without the twenty-four hour call out. That was killing him. Let him just keep things slowly ticking over.'

'You know more about running the business than I do, little tomboy. You know who's behind this don't you?'

'Of course I do. It's Lorna. She's got some pull at Lichfield. Voluntary visitor, daughter of the one-time C.O. widow of a Grey Jackets hero. I'm going round to thank her this evening. See you, Tommy, I love you.'

Lorna sat in the waning sun on the patio with Jerome in her arms. The phone rang. 'Auntie Lorna?'

'Veronica, my sweet child.'

'Can I call round?'

'Of course.'

'I'm leaving now.'

She took the well-worn path across the oval and spied Lorna emerging from the cedar trees, right onto the road.

'This is a bit daring isn't it, Auntie Lorna? Out on the road in nothing but a sun hat and a little baby.'

'It's been so hot today. I never dress when it's hot. Let's walk back to the kitchen. Isn't this a lovely little lad? He gets more handsome every day.'

'Vonika,' Jerome said.

'Isn't that nice?' Veronica said.

'Yes he's a clever boy. You're a clever boy aren't you, but you've got to go back to your mummy now. Your step-daddy's gone back to be a soldier. Come on, young fellow.' Lorna took Jerome through the dividing door and handed him over to Sarah.

'You'll have two like that, Veronica, a boy and a girl they'll be two little rascals too.'

'I hope so. Are you really clairvoyant, Auntie Lorna?'

'Not to the point of exact accuracy. I see things, images, people, events. Some of the visions are meaningless.'

'Like what?'

'You always were a curious child. Let me pour out two glasses of wine first. Where was I?'

'Meaningless visions.'

'That's right but eventually, sometimes after twenty years or more, the image reveals its meaning. The other night I saw a rainbow. One by one the colours of the spectrum disappeared in order – red, orange, yellow, green, blue, indigo and violet and as each band floated away it seemed to twist and turn like a huge piece of cloth changing shape in the wind. Ralph was with me in the dream.'

‘The reason I called Auntie Lorna, was to thank you.’

‘For what?’

‘For using your influence in getting Tommy his home posting.’

‘Was that I?’

‘I think it was.’

‘Yes, I spoke to a dear friend, no less than retired Lt Colonel Arthur Wood, the most charming, good-looking man in the regiment at one time. The men called him Clark Gable.’

‘I bet he was putty in your hands, Auntie Lorna.’

Ralph settled down to military life again. He had to take his turn for guard duty and duty clerk. In other respects his off duty time was his own. With the battalion still building up to full strength it seemed that nobody really knew who was there and who was not. Some men thumbed it home every evening and got back before muster parade next day. He and Lorna agreed that coming home every night was a waste of time and effort. Lorna remarked that there must be a lot of lovelorn young men at Lichfield, especially since most of them had already had a big chunk of disembarkation leave.

Most evenings Ralph and two of his cronies, Freddy Keynes and Graham Scott, would walk into Lichfield or Tamworth with vague ideas of picking up women. They never did. They never even got on speaking terms with the elusive female sex. The standard night out was a long walk, three pints and a long walk back. Having accepted that the odds on picking up a girl were a hundred to one they regarded their walks in the balmy evenings as exercise and therapy. They talked a lot about their futures. Graham would be going to Wadham College, Oxford in a matter of weeks. He was seeing his time out.

‘What will it be like going back to school again?’ Ralph asked.

'How will you get on with eighteen year olds who've done nothing, been nowhere?' Freddy asked.

'How can you hang on without a proper job until you're twenty-four?' Ralph added.

'How will you tolerate the jumped-up little political activists with beards and sandals and smoking foul pipes and trying to change the world?' Freddy wanted to know.

'Are you going to give me the chance of getting a word in?' Graham demanded. 'In answer to your questions, I don't know. I simply don't know. I shall try to settle in and take what comes – a bit like the army.'

'Except that you get paid in the army.' Freddy had the last word. They walked on through the Staffordshire countryside. Summer died.

September came. Ralph wangled himself three days leave. It was to be his last time off before shipping out to Germany. He got out on the road early and was at Stanhope Hall at ten o'clock as he had promised. Lorna was waiting for him on the road at least fifty yards from the avenue of cedar trees. She wore a sun hat and nothing more. 'This is a bit risqué is it not, dear Lorna? A good job there are no cars coming.'

'Let them come. This is my land. This road was put through without my father's permission.'

She took his hand and they walked back to the kitchen entrance. She took a bottle of beer from the fridge, opened it and passed it to him.

'I can see that you've been a good lad and got your exercise in, my handsome man.'

'I usually walk into Lichfield or Tamworth with a couple of mates each evening. We have three pints at any old pub and walk back. It may not sound exciting but it's enjoyable. We talk about all sorts of things but mainly our futures.'

'You're not as apprehensive about your future as you were, are you? Not since you're meeting with Bryn. You're looking relaxed and healthy.'

‘So are you Lorna. Veronica says that you look radiant.’

‘I *looked* radiant – past tense. Only one man can make me look radiant and that’s you, Ralph Tucker and I’m sure you will. Do you see much of Stanley?’

‘Sometimes in the Naafi or the Church Army. We have egg and chips together. He’s very morose. He pines for Sarah.’

‘I know he does and so does Sarah. I’m happy that they’re so in love, but I’d like them to try and act like adults. I told them how long I had had to be without you and how long Veronica waited for Tommy. Apparently Sarah and Stanley’s love is *different*. It’s on a higher plain. What a load of nonsense.’

‘It’s a wonder Stanley doesn’t do what a lot of blokes do – thumb it home each evening and get back for muster parade.’

‘He’s done that a few times too,’ Lorna said.

‘Are you home, Mother?’ Ralph shouted.

‘I’ll be there shortly.’

She appeared in the hall dressed in a navy blue jacket, skirt and crisp white blouse.

‘What do you think?’

‘Very smart. The outfit gives you an aura of a successful career woman.’

‘Do you think the skirt’s too short?’

‘It is a little, but you’ve got good legs so you can get away with it.’

‘Those were my thoughts also. Not like Lorna Pitt’s legs. They’re like tree trunks.’

‘Now, now Mother.’

‘Surely I’m allowed to criticise my best friend. But let us not deviate from the main point. This uniform is now standard compulsory dress for all employees at all branches of Appleby, Andrews and Pearson, sometimes known as ‘apples and pears’.

'You will have a secretary, Ralph, once you commence your commercial career. Some secretaries are brazen hussies despite their sombre dress. My seventh best friend Dawn and my ninth best friend Brenda both fall into this category. If either one of them saw you, Ralph they would literally be fighting each other to sit on your lap.'

'Hope so.'

'Don't be facetious. This is serious; these pushy women would squirm and wiggle and wriggle all over you, showing their knickers and everything, but you lay a finger on *them* and boy, you're in big trouble and you'd get the sack on the spot. So my advice to you is to keep your hands behind your back. Do you want me to act it out for you?'

'I think I've got the idea, Mother. If I need any help when I get my first secretary, I'll phone you.'

'I know you will darling. Now we come to the second point – your posting to Germany. There is something you have to be very careful of.'

'What's that, Mother? Does it involve women squirming all over me?'

'Who knows whom or what it involves: it's to do with espionage. There are literally hundreds of East German spies in West Germany. Their aim is to destabilise the present West German government so that when Germany is finally reunited it will be an Iron Curtain country instead of being a western European country.'

'This is pretty heavy stuff, Mother. Where did you get your information?'

'From a lady at the bus stop.'

'What's her name?'

'I can only refer to her as X2.'

'What does she do?'

'She works for MI5 under cover. To all intents and purposes she sells fruit in Walsall market using the alias Gladys Onions.'

'Not X2.'

‘No. That’s her name within MI5. Don’t make it *too* complicated. She’s given me some tips, which I’m passing on for your own safety. Firstly, be careful of befriending anybody with a walking stick. It probably contains poisonous darts, which are set off by pressing a button on the handle. Secondly, stay away from frauleins. If you *do* have to have anything to do with them, keep your eyes on your drink. Do not go to the toilet. They’ll spike your drink while you’re away. Thirdly, be very careful what you eat when out of camp. Don’t touch sausages, especially those giant ones. They’ve almost certainly been injected with poison.’

‘But the Germans eat them, don’t they?’

‘Yes, of course. They eat the ones that haven’t been tampered with. The poisonous ones reserved for the British Army have a mustard stain on them. Be careful, my son.’ She kissed him goodbye.

Ralph made his next call to Nan Tucker short and sweet. His mother’s lecture on spies and secretaries had left him bemused and tired. What a strange, slightly dotty woman she was becoming. Yet he loved her dearly as did they all – Ralph, Hugh and Veronica.

‘Your dear mother may make some unusual demands of you sometimes, Ralph,’ his father had once told him. ‘If she does, just do what she asks. Whatever it is that’s going wrong, I’m hoping that love will contain it, if not cure it, and there’s plenty of love around in this house.’

Hugh put things well, Ralph thought.

Ralph and Lorna lay together on the bed which, to quote Lorna, had seen so much jolly good fun. There was no jollity now, only precious silence. The leaves had started falling. The lawns and the Oval were a carpet of gold. Gold too was the shaft of light from the window that shone upon his golden lady – the Guarani warrior, the show-off, the clairvoyant, the bare-back rider, the swimmer, the boozer who never ever had a hangover. He wondered what she would do. He knew that she would make her mark wherever she went or whatever she did. He wished her well. She had said that their parting should be dignified There would be no tears. Spiritually they might not ever part. There would forever be a great mystery about her and about her glorious eccentricities.

They fell asleep and did not wake until sunrise. She arose and stood before him just as on that long ago day of the garden party. She held her lusty pose for five full minutes before sitting demurely on a chair, a woman of self-proclaimed, unsurpassed beauty and who would argue with that. It was over.

The battalion was back up to strength. They were granted freedom of several Midlands towns. To the tune of 'Come Lasses and Lads',' the Grey Jackets and their regimental band marched through Walsall, West Bromwich, Wolverhampton, Bilston and Lichfield.

The advance party had already gone out to Germany. The Battalion followed in September 57 via Harwich and the Hook of Holland to Lüneburg, a town between Hamburg and Hanover. Their new home was renamed Whittington Barracks. Whatever its origins (presumably built in the thirties when Germany was preparing for war), it was a spacious, clean and not unattractive complex of buildings – a far cry from the bleak, cold Victorian clusters of buildings that housed infantry regiments in Britain. Headquarters block, where Ralph was to live, had more of the atmosphere of a university hall of residence than a barracks. Ralph shared a room with the pay corporal. No single room housed any more than four men. One complete floor on every block was given over to showers; steaming hot water cascaded down from the apertures in the ceiling. Luxury indeed, hot water having been non-existent in Cyprus. As many as fifty or sixty men would be under the showers at any given time. Saturday morning after the cross-country run, was the most popular time when everybody let go and roared out 'Heartbreak Hotel' and 'Hound Dog'.

Headquarters block had a complete empty floor, which the men used for five-a-side football. Five-a-side became anything from four-a-side to nine-a-side, according to how many turned up. There was also a lounge with armchairs where one could read, chat, listen to the radio or simply sit around.

Pay was either in Deutschmarks, BAF money or a mixture of the two. BAF money was bulky because it consisted of notes down to as low as three pence. A pocket full of BAF (British Armed Forces) was not worth a lot and could only be spent in service establishments like the YMCA, the Naafi or the Globe cinema, where it was possible to do some exchange dealing with German teenagers who wanted to see the latest films.

Chapter 25

Germany

When Ralph looked back on his time in Germany, much of it was a blur, unlike Cyprus where the images were clear, colourful and bouncing around his memory by the hundred. Soldiering in Germany was as dull as peacetime soldiering could be. Lüneburg was as rudimentary as any English garrison town. Maybe the architecture was more ornate. A few events stayed in his mind, the first one being the 'scheme' in which they participated at a place called Soltau Plain. It was enacted in freezing weather in February 1958. The Danish army was involved and so were some US army personnel, who brought with them a mobile ice cream parlour, mobile diner and mobile cinema. Obviously, in temperatures below freezing a good supply of ice cream was a must, so was a night out at an open-air cinema watching a film about a chain gang.

Nobody seemed to have a clue what they were doing. The fact that three huge white vehicles had been introduced to the 'battle field' gave the whole thing a farcical touch. The Orderly Room was there in force. Nobody knew why. Ralph decided it might be a good idea to start playing soldiers. He gathered together as many inactive administration personnel as he could find, led them out to vast snow-covered field and ordered them to spread out in 'open order' and advance toward a ramshackle wooden shed about a hundred yards away. They charged across the open ground with bayonets fixed towards the shed and surrounded it. Amazingly, they seemed to have turned a futile theatrical piece of piss-taking into a successful operation as one by one a section of Danish soldiers emerged from the shed and were ordered to lay down their rifles.

A group of officers arrived. It included Lt Colonel Irons, still referred to as the 'new CO', and the Brigadier.

'Who's in charge here?' The Brigadier asked.

'Me, sir. Corporal Tucker.'

'Well done, Tucker!' He turned towards the CO and said, 'This is what we need. A bit of flair. Note the name – Tucker. Send a runner to HQ – someone intelligent – and let them know that we've taken target W or is it target M?'

'I think you've got the map upside down, sir.'

Another clear memory from the Germany days was Ralph and Freddy's weekend in Hamburg.

As a reward for excelling themselves on Soltau Plain, the Orderly Room staff were personally congratulated by the new CO. Ralph and Freddy, as the main instigators, were awarded a weekend pass to Hamburg.

It was March and still very cold. They dressed in the warmest civvies they owned, which in their case were T-shirts under check shirts under pullovers, and *still* they were cold, but they figured, that they'd either be walking around energetically or would be in cosy, warm Bierkellers. They looked upon the trip as an adventure. In that respect they were of a similar mould. Even if it turned out to be dull, they would give their mates an embellished version of events. They had particularly looked forward to seeing a 'real German city' as Ralph described it.

They arrived in Hamburg ravenously hungry and soon found a large modern restaurant – all shiny leather and chrome. They had a very Teutonic meal of huge sausages, gravy and so much cabbage that they need extra side plates. They had apfelstrudel for sweet and washed down the gigantic meal with two foaming jugs of ice-cold lager. The restaurant was half empty so they ordered more lager and sat at their window table watching the world go by.

Eventually they left the restaurant to continue their wandering. They were sinking lager at quite a pace and this was why some of their memory broke away into fragments. Ralph remembered being in a market place where there was a bear in a cage, or was there?

Inevitably they drifted towards the Reeperbahn, reputedly the red-light area, and walked into a bar. They ordered two beers which, when the Deustchmarks were converted to sterling, were very expensive.

'This place is a big con,' Freddy protested. 'We've just paid nine quid for two beers.'

'We're here now, Freddy.' Ralph told him. 'We'll stick it out. Don't worry too much about money. I've got some in reserve in my secret pocket. See! Stitched in. You'd have to pick away at the cotton to get at the money.'

There was a film showing on a large screen. Scantily dressed young ladies walked suggestively along a catwalk. Each wore a type of fruit hanging from a cord covering the obvious – a banana, an apple, an orange; it looked like artificial fruit. These same ladies were acting both as waitresses and dance partners. So Ralph and Freddy were getting a double 'come on' from screen stars and actuality.

'It's making me feel depressed, Freddy,' Ralph said. 'My Lorna is unclothed throughout the summer. She is a magnificent sight. She is sensuous, superbly sculptured, a woman of unsurpassed beauty, an enchantress, an exciting woman. Am I getting drunk, Freddy? What I'm saying is that these tarty, gormless women disgrace the female form.'

'You're taking it all too seriously,' Freddy said. 'Here's Miss Banana coming over to our table.'

She began to bombard them with questions. Were they Swedish? No? Were they Latvians? Finns? Were they businessmen?'

'We're Canadian,' Freddy said.

Questions continued. Were they businessmen? Were they ice hockey players? Were they lumberjacks?

'We're fishermen,' Freddy told them. More questions followed. Did they fish for salmon? Were they whalers? Were they from Quebec? Were they Red Indians?'

Freddy finally broke. 'Of course we're not bloody Red Indians.'

A very large black suited man walked over to Miss Banana and muttered in German.

'He told me that you have to buy me a drink for thirty Canadian dollars, then leave.'

'Let's get out of this poxy place, Ralph.'

Ralph took two £5 notes, screwed them up and handed them to Miss Banana on the way out. They ran like mad and turned down an alleyway.

'Black suit fatso's after us,' Freddy said. 'There he goes. He went past the alley. He's still on the main street.'

They took refuge in a tattooist's shop.

'Bet you I'll have a tattoo,' Ralph said.

'It's not a bet. If you want one have one.'

Ralph took a seat and picked out his tattoo, which was to be two bluebirds with a banner in their beaks. The banner would bear the words MOM & DAD. He paid for the tattoo in advance as seemed to be the custom. Who could blame the tattooist for getting his money up front? The clientele, who were mainly from the Baltic States, looked big, rough and dangerous.

The tattooist got to work on Ralph's forearm. When he got as far as the second bluebird Ralph shouted 'enough' He felt faint. The tattooist stuck a piece of lint over the tattoo and told him that it would bleed for a while and then form a scab. When the scab fell off it would be there for life.

'Come on, Ralph,' Freddy said wearily. 'Let's get back to the railway station, sleep the booze off and get a train early tomorrow. Give every club and Bierkeller a wide mark. Old black suit fatso'll be at his door. The scary thing is *which* door?Incidentally how much money did you give him?'

‘Ten quid.’

‘Ten quid’s okay.’

‘Not in BAF money, it isn’t.’

‘You mad bastard. Let’s get out of here. I’ve had enough of this ‘real German city’ and I’m freezing cold.’

So much for their weekend in Hamburg.

‘But it’ll make a good yarn,’ Ralph said.

Another incident from his days in Germany stays in his memory. It was only trivial but it had implications. He and Freddy were late walking home from their drinking den, the Ilmenaugarten. The RMPs spotted them, told them that it was ten minutes after 2359 hrs. They were subsequently charged. Freddy was given a reprimand for being out of bounds. For the same offence Ralph was severely reprimanded. Such a punishment was a ‘Regimental Entry’ which Ralph thought too tough for such a minor offence. Major Le Breton explained to Ralph that the nature of the offence did not affect the decision, lit was the fact that he was the Orderly Room corporal and was supposed to behave correctly, which he had not done in this case. The Orderly Room were ‘just not supposed’ to break the rules.

The posting to Germany had been a boring interlude. Regular correspondence was deemed unnecessary to a great extent. Veronica had sent the annual report on Nan Tucker’s Christmas party. It was repetitious.

Except for a letter about her possible weekly column in the *Express*, Lorna did not write. She could see no point. The debate was over.

Uncle Bryn wrote in early August 1958 that the flat was ready for occupation – fully furnished, big TV, shower and toilet, own private entrance. He also informed Ralph that he had paid Lorna £25 for the green Morris Minor on Ralph’s behalf and would need immediate remuneration. The car was now parked outside the flat and Bryn started it up each day. Relevant paperwork was in the glove box.

His mother wrote to him every fortnight. She still had her obsessions with East European spies. The letter she sent him in April was typical, and read:

My beloved and truly wonderful son,
I read your letter about your weekend in Hamburg with some annoyance. Why have you had yourself tattooed? It's very common. I'm rather glad that you felt faint after the first bluebird was completed. At least you'll only have a very small tattoo. You don't seem to be heeding my advice. You ate huge sausages in Hamburg. You were lucky you didn't get poisoned. And what's this about fiddling a restaurant out of money. That could have created an international incident. I can see the headline now, 'British soldiers rob restaurant – World War III can be avoided says German Chancellor.' I told Gladys the whole story. She knew about it. The man you refer to as black suit fatso is a Bulgarian and leader of a vicious gang. You won't be able to go back to Hamburg for many years, if ever. I should lie low. We'll have to be careful not to put anything controversial in our letters in case they're censored. You're very lucky that your mother has friends in MI6. (Gladys *was* in MI5 but she's been promoted she is no longer X2. She is X2.7 but I shouldn't be telling you this.
All my love and be careful,
Your devoted mother

The day came for the intake of 24th August 1958 to ship back to the UK. It was over for them, the RSM's parades, the Saturday morning cross-country, the meaningless exercises, tramping through the forest, wandering aimlessly around Lüneburg on Sundays.

Twenty-five men had left a month earlier to attend a civil defence course at Millom in Cumberland. Others, like Dennis, would be arriving from various postings. Thus there was a small party of ten which included six full corporals. Ralph was not promoted to sergeant for his last few weeks because of the 'out of bounds' incident. Theoretically Ralph was the draft conducting corporal but, in reality, they were all pals together irrespective of rank. They considered themselves civilians. In fact, it was the 'in' thing not to put ones rank on suitcases and return to the title Mr.

The draft finally arrived back at Whittington after what had seemed a marathon journey by train and ferry. They had done the sea journey from Hook of Holland to Harwich in a rusty old tub called Prins Rupert. They were put in the bowels of the ship. The weather was stormy. The refrigeration had broken down. They drank warm beer. Almost every serviceman on the ship was seasick. There was vomit everywhere. They were glad to be off the ship in the early hours to get the train to London and change for Lichfield Trent Valley.

It was too late to check into the Guardroom so they mutually agreed to be at the Depot at 0800hrs next morning. For the rest it was boring procedure. They were sent home with instructions to be at the depot at 1000 hours next day in civvies with all their kit. They were allowed by the QM to keep one pair of boots, socks, braces, their tropical blue pyjamas, one shirt and one pair of denim trousers. They had their release medicals, collected the documents for the whole party, made their way to Walsall Territorial Army HQ in Whittimere Street, handed over the documents and became civilians again. So this was it? Back in the same old town. Back in the same old clothes they'd gone away in. So this was the day of celebration that had been stencilled on their brains for three years. How did they feel? Miserable!

'How do you feel Ralph?' Tommy asked. 'How do you feel on this day we've all been waiting for and dreaming of?'

'I feel empty.'

'So do I. D'you know what? I wanted to put that uniform back on today. I wanted to look immaculate and march with a spring in my step over to my squad of recruits and get the lazy bastards scampering here and there to the instructions of Sergeant Ward. Then I realised that that was all over. I put on my civvies, items of which are over three years old, and I felt a nobody. Nobody to instruct, guide, encourage, help, warn, criticise, remonstrate with. I have to face reality, Ralphy. Tomorrow is the official start of Ward Brothers. We work to Lorna's business plan. It's going to be tougher than the army but I'm determined. I'll do it.'

'You'll do it, Tommy. You're the stubbornest man I ever knew. Let's not hang around here though. Let's head for the pub. Which pub, I hear you ask. It's only five thirty. Shall we walk into Caldmore and grab the big table at the Windmill?'

Stan, Dennis, Tommy and Ralphy thought it was a good idea. Carrying half empty suitcases they ambled their way to their favourite watering hole.

'Good old Walsall,' Tommy said. 'I bet you dreamt about it didn't you, Dennis, when you were in that dump, Paris?'

'Paris is a magic city. Walsall? Good and bad I suppose. My rather warped opinion at the moment is that you can stick Walsall up your arse.'

They reached the Windmill, positioned themselves around the big table.

'Your round, Dennis. You were out there watching the can-can and strolling down the Chauncey Lisa or whatever it's called while we lay in our tents listening to the cries of "Cha Wallah, Cha Wallah".'

'Sorry lads, I can't buy a round. I've only got French money on me,' Dennis explained.

'Crafty bugger,' Stan said.

'Only joking. Only joking. I'll get 'em in,' Denis said.

'Cheers lads,' Dennis said and quaffed at least a third of his beer. 'What shall we drink to?'

'Well,' Tommy said, 'we can drink to Tommy Ward or am I supposed to drink to myself?'

'What are you waffling on about, Tommy?' Stan asked.

'Veronica's pregnant,' Tommy replied.

'That's great news,' Ralph said. 'I shall have a little nephew or niece. What will it be, I wonder?'

'Consult the oracle,' Stan suggested. 'Ask Lorna. She's almost psychic.'

'Not on everything, Stan,' Ralph said.

'We'd rather not know, lads,' Tommy pleaded. 'We're having a lot of fun guessing and thinking of names. It's nice to have a few surprises in life.'

Ralph took his leave to call his mother.

'Hallo?'

'It's Ralph, Mom.'

'My darling son! Shall you be staying here tonight?'

'That's exactly why I'm ringing. I can't stay at Stanhope Hall anymore. I don't feel up to moving into the flat. I'm having a reunion drink with Tommy and everybody. I'm about twenty minutes away, but I don't know when I'm leaving. It would be too much if I asked you to hold dinner for me.'

'Your dad and I will eat now. Get home no later than nine thirty and we'll have a little drink together.'

'Thanks a lot, Mom. See you at nine thirty.'

Ralph rejoined the table.

'Let's hear what you've been doing, Dennis,' he said. 'It seems an age since we all took the piss out of you way back God knows when. We were just jealous. So tell us what happened.'

'I've been dying to. The job with 'SHAPE' was purely security – manning offices, doing guards, lock-ups, patrols, and some ceremonials. There were a mixture of nationalities – Dutch, Canadians, Yanks, English of course, and French.

I never bothered to make friends. I was in Paris with a fair bit of free time. That's all I cared.

'I took to being a bit of a loner. I badly wanted to improve my schoolboy French so what better opportunity would I have than to ramble the streets of Paris talking to all and sundry in parks, bars, restaurants and shops. I was laughable at first, but as time passed I could hold a conversation in French albeit multiple errors and mispronunciation being plentiful. I liked the life in Paris, simply sitting outside nursing a cold beer and watching life pass by is glamorous. I spent a lot of time in the Champs Elysées, watching street entertainers and buskers. A lot of them were from French possessions like Guadeloupe or Martinique. They put on dance acts. They seemed to be made of rubber.

'I never saw any singers. I thought I'd spotted a gap in the market. One Saturday when I'd had a fair amount to drink, I got to my feet and started belting out Elvis songs. I thought that I'd be told to shut up but that didn't happen. People started chanting, 'Elvis, Elvis, Elvis' and put money into my empty beer glass. I announced 'Je serai ici mardi.' When I arrived at the same place the following Tuesday evening, there was a small gathering. I stood up and said, 'Je suis L'Elvis nouveau'. I put my hat down on the pavement and went through the same repertoire and collected the equivalent of four quid.

'I loved – and still love – Paris. I had a little girlfriend. I wanted to call her my Tomboy so I tried to put it in French and said, "Vous êtes comme un garçon s'appelle Thomas".' She was doubled up with laughter. 'We settled on our own word –'Tomboi'. Even that she did not understand but the name finally stuck. "Mon Denis" she would say, and I would whisper, "Ma Tomboi". She lived in an old house not far from my pitch. She had only a tiny room, but she was happy. I could scoop her up with one hand and sit her on my shoulder. She loved that. We walked many a mile like that. I tried to persuade her to come to England with me, but she said she would not fit in. She was a child of the Paris streets. Sometimes I called her mon petit moineau – my little sparrow – like Edith Piaf. I may go back to France. Who knows?'

'Paris might not be so romantic, second time around,' Tommy told him.

'You're right there Mr Common-sense-man. How would I make a living? I shall go back when I'm rich and famous and find my little sparrow and whisk her off to my mansion in the south of France.'

'You've become quite the romantic, Dennis,' Ralph said.

'Yes I have. I've become a bit like you. You were always the dreamer of us all – you and Duggie. We should drink to Duggie.' He raised his glass and reverently they said, 'To Duggie'.

'I shall travel,' Ralph said. 'I shall go to Australia, New Zealand and maybe the South Seas. I'll stay in Blighty for a while though. I'll get some qualifications behind me and leave when I'm about twenty-five. Early enough I reckon. That's what Duggie and I were going to do so I'll do it for him.'

'And now we come to Stan the man. You're a war artist or so I hear.'

'Yes, in a way, though I hope to God there are no more wars to draw and paint. I'm looking at being an artist in the long term. In the meantime, I'll put in fair bit of casual time with Jeff Pyke at QBS. All in all, I suppose we're all in the same boat: Tommy's business, my career as an artist, Ralph's qualifications, whatever they are and Dennis's acting success. They're all long-term projects. Let's hope we all get there.'

'You've put it well, Stan the man,' Dennis said. 'Let's keep in touch.'

The party broke up. Ralph picked up his battered suitcase and ambled home. It had been three years and more since he had thought of it as home, but home it truly was.

His mother had been watching from the window. As soon as she saw him coming down the drive, she ran to the front door to open it and let him in. She took him tightly in her arms.

'My son, my son, my handsome son. You're home. You're home, not Stanhope Hall or Whittington Barracks but here, the first, home!'

She was wearing the same brief cocktail dress that she had worn one Christmas to the express disapproval of Nan Tucker.

'You've got your naughty dress on, Mother.'

'Do you like it? Yes, of course you do.'

'You're looking great.'

'Is my beauty on a 'higher level' as Lorna Pitt would say?'

'Now, now, Mother.'

Hugh came in and greeted Ralph.

'Put your suitcase down over there, son. If there's any dirty washing there, your Mom will see to it. She'll be delighted to have one of her little scamps to wash for again. Now then son, we've got drinks on the table and I believe that your overjoyed mother has made you up a nice plate of sandwiches.'

Hugh poured out three large whiskies. They drank for a while. Ralph, who was ravenously hungry, wolfed down his sandwiches in minutes, and was told off for his disgusting table manners.

'Thank God that you're out of the army,' Margaret said. 'I want to see the well-mannered boy that left me back in 1955, not a navvy scoffing his cheese sandwiches by the roadside.'

'Sorry, Mother. I hadn't eaten all day.'

'I've been having a chat with Bryn,' Hugh said. 'He was expecting you to move in tomorrow.'

'That's correct. I *shall* be.'

'I know that was your plan. However, I'd like you to take your mother away for three nights at the place we went to a while ago – Rockingham on Sea. I can't get the time off work. You've got plenty of time to settle in and get a job. Three days is nothing in the long run.'

'Long run is something I've been hearing a lot of over a period. I'd love to go. It'll be great. I really loved the place. And why not get the little break in when we can? Once I start applying for jobs, I shall need to be on the spot. Anyway, I owe Mom a lot of my time.'

'Will the old Morris Minor make it?'

'Of course. It made it down to Devon enough times. It'll make it to the South Coast. I'll pick it up from Bryn's. This is a special day for me,' Ralph said. 'It's my first full day as a civilian.'

About the Author

David Stant spent his early years in Walsall, birthplace of the great humorous writer Jerome K. Jerome of *Three Men in a Boat* fame. He attended Queen Mary's school for boys where he failed comprehensively to make his mark. He served two years National service in the 1st South Staffords plus four years in the Territorials. He served in Cyprus at the time of the EOKA terrorists and in Germany (BAOR) British Army of the Rhine. He finished with the rank of Sergeant.

In 1962 he emigrated and spent nine years working in Australia, New Guinea, New Zealand and Fiji, returning to England in 1971. For most of his working life he has made his living in the shipping and forwarding business (the international movement of goods by land, sea and air). He retired in 1997. He still had a wanderlust and took his late wife on several cruises. He lists travel as an important spare-time activity, along with walking/rambling, trying to keep fit, painting and poetry. Since his wife's death he has lived alone in Sutton Coldfield. He has two adult stepchildren and five grandchildren.